INTO THE FIRE

INTO THE FIRE

Asian American Prose

**Edited by Sylvia Watanabe
and Carol Bruchac**

Greenfield Review Press

Publication of this book has been made possible, in part, through a Literary Publishing Grant from the Literature Program of the New York State Council on the Arts.

Introduction copyright © 1996 by Sylvia Watanabe.

Library of Congress #94–79476

ISBN 0–912678–90–9

FIRST EDITION
Printed in the United States of America.

Cover and book design by Vivian L. Bradbury.
Cover Illustration by Wakako Yamauchi
Typeset by Sans Serif, Ann Arbor, MI.
Printing by Thomson-Shore, Dexter, MI.

Distributed by The Talman Company, Inc.
131 Spring Street
New York, N.Y. 10012
(212) 431–7175 Fax: (212) 431–7215

CONTENTS

Introduction

Sylvia Watanabe ix Out of the Frying Pan
Carol Bruchac xii Seeing the Fire

Part I ORIGINS

Nora Cobb Keller 3 Mother-Tongue
Shirley Geok-lin Lim 11 Hunger
Larissa Lai 21 Water, and Other
Measures of Distance
Dung T. Nguyen 33 Night
Vince Gotera 39 Returning Fire
Jason Laus Baluyut 51 The Storyteller
Chitra Divakaruni 69 Clothes

Part II ISLANDS

Sylvia Watanabe 85 A Conversation with Eric
Chock and Darrell Lum
Lois-Ann Yamanaka 99 Dominate and Recessid
Jeans
R. Zamora Linmark 105 Our Lady of Kalihi, Mama's
Boy, and Dreamhouse
Darrell Lum 113 Giving Tanks
Marie Hara 119 You In There
Cedric Yamanaka 127 The Lemon Tree Billiards
House
Garrett Hongo 139 Sunbird

Part III SURVIVAL

Wakako Yamauchi 149 Otoko

William P. Osborn and Sylvia Watanabe	163	A Conversation with Wakako Yamauchi
Jeanne Wakatsuki Houston	175	O Furo
Hisaye Yamamoto	187	Eju-Kei-Shung! Eju-Kei-Shung!
William P. Osborn and Sylvia Watanabe	197	A Conversation with Hisaye Yamamoto
Ruth Shigezawa	209	Three Steps A Minute
Sesshu Foster	219	City Terrace Field Manual
Joseph Won	225	Over Here Is Where I Am
Marianne Villanueva	235	Bad Thing
Carol Roh-Spaulding	247	Pages from the Notebook of a Eurasian
R. A. Sasaki	255	A Dictionary of Japanese-American Terms
Neela Sastry	263	Tremors
Shawn Wong	273	Fear of Flying
Shawn Wong	287	Reflections

Part IV HEARTLAND

Usha Lee McFarling	301	Cooking Lessons
Mabelle Hsueh	307	A Platter of Steaming Dumplings
Kiyoshi Young Najita	315	Dovetailing
Connie S. Chan	323	Journal Entries

Part V FULL CIRCLE

Alan Wald	341	Introduction to H.T. Tsaing
H.T. Tsiang	345	The Hanging on Union Square
Adrienne Tien	359	Tangents
Leslie Lum	369	Sam
Thelma Seto	381	Inshallah

ACKNOWLEDGEMENTS

In all cases, unless noted, permission to reprint previously published work has been granted by the individual authors. We are grateful to the magazines and publishers listed below for their commitment to the writing of Asian American authors.

Marie Hara: *You in There* first appeared in SISTER STEW, *an Anthology of Women Writers*, Bamboo Ridge Press, Honolulu, 1992.

Adrienne Tien: *Tangents* first appeared in THE PORTABLE LOWER EAST SIDE in 1990.

Shawn Wong: *Fear Of Flying* from AMERICAN KNEES, Simon and Schuster, New York, 1995.

Hisaye Yamamoto: *Eju-Kei-Shung! Eju-Kei-Shung!* first appeared in THE RAFU SHIMPO Supplement in Dec. 1980.

Lois-Ann Yamanaka: *Dominate and Recessid Jeans* first appeared in BAMBOO RIDGE #57, Winter 1993.

Wakako Yamauchi: *Otoko* first appeared in SOUTHWEST REVIEW, 1992.

INTRODUCTION

OUT OF THE FRYING PAN

THE TERM ASIAN AMERICAN* includes a variety of groups with distinct cultural identities and, occasionally, bitter historical antagonisms. While the wounds of history run deep, as Nora Cobb Keller's "Mother Tongue" and Vince Gotera's "Returning Fire" remind us here, these antagonisms have been somewhat tempered by resettlement in America and a commonality of experience arising from the often brutal contact with mainstream society. Such contact is perhaps most starkly chronicled in Wakako Yamauchi's autobiographical story, "Otoko," about the Japanese American internment during World War II, and in Sesshu Foster's "City Terrace Field Manual," which describes the exploitation of itinerant agricultural workers in California. Other forms of culture contact that surface repeatedly throughout this collection include the experiences of language learning, of being "named," of attempting to deal with competing belief systems, of fashioning a sense of self in an environment where one's identity is persistently elided, and of searching for home in a nation where Asians are identified, *a priori*, as foreign. Shawn Wong's novel excerpt, "Fear of Flying," takes on all of these issues and depicts, with wit and unsparing honesty, how they function in the psychology of internalized racism.

However, all this is not to suggest that *Into the Fire* is merely a book about issues; it is filled with memorable situations and characters. Among the most memorable and surprising of these characters are the old *issei* farm laborer in Ruth Shigezawa's "Three Steps A Minute," and the female protagonists of "Clothes" by Chitra Divakaruni and "O Furo" by Jeanne Wakatsuki Houston.

One of the most exciting things about being an editor is the opportunity to discover new voices. Those whose fiction is first being published here include Mabelle Hsueh, Dung T. Nguyen, Usha Lee McFarling, Joseph Won, and Jason Laus Baluyut.

Expanding the scope of the book to include non-fiction has also given us the opportunity to share a less-familiar side of more established writers like R. A. Sasaki and Hisaye Yamamoto. When viewed as a whole, the work gathered in this collection not only includes a variety of individual voices and narrative genres, but also spans a great part of the century—from the 1930's to the present—as well as a geographic region covering a major portion of the globe.

During the process of organizing our selections and putting together a table of contents, Carol Bruchac came up with the idea of dividing the material into five sections based on narrative setting. These sections follow a circular structure—beginning on the Asian continent, moving across the Pacific to Hawaii, continuing west across the continental United States, and finally, returning with Thelma Seto's story, "Inshallah," in the direction of the old world.

By attaching the issue of place to the narratives themselves rather than, as is usually done, to the origins of their authors, we foreground the relationship among these narratives within a larger, diasporal process. This approach is not meant to exclude the consideration of authorial origins. However, our initial attempts at organization showed this consideration to be most useful when applied to the work of writers like Darrell Lum, Lois-Ann Yamanaka, or Marie Hara, who have a strong sense of identity with and long-term commitment to a particular locale. Such a focus seemed much less meaningful in the case of a Connie Chan or a Garrett Hongo, who retain their ties to place, but write from a more distanced and global perspective.

The use of ethnic categories proved to be similarly problematic. How does one classify the work of Carol Roh-Spaulding, who is of mixed Korean and European descent? Or of Joseph Won, a Japanese Chinese American, who has lived in every major region of the United States? And for that matter, how does an author's choice of subject matter relate to such schemes of classification? Is *The Hanging on Union Square* by H.T. Tsiang to be considered a Chinese-, or even, an Asian-American novel, when it contains no Asian characters and is not about an "Asian American subject"? Furthermore, while Darrell Lum and the other writers from Hawaii retain a clear connection to place, they are not so easy to pin down in terms of ethnic or cultural identity. Over a fourth of the three hundred-plus submissions that Carol and I received were by writers of mixed descent, with many others also defying essentialist classification schemes.

There are presently no satisfactory models for describing the polyglot complexity of contemporary Asian American literature. As many critics have pointed out, the melting pot analogy too easily dispenses with difference, while the metaphor of the cultural mosaic does not allow for the exchange of influences between groups. The title of this book comes from the mixing of the well-worn metallurgical and cooking metaphors—as in, out of the melting pot into the fire.

This leap into the flames seems an appropriate analogy for the process of trial and transformation described in so many of the stories here—to say nothing of the dangerous business of editing an anthology. It has been a privilege to work with Carol Bruchac on both this book and on *Home to Stay*. From her I have learned that a literary tradition is vast and unfinished—composed of all the writers writing in it—a thing fashioned out of fire.

Sylvia Watanabe
Grand Rapids, Michigan
November 1995

*Note: The editors have followed the preferences of the individual authors in hyphenating terms which designate American ethnic groups.

SEEING THE FIRE

The four year project which resulted in this book began with our wish to combine the best of what we at The Greenfield Review Press felt had been two of our most outstanding books—our 1983 collection of Asian American Poetry *Breaking Silence* and our 1990 anthology of Asian American Women's fiction *Home to Stay*. Our plan was to do a comprehensive anthology of contemporary Asian American fiction and poetry.

Walter Lew and Joseph Bruchac agreed to act as poetry editors while Sylvia Watanabe joined me as the co-editor for fiction. Submissions, very strong submissions, poured in and we found ourselves with a dilemma. To publish a book that included all the worthy material was beyond our resources. We had to either reject a great deal of good work or redefine our goal. We soon realized that what we had was two books—one fiction and one poetry. Walter Lew took on the responsibility of not only editing but also publishing the poetry anthology with his new press Kaya Productions.

Sylvia and I continued to read work as it came in, but a long period of distraction and reorganization began in our lives and in our business. Everyone is probably familiar with the difficulties now besetting small presses, not only problems of finance and diminishing public support but also related issues of distribution, record-keeping and increasing work loads. The fact that we also were the fiscal agents for a major conference of Native American writers called Returning The Gift in 1992 only compounded things. Our book of Asian American fiction was virtually ignored for months on end. It was moved from my office to our home—a quiet place on an Adirondack ridge overlooking a pond. It sat in an old wooden fruit box as seasons changed and major decisions were being made in the publishing world. Those changes were so dramatic that we considered ending The Greenfield Review Press after having done it for over a quarter of a century.

Finally, however, new energy arrived. We hired our son, James, just out of college. He brought fresh ideas and new approaches; he was willing to blaze new trails, to travel and do all those things necessary to keep a small business alive in the age of "category killers." Small successes began. We signed a contract with a national distributor. We received a grant from the New York State Council on the Arts. Our book seemed possible again.

So, in the fall of 1995, final decisions were made and the manuscript went off to be typeset. So many years had slipped by that I had been finding it hard to feel connected to the book as a whole. Then a wonderful thing happened. I began the process of proof-reading the 380 plus pages and, during one glorious week of brilliant fire-filled foliage in the foothills of the Adirondacks, the collection took shape and fell together with its own bright colors and startling diversity. I saw that *Into The Fire* was a book which had grown to have a life of its own, a magical series of journeys which travel nearly the whole world, a globe-circling collection that honors the many facets of Asian American life with its history, its courage, its wisdom, humor and strength. My hope is that many others will travel that same road with this book, learn from its many voices, feel the fire of these stories.

Carol Bruchac
Porter Corners, New York
November 1995

Part I

Origins

Nora Cobb Keller

MOTHER-TONGUE

THE BABY I COULD KEEP came when I was already dead.

I was twelve when I was murdered, fourteen when I looked into the Yalu River and, finding no face looking back at me, knew that I was dead. I wanted to let the Yalu's currents carry my body to where it might find my spirit again, but the Japanese soldiers hurried me across the bridge before I could jump.

I did not let them get too close. I knew they would see the name and number stenciled across my jacket and send me back to the camps where they think nothing of using a dead girl's body. When the guards started to step towards me, I knew enough to walk on, to wave them back to their post where they would watch for other Koreans with that "special look" in their eyes. Before the Japanese government posted the soldiers—"for the good of the Koreans"—the bridge over the Yalu had been a popular suicide spot.

My body moved on.

That is why, almost 20 years after it left my spirit behind at the recreation camp, my body was able to have this baby.

Even the doctors here say it is almost a miracle. The camp doctor said I would never have a living child after he took my second one out, my insides too bruised and battered, impossible to properly heal.

So this little one is a surprise. This half-white and—though she doesn't know it yet, and may never know since her father thinks otherwise—half-Korean child. She would be called *tweggi* in the village where I was born, but here she will be American.

When the missionaries found me, they thought I was Japanese because of the name, Akiko, sewn onto the sack that was my dress. The number, 41, they weren't sure about and thought, perhaps an orphanage? They asked me—in Korean, Japanese, Chinese, English—where I came form, who my family was, but by then I had no voice and could only stand dumbly in front of their moving mouths as they lifted my arms, poked at my teeth and into my ears, wiped the dirt from my face.

She is like the wild child raised by tigers, I heard them say to each other. Physically human, but able to speak only in the language of animals. They were kind and praised me when I responded to the simple commands they issued in Japanese: sit, eat, sleep. Had they asked, I would also have responded to "close mouth" and "open legs." The Jungun lanfu camps trained the women only what they needed to know in order to service the soldiers. Other than that, we were not expected to understand, and were forbidden to speak, any language at all.

But we were fast learners, and creative. Listening as we gathered the soldiers' clothes for washing or cooked their meals, we were able to surmise when troops were coming in and how many we were expected to serve. We taught ourselves to communicate through eye movements, body posture, tilts of the head or—when we could not see each other—through rhythmic rustlings between our stalls; in this way we could speak, in this way we kept our sanity.

The Japanese say Koreans have an inherent gift for languages, proving that we are a natural colony, meant to be dominated. They delighted in their own ignorance, feeling they had nothing to fear or learn. I suppose that was lucky for us, actually. They never knew what we were saying. Or maybe they just didn't care.

I'm trying to remember exactly when I died. It must have been in stages, beginning with my birth as the fourth girl and last child in the Kim family, and ending in the recreation camps North of the Yalu. Perhaps if my parents had not died so early, I might have been able to live a full life. Perhaps not; we were a poor family. I might have been sold anyway.

My father was a cow trader. He traveled from village to village, herding the cows before him, from one farmer to the next, making a small profit as the middle man. When he was home, my older sisters' job was to collect the dung and, after we parceled out a small portion for our own garden, sell the rest to our neighbors. Sometimes we dried the dung for fuel, which burned longer and cleaner than wood. Most of the time, though, we used sticks that my sisters collected from the woods.

My job was to help my mother wash clothes. We each had a basket, according to our size, which we carried up the river we called Yalu Aniya, Older Sister to the Yalu. Going up was easy, the load light on our heads. Coming home was harder since not only were the damp clothes heavier, but we were tired from beating the clothes clean against the rocks. I remember that as we crouched over our wash, pounding out the dirt, I pretended that my mother and I sent secret signals to one another, the rocks singing our messages only we could understand.

My mother died shortly after my father. I didn't see my father die; he was almost 20 miles away. As with his life, I know about his death primarily through what others have told me. The villagers that took him in say he died of a lung disease, coughing up blood as he died. They also said he called for my mother.

She was always a good wife; she went to him quickly in death, just as she did in life. One night after we had carried home the wash, she kept saying how tired she was, how tired. Come, mother, I told her, lie down. I kept asking her what could I do? Do you want soup, do you want massage? Till finally she put her hand over my mouth and guided my fingers to her forehead. I stroked her softly, loosening her hair from the bun she tied it in, rubbing her temples where I could feel the heat and throb of her heart beating. Even when the erratic tempo slowed, then finally stopped, I continued to pet her. I wanted her to know that I loved her.

I touch my child in the same way now; this is the language she understands: the cool caresses of my fingers across her tiny eyelids, her smooth tummy, her fat toes. This, not the senseless murmurings of useless words, is what quiets her, tells her she is precious. She is like my mother in this way.

Because of this likeness, this link to the dead, my daughter is the only living thing I love. My husband, the missionaries who took me in after the camp, my sisters, if they are still alive, all are incidental. What are living people to ghosts, except ghosts themselves?

My oldest sister understood this. When my second and third sisters ran away together to look for work as secretaries or factory workers in Phyongyang, my oldest sister tried to keep father's business going by marrying our closest neighbor. They didn't have much money, but they had more than us and wouldn't take her without a dowry. How could they buy cattle without any capital, they reasoned.

I was her dowry, sold like one of the cows before and after me. You are just going to follow second and third sisters, she told me. The Japanese say there is enough work for anyone in the cities. Girls, even, can learn factory work or serve in restaurants. You will make lots of money.

Still, I cried. She hugged me, then pinched me. Grow up now, she said. No mother, no father. We all have to make our lives. She didn't look at my face when the soldiers came, didn't watch as they herded me onto their truck. I heard them asking if she didn't want to come along; your sister is still so young, not good for much, they said. But you. You are grown and pretty. You could do well.

I am not sure, but I think my sister laughed. I hope that she had at least a momentary fear that they would take her, too.

I am already married, she said.

I imagine she shrugged then, as if to say, what can I do? Then she added, my sister will be even prettier. She didn't think to ask why that should matter in a factory line.

I knew I would not see the city. And I think my oldest sister knew, too. We had heard the rumors: girls bought or stolen from villages outside the city, sent to Japanese recreation centers. But still, we did not know what the centers were like. At worst, I thought I would do what I've done all my life: clean, cook, wash clothes, work hard. How could I imagine anything else?

At first, that is what I did do. Still young, I was kept to serve the women in the camps. Around women all my life, I felt almost like I was coming home when I first realized there were women at the camps, maybe a dozen. I didn't see them right away; they were kept in their stalls, behind mat curtains, most of the days and throughout the night.

Unless they had to visit the camp doctor, their freedom outside their stalls consisted of weekly baths at the river and scheduled trips to the outhouse. If they needed to relieve themselves when it was not their turn to go outside, they could use their special pots. It became my job to empty the pots. I also kept their clothes and bedding clean, combed and braided their hair, served them their meals. When I could, I brought them each a dab of grease which they would smooth over their wounds, easing the pain of so many men.

I liked caring for the women. As their girl, I was able to move from one stall to the next, even from one section of the camp to another, if I was asked. And because of this luxury the women used me to pass messages. I would sing to the women as I braided their hair or walked by their compartments to check their pots. When I hummed certain sections, the women knew to take those words for their message. In this way, we could keep up with each other, find out who was sick, who was new, who had the most men the night before, who was going to crack.

To this day, I do not think Induk—the woman who was the camp Akiko before me—cracked. Most of the other women thought she did because she would not shut up. She talked loud and non-stop. In Korean and in Japanese she denounced the soldiers, yelling at them to stop their invasion of her country and her body. Even as they mounted her, she shouted, I am Korea, I am a woman, I am alive. I am seventeen, I had a family just like you do, I am a daughter, I am a sister.

Men left her stall quickly, some crying, most angrily joining the line for the woman next door. All through the night she talked, reclaiming her Korean name, reciting her family genealogy, even chanting the recipes her mother had passed on to her. Just before daybreak, they took her out of her stall and into the woods where we couldn't hear her anymore. They brought her back skewered from her vagina to her mouth, like a pig ready for roasting. A lesson, they told the rest of us, warning us into silence.

That night, it was if a thousand frogs encircled the center. They opened their throats for us, swallowed our tears, and cried for us. All night, it seemed, they called, Induk, Induk, Induk, so we would never forget.

Although I might have imagined the frogs. That was my first night as the new Akiko, I was given her clothes, which were too big and made the soldiers laugh. She won't be wearing them much, anyway, they jeered.

Even though I had not yet had my first bleeding, I was auctioned off to the highest bidder. After that it was a free-for-all and I thought I would never stop bleeding.

That is how I know Induk didn't go crazy, she was going sane. She was planning her escape. The corpse the soldiers brought back from the woods wasn't Induk.

It was Akiko; it was me.

My husband speaks four languages: German, English, Korean and Japanese. He is learning a fifth, Polish, from cassette tapes he borrows from the public library. He reads Chinese.

A scholar who spends his life with the bible, he thinks he is safe, that the words he reads, the meaning he gathers will remain the same. Concrete. He is wrong.

He shares all of his languages with our daughter, though she is not even a year old. She will absorb the sounds, he tells me. But I worry that the different sounds for the same object will confuse her. To compensate, I try to balance her with language I know is true. I watch her with a mother's eye, trying to see what she needs—my breast, new diapers, a kiss, her toy— before she cries, before she has to give voice to her pain.

And each night, I touch each part of her body, waiting until I see recognition in her eyes. I wait until I see that she knows that all of what I touch is her and hers to name in her own mind, before language dissects her into pieces that can be swallowed and digested by others not herself.

At the camp, the doctor gave me a choice: rat poison or the stick. I chose the stick. I saw what happened to the girl given the rat bait to abort her baby. I did not have the courage then to die the death that she did.

As the doctor bound my legs and arms, gagged me, then reached for the stick he would use to hook and pull the baby, not quite a baby, into the world, he talked. He spoke of evolutionary differences between the races, biological quirks that made the women of one race so pure, and the women of another so promiscuous. Base, really, almost like animals, he said.

Rats, too, will keep doing it until they die, refusing food or water as long as they have a supply of willing partners. The doctor chuckled and probed, digging and piercing, as he lectured. Luckily for the species, Nature ensures that there is one dominant male to keep the others at bay and the female under control.

I followed the light made by the waves of my pain, tried to leave my body behind. But the doctor pinned me to the earth with his stick and his words. Finally, he stood upright, cracked his back and threw the stick into the trash. He rinsed his hands in a basin of water, then unbound my hands and mouth. Those rags he put between my legs.

Fascinating, he said thoughtfully as he left the tent. Perhaps it is the differences in geography that make the women of our two countries so morally incompatible.

He did not bother tying me down, securing me for the night. Maybe he thought I was too sick to run. Maybe he thought I wouldn't want to. Maybe he knew I had died and that ropes and guards couldn't keep me anyway.

That night, with the blood-soaked rags still wedged between my thighs, I slipped out of the tent, out of the camp. Following the sound of my mother beating clothes against the rocks, I floated along the trails made by deer and found a nameless stream that led, in the end, like all the mountain streams, to the Yalu.

Nora Cobb Keller is a Korean American free lance writer whose short fiction and critical essays have been published in several journals. She lives in Hawaii with her family and writes when the stories start invading her dreams. She holds a Masters Degree from Santa Cruz. "Mother Tongue" is part of a novel that she is currently working on.

Shirley Geok-lin Lim

HUNGER

ONLY TWO DAYS since Mother left. The freedom seemed like forever. More room for running. More time for staying awake, games, play. Was she glad? Was she sad? There was never time for thinking though the day was long, longer as the afternoon drew on and on towards meal time, longest in darkness when the odors of soy, pork, ginger, garlic and sweet cooked rice lingered on and on in the empty rooms downstairs, like a vague ache in her crotch, a burn in her chest, and followed her to the bedroom to lie down beside her in the brown faded dark of the bottom half of the iron double-bunk bed that had been so fashionable only a few years ago.

Three days next morning. She tightened the uniform belt. Suweng's mother was a washerwoman, but in her hand Suweng had a piece of white bread spread thick with margarine and sprinkled with sugar. She wasn't in her A class. Suweng was a B class girl, but her uniform was starched and ironed, the creases sharp and straight, the folds thick like the slice of bread and the yellow margarine spread with a fat knife.

The starch made the royal blue cotton gleam, like the fat sugar crystals glistening on the margarine on top of the bread.

She had seen Suweng eat that slice of bread walking ahead of her across the bridge to school a few weeks ago when they had first moved to Grandfather's house. Even then she had been hungry. Mother had given her two manie-piah biscuits and some boiled water. Brown, crisp, flat, dry, round, pricked, sugary, crackling, each half the size of a palm—you could buy ten for five cents. She had watched Suweng eat her slice of thick, soft, oily bread. She walked beside her and began talking, watching as Suweng put the last wedge of bread in her round greasy mouth.

Now she waited for Suweng in the middle hall and watched as Suweng's mother spread the margarine on the bread. The margarine tub was huge, almost as large as those square tins of fancy English biscuits they had when they had money and lived in the bank. Now she didn't even have those two manie-piah biscuits for breakfast.

Perhaps she was hoping Suweng would not be able to finish her bread and would give her the leftover. Perhaps she hoped the washerwoman would offer her a slice. At every house from every open and half-opened door she smelled the fresh yeasty dough of white bread, the clean alkaline of sugar crystals. The morning was full of food, and she was hungry.

By the next week she had stopped walking with Suweng. She could walk faster, easier, without Suweng who strolled lazily munching her bread. Swiftly she passed the half-opened doors from where warm scents of toast and coconut cakes wafted towards her thin chest. She did not care to pause to breathe the full aromas of black coffee, that clear scent of pandan-scented coconut-boiled rice that made her stomach lurch. The houses were rich, concealed behind gold-leafed carved doors and windows, like her Grandfather's house had been, even in her memory which seemed now so short, so immediate of quick movement and sunshine.

This was freedom. To walk at a fast trot to school, to think ahead only to the day, the play, the books, the next day, the play, the books. Not to think of where she was but how she must go. Quickly she crossed the little bridge, breathed the sulfuric smell of putrid riverine sediment. This is not it, she thought. The Angsana trees were heavy with yellow blossoms. The tiny petals littered a stretch of the park, the morning air was acid sharp with their efflorescence and decay. Yellow pollen like gold dust dotted the ground. To the right the Straits of Malacca were always blue or grey, colors as steadfast as her heart as she walked rapidly to school. I am steadfast, she thought, exhilarated, I am myself, no one is me, I am alone. She forgot she was hungry walking between the weight of the blossoming Angsana and the empty blue space of the morning sky and the Malacca Straits.

So quickly she had forgotten about Mother. Poor Mother who cried that morning in Auntie's house after she had pulled her in as she was passing by on her way to school and had given her a glass of Ovaltine and a slice of bread and marmalade. Very good marmalade, form Sheffield, England. It had strips of bitter peel and was shining clear orange, just the way she liked marmalade. But that was only one morning. Mother wasn't at the window of Auntie's house the next day nor the next, nor the next, and so on. Mother had gone someplace, gone away. Now she walked quickly past Auntie's house with its closed gold-leaf carved windows and doors and tried not to think about the marmalade.

Sister Finnigan was a tall scarecrow. Her eyes were bright blue, little shifting chips of precious star sapphire behind the steel-rimmed glasses. Mother had taken her to many jewelry stores. She had sat in front of the long glassed-in counters and stared at the colored stones, watery aquamarine, flushed pigeon rubies from Burma, the bland green jade best for carved peaches and buddhas, and dense yellow tourmaline from Brazil. It was the colorless stones that cost the most: clear as nothing else in the world. No blue, no grey, no yellow, the hardest stone in the world Mr. Koh, the man behind the glass counters with his abacus and little magnifying glass, had told her. No-color, clear as clear, like looking through water and seeing no bottom, no sky, no eyes looking back, the impossible clear that is still not nothing, that has been chipped and chipped till the planes tilt like crazy mirrors refracting each other, till their cross-reflections catch dizzy fire, and what you saw then was this blaze, this spark that sprang up at you and pulled you in. But it was just a stone, a stone with no color. Now Mother had been gone for weeks she was becoming like that stone, she was becoming no-mother, a memory clear as clear and Chai knew she was forgetting her, as if Mother had no reflection in the bottom of her memory or in the sky above. Sister Finnigan's blue star-sapphire eyes snapped and pulsed, although not as blue and steadfast as her own heart.

She sat on the floor by the classroom door and sewed a row of back-stitches, hemming handkerchiefs. She had to unpick the first row. You're taking too much cloth in the stitch, Sister Finnigan said, turning the handkerchief over to show the way the stitches bunched up on the seamless side. Pick only a thread, she said, her long white fingers pushing the needle smoothly through the cotton, sliding through a thread of the weave, and don't pull tight. She turned the cloth over to show where the stitch had closed the seam, not even a faint shadow of the thread showing. Invisible, it must be invisible, she said.

Try as she would, she could not do it. The handkerchief was for her father. Invisible, she thought, pick only a thread, leave smooth. But the needle was huge and clumsy and wouldn't obey her. It broke off the thread of the weave and left cloth scars. Her anxious fingers printed smudges of pencil grey lead and grime. After Mother left, she didn't take a bath everyday, sometimes it was three days before she felt grubby enough to strip and pour buckets of well water over herself. There was no soap and Father rinsed their clothes and dried them on Saturdays and Sundays. Sister Finnigan fixed her chipped blue eyes on her crumpled uniform, the socks she slipped lower each day into the canvas shoes so as to hide the spreading grey heels. So she sat right by the doorway, as far as she could from Sister Finnigan's stinky black robes as Sister perched on her desk showing the eager girls how to turn daisy petals, knot bachelor buttons, cross-stitch a satin oval, and ruffle and gather smocks and aprons. She could only hem a handkerchief, and she could not go beyond the second seam.

Still, sewing was alright. It was better sitting in class an A girl than in the room at night without Father or Mother there. Her brothers slept in a different corner. She never remembered in the afternoon if she had changed into pajamas or had just fallen asleep in her skirt and blouse waiting for Father to come back. She kept the handkerchief in her desk, and she never finished it, and Sister Finnigan forgot about her poor back-stitches because she memorized the Book of Luke and recited each chapter that was asked for perfectly as if she had swallowed the book and had only to open her mouth to find the page and rattle off verse and chapter. Being an A girl in class was much better than being a girl at home.

Father had forgotten about her too. He forgot she walked to school every morning without breakfast, that he hadn't given her money for lunch, and that she hadn't taken her bath before he slipped out each night some place.

She was beginning to forget she was hungry. They must have eaten at night. Something some auntie gave them. In the morning she washed by the well with a bucket of water smelling slightly of sulphur and hurried past the splendid houses of gold-leaf closed doors and across the bridge. It was the bridge that brought her to herself, across to the Angsanas in the park and the long consoling line of blue and grey Straits water. Once across the bridge she began reciting the Book of Luke, long mouthfuls of words. Sister Finnigan loved her for the Book of Luke. She had this secret machine inside her that could eat up books, swallow them whole, then give them back in bits and pieces, as good almost as before she ate them.

She didn't look up at the Angsanas anymore, all their flowers were gone and only dry brown rustling seeds hung down and scattered by her feet. Some auntie, her mother's sister, had told her that the seeds were devil shoes. The auntie had peeled the tough fibrous brown covering and showed her the tiny shoe-shaped seed. Don't you put any in your pocket, Mother's sister said. The devil will come to your house looking for his shoes. She had been afraid when the auntie told her this, she had put that little shoe in the pocket of her pajama that night. Mother was still with them then, she had not been hungry, only naughty. She fell asleep frightened that the devil would come, but the next morning the shoe was still in her pocket and then the pajama had been washed and the shoe disappeared.

Things disappeared all the time now. First it was Mother, then her doll with the round blue eyes over which pink plastic lids tufted with tough bristle-lashes could fall as you pushed her head down. She had forgotten about her doll in the freedom which Mother's disappearance brought. All those hours of afternoon play by the river's muddy flats, the grubbiness between her toes that nobody scolded her for. Then she saw Ah Lan carrying the doll; Ah Lan said it was her doll, but she recognized the red blemish on one upper arm which she had always pretended was a vaccination mark. It was her own doll, with shining yellow stringy hair springing in clumps from the hard plastic head, and the straight fat legs that could move only from the hip like the German soldiers in the old war movies. She was sad the doll no longer belonged to her, it had been her doll and she never saw it again after that afternoon she asked Ah Lan to show her its upper arm and pointed out the red patch on it.

She went to class every day. Sister Finnigan loved her. She sat in the front row and read all the books. One day, after recess, it was so hot she felt faint. She thought she saw Sister spread out her arms. The black robe fell like a cloak from her arms, it ballooned like a cape, like furry black wings, and Sister rose towards the ceiling, her face still calm and smiling, the blue eyes glinting like pieces of sky. There was a little dribble of spit by the corner of her mouth, she had fallen asleep, and Sister Finnigan was still leaning against the desk reading a passage about the Seven Years War. She had felt really hungry then, as if she would die if she didn't have something to eat immediately, but she knew she wouldn't. She hoped Sister Finnigan would not catch her sleeping in class, so she stretched her eyes wide open and rolled the pupils around like marbles to keep awake. Instead she felt nauseous. She kept her eyes on the page and tried drinking in the words. The next period was library hour and she knew there were all kinds of adventure books in the cupboard she hadn't read yet, so if she could wait till then she would be able to forget about being hungry.

It was getting harder to play in the afternoon. She was tired and weak a lot. She waited every evening for Father to come home from work. Then Auntie gave them their meal. Her brothers ate so much rice, three plates full of rice. She couldn't eat that much. Her stomach hurt her after the food, although she had been waiting all day to eat.

She waited in the morning as she walked past the park with its long green sweep of grass lying beside the pulsing

Straits waves. Now it was a kind of loneliness. She sang to herself as she walked, and kept her head down as she passed the crowded areas where other children who went to other schools were noisily crowding around the ice-cream man, the Indian peanut seller, the pushcart on which the peddler was quickly grilling coconut waffles. The fruitsellers had baskets of golden langsats, egg-shaped crimson rambutans spiky with dark hair. They had split open dark red juicy watermelons dotted with shiny black seeds, gleaming yellow jackfruit, plump and ribbed, and light green guavas with pink seedy hearts. She kept her head down as she passed, only lifting it high to sing to herself when she was safely alone under the umbrellas Angsanas.

But she still had to go through recess every day. She waited till the girls had rushed out and pushed their way to their favorite stalls. Some bought fried noodles or sardine sandwiches or rice cakes. Others brought bread and jam and spent their money on syrupy ice drinks or sweets. She waited in the classroom till she thought they had finished eating, then she went out to play with them. She was ashamed she could not eat with them. It wasn't that she was hungry, although of course she was, but she was more ashamed she had no money for food.

Only after she got home did she feel hunger. Her stomach made so much noise crying for some food that she shouted louder as she played to hide its noise. Her brothers played more and more in the streets. They ran further and further beyond the house. They always came home before Father did, before it became night. Away from their house and the other gold-leafed covered doorways, the streets were narrow and the houses crowded and small. She was running down the narrow street going home when the old man waved at her. He was very old and thin, an opium smoker, she thought, like her uncle in the big house. She hurried after her brothers, she was so hungry she didn't wave back.

The old man was sitting on a bench outside the small house the next afternoon.

They had found some seahorses in the Straits water beside the seawall. They knew it was dangerous to walk that far out on the seawall, but a whole crowd of them had gone anyway. She was timid at the close sight of so much water. The seawall was about eight feet high and the Straits came up almost to the top of the wall. On the landward side of the wall it was all steaming mud. Wrinkled mud-skippers leapt from mud-hole to mud-hole like her bad dreams in the morning; they were grey like the mud come alive, and they had loose flaps of warty skin, flopping open mouths, and waggling tails; they were creatures from the stinking revolting mud. Immediately on the other side of the wall were the clear Straits waves, so bright in the burning afternoon sun that it hurt her eyes to look at them too long. They were blue like the sky brought close to hand, yet they were no-color when she put her face down to look. Her brother had found a Players Cigarette tin and had tied a string through a rusted hole in its side. They had thrown the tin into the water and dragged it alongside as they walked along the seawall. Then they found two tiny seahorses swimming in the tin when they fished it out.

The seahorses swam bravely up, their horse-heads held up high. From their curving flanks fringed fins fluttered like mermaids' fans. She fancied they were ladies dressed for a ball; there they would dance and never ask about dinner the way she would never ask her aunties about food. She was a machine like the sea, churning her own salt, licking the sweet salty flavor of her body in secret at night when hunger woke her. The seahorses waltzed, strange tiny women in a tinful of water. She wanted them thrown back into the huge sea, she wanted to keep them to show father, she wanted them to wink at her, she knew them very well. But they curled like grey grubs and died, floated in the leaking tin, ugly things.

She was running away from her brothers who had caught and killed the seahorses and who wanted to stay by the wall to catch more of them. Whatever for? They would only sail for a few beautiful moments, then turn on their sides like capsized boats, only they were already in the water, and die. So there. She wasn't staying to watch that. When she saw the old man sitting on the bench just like yesterday. Only this time he had a giant guava in his hand, as big as her two hands, and he was smiling. She could see he didn't have a tooth in his mouth, he was so old, he must be somebody's grandfather.

He waved the guava, saw her stop, held it out to her. It was light green, ripe, that's when they're the sweetest. She knew because of the times Mother had taken her to Grandmother's house and she had picked the fallen guavas in the garden. Now Mother was gone, and she would never visit Grandmother's house. Had Grandmother died and no one had told her? But that was because she was only eight. Grandmother's guavas were never so large. She wanted it not to bring home to Father but to eat it like she ate all those little sweet guavas in Grandmother's garden when Grandmother was alive.

The old man handed her the guava and tugged at her to follow him. The front room was empty and dim, it didn't look like anyone lived there. He put his hand under her dress and stroked her front. She didn't think anything of it. He was shivering, the folds of his face matching the folds of his arms. She didn't know skin and flesh could drip and drape like spotted grey cloth over a body. He put one hand through her sleeve and twisted her nipple. It didn't hurt, but she moved away then ran out.

The next day, he was sitting by the bench waiting for her she knew. This time he had a ten-cent coin, all shiny and new, and she stayed just a little longer while he stroked her arms and chest, his eyes shut mysteriously. But when he called to her the day after and the days after the day after she ran past without looking. He had only money to give her, and the ten-cent coin did not make up for the terrible pleasure of ignoring his pleading eyes and wavering hand.

I am so pleased to be included as a short story writer, for it helps to confirm one lesser-known identity in the public selves willy-nilly conferred on me, as poet, scholar, editor, teacher, mother and woman. Although I have only one collection of short stories, *Another Country* (Times Books International, 1982) to my name, the short story continues to be my "other country" which I return to no matter how briefly for the pleasures that only fiction writing can offer. The promise of intensity, the remembered suppleness in the prose of Mansfield or Chekhov, the tantalizing sugges-

tions of subterranean conduits between narrative form and psychic/community/historical breaking secrets—these are just a few of the temptations that keep the short story a disruptive pleasure force for me. May the force be with all of us?

My first book, *Crossing the Peninsula,* received the Commonwealth Poetry Prize, 1980. I won the Asiaweek Short Story Second Prize in 1982, and *The Forbidden Stitch: An Asian American Women's Anthology,* which I co-edited received the American Book Award, 1990. Besides my three volumes of poetry and one collection of short stories, I am completing a book of memoirs for Feminist Press (New York), tentatively titled, *Moving Her Self: Memoirs in Postcolonial Geographies.* I am also on the editorial board of *Feminist Studies,* and am co-editing its special volume, *Whose Asia, Who's Asia,* for Fall 1993; and am on the advisory boards of *Calyx* and *Belles Lettres,* two well-known feminist publications in the U.S. In 1991/92, I edited or co-edited *Approaches to Teaching Kingston's The Woman Warrior, One World of Literature* and *Reading the Literatures of Asian America.* I am presently preparing a new collection of poems, *What the Fortune Teller Didn't Say.* I am currently Professor of English and Women's Studies at the University of California, Santa Barbara.

Larissa Lai

WATER, AND OTHER MEASURES OF DISTANCE

1. BLOOD

MY MOTHER'S BLOOD thundered in my ears and in my heart, which still beat in sympathy with hers. It skipped out of time the moment the promise was made, then fell back again into perfect synchronicity. The day I was born, the rhythm began to separate again, slowly finding its own pace and then rushing back to meet hers, reeling out and rushing back over and over, until the pressure from within became too great and the outside world wailed for me to enter it. Light flooded into my body so fast that my eyes stung and watered. For the first time, I felt small and fragile, confined within my own skin.

The colour of blood is the colour of luck, the colour of life. They say my father's heart was rich with all three the day he died. I am amazed how quickly the body can be turned to ashes, the blood turned to steam. We light incense to make the steam fragrant. The colour of death is no colour at all, only the traces of a concentrated essence going up and up. It finds its way past our lips, straight into the bloodstream.

The funeral was already over by the time the news reached me. I asked the housemother for a day off to go up to the Temple of Shifting Vapours to burn incense and paper money for his soul. It was raining that day, as it had been the day my mother died. My oiled-paper umbrella was still good, although three of the spokes were broken. I put on heavy shoes and a big coat and set off. In town I bought a large roll of joss sticks and many stacks of paper money, purple, turquoise, yellow, orange and red. I bought a whole chicken and a few oranges, which however, were slightly shriveled, and no doubt sour. The rain had come quite suddenly and the ground was still warm. Steam rose up from the earth like little wisps of lost souls, making the path hard to see. The air smelled of iron—freshly turned soil? or was it blood? If it weren't for that smell, one might indeed believe that the temple was in the clouds, suspended high above the mortal world, floating there in its arbitrary location.

I was greeted by a young novice. She seemed to be still unaccustomed to the robes. They weighed her down, keeping her close to the earth, to the cool stone floor which was in need of mopping. The muddy footprints of a recent visitor were still discernible. As we approached the main pavilion, I could hear the cooing of doves. A short slim snake darted past me on the right. Another shot right between my feet. I nearly cried out in shock. Suddenly a panic of white wings fled past my face. Doves. A thousand of them. And a thousand snakes. A patron is doing a ritual for her mother-in-law, the novice explained. A rich and beautiful patron, she added, with a shy half-smile. I looked at her and felt compelled to smile back.

The novice suggested that we should wait for her to finish, if that would be alright with me. I agreed, so we stood behind a pillar and waited for the woman to finish kowtowing, three sticks of incense in her elegant hands. Her white silk robe moved as she did, always just a moment behind, remembering each motion after it had already passed with a kind of sadness. Even under the high ceiling of the temple, she seemed tall. She wore an expression of deep concentration which intensified whenever she paused for a moment to take the effects of the ritual in. A few snakes still twisted around the base of the large ornate Buddha, whose head almost touched the ceiling. There among the rafters three doves fluttered, still desperately searching for a way out. Sometimes, said the novice, they die of exhaustion and just fall, like that, onto the stone floor.

When she was finished, the woman strode out of the temple with a walk that suggested royalty. As she breezed past me, something cool flooded through my bloodstream like a thousand tiny birds. My breath darted into my mouth before I could stop it. The novice gave me that funny half-smile again, but I pretended not to notice.

I lit the incense for my father and placed it in the sandbox beside hers. Hers was still smouldering steadily. I laid out the chicken and the oranges. I put the paper money into the burners and lit them, watching the bright colours dissolve in the orange light, and the smoke spiral up, past the three doves, still fluttering, up to where my father was waiting. For a moment I thought I detected a trace of the herb shop smells flowing under in the fragrance of the joss sticks. Then it was gone. I knelt on the cold floor for a long time.

The sky had already begun to darken when I began my descent, and it was raining steadily. Quietly, I cursed myself for not having been more careful about the time. My shoes, by this time, were damp both inside and out. I shivered a little from the cold. Two more spokes of my umbrella had broken. I scrambled down the hillside, not wanting to get caught by the pitch dark of a rainy night. A moderate wind came up from the North, blowing rain under the umbrella. My coat was beginning to soak through when ahead of me on the path I noticed a lantern swaying with a step I thought I recognized. It was the woman who had made the dove and snake offering! I considered whether I should approach her, but thought better of it. The lamp stopped swaying. It glowed evenly from a fixed position on the path. She was waiting for me.

Dear Hsuan-Chi,

For her crucial scenes, David Lean always starts with daffodils. Or is it sunflowers? Something yellow. Will Yuri ever leave his dark, beautiful wife Tonia for her, or will she drift away from him towards some tragic end? Those beautiful Russian names. Lara. Larissa. The movie Dr. Zhivago came out in 1966, the year before I was born. Yuri didn't leave his wife. Years later he sees Larissa on the street but dies of a heart attack before he can approach her. I have never looked good in yellow.

My mother gave me the name, but I want to tell you about my grandfather on my father's side. He has always loved Hollywood. My father is named after Ingmar Bergman. My cousin is called Isabella. (I saw Isabella Rosellini once. She came with David Lynch into a cafe where I was working.) I have an Auntie Marilyn, and Auntie Marlene, and Uncle Grant and an Auntie Judy. Who woke up where the clouds were far behind, first? I come from a nomadic family. Always waking up somewhere else.

I have two Chinese names, one my Yeh Yeh gave me and one my mother gave me. I can't pronounce either of them correctly.

In David Lean's movie, Larissa is played by Julie Christie. She has freckles and beautiful long red hair, parted on the side in a way that is quite fashionable now. Since moving to the West Coast, I have met quite a few young women about my age called Larissa. Once, I met a Larissa who was older than me. She was the wife of an old friend of my parents. She was from Russia, for real.

2. A PURCHASE

I have been thinking of my father a lot in these last few months. I think of the herb shop, the little drawers of leaves, stems, roots, flowers, insects, bones, horns, claws, viscera. . . . The smell of medicine always makes me nostalgic. They said my father was strange. That he would regret teaching me to read when I was five, that my water clear soul would murk over and fade away, and that I would never marry. He said I have my mother's face, the same forehead, the small, slightly pointed nose. I can't remember her at all. Can't remember her holding me. Can't remember her walking me out into the garden in spring to watch the cherry trees blooming. Can't remember how the fog came in like the tide and stayed for months one unusual autumn, taking her life when it ebbed out.

What I do remember is the magic leaving my father's hands. There was a time when it seemed there was nothing he couldn't cure, with just the right mixture of this root or that, the essences of flowers, plants or animals. My mother started bleeding on the inside and he couldn't stop the flow. The house filled with steam from this or that infusion boiling away in the kettle. In fact it reeked of steam and the rich fetid smells of life, the way you would expect it to smell deep beneath the earth where the soil is rich and gently heated by the planet's insides bubbling. Strong and bitter as blood. I imagine my mother must have begun to smell that way too, stinking of life until the moment she died. I don't think that smell ever left the house, although it diminished after her death to the faintest odour, that would occasionally bloom with the pungency of memory when I would shake out sheets that had been in storage for a long time. I don't remember her, but I remember that smell. It never entered the house with that intensity again.

After her death, he began to get the prescriptions wrong. His hands became clumsy in the measuring, his nose lost the ability to determine quality herbs from stale ones. His vision grew blurry. His eyes lost his ability to distinguish the various shapes and sizes of the raw materials he used to make his medicines. It was as though his senses were retreating deep inside the temple of his body, renouncing the world in favour of a lifetime of mourning.

He would come alive sometimes at night. He would collect the oddest assortment of objects—strange flowers in the deepest reds, plants with thick green leaves, mushrooms in brilliant oranges and russets, which must surely have been poisonous, branches that smelled sweet when burned, and sometimes even small animals or lizards, still wriggling. None of the traditional paper money or candles. Occasionally he would use incense I had bought at the market, if it was within easy reach as he stumbled through the kitchen into the backyard. He would set his offerings on fire, fully expecting the smoke to journey straight to heaven and bring her back to him.

He would sit up late into the night waiting for her. It terrified the neighbours.

Eventually she came for him, beckoning once and then not turning her head again until they had passed through the gates of paradise.

When a younger herbalist with a pretty and very much alive young wife set up business on the other side of town, business slowly began to drift in his direction, as gently as the wind changes with the turn of the seasons. As his business dwindled and he found he had more time on his hands, his nocturnal rituals increased in frequency. It was unlikely that a marriage would be arranged for me at this rate, so I began to consider alternatives. There was a rumour of a village in the West inhabited only by women.

I have always had trouble distinguishing what is a story from what is real.

I arrived at a more practical solution late one night after a bout of tossing and turning. The wet smell of burning flowers and branches and mushrooms found its way into my head. Outside the window, my father was sitting on the edge of a fire, looking for all the world like a ghost. His hair needed trimming and he was as thin as a hungry dog. I almost wished my mother would appear and put him out of his misery.

In the morning, he was more or less himself, although his eyes were tired.

"Father," I said, "how is the shop doing?"

"You know it is not doing well," he answered.

"Yes, I know," I said. "I think that if you had a little money to invest, you might still make a go of it."

"Perhaps so," he said.

"If you sold me to a teahouse it might make the crucial difference."

His hair suddenly became a white forest. I wondered if it had gone from black to white at that precise instant. "My only daughter," he said, "how could I?"

"If you don't there will be nothing left for me here either. You won't be able to afford a dowry to marry me off. If you don't get another chance the shop will fold, even assuming I could manage it on my own, after you have gone. If you sell me, I will at least be guaranteed of a roof over my head, and you will have another chance with your business, or at the very least, something to retire on."

He sighed. "I knew it was a bad omen," he said.

"What?"

"Do you remember Chiu the oil seller?"

"Just a little," I replied.

"We were good friends before you were born. When your mother and his wife got pregnant at the same time, we promised that our children should marry. But then both women gave birth to girls. We should have known not to make promises under such uncertain conditions. I must be haunted by a fox!"

A well-known tea house took me because I could write pretty lines. I sent my father the money.

What is the value of human life? We are made up of so much water.

I have a nightmare about the ocean. Not a nightmare exactly. A dream then.

I am walking along a sandy beach. It's warm and the sun is bright. Large rocks stick up from the sand like teeth, twice my height. I weave among them. They hide where I have come from, where I am going. Finally I come to a wide open area that is all grey rock, stepping down in wide plateaus to the edge of a cliff, which drops impossibly down to where the sea is waiting. I lie on the cliff's edge and wait, for what, I'm not sure. I don't notice the water begin to rise.

It comes up behind me making small animal noises. By the time I notice it, I have to hurry, but the plateaus aren't so wide after all. I'm climbing trying to find footholds in an increasingly steep, increasingly smooth rockface. The sea is a thousand greedy hands, grabbing.

The woman I am about to tell you about was not afraid of the sea. She was afraid of the moon. The way it tugs at our blood always. "It seems incredible that the moon does that," she said, watching the sea enter a narrow gorge it had cut for itself in the black rock. It swerved hard against the rock we sat on and sent salt water flying into our eyes. "The sea survives all droughts and floods and still, the moon can make it move. Have you ever thought about that?" What about our blood? I wanted to ask. How can something clutch at us from such a great distance? Now I want to ask her if that's how fate works, but she isn't here.

Dear Hsuan-chi,

You have worked in these places. And yet your story comes back so romantic. Where is the truth there? Is it time that cauterizes the raw bleeding edges? Or that the men who wrote about you never understood? I admit, I too am inventing you.

Presently in Thailand, whole villages lose all their women and many children to a sex trade industry that caters to tourists from the Western industrial world. Companies, American and Japanese, send their employees on packaged sex tours to the Philippines, Thailand, Taiwan and South Korea. Can you imagine a trafficker descending from a helicopter like a fairy godmother into a village with gifts of baubles, make-up and other finery? When she leaves, she leaves with several young girls in tow.

Do you remember the story of Li Chi? I think of her climbing the stony hill up to the serpent's cave, in silk, perhaps, white silk, the colour of death. The serpent had already devoured nine virgins, one a year, voluntarily sent so that crops would continue to grow. Up the hill she goes, her white dress mimicking every motion she makes like a slow shadow. There are rice balls in her pockets, a sword in her hand, and a snake hunting dog at her sides. With the rice balls she distracts him, the dog attacks him and the sword in the hand goes in for the kill.

But what had made this possible for her, and not the other nine victims? She was the daughter of an official, where they were the daughters of workers and criminals. What made it possible for her? Class privilege? Her beauty? Or the fact that she was a heroine in an epic tale?

In Ottawa Magazine two years ago, there was a story about a journalist who disappeared in Thailand. He was a good man who felt sorry for the women who worked the bars there, and had gone to do a story on them. Because his good heart aches so much, he feels he must stay and help them, so he opens a brothel of his own in Bangkok. Years later, a second good-hearted journalist goes to look for him, and comes back saying he did the best he could, he did the best he could. . .

The serpents are hungry, the cave itself is hungry, hungry, hungrier . . . and the serpents heads are multiplying. . .

How were you to know that the merchants and scholars you met would grow into these corporate monsters, their eyes running LED spirals of numbers, spitting them onto the floor of the stock exchange to put a price on everything in the so called Third World, in order to take it away? The only things women have left to sell are their bodies and their children. So the monster takes, not one virgin a year, but one hundred thousand. Where are you in this, my epic heroine? Where am I?

3. ROSES

The woman with the lantern smelled subtly of roses. She asked my name. When I told her she seemed pleased. My husband reads your poetry, she said. He quotes your lines to me sometimes. Although her umbrella is glossy and whole, the rain has drenched her clothing also. In the light of the lantern, I can make out the shape of her body beneath her damp dress.

Later that week, I was introduced to a traveling scholar. He was tall and his skin was luminous as the surface of a lake. He looked at me with a light in his eyes which made me think perhaps he was remembering someone else. His gaze weighed on me. I wasn't sure whether to be worried or pleased.

We played chess until late in the night. Some men, when they discover that I play chess, find it distasteful, since it is not a very ladylike game. But this scholar seemed to enjoy it immensely. I watched his hands as he lined up his men, his horses, and his cannons. His palms were narrow, the fingers long and nails clipped so that they were round and pink with neat white borders. They moved with a decisive swiftness that made me think of carp, darting about to capture bits of bread tossed into their shallow pool. He beat me once, I beat him twice. He complained of faulty horses, and suggested we play a game of rhymes instead.

He asked if he could stay the night, but I said no. As a rule, I didn't sleep with the clients. Since I earned my keep with my poetry and other amusements, Mrs. Ho didn't pressure me.

He came again the next night, saying that the roads were too muddy to travel. He brought me a gift—a packet of rose scented incense. I lit some. The smoke and sweet odour filled the room like fresh air from a place far away. I found myself remembering a rainy dusk on the hill leading down from the temple, and a figure standing on the path. I pushed the memory away, recalling that I was working and ought to put my energy into that. It would not, I thought, be at all unpleasant to have this man as a patron. He asked me if I could sing. I told him I had been studying with one of my sisters who had been an opera singer. Spiders scuttled from my elbows to my wrists. I don't often get nervous. I wasn't sure whether it was because singing was a relatively new thing, or because I was so anxious to please my guest. I stood up conscious of the weight of my embroidered sleeves, and then the weight of the whole garment, the way it flowed blue to the floor cascading birds and flowers. The silk lining began to feel rough and slightly sticky against my skin, and I noticed my hands were not as steady as usual. When I opened my mouth, the voice began to come. It was frail at first, conscious of itself alone in a quiet room. Then it grew to fill the space, a creature unto itself, streaming from my lungs with the force of a tidal wave. It enveloped me firmly, guiding me through myself like a long path to the ocean.

The next day there was a typhoon. It started slowly on a mountain far away. Then the rain came smashing onto the street like eggs. It moved over our heads and was gone like a great beast, passing through the sky. The air was filled with steam. Next the wind came, bringing shards of rain, cutting wildly into the air, making gashes in trees and houses, pushing people to the ground like an angry tiger in a great hurry to lay the blame on someone. I stayed in my room and lit some of my new friend's incense to calm my nerves. Outside, earth and water and leaves and branches slammed into the side of the building. I thought I would go to bed early to try and hide from the storm, and had just begun to undo my hair when I heard Mrs. Ho calling me. Quickly, I rearranged my hair and went out into the foyer. The scholar was there. He was drenched to the bone, and his clothes were streaked with mud. No sedan would take him, he explained, so he had walked.

I suggested he might like a warm bath. He seemed suddenly to grow shy. His clothes were dripping, leaving murky puddles on the floor. I felt something like generosity well up inside me, and offered to bathe him myself. He agreed, but made me promise that whatever I saw, not to hate him. I laughed, somewhat surprised at what I assumed to be a vulgar reference. I promised. When the water was hot, he went into the alcove alone, and drew the screen. I watched his shadow undress. A long back emerged, a little crook where the waist went in and a hip flared out. There was something familiar about the shape. Then, he stepped into the tub and called to me. I went behind the screen. Slightly distorted by the water in which it was immersed was the body of the woman with the lantern.

"Remember your promise," she said, unable to read my face.

"I don't hate you," I said.

Somehow, I had expected it, all those brief flashes of thinking I had seen a hand move that way before, or known someone with a similar step. I didn't know what to say. Outside the wind whirled like a mad dancer and the rain clattered, clamouring to get in. It seemed so far away. I picked up the bar of soap and rubbed it between my palms. I like the way a half-used bar of soap feels, all smooth and irregular from contact with hands and water. The smell of sandalwood and steam rushed into my lungs as I smoothed it over her shoulders, her chest, into the soft space between her breasts. Her skin was smooth and stretched taut over her flesh, fine over the lip of her collarbones. Even with the temperature of the bath, there was a heat which came distinctly from her body. It seemed to seep through the skin of my palms, up my wrists to my elbows and flood straight into my heart. Then the room was quiet, only the sound of bathwater lapping and my blood roaring in my ears.

I bent over the tub and kissed her. She pulled me into the water.

Larissa Lai was born in La Jolla, California where her parents were graduate students from Hong Kong. She came to Canada (St. John's, Newfoundland) in 1972, as a child of university professors—part of the "Third World brain drain" that occurred in the late 60s and 70s when North American universities were expanding.

Currently, she lives in Vancouver where she works as a community activist, writer, editor and critic. Her articles and essays have been printed in *Fuse, Video Guide, Harbour, Rungh, Yellow Peril: Reconsidered, Matriart* and *Kinesis*, as well as a number of art catalogues. Her poetry and fiction have appeared in numerous journals including *West Coast line, CV2, Matrix, Room of One's Own, Bamboo Ridge, Estuaire* and the *Capilano Review*, as well as the Chinese Canadian anthology *Many-Mouthed Birds*.

She curated the exhibit *Telling Relations: Sexuality and the Family* featuring the work of seven woman of colour artists at the **grunt gallery** in June 1993 and *Earthly Pleasures*, an exhibition of work by Asian Canadian women dealing with notions of pleasure, desire, consumption, class, family, food, sex, childhood, memory and history in June 1994.

She was one of the organizers of the Vancouver conference, *Writing thru Race*. In the late spring of 94, while the regular editor was in South Africa covering the elections, she and Lynne Wanyeki edited *Kinesis*, the newspaper of the **Vancouver Status of Women**, where she has been a frequent contributor. She currently edits *Front*, a Vancouver-based arts magazine, and is working on her first book, a novel tentatively entitled *When Fox is a Thousand*, to be published by **Press Gang Publishers** in the fall of 1995.

Dung T. Nguyen

NIGHT

"MAI! DẬY! Mau lên! Dậy! . . ."

"Mai! Wake up! Quickly! Wake up! . . ."

Mai's eyes opened suddenly in the dark. She felt Nội's small bony hands gripping and shaking her shoulders. Several moments passed before Mai became fully conscious and she finally understood her grandmother's quiet yet urgent whispers coaxing her to wake up. Once she noticed that Mai was awake, Nội turned around and swiftly pushed aside the green netting that was draped over and around their bed to keep away the mosquitoes. Mai sat up and rubbed her eyes, trying to adjust to the darkness. She followed Nội out of bed. She slid her feet across the floor looking for her new slippers—the bright yellow plastic ones with the large stiff flower that covered her toes when she put them on. Má had given these to Mai when she came from Saigon to visit her two weeks ago. The other presents included little packages containing small round candies that came in different colors. Each candy was shaped like a pill and had the letter "M" printed on it. Mai would put the candy, one at a time, into her mouth and suck on it until the white "M" disappeared and the brown chocolate center had softened and dissipated on her tongue. Muttering under her breath, Nội had said, "Your mother must have gotten them from the Americans."

A high-pitched sound punctuated with a loud BOOM made the earth vibrate underneath Mai's feet. Trembling with fright, Mai forgot about her slippers and ran towards the *hầm*, where Nội was already sitting. The *hầm* was a shelter that was as familiar to Mai as it was to her grandmother on nights like this one. It was hidden behind some heavy curtains that were adjacent to the end of the bed. Inside the curtains, there was a tall wooden bed with books, trunks, suitcases, and even bags of rice cluttered on and around it. When the bombs exploded and the guns fired in the night, which happened quite frequently in this small village, perhaps once or sometimes twice a week, Mai and Nội would hide in there, underneath the bed, behind the bags of rice, the trunks, and the suitcases until the explosions and firings ceased. They were lucky some nights when it wasn't too long before they could resume their sleep. Some nights, they would be in the *hầm* for a long time before it was over.

Mai lowered her small body and crawled underneath the bed, not forgetting to place some boxes in front of it. Nội had already lit the small kerosene lantern, making it easy for Mai to find her usual spot in the corner, one directly opposite from where Nội was sitting. The shelter was Mai's favorite spot in the one-room house. She would play there by herself during the day, or sleep, or hide from Nội and her incessant mumblings.

"Shhhh! Be quiet! Why must you make so much noise? You are always so clumsy," Nội whispered in an annoyed tone. She took out her rosary, which was always in her pocket, and started to pray in low whispers.

Over Nội's prayers, Mai could hear the explosions. Some sounded as if they were coming from nearby and others from further away. Sometimes they were spaced far apart. Sometimes they followed one another in quick succession. In between the explosions, Mai could still hear the crickets singing. The rhythm of their chirping did not seem to be affected by the thunderous roars. She wondered if the crickets were scared or if they were used to these episodes, like she was. She would be scared if she had to be outside in the grass, in the midst of the bomb raid. The dogs from the neighborhood started barking. She thought it was funny how one would bark first, and then another from somewhere else would bark as if responding to the first one. Perhaps the dogs were telling each other how scared they were. Mai glanced over at Nội who was earnestly mouthing the words of the Hail Mary and moving her fingers methodically across the rosary beads.

"Crrreakkk!"

Both Nội and Mai leaned forward. Mai recognized that familiar sound, the sound that the bamboo gate made when it was being opened. A few seconds later, she heard fast footsteps on the soft earth outside, circling towards the back of the house. The chickens screamed. From the *hầm,* Mai and Nội could hear them moving about in their cages and their wings flapping as if they were trying to fly out of their cages. Then, the footsteps stopped. Mai tried to be as still as possible so that she would not miss any sound of movement from outside. Through the space between two boxes and the space where the curtains did not meet, she could see the back door. The bolt of the door rattled and the door made a slight sound as if someone was leaning against it from the other side.

Although the house was built of soft cement and the roof of woven palm leaves, the doors were unusually heavy and solid. they were made of some kind of metal that Mai liked because they were cool to lean on, especially in the summer. Who could be out there? What was he doing? Where was he? Even though there had been numerous bomb raids before, Mai had never encountered intruders. She tried to reassure herself that she didn't hear anything. Maybe she imagined the sounds. Maybe she was still asleep and had dreamt the whole thing. Just that afternoon, Mai had been taking a bath outside that door in the sunshine. She hated taking baths outside. She always felt that someone was watching her naked body. Although she was twelve, Nội was still helping her bathe because she didn't trust that Mai could get herself completely clean.

"Like this! You have to rub your skin like this to get all of your dirt out! You know, you are very dirty. If only your mother knew how hard it is to feed you and take care of you. The money she gives me is just not enough. Only your father in heaven sees how hard it is for me. Just rub hard. Look at this! See how much dirt there is!" Mai watched Nội rub her arms and legs with her forefinger until the tiny bits of what Nội called dirt rolled off and were washed away by the water.

"Especially this part! This part is the dirtiest part and you have to rub especially hard." Nội was rubbing the inside of Mai's thighs so vigorously that the skin there started to feel raw. Mai wanted to cry because of the pain and because she felt strange that Nội was touching her there. She started rubbing herself but no matter how hard she rubbed, the darkness there defied her and would not go away.

In the midst of the sounds of guns and bombs, Mai heard a voice from outside, calling to somebody. But it didn't belong to the intruder outside. It was from farther away.

THUMP! THUMP! THUMP!

The door shook harder. Nội blew out the kerosene lamp. Mai was consumed by panic and fear. She was sweating. Every part of her body trembled. Then her body went limp. Trying to regain her composure, she thought to herself, "Just be still! Whatever happens, it will be alright. No matter what, it will be over . . . It will soon pass . . . Just like it did that time when Ba touched me there too, when he was alive, the two of us lying in the hammock in the afternoon sun and Nội was sitting across the room sipping tea and staring out the window . . ."

. . . hail mary full of grace the lord is with thee blessed art though among women and blessed is the fruit of thy womb jesus holy mary mother of god pray for us now and at the hour of our death amen. . .

Another explosion! Mai raised her head to listen. It was not a bomb. It was thunder, and rain was now falling heavily on the earth and on the leaves. The bombs stopped. The door stopped rattling. Fifteen minutes later she heard a bomb explode from far away. And then, nothing. Just the rain and the periodic cracks of thunder. Half an hour, an hour later, still nothing. Nội and Mai pushed away the boxes in front of the shelter and slipped back into their bed.

"Get up! You're a big girl now, you know? Twelve years old, almost thirteen, and still sleeping in late. When you get married, do you think your husband is going to allow it?"

Nội was sitting on the front stoop, drinking her morning tea. Her voice rang out loud as she stared into an empty space in her front garden. Then, turning her head towards the house, she yelled,

"Get up! Are you going to sleep until noon?"

Mai scowled as she heard Nội's rancorous voice. She stirred a bit before climbing out of bed. She walked out to the back-yard to brush her teeth and wash her face. Remembering the strange events from the previous night, she stopped to look inside the chicken coop. The chickens huddled together in a corner. The bowl of water had spilled over and feathers covered the floor of the coop. She looked closer and saw that the feathers were speckled with blood. When she opened the cage and took the chickens out to examine them, she saw that some had cuts on their wings and other parts of their bodies.

Mai sighed and put the chickens back into the cage. She took the empty bowl to fill it with water. It was a beautiful day. The sun was shining so brightly as if the darkness had never been. The hibiscus hedge was full of blooms. She came closer to one of the flowers to admire it. It was magnificently red. The petals were wide open, but still holding a pool of water in the center. It was probably rain from last night, Mai thought. She looked around some more and was amazed that everything was in place. The only evidence of the raid and the silent intruder were the feathers lying in the chicken coop and the water pooled in the hibiscus.

I was born in Vietnam and lived there with my family until April 1975 when the war ended. After spending several months on the Pacific Ocean and in Thailand and Taiwan as refugees and "boat people," we eventually arrived in the U.S. My family was finally resettled in Michigan. I remember my parents working very hard to raise five children in an environment that was, to say the least, very foreign to them.

I currently live in New York City where I am a graduate film student at NYU. Telling stories—with either words or images—is a relatively new endeavor for me, especially considering that I studied molecular biology as an undergraduate. My motivation to write and to make films comes from a desire to recuperate a sense of beauty amidst the loss and grief endured by many Vietnamese people whose experiences I seldom read about or see on the screen. In recreating the lives of my characters I hope to celebrate the small gestures of resistance that are apparent in everyday activities. Although it is often difficult and sometimes even painful, writing is a way for me to rediscover, to heal, and to understand.

When I am less busy, I like to indulge myself by going to see as many movies as I can or by getting addicted to "trashy" TV programs like soap operas and game shows. Otherwise, I love to knit, cook, bake, and go out for Vietnamese food with my husband and sisters.

Vince Gotera

RETURNING FIRE

THE HEAT AND HUMIDITY blasted Bogey Reyes in the face as he stepped off the C-130. It was déjà vu—like 187 days ago, when he's stepped off a Braniff airliner into a wall of heat that took his breath away, hoisted his OD duffel bag up onto right shoulder, then double-timed off the runway at Tan Son Nhut Airport. Vietnam. The 'Nam. In country. Three fucking hundred sixty-five virgin slots left on his short-timer's calendar. A damn FNG. A *fuckin' new guy*—a red, white and blue target painted on his back. And now, walking off another plane at Clark Field in the Philippines, the customary black AWOL bag bumping his leg rhythmically, he paused to look around: the wide spaces of concrete and tarmac, waves of tropical heat shimmering over the macadam apron where the C-130 sat like some hulking dead albatross. "Jesus H. Christ. Just another 'Nam," he said, slipping his Zippo out of his pants pocket. "Land of my forefathers, Land of the Morning—just another Viet-fucking-Nam." Bogey lit up a Salem and stood there for a moment, idly fondling the lighter's chrome surfaces. Hell of a place for a week of R and R. Though he didn't know those grunts he'd flown here with, he'd bet his last RPC that they would soon be on a search-and-clear mission on the streets of Manila, hunting round-eye prostitutes. Bogey planned to be on a train to his father's village, a little farming and fishing hamlet near the Lingayen Gulf. He was on a pilgrimage, like any good Pinoy. Bogey flipped the Zippo into the air, where it flashed in the noon sun for a shining moment, and then plucked it out of the sky. He turned and walked into the Clark Field terminal.

The train to San Fernando smelled like pigshit and *bagoong*. Bogey's mother—a nurse who'd been raised on a dairy farm a few miles from Cedar Rapids, Iowa—loved all things Filipino except for *bagoong*—a salty fermented fish paste which his father had dearly loved. At least so he'd been told: Bogey's father, Raymundo Reyes, had died when he was a mere toddler. In 1939, Bogey's mother, a dewy-eyed eighteen-year-old farm girl named Margaret Fisher, had become intolerably weary and bored with her parents' acres of corn and pasture; so she had taken the unprecedented step of attending nursing school in Des Moines and shipping off to the Philippines to work at a leper's hospital run by Presbyterian missionaries. The religious connection was really only to mollify the folks; what Maggie was really seeking was high adventure in the South Seas. She had subsisted as a young girl on romantic novels about places like Sumatra and Fiji; her favorite was *The Hurricane*, and Maggie would have wanted nothing more than to be lashed to a tree by a clear-eyed, handsome and muscled Samoan boy while monsoon winds whipped the ocean into gigantic waves that threatened to engulf the island of their tryst in paradise. Instead, all she got was World War II, long hard hours at a military hospital just outside Manila, a hospital that was first the U.S. Army's and then later taken over by the Japanese (she had refused to leave her patients when the other American nurses were evacuated). Maggie miraculously avoided harm during the Japanese occupation, and when the hospital had been reclaimed by the Americans, she had tended a brown-eyed Filipino infantryman named R. Reyes, or Rey-Rey as his friends called him.

Raymundo Reyes had been a college student who became a Philippine Scout during World War II. Reyes and his unit had fought valiantly and with honor, as they say, under General King until his surrender of Bataan on 9 April 1942 and the infamous Death March which followed it. Rey-Rey, a corporal, contracted some rare jungle disease in the concentration camp—a disease that manifested itself in occasional but chronic bouts of malaria-like symptoms. It was because of one of these attacks that he had ended up as Maggie's patient. The rest is, as they also say, history: a whirlwind romance, rendezvous after secret rendezvous in the moonlight of Intramuros—the old Spanish presidio—and morning strolls at Quiapo market, a sparkly Catholic wedding with a few friends at the Church of Our Lady of Antipolo, and then they honeymooned Stateside, as the expression goes. Rey-Rey had become a naturalized American citizen as a result of his wartime service, and he and Maggie settled finally in San Francisco in 1947.

On All Saints' Day, 1949, Maggie gave birth to an eight-pound-five-ounce baby boy, whom they christened Humphrey Bogart Reyes. When Bogey was three, Rey-Rey had another one of his chronic attacks and died. Humphrey being no name to grow up with in San Francisco—his classmates began to call him "Humpty-Dumpty" in third grade—"Bogey" became the boy's name of choice. He had a fairly uneventful childhood, except that he remembered he saw his mother rather seldom, since she never remarried and had to work long hours at General Hospital. So Bogey knew next to nothing about his father's background and life. All he knew was that at Polytechnic High—the toughest, rowdiest school in the city—he had to fight every single day. Whites and blacks both were continually hassling Bogey because he wasn't white and he wasn't black. "Hey, Hirohito!" a blond-haired boy had called him one morning at the basketball courts; switchblades swiftly sliced the open air, and Bogey had ended up flat on his back for a week at his mother's hospital with a punctured lung. The Filipino kids—the Flips—they didn't consider him one of their own, either. His nose was just not flat enough, his lips a bit too thin, his hair just a shade too fair. So for Bogey, "Flip" became a nasty word. Just some more people he had to fight.

Nevertheless, Bogey couldn't help but wonder about his father and the Philippines. Perhaps he never really connected the Flips who called him undecipherable Tagalog names in the hallowed halls of Poly with the postcards of outrigger boats and emerald-green volcanoes that would occasionally come to his mother from her old friends in the Philippines. After Bogey graduated from high school, his Uncle Sam sent him a congratulations card that started out "Greetings"—he was instructed to report to the Oakland Induction Center at the end of the summer. Bogey gladly signed up and found himself a few months later in the 'Nam. He was only a hop, a skip, and a jump—as they say—form his father's homeland.

So now Bogey found himself on a Philippine train, and it smelled like pigshit and *bagoong*. There were other smells too: under the passenger seats all around him were chickens being transported in large domed baskets, people eating their lunches of bagoong and rice or their snacks of *suman*—sweet sticky rice steamed in a wrapping of banana leaf—all melding with the pungence of fertilizer from the fields swooping by beyond the train's windows. The air was filled with a strange cacophony of noises: the staccato gobbledygook that was, to Bogey, how Tagalog and Ilocano sounded, mixed with the strident squawks of chickens, the piercing squeals and bleats of pigs, and the high-pitched screams of children running up and down the central aisle of the passenger car.

In the middle of this vortex of sensation, Bogey could only marvel at how much these Filipinos seemed, to him, Vietnamese. The green rice fields outside with their paddy berms punctuated by an occasional *nipa* hut seemed just like the boonies he had been humping for the last six months. He found himself expecting incoming from the tree line—rockets, maybe, or mortars—and kept having sudden panic attacks when he would alternately realize that he didn't have his flak jacket and then that he didn't need it here. Every time he would drift off to sleep, he felt like he was walking through some ville in Vietnam, the mama-sans and their kids all in black pajamas, peeking out of their sorry hootches . . . the same smells, the same smells. Lock and load one magazine. Then pivot in place, trigger finger jamming, rocking and rolling, bullets spraying everywhere and every which way, the Vietnamese pigs like miniature rhinos running and falling over, mama-sans huddling over their screaming children—blood, blood, blood.

"What the fuck!" Bogey screamed, jumping to his feet . . . somebody had touched his arm.

The man who'd been sitting next to him had also bolted, jumped up, and was now staring at him, wide-eyed his voice quivering, "Sorry, Mister. You . . . you were moaning, and I thought . . . I thought . . ." The man trailed off, then looked abruptly away.

Bogey looked around the passenger car. Everyone was staring at him; even the kids, the pigs, the chickens had all quieted down. As if by signal or conspiracy, they all averted their eyes. "You're all gooks, you know that?" he yelled. "Just gooks. The things that happen when you don't have your weapon!" Bogey reached for the Zippo and shook out a Salem, his hands trembling just a little. "Just motherfucking gooks."

"Here, you will sleep here," Uncle Mariano pointed out Bogey's room, a *nipa*-walled cubicle equipped with a sleeping mat or *banig*, and a mosquito net. In the corner, a small wicker table held an ancient kerosene lamp. When Bogey had stepped off the train a half hour earlier at this small whistlestop called *Batong Ginto* partway between the cities of Bauang and San Fernando, his uncle (not actually a relative but rather his grandfather's godson, nevertheless an uncle by Filipino reckoning) Tio Mariano had been waiting. Mariano Jacinto was a small man, not even five feet; his eyes looked almost Chinese, and on his chin, he had a few wisps of white beard. His shoulders were rounded, and he walked with a stoop. In fact, he limped and leaned visibly on a gnarled walking stick he held in his left hand. "An old war wound," Tio Mariano explained, "I stepped on a Japanese mine, but it did not have much powder. I was lucky. Your Papa carried me on his back, along with both our rifles and ammunition, gas mask, five miles through the jungle to get me to a doctor. Very strong man, your Papa." Bogey, however, could not shake an anxious, nagging feeling that, if they had been standing in Vietnam that very moment, this man—his father's buddy—would have been Vietcong. He imagined Tio Mariano in black pajamas rather than white cotton shirt and bright red neckerchief, rough serge pants; Bogey could almost see him bent over a work table deep in some Vietnamese tunnel, arming booby traps with stolen G.I. material or sharpening bamboo sticks to be smeared with human shit. Bogey shook his head sharply, as if to clear the image from his brain.

"And here, this is your *pinsan*, my daughter Carmelita . . . Mely." The woman standing at the bottom of the bamboo stair was lovely—soft clear skin and straight white teeth, blue-black hair cascading past her slim shoulders, bright almond-shaped eyes like Tio Mariano. *Slant-eye*, Bogey thought. He looked past Mely to the house: a large house on stout six-foot bamboo stilts, the walls made of intricately woven *nipa*, certainly large enough to contain several rooms, unlike the smaller one-room *nipa* huts they had walked past. A split-bamboo verandah surrounded the entire house at the top of the bamboo stairway where Mely was waiting. A thought flickered at the edge of Bogey's consciousness: *Just another hootch, another goddam hootch*. Mely smiled and dropped her eyes.

Over the next two or three days, Bogey began to feel more and more relaxed. His taut nerves were loosening up, their knots untying. Evenings, he and Mely would stroll down by the beach, watch the village boys climb coconut trees and hack coconuts loose with their *bolos* and machetes. They would look out across the Lingayen Gulf, the sun floating like a purple salted egg over the South China Sea, the sky streaked with vermillion and pink clouds, and Bogey could hardly believe that he was looking towards Vietnam. That at that moment, grunts in his company were checking their stuff—Claymore mines, flares, tracer rounds. That they were preparing to set up listening posts, guard the perimeter of Fire Base Jezebel. And here he was with a beautiful woman, talking of their separate childhoods, their vastly different lives, talking of the horrors of Vietnam, of how the fog rolls in nights in San Francisco. She giggled a tiny laugh when he described the flower children in the Haight Ashbury, patchouli oil and giant daisies, the

Grateful Dead and the Charlatans putting on free concerts in the Panhandle. He smiled as she recounted to him stories of religious festivals, of candlelight processions through the streets of Bauang City, of the blue-and-silver statue of the Blessed Virgin carried by the strongest men of this village whose name meant *rock of gold*. Then they would walk along the waterline, their hands touching briefly in the indigo air just after sunset. Once, they came upon some beached fishing boats and laughed together at the name painted on one: *Bogart*.

On the fourth night, Bogey dreamt of the 'Nam. As squad leader, he was collecting his grunts. The platoon had been ordered to hump to a remote ville to check on rumors of Vietcong activity. *Fucking commie sypathizers, all of them,* he thought. The platoon sergeants had brought all the residents and lined them up at the edge of a rice field: not one able-bodied man among them . . . all wizened grandfathers and old women, or young wives with filthy babies. Where were the young men? Vietcong, each and every one. Then Smitty discovered a tunnel entrance under one of the hootches. A dull boom sounded and then another as they slung frags into the tunnel. "Get yer Zippos out!" Bogey yelled, and as the Vietnamese begged, "Please, G.I." or screamed "You number 10, *dien cai dau*," he flicked the Zippo's small wheel and a yellow sheet of flame engulfed the first hooch. Bogey was stoked to the max, he had been made for this. He was King of the Mountain. He was headman of the Zippo squad. The Vietcong scared their children with stories about him: the Bogey Man. Then he felt a funny tingle in the hand which held the Zippo. Bogey looked down. The skin on his right wrist, his forearm, was mottling, writhing, tightening—it was turning gray and purple, a reptilian, knobby carapace. As he watched, fascinated—thinking *acid flash*—his skin burst painfully into flame, crackled and burst, oozing some vile-smelling liquid—Bogey began to scream—the lizard skin and the flames were traveling up his arm, engulfing his shoulder—his fatigues, his boots were burning off with an oily smoke—around him, no one paid any attention, his men setting fire to hootch after hootch as the villagers wailed—Bogey was almost afraid to look down at his body—the skin of his legs was hardening and then exploding in fire—he looked down and screamed—still no one noticed—the burning skin was triangulating on his cock and balls—a thousand cicadas were buzzing in his head—someone was screaming, "Stop! Stop it! For God's sake, Stop!"—his shriveled penis and scrotum were turning green and barky like an alligator's back—it felt like a hundred bees were stinging his crotch—the heat of an imploding sun centered on his groin, ground zero—

"Bogey? Bogey? Are you okay?" It was Mely, her cool fingers caressing his temples. Bogey shuddered and came out of the dream, sobbing. She lay down next to him and held him in a tender but firm embrace. Bogey turned his eyes towards her and saw the gold flecks glittering in her dark eyes. He hid his face between her breasts.

At breakfast Tio Mariano handed Bogey a small, slim notebook. Its leather cover was moth-eaten in places, but the paper inside was in good condition. "This was your Papa's, Bogey. It is his journal. He kept it during the war. I want you should have it. I think you need it now." Bogey went to his room and began immediately to decipher his father's scrawled script, dipping in and out, reading here and there in the journal.

Today we found a Jap cache of food. We took a case of condensed milk. What a luxury! We ate about two or three cans each of the milk. And then we got pinned down in a crossfire. Retreat, Retreat! ordered Lieutenant Gutierrez. So we ran through the jungle, and the bullets were singing like little wasps over our heads. And as we ran, we all began to have diarrhea. My stomach was boiling. Ay, naku! No time to stop. We just ran and ran. Literally. Later, we all had a big laugh about it as we washed out our uniform pants in a river. Johnnie recalled the sapper they had shot at Jezebel a couple of months back, how they had found a pack of Marlboros and two Pepsis in his little black pack. But then he also remembered burning barrels of shit, the stench and the smoke. He had always given his stinky uniforms to the Vietnamese washwomen, and now Bogey wished he could have washed them himself with his buddies in the river. A smile broke out like sun streaming through clouds as he imagined the incredible event of dodging a hard rain of bullets, shitting sweet milk all the way.

After General King's surrender last week, we burned our uniforms and began pretending to be farmers or fishermen. God help us, we can be shot now as spies: Mariano and I, Pabling, Francisco, Lieutenant Gutierrez, Charlie, and Duling-duling. It's becoming too dangerous. On 13 April, a farmer told us the Japs were setting up roadblocks and checking the right index fingers of all able-bodied men. And if you had a callus there, they would bend you over right in the road and cut off your head with a samurai sword. No trial, no bullshit. So that morning, all seven of us decided to hide out in the jungle, but we had no food. Last night, we found a wagon full of Jap provisions—canned goods. But the Japs had bolted an iron cage on top of the wagon. And none of the cans would fit through the bars. And the wood was very tough. We had been on half-rations for months even before the surrender, so we were too weak to cut through the wood. But you never know what a hungry man can do. Mariano reached through the bars and picked a can of evaporated milk, and he squeezed it and squeezed it until it could fit through the bars. Bogey remembered how he had set fire once to a hootch filled with rice, probably an entire harvest. He began to cry silently.

Tio Mariano was standing at the door. He smiled gently. Then he opened his right hand to show Bogey the scars like gnarly vines in his palm, on the insides of the fingers. For the first time, Bogey noticed that the hand was slightly deformed, misshapen, spatulate fingers hooked ever-so-slightly like small scythe handles. "We were in a bunker far back in the jungle, maybe two weeks after the surrender of Bataan. A Japanese grenade came in through the fire window. We had nowhere to run. Everyone just froze. I reached down and held that grenade tight as I could, and it went off in my hand, but I kept in the blast. Maybe like that mine that crippled my leg, it had too little powder. I don't know. But after that, we knew we must give up. Your Papa and I both ended up in the Death March. I don't know how, but Rey-Rey was able to keep that book. The whole time in the concentration camp. Wait here, I have something else to give you." Tio Mariano went back out of the room and Bogey flipped to another page near the end of the journal.

Our prisoner-of-war camp is a horrible place. There is very little food. Sanitation is terrible. Everyone has dysentery and beri-beri. It might almost be better for your head to have been chopped off for lagging behind when the Japs marched us to this camp. But this morning I gained hope again. I do not know what today is, but I know we have been here for several months. This morning, a guard at the fence beckoned to me. I thought, oh no, what foolishness will I have to face now? But he only wanted to give me a cigarette. It was a Camel. I wonder where they get Camels? He gave me the cigarette and smiled. I realized he is only a boy. Probably no more than eighteen or nineteen. And he is lonely. As we are too. Friend, he said to me in English but with a thick accent. Friend. Hai, I answered, arigato.

"I have one other gift for you," Tio Mariano came back with a long bundle wrapped in cloth. "This also was your Papa's." He unwrapped an old but meticulously clean rifle—twenty years old if it's a day. "This was your Papa's hunting rifle. He bought it on the black market after the war. 1946, maybe. It's a converted military rifle, a Garand. We don't know whose it was originally. Your Papa liked to think that it had been the rifle of one of our dead comrades, Lt. Gutierrez or Francisco or maybe even Duling-duling—"Old Cross-Eye" we called him in English sometimes. Your Papa gave me this rifle when he married your Mama. He said, Mariano my brother, you keep it for me, but he never come back. Now it is yours. Tomorrow you will have to leave for Clark Field so you will not be AWOL, ha?" Tio Mariano left, and Bogey sat there until dark, his legs folded in lotus position, the rifle nestled in his lap, and read his father's journal from beginning to end.

Bogey's last R-and-R morning dawned magnificently. The eastern sky was a pale mauve, shading to a deep purple at the western horizon; the silhouette of mountains and pine forests stood crisply against the dawn like a serrated blade. The air was sharp and cool. Bogey was still sitting in lotus, book and rifle carefully arranged on the floor in front of him like two precisely placed stones in a Japanese garden. He got up and began to pack his stuff in a rucksack he had purchased in Bauang City two days before, when he and Mely had gone on a little shopping junket.

Mely came out of her room to prepare breakfast, and they met, held hands at arm's length. Then he kissed her gently, first on the forehead, then on the lips. She closed her eyes. "I love you," he whispered. "Please wake up Tio Mariano, okay?" She roused her father, and they both went outside. There was Bogey: rucksack and rifle, hiking outfit of heavy broadcloth, hiking boots. His class A's were folded neatly on the verandah next to his spit-shined low quarters.

"Thank you, Tio Mariano. You're one hell of a wise man. So you must know, and Mely, you know too, that I can't go back to Vietnam. It would shame my father's ghost—his memory. I feel as if evil now runs in my veins like poison. But I'll be back someday. Mely, I love you. Please understand." Mely slipped down the stairway in her bare feet and gave Bogey a last kiss. Tears slid down her cheeks. Tio Mariano nodded his head slowly, his own eyes glistening.

Bogey held her hand for a brief moment, then turned to walk east toward the mountains, toward the peak of Mt. Pulog. After a few steps, he stopped and looked back. Then he fished the Zippo out of his pocket and pitched it in a low arc towards the beach. As it spun through the morning air, it lit up briefly like a miniature comet, then disappeared. Bogey turned back towards the rising sun.

"Returning Fire" is the first story anyone's ever accepted, and I'm ecstatic to be here. I'm better known as a poet. In 1993, I won a creative-writing fellowship in poetry from the NEA.

I was born and mostly raised in San Francisco. I say "mostly" because my family moved to Manila for several years when I was a young child. Consequently I have some pretty bizarre, magical-realist memories of the Philippines.

Now I live and work in Arcata, California, nestled between giant redwoods and the beach. My official gig is being an English professor at Humboldt State University, where I direct the creative-writing program and teach ethnic literature.

My wife Mary Ann and I have three daughters—Amanda (6), Amelia

Mary Ann Blue Gotera

(3), and Melina (1). I also have son from a previous marriage—Marty (22).

As far as the usual "bio-stuff" goes . . . My book of criticism, *Radical Visions: Poetry by Vietnam Veterans*, was published by the University of Georgia Press in 1994. A poetry collection, *Dragonfly*, is forthcoming from Pecan Grove Press. My poems have appeared in such lit-mags as *Kenyon Review, Caliban, Ploughshares*, and others. I'm the poetry editor of the journal *Asian America*.

Really, I'm just glad to be on the Greenfield bus. We're all rolling along, having an honest-to-goodness adobo and sushi picnic. Ride on, everybody.

Jason Laus Baluyut

THE STORYTELLER

IT WAS THE SUMMER of my eighteenth birthday. My parents and I had flown into California from Michigan to visit relatives and catch up on old times, or so my mother said—although I had been witness to enough of her strained conversations with my father, enough of her frustrated long-distance arguments with the folks in L.A., enough of the lines of tension that defined her movements as she packed our suitcases for the trip, to know that this was anything but an innocent family vacation. This was, more than anything, a business trip, regarding the same subject which had kept the members of my mother's family feuding for years: who would assume responsibility for my mother's mother, who would feed her, who would wash her and move her as her limbs daily lost their strength, who would describe for her the world she could no longer see with her own eyes; and finally, whenever she died, who would hold the title to the land she owned in Manila which—so legend had it—had once belonged to the first *encomenderos* who arrived, with their soldiers and their Jesuit priests, at the virgin shores of the country.

I had grown up in the shadow of my mother's arguments with her brothers. I had played and laughed and gotten into fistfights and fallen in love in Manila's noisy and dust-choked streets as Mama made phone calls in the shadows of the ancestral house, wrote letters to Uncle Teodoro and Uncle Emmanuel who in my youth had already made new lives for themselves in the States, held meetings with her remaining three brothers in the old family dining room that had grown damp and dusty with neglect and was invaded by a perennial chill. Always, when I came in at dusk scratched and filthy from play or weary from school, I would pass by the dining room on my way upstairs to the family bedroom and catch a glimpse of Mama sitting there, alone or with her arguing brothers, her brows knitted together and her mouth compressed in a tight line that tried to keep in the tension that rose from her throat and brimmed in her eyes. I had never allowed myself to dwell on it. But at night, as I drifted to sleep between the silent forms of my parents, I connected Mama's restless stirring with the coughing and the sing-song babbling that came from the room below, and my thoughts turned to the old woman there who was slowly fading from the world. My *Lola* Silang is dying and Mama is sad, I thought, because no one wants to save her.

A decade later still no one did. My mother's family had dispersed, scattered like seeds into destiny's various corners: Uncle Fidel married the grand-daughter of a *gobernador* and moved away to one of the country's far provinces; Uncle Teodoro wrote from the States and told us how the latest earthquake had all but devastated his restaurant business; Uncle Manny announced from Berkeley that he had graduated from his medical studies; and Uncle Ignacio lay peacefully under the grass of Loyola Memorial Park, dead four years from a stray bullet in the revolution. That was the last straw for Mama; she swore at Ignacio's funeral that her son would never be raised in a place so thick with shotgun politics, and the same wave of panic and political upheaval that had claimed my uncle's life swept my parents and me to the United States, to Michigan, where we settled down with the blessings of the Department of Immigration and tried as best we could to stitch the patches of our lives back together. And through all the cataclysms, the marriages and deaths and revolutions that tore my mother's family apart, Lola Silang remained in the darkness of the ancestral house in Manila, singing her hymns softly to herself, her eyes dimmed by a descending cloak of shadows, her mind unravelling into a chaos of memories and dreams.

Only Uncle Eduardo stayed with her now, and when Mama found out how her youngest brother had surrounded the old mansion with German shepherds and kept Lola Silang confined in her room like a prisoner with the barest provisions, she flew into a rage. She began anew her correspondence with her brothers, denouncing Eduardo for his lack of love and respect for an old woman, for his base greed for property and his devil's patience as he waited for her to die. And it was devil's patience indeed, said Mama, for he had been waiting quietly for years—ever since the shadows began to encroach upon Lola Silang's eyes and the quivering sickness first touched her nerves, when he decided to approach her with a cool smile on his lips and tell her fervently that her favorite son was going to do her proud, was going to ignite a Charismatic movement among the heathen of this backwards country, was going to build churches upon the rocks and in the valleys all dedicated to the God she loved. Lola Silang believed him in her religious delirium, Mama recalled aloud whenever she could get me to listen; she believed him, hung a halo of praise around him whenever his name came into her head, and in a muddled ecstasy signed her name to any sheet of paper that Eduardo pushed in front of her.

"God knows how hard I've had to fight that bastard brother of mind," Mama would tell me in the quiet hours of the night as she sipped her *kape*, her mouth drawn into that tight line of pain. "God knows how long and how hard. You should be thankful your cousin Lita's a practicing lawyer in Manila and that she'd do these things for free, or we'd be up to our necks in debt before you've even started your life . . ." And she would lapse into the foreign tongue of lawyers, trying to explain to me the world of affidavits and contracts and litigation and how much she'd gone through in her battles with Eduardo in the arena of the courts, while I sat nodding next to her and noticed only the bitter shape of her mouth, the eyebrows furrowed like scars over old pain. The legal skirmishes alone couldn't possibly have caused such deep sadness, I thought. I remembered then those distant nights in the ancestral house, when my grandmother and my three uncles and my parents and I occasionally sat down to a communal dinner in the chill of that dusty room, when Lola Silang offered smiling words to Fidel and Ignacio and heaped upon Eduardo all the benedictions worthy of a servant of the Lord, and I thought I understood. She never turned her face in Mama's direction, never acknowledged Mama's kind attentions, never spoke a word to her except in resentment or accusation—you, who are always trying to turn me against my Eduardo, you, who married that good-for-nothing *impakto* from the projects, you, who would have done great things for the Lord had you been a son, you, my useless, useless daughter. As Mama sipped her *kape* and talked of litigation I saw scorned love inside her downturned eyes, like an eternal tear that survived a journey across the sea and the hardships of a harsh northern land, to well up within her once more in hours of anger and remembrance.

And now the cause of her pain was here. On the summer of my eighteenth birthday Uncle Eduardo called from Manila and told Mama that their mother had fallen extremely ill, that she could no longer speak nor walk, that she refused to have herself moved from place to place and simply lay stiffly and stubbornly in bed, letting the teaspoons of baby food which the hired help fed her trickle out of her mouth and down her cheeks. He'd talked to all the doctors, exhausted all his resources, he said, and didn't know what else to do; so he'd bought two one-way tickets to California and was sending Uncle Fidel to take Lola Silang there, where he knew that Uncle Manny—now a certified doctor, after all—would give her the proper attention. "*Ang walanghiya,*" Mama cursed Eduardo as she put down the receiver. "All those years treating her like a prisoner, like a dog from the streets, and now he wonders why she's so sick, doesn't even have the guts to face up to what he's done. Now he's sending Del to dump her here, like garbage, just like garbage, and he's expecting us to fix all his mistakes."

I watched her from the next room, listened quietly to her anger. She didn't mention that with Lola Silang and the surviving brothers gathered together a thousand miles away, Eduardo could easily snatch up the rights to the ancestral property the moment the old woman died, but I knew that Mama couldn't escape that realization. That was part of the fabric of her pain—the tension between love and strategy, the difficulty of treating Lola Silang as a pawn in a war for property and at the same time as a mother, to be cherished purely and simply, on the heart's unconditional terms. Mama gave voice to none of this, although her body sagged in a curve of weariness; but she straightened herself up, lips firmly together, told Papa to ask for vacation leave from the office the next day, and dialed the airport to make the earliest possible reservations for Los Angeles. While she waited on hold, the receiver cradled against her cheek, she saw me standing in the doorway and knew that I'd heard everything. But she smiled anyway, putting on a face to revive the dying cheer that still lingered from my birthday celebration a few days back, thinking perhaps that I deserved a life untainted by her sorrow. "Pack your bags, Pepe," she said. "We're going to see relatives and say hello to Uncle Emmanuel, you haven't seen him in a long time. And Lola Silang will be there too, I bet she'll be really glad to see you."

Uncle Manny stood at the entrance to his compact house, his giant, thick-boned frame barely contained in the doorway, and greeted us with outspread arms. "*Oy*, Alma, Federico!" he beamed, and in the brilliance of that smile there could be nothing wrong in the world. Papa laughed and waved hello. Mama simply smiled and said nothing. She touched her younger brother's arm to acknowledge him while her restless eyes looked beyond him into the house, as if trying to seek out her mother's presence. "Long time no see, *ha?*" Uncle Manny continued. "And who's this? *Diyos ko*, who is this fine young man? Not Pepito, is it, not my little Peping? My God, Pepe, how you've grown!"

I found myself crushed, without warning, against the hard warmth of his barrel chest, his arms squeezing all air and self-conscious aloofness out of me. "For you, Uncle Manny," I said when I had regained my breath, "just for you I'll let myself be called Pepe. All my friends call me Johnny."

"*Johnny*?" he boomed, his eyes wide with laughing disbelief. "Not even Jose Lorenzo, your given name? My God, that's
worse than what these *Amerikanos* have done to me, shorten-
ing my name to Manny. What have you done to this boy, Alma?
Only here four years, and already he's speaking with the perfect G.I. Joe accent. Took me sixteen years to wash that Filipino thickness off my tongue, and I still don't speak as good as
he does. That's a real risk at work, you know, being misunderstood by the patients, and someday God knows when they're
going to take pills when I just ask them to grab pillows."

I laughed along with my parents as Uncle Manny showed us
in, but I felt a twinge of discomfort at the joke. He had drawn a
line between my roots and the roots of the people I found
around me, and it was a division I had not yet discovered how
to deal with, a quivering high wire that I toed everyday, hoping
not to fall. It had been a tremendous ordeal when I first arrived
in Michigan, practically a child unschooled in the ways of the
country, enduring the slow passage of the weeks and months
and seasons as I bore the secret stares of strangers, heard their
laughter at my accent and my ignorance, struggled with textbooks that chronicled the history they knew so well, and
glimpsed the reflection in the locker-room mirrors that told me
I had dull black hair and too-dark skin and narrow, lusterless
eyes. It had taken me four years to abandon my ethnic luggage
at the station of my alienation and loneliness—four years to exchange the warmth of a brotherly embrace for the cool aloofness
of a limp handshake or a distant nod, to master the strangers'
catchwords and speak with ease of their loves and lusts and
griefs, to finally come into a circle of acceptance whose cocky
smiles and approving eyes banished the self-loathing like bon-
fires against the darkness and allowed me to forget, at least in
waking hours, that I was a shipwrecked alien from another
world named Jose Lorenzo Guzman.

But four years are not enough to wipe out a lifetime of
memories deeper than blood. In the middle of the night I would
wake from dreams of childhood joys and fears, of feasts of *balot*
and *lechon* and *pancitmalabon* and the unforgotten bliss of the
belly, of running through the uncut cemetery grass under the
gray November sky of All Soul's Day, of playing *patintero* with
grimy, dust-cloaked playmates in the noisy neighborhood

streets, of people waving blood-red banners and marching en masse from their homes to form a barricade of bitter and hopeful faces against the rumbling of distant tanks; and as these images faded from my head I would find my solitude and confusion present in the darkness of my room, undiminished, crouched in a corner like a beast of shadows and watching me with silent , questioning eyes. In those naked hours I knew that the high-wire act had never ended—that it continued still, suspending me above a chasm between two worlds as I nervously thrust out my arms and tried to learn how to fly.

Uncle Manny's voice was low and his tense eyes belied the cheer in his broad smile. "Mother's in the kitchen with Del and Dodi," he told my parents. "Eduardo hasn't called since the day he told me he'd bought the tickets. I've tried calling him but no one ever answers. And Mother, she's . . . well, I don't know just how bad it is, I haven't diagnosed her formally yet, but it doesn't look good. She still has spells of, well, clearheadedness, as clear as she'll ever get in her condition. But *Diyos ko*, sister, how bad she's gotten, it really breaks your heart . . ."

Papa put his hands on Mama's shoulders, as if to absorb some of the tightness there. "Why don't we all just go in together and say hello and see how she is," he said, "and then Del and Dodi can just join us and talk about old times." Uncle Manny nodded and led us into the kitchen, where Uncle Fidel and Uncle Teodoro stood up to greet us with embraces and with the how-have-you-beens that accompany reunions.

Lola Silang sat motionless in her battered wheelchair, her eyelids crumpled shut, blind to the midday light that poured in from the windows thrown open to the California summer. "She's been like that ever since she got here," Uncle Del said quietly as Mama knelt down beside her and looked at her wilted face, a faded map of lines and creases that charted the territory of her ancient pain. "Once, here, she spoke," he continued. "It was in the middle of the night, and she was giving an oration to an invisible audience of women, telling them they were all her sisters and that she had gathered them there to call them to arms, to help their men fight off Magellan and his *conquistadores*." He shook his head. "And once, on the plane, she called for me and I said I'm here, Ma, and she said she was so sorry that I'd died in the womb, that she'd tried so hard to bring me out alive." Uncle Manny smiled broadly at this and murmured, "She still knows she loves her kids, at least that's something," but his eyes remained sad. "Aside from that," Uncle Del continued, "nothing. She's been sitting there like a stone, and God knows if the sunshine and the short trips in the car are doing her any good." Mama stayed on her knees and took her mother's limp hand in hers, whispering, "Mother, it's me, Mother, it's Alma," as if she were gently calling her back from a wilderness.

I stood by the doorway to the kitchen and regarded my grandmother from a distance, invaded by unwanted memories. Lola Silang was part of the fabric of my pain as well: the old woman was a cornerstone in the house of my childhood, an embarrassing mark upon my life that I had tried to come to terms with or disguise or erase like an unwanted tattoo, a scar in a secret place. I could not remember feeling anything positive at all towards Lola Silang, anything that would offset the shadow she had cast upon my youth. My earliest memory of her was an odor, the sickening too-sweet stench of the uncapped perfume bottles and medicine vials that lined the shelves and cupboards of her room. It oozed out from underneath her door and assaulted my nostrils as I passed by on my way to or from the streets. When she still had full use of her limbs she would appear silhouetted in the rectangle of the doorway and beckon me towards her in a voice made unearthly by the echoes of the house—the voice of the wrinkled ghost with the heavy cloying smell, the phantom who lurked in my childhood nightmares. As I grew older Lola Silang shed her ghostly garb and became for me the earthly villain, the heartless crone who despised my father and caused my mother grief, the source of Mama's frustrated correspondence and nightly arguments with her brothers—threads in the tapestry of anger that formed the backdrop of my days. Finally, as night took her eyes and her mind, even this illusion of villainy dissolved and I saw clearly the emaciated limbs, the shrunken frame, the deep furrows in the face of an old woman whom Mama often had me wash and feed like a helpless infant and whose delirious silence acknowledged no help. She became a ghost once more, removed from this world, lost in a realm of shadows that she imagined to be real. More than anything, she was for me an annoying inconvenience, an unthinking cancer that ate at my mother's soul, a feeble creature made small and useless by her age.

And now she looked smaller still. I stood across the room and stared at her, wondering, as I often did secretly, if it would not have been better for Lola Silang to collapse without noise or fanfare into a heap upon the earth, to release her daughter from her misery and grant her warring children peace.

"O, pictures na, pictures everyone! It's mandatory, I insist! A group picture of Mrs. Priscilla Sanchez and what's left of her kids, courtesy of my brilliant nephew," said Uncle Manny, tossing me the camera with a wink. "Some shots can take away from this family, like the one that took Ignacio," he added in one of his ceaseless attempts at wit, "but other shots hopefully can preserve it."

I doubted that silently, as Uncle Manny wheeled Lola Silang into his sunlit garden and marshaled everyone into position, Papa and Uncle Del and Uncle Dodi and himself flanking my grandmother like soldiers, Mama kneeling beside her as if still begging for her withheld love. I doubted that as I peered into the viewfinder and saw their smiles pretending to unity while their eyes betrayed their discord, their unconnected solitudes. "Say cheese," I said as I clicked the shutter open, and in my mind I saw other scenes from other photographs, gray and faded portraits that I'd once come upon as I was idly going through my parents' shoeboxes filled with memories. In those photos Lola Silang sat in the courtyard of the ancestral house, her husband standing beside her and her children at her knees, Teodoro and Ignacio and Fidel and Alma and Emmanuel and Eduardo all suppressing their forbidden laughter and standing in awkward, formal poses that barely contained their youth; and at the center of her family Lola Silang smiled with quiet dignity and conscious grace, held her head high and looked out of the portraits as if to tell their audience *this* was a family, *this* was tradition, *this* was joy. As I took their picture in the garden, I wondered what they had lost, and what had been lost to me.

They left shortly after that, Papa and Mama and her brothers, to have lunch at one of Uncle Dodi's restaurants and see a bit of the town and discuss the perennial question of Lola Silang. "Take care of your grandmother for us, Pepe, we won't be long," Uncle Manny had said before leaving. "Give her lots of sunshine and air and water, if she'll take it, and talk to her, sometimes it does her some good and makes her open up. Like a plant in bloom." I laughed, and asked him if that was his professional opinion; he chuckled and shook his head, but looked at me with those eyes, incongruous to his smile, which said that perhaps sunshine and water and conversation were the last hope she had. They piled into Uncle Dodi's van, then, already murmuring among themselves about Eduardo and lawsuits and land. The sound of the motor died away, eventually, and a hush fell upon the garden, broken only by the chirping of a sparrow or my quiet sips of water or the faint hiss of Lola Silang's breathing as she sat in her wheelchair, with me on a stool beside her, in the middle of a square of green space that glowed with summer. "It's really beautiful out here," I said to Lola Silang, to no one in particular.

My grandmother stirred. "Mmm, beautiful," she murmured, mildly startling me. Then, as if she could discern shapes within the shadows that caged her, she furrowed her brows and slightly moved her head from side to side. "*Sino 'yan*? Who's there, *ha*? Why don't you show yourself?"

I patted her hand in reassurance. "Relax, Lola. It's just me, I'm keeping you company for a while." I listened to myself as I spoke. Without meaning to, I had slipped into the heavily-accented English that I'd used in the past to speak to elders as a sign of deference. I'd always felt that my native Tagalog was too intimate, rolled off the tongue too quickly and with too much of a sense of conspiracy; G.I. Joe English, on the other hand, was hard and rude on my elders' ears, a staccato gibberish that for them evoked memories of imperialism and deceit. So I'd decided to compromise, long ago, with the stumbling Filipino *Ing-leesh* that conveyed my respect to the older folks and endeared me to their hearts. As I found myself compromising now, after all these years of wearing only proper English on my tongue, calling out to my grandmother as my mother had before me: "It's me, Lola, it's me, your *apo*, it's Pepe."

Her voice seemed smaller too, as if it had atrophied with her long silence. "Ay, Pepe, Pepe, is it really you, my child?

Come here into my room, come here where I can see you, sit down here beside me so we can talk."

"Your room? Ah," I said, understanding. She had turned me back into an eight-year-old, transported us back to the room in the ancestral house where the shadows stood brooding in the corners and the fumes of mingled medicines choked the stagnant air. I decided not to tell her where she was. The past was her last refuge, and I had no wish to be cruel. "Okay, I'm here, Lola. I'm right here."

"Can you still recite it, my little Pepito? Can you recite it for me?"

I had no idea what she meant until, softly, she began to hum. And then I remembered: Lola had summoned me many times to her room, sat me down on her lap as I squirmed in restlessness and secret terror, lifted the Bible from her dresser with reverent hands, and, turning now to this chapter and now to that, taught me passages, psalms, hymns. One psalm, the twenty-third, she recited over and over with such emphasis and such fervor that despite my terror at the wrinkled ghost the words embedded themselves in my memory; and then she sat back, humming the melody to the *Ama Namin* that early churchgoers sang on Sunday, and listened to me struggle to repeat the psalm to her.

She was humming the *Ama Namin* now, a melancholy air that wove itself into the silence of the garden, and almost against my wishes the words came to mind, came to my lips. "The Lord is my shepherd; I shall not want. He maketh me to lie down in green pastures; he leadeth me beside the still waters. He restoreth my soul; he leadeth me in the paths of righteousness for his name's sake. Yea, though I walk in the valley of the shadow of death I shall fear no evil . . ."

I faltered, searching for the words, and stopped. Lola Silang stopped humming as well, and burst into a laughter that surprised me with its vitality. "Poor Pepito," she gasped, "still trapped as always in the valley of the shadow of death."

I smiled, half-heartedly, thinking of the tightrope that stretched over my personal abyss, and a quiet gloom overcame me. "Ah, Lola, who knows? Maybe you're right. If you only knew how true that is, maybe you wouldn't be laughing so much."

"Ay, Pepito," she said, "you're too small to be thinking about such big things."

She disconcerted me. For most of my years I had known her face to wear no expression save bitterness, save anger, save a haughty, frowning pride. Then, as she descended into her shadows, I grew accustomed to the stoic mask that hardened on her features, the jaw thrust stubbornly forward in defiance of the efforts of bewildered doctors, the eyes screwed shut against the sight of her crumbling family, the quarrels of her errant children. But in the garden illuminated by the softening light of afternoon, I had seen her laugh; and now, as she sensed my self-pity, her worn and wrinkled features bore a compassion I had never seen before, startling in its newness. "You're too small for such big thoughts," she was saying. "You let God take care of you, Pepito, like he takes care of the smallest of his creatures. And after God, your family. Your family will always protect you."

"Family." I scowled, involuntarily, and wondered if she could sense it; and I almost told her point-blank, you don't like my family, Lola, you despise your own daughter and the man she married. I swallowed the words before they could be uttered. Whatever reasons she had for denying her love to Mama seemed beside the point now; she was old, and would take her petrified loves and hatreds to her grave. "Tell me about my family, Lola," I said instead.

"Your family," she replied, cackling at her own private joke, "is a flock of chickens running around in the backyard when the master is gone." She wheezed, trying to catch her breath, as laughter shook her. "Ay, Pepito! When your *Lolo* Enchong comes home from *sabong*, he will tie all those chickens' heads together and teach them how to behave. He will bring order to his house, and he will sing praise to the Lord on Sundays. Oh, you should hear your Lolo Enchong sing, Pepito! His voice is like thunder, ringing from the mountains, ringing in the high heavens. His voice is like the voice of God himself, as God was once heard speaking in the wilderness. *Ay*, Pepito, when your Lolo Enghong comes home, then you will hear the thunder in his voice and see the fire in his eyes, and then he will tell you about your family . . ."

I sat, listening, dumbfounded. Lola Silang rambled on, describing Lolo Enchong for me, the grandfather who never lived to see my birth—bringing to life his vigorous hands, his fat man's laugh, his mane of silver hair, his booming baritone which drowned out the rest of the choir and rocked the walls of the church, the curt *pok-pok* of his cane on the wooden floors of the ancestral house, the monstrous snores that rattled the bedroom at night, the fiery, flashing eyes that ran in both sides of the Sanchez family and diminished with the generations. And from her disjointed phrases and fragmented recollections, I pieced together stories. How Lolo Enchong drank ten cups of *kape* at six o'clock every morning before he was awake, how he drained a bottle of gin every night at eleven before he could fall asleep, how he'd once smashed Ignacio across the cheek when he discovered him doing the same. How he'd ordered, on a Valentine's Day, a truckload of roses for Lola and a bouquet of *sampaguita* flowers for Mama, all costing a small fortune that put him in debt for a year despite his considerable wealth. How he'd once carried a sick Teodoro six miles to the hospital on foot, in the driving rain, when his car broke down after the first four miles. How he'd seized a student making noise at the back of his class and thrown him bodily out the window, ensuring perfect behavior from his class for the remainder of the year. How he'd celebrated for weeks, with wine and song, with his neighbors and his students and his colleagues, when he was declared the champion *sabongero* of the town, his fighting cocks standing bloody but undefeated in the sandy arena. How he had done all this and so much more, as Lola Silang fed me on her memories, until I could no longer help but believe in the powerful existence of Don Lorenzo Sanchez.

I had asked about my family. She gave me stories of the family I never knew, the generations that had long since faded from all memory but hers; and she spoke of them in the present tense, as though they were still alive, with an immediacy and an informality that implied that the dead were not dead, that they had simply gone to market for the day and would return by nightfall to chat with Lola in her world of shadows. Lolo Enchong first, and then the others—her brothers and sisters, her mother and father, her uncles and cousins and aunts who grew larger as they receded further into legend. Maximilio, who fought with the guerrillas in the Filipino-American war, and Teofilo, who betrayed him to the puppet government. Eulalia, driven mad by her husband's affairs, who roamed the streets at night moaning and tearing at her hair and finally returned home and set her children on fire. Ramon, the poet, who wrote for his lover songs so beautiful that men cried when they heard them, and sang them to warm their souls in the darkest hours of the night. Lucia, whose grave was decorated with ten thousand flowers, one for each of the souls she'd saved with her medical arts when the bubonic plague hit the town. Benjamin—*ang relihiyoso*, Lola called him—who rose to become the highest Catholic bishop in the country and whose illegitimate children scattered across the land, gazing at the world with their fierce, flashing eyes. Rebeca, *ang rebelde*, who trained a secret battalion of women in the mountains during the Spanish-American war and led them to slaughter a thousand troops, without the aid of the foreigners, before the final destruction of the Spanish fleet.

The waning light turned my grandmother's hair a softly-glowing silver as she talked on into the afternoon, as animated as her stiff and feeble limbs allowed her to be, gesturing with her gnarled and trembling fingers and tracing portraits of the dead in the hushed garden air. That day, as I watched her and touched the vivid surface of her memories, I saw Lola Silang as I had never seen her before. She wasn't simply a victim, I thought, a limp and sightless rag doll tossed about in the battle for her soul and for her land. She was a survivor, a storyteller, who held her history together even as it tore her apart. These stories, I realized, were what she'd guarded all this time in her silence, a treasurehouse of secret memory that sustained her through the long years of darkness.

"Listen to me now," she was saying, "listen to me, Pepito. I will tell you now about my grandfather, that brave, wonderful man, are you listening, *ha*, Pepito? Because when he comes home from the war, when he defeats those bastard *Amerikanos*, those devil troops, he will take you and me and my mother and my grandmother into his big, strong arms and we will dance to his beautiful music on top of the bird-hill, higher than the treetops, Pepito, higher than the clouds."

She went on, her rambling voice a trembling enchantment, and from the images she wove I deciphered the last and the oldest of her stories—how in the last wounded days of the Spanish-American war a tall, nameless stranger with blue eyes fierce as lightning arrived at her grandmother's town. He was a demon, some said; others said that he was a messenger from God, an ivory-skinned archangel come to save the souls of the town; others, less given to superstition, guessed from gossip and from the news telegrams from the capital that he was a legendary Spanish general, defeated but still terrifying in his raging pride, driven from his fortifications in Manila and retreating slowly to the sea. His troops had abandoned him along the way, and now, alone, he made his way resolutely from town to town, heading towards the port where his ship waited to take him home. Spies watched him nervously to make sure he was not about to organize an attack against the capital, and they tracked his progress across the provinces by the birds that fell out of the sky—for the fearsome power of his eyes was such that as he strode, his head held high, his withering gaze killed the birds in mid-flight and made them decay into dust and bone as they spiraled to the earth. He did not get any further than my great-great-grandmother's town, however, because when he heard Andalusia Santamaria sing, when he saw her move with the pure grace that took men's hearts away, when he saw her tangled midnight curls and her dark eyes which were unafraid to look into his own, he knelt before her and declared his love with a feverish passion that lasted for years as he stayed in that town, as his lightning gaze continued to cause birds to rain from the sky, as he spent his remaining time with Andalusia in the highest ecstasy a lover could possibly know until sickness took him and he died, unwedded, in her arms. She buried him at the entrance to the town, on the hill of bird bones that had grown constantly during the years of their bliss, the same hill on which they had danced every night to faint strains of music that wafted in on the wind, whispering their love to each other under the blue eye of the moon.

"You must remember, Pepito," Lola Silang said, "you must remember to ask your great-great-*lolo* to take you to the hill, to take you dancing there up high where you can see the rest of the land, yes, where you can see the mountain of roses over there, see what your Lolo Enchong gave me once, and there, Eulalia's house on fire, *ay, kawawa*, poor girl, and there, Ignacio's grave and my Eduardo's wonderful churches. There, do you see, do you see," she said as she trailed off into silence. In the stillness of the garden her stories shimmered in the fading light.

"*Hoy!* What are you doing?" she shouted suddenly, sinking further into her delirium. "What are you doing, Pepito, *bataka*? Don't stand there, you'll fall! *Diyos ko*, come back from the edge, be careful!"

"I'm here, Lola, I'm right here, I'm not going anywhere," I said, grasping her hands to calm her down as I looked, startled, into her face. Her unseeing eyes were open for the first time, dark pools coated with white mist, shifting and roving about as if they followed the contours of her landscape of shadows. I wondered what she saw as I held her, whispered to her, stroked her withered arms. "Don't fall, don't fall," she murmured as the afternoon deepened, as the first star winked open in the sky.

By evening Papa and Mama and her brothers were back, and Uncle Manny apologized to me for the long wait. They'd returned in sullen silence, and the frowns they wore told me that they'd fallen into one of their arguments, painful, guilt-laden, and unresolved, as always. We ate dinner, and Uncle Manny helped Lola Silang into bed before seeing us to the door. Uncle Del and my parents and I rode back with Uncle Dodi to his house, where we would stay for the remainder of our trip.

I asked Mama that evening if she would enumerate for me all of her relations whom she could remember; she smiled, glad to be asked something that took her mind off her pain, and rattled names off the top of her head as I jotted them down on sheets of paper. Later, as my parents slept in the next room, I put the sheets together, drawing lines from brother to sister, from mother to son, until I had constructed an elaborate family tree that glittered with names and the promise of history. Mama was not good at telling stories. The names of most of her kin were just names to her, with no tales lurking beneath the sound of the words—just dates of births and deaths, at most, and documents of who was married to whom. But I filled in the hollow names with my grandmother's stories, gave the dead their flesh and bones again to hover above me and confess their secret lives in the silence of the room, felt the penciled web of relationships tremble and come alive and include me in its vibrant unity.

Two weeks later, when we had returned to Michigan, when the breathless voice of Uncle Manny at the other end of the line told my tearful mother that Lola Silang had died quietly in the night, I took out the folded sheets and gazed at the names once more, tracing with my finger the lines of relationships in which so much of my grandmother's memory was contained. All this time, I realized, I had been judging my life by measuring the distance I could put between her and myself, denying her blindness and her prayers and her stories and her hymns as I lost myself in a cacophony of foreign tongues, a chaos of strangers, trying to forget my name. Listening to my mother weep, I wondered if she would forget her name as well, if she and her warring brothers would drift silently apart and break the last threads that kept their family from oblivion, if somehow Lola Silang were the core that held the web of names together, without which the names would snuff themselves out, leaving wisps of smoke in the air.

That night I dreamed of my great-great-grandmother's town. I walked upon a landscape of bones, and wherever my foot fell the carcasses stirred and sprang to life—ravens and crows and nightingales, robins and sparrows and eagles and hawks, launching themselves into the air, one by one, until the sky was crowded with wings.

Born in the Philippines in 1973, Jason drifted through a patchwork childhood of puto and pizza, Aesop's fables, the Apostles' Creed, martial law, Lea Salonga and Sesame Street on network TV, typhoons, fiestas, first love, a People's Revolution. His parents, though artists and wordsmiths themselves, sent him to the prestigious Philippine Science High School hoping that he acquire a taste for engineering or medicine—but made the mistake of reading him excellent stories and buying him a typewriter in his youth.

He has wanted (perhaps unwisely) to be a writer ever since. In 1989 he immigrated with his family to the United States.

Jason is now on his last year at the University of Michigan's Residential College, where he studies comparative literature and creative writing. His fiction has won several prizes—including a Hopwood Award—and he plans eventually to pursue a postgraduate degree in literature across cultural boundaries. He shares an Ann Arbor apartment with five friends and a tyrannical cat. He dabbles in drawing and songwriting, dreams in Spanish, and is discovering the joys of opera.

He dedicates this story to his parents, to his grandmother Ester, and to the memory of a dear friend.

Chitra Divakaruni

CLOTHES

THE WATER OF THE WOMEN'S lake laps against my breasts, cool, calming. I can feel it beginning to wash the hot nervousness away from my body. The little waves tickle my armpits, make my sari float up around me, wet and yellow, like a sunflower after rain. I close my eyes and smell the sweet brown odor of the *ritha* pulp my friends Deepali and Radha are working into my hair so that it will glisten with little lights this evening. They scrub with more vigor than usual and wash it out more carefully, because today is a special day. It is the day of my bride-viewing.

"*Ei*, Sumita! Mita! Are you deaf?" Radha says. "This is the third time I've asked you the same question."

"Look at her, already dreaming about her husband, and she hasn't even seen him yet!" Deepali jokes. Then she adds, the envy in her voice only half-hidden, "Who cares about friends from a little Indian village when you're about to go live in America?"

I want to deny it, to say that I will always love them and all the things we did together through my growing up years—visiting the *charak* fair where we always ate too many sweets, raiding the neighbor's guava tree in the summer afternoons while everyone else slept, telling fairytales while we braided each other's hair in elaborate patterns we'd invented. *And she married the handsome prince who took her to his kingdom beyond the seven seas.* But already the activities of our girlhood seem to be far in my past, the colors leached out of them, like old sepia photographs.

His name is Somesh Sen, the man who is coming to our house with his parents today and who will be my husband "if I'm lucky enough to be chosen," as my aunt says. He is coming all the way from California, where he lives. Father showed it to me yesterday, on the metal globe that sits on his desk, a chunky pink wedge on the wide of a multi-colored slab marked the *Untd. Sts. of America.* I touched it and felt the excitement leap all the way up my arm like an electric shock. Then it died away, leaving only a beaten-metal coldness against my fingertips.

It struck me then that if things worked out the way everyone was hoping, I'd be going halfway around the world to live with a man I hadn't even met. Would I ever see my parents again? *Don't send me so far away*, I wanted to cry, but of course I didn't. It would be ungrateful. Father had worked so hard to find this match for me. Besides, wasn't it every woman's destiny, as Mother was always saying, to leave the loved world of girlhood for the unknown? She had done it, and her mother before her. *A married woman belongs to her husband, her in-laws.* Hot seeds of tears had pricked my eyelids at the unfairness of it.

"Mita Moni, little jewel," Father said, calling me by my childhood name. He put out his hand as though he wanted to touch my face, then let it fall to his side. "He's a good man. Comes from a fine family. He will be kind to you." He was silent for a while. Finally he said, "Come, let me show you the special sari I bought in Calcutta for you to wear at the bride-viewing."

"Are you nervous?" Radha asks as she wraps my hair in a soft cotton towel. Her parents are also trying to arrange a marriage for her. So far three families have come to see her, but no one has chosen her because her skin is considered too dark. "Isn't it terrible, not knowing what's going to happen?"

I nod because I don't want to disagree, don't want to make her feel bad by saying that sometimes it's worse when you know what's coming, like I do. I knew it as soon as Father unlocked his mahogany *almirah* and took out the sari.

It was the most expensive sari I had ever seen, and surely the most beautiful. Its body was a pale pink, like the dawn sky over the woman's lake. The color of transition. Embroidered all over it were tiny stars made out of real gold *zari* thread.

"Here, hold it," said Father.

The sari was unexpectedly heavy in my hands, silk-slippery, a sari to walk carefully in. A sari that could change one's life. I stood there holding it, wanting to weep. Because I knew that when I wore it, it would hang in perfect pleats to my feet and shimmer in the light of the evening lamps. It would dazzle Somesh and his parents and they would choose me to be his bride.

When the plane takes off, I try to stay calm, to take deep, slow breaths like father does when he practices yoga. But my hands clench themselves onto the folds of my sari and when I force them open, after the seat belt and no smoking signs have blinked off, I see they have left damp blotches on the delicate crushed fabric.

We had some arguments about this sari. I wanted a blue one for the journey, because blue is the color of possibility, the color of the sky through which I would be traveling. But mother said there must be red in it because red is the color of luck for married women. Finally, father found one to satisfy us both: midnight blue with a thin red border the same color as the marriage mark I'm wearing on my forehead.

It is hard for me to think of myself as a married woman. I whisper my new name to myself, Mrs. Sumita Sen, but the syllables rustle uneasily in my mouth, like a stiff satin that's never been worn.

Somesh had to leave for America just a week after the wedding. He had to get back to the store, he explained to me. He had promised his partner. The store. It seems more real to me than Somesh—perhaps because I know more about it. It was what we had mostly talked about the night after the wedding, the first night we were together alone. It stayed open 24 hours, yes, all night, every night, not like the Indian stores which closed at dinnertime and sometimes in the hottest part of the afternoon. That's why his partner needed him back.

The store was called *Seven Eleven*. I thought it a strange name, exotic, risky. All the stores I knew were piously named after gods and goddesses—*Ganesh Sweet House, Lakshmi Vastralaya for Fine Saris*—to bring luck.

The store sold all kinds of amazing things—apple juice in cardboard cartons that never leaked, American bread that came in cellophane packages, already cut-up, canisters of potato chips, each large grainy flake curved exactly like the next. The large refrigerator with see-through glass doors held beer and wine, which, said Somesh, were the most popular items.

"That's where the money comes from, especially in the neighborhood where our store is," said Somesh, smiling at the shocked look on my face. (The only places I knew of that sold alcohol were the village toddy shops, "dark, stinking dens of vice," Father called them). "A lot of Americans drink, you know. It's a part of their culture, not considered immoral, like it is here. And really, there's nothing wrong with it. Why," he continued, touching my lips lightly with his finger, "when you come to California, I'll get you some sweet white wine and you'll see how good it makes you feel. . . ." Now his fingers were stroking my cheeks, my throat, moving downward. I closed my eyes and tried not to jerk away because after all it was my wifely duty.

"It helps if you can think about something else," my friend Madhavi had said when she warned me about what most husbands demanded on the very first night. Two years married, she already had one child and was pregnant with a second one.

I tried, but his lips were hot against my skin, his fingers fumbling with buttons, pulling at the cotton night-sari I wore. I felt as though I couldn't breathe.

"Bite hard on your tongue," Madhavi had advised. "The pain will keep your mind off what's going on down there."

But when I bit down, it hurt so much that I cried out. I

couldn't help it although I was ashamed. Somesh lifted his head. I don't know what he saw on my face, but he stopped right away. "Shhh," he said, although I had made myself silent already, "it's O.K., we'll wait until you're ready." I tried to apologize but he smiled it away and started telling me some more about the store. And that's how it was the rest of the week until he left. We would lie side by side on the big white bridal pillow I had embroidered with a pair of doves for married harmony, and Somesh would describe how the store's front windows were decorated with a flashing neon Dewar's sign and a lighted Budweiser waterfall *this big*. I would watch his hands moving excitedly through the dim air of the bedroom and think that Father had been right, he was a good man, my husband, a kind, patient man. And so handsome, too, I would add, stealing a quick look at the strong curve of his jaw, feeling luckier than I had any right to be.

The night before he left, Somesh confessed that the store wasn't making much money yet. "I'm not worried, I'm sure it soon will," he added, his fingers pleating the edge of my sari. "But I just don't want to give you the wrong impression, don't want you to be disappointed."

In the half-dark I could see he had turned toward me. His face, with two vertical lines between the brows, looked young, apprehensive, in need of protection. I'd never seen that on a man's face before. Something rose in me like a wave.

"It's O.K.," I said, as though to a child, and pulled his head down to my breast. His hair smelled faintly of the American cigarettes he smoked. "I won't be disappointed. I'll help you." And a sudden happiness filled me.

That night I dreamed I was at the store. Soft American music floated in the background as I moved between the shelves stocked high with brightly colored cans and elegant-necked bottles, turning their labels carefully to the front, polishing them until they shone.

Now, sitting inside this metal shell that is hurtling me through space towards my husband, I try to remember other things about that night: how gentle his hands had been, and his lips, surprisingly soft, like a woman's. How I've longed for them through those drawn-out nights while I waited for my visa to arrive. He will be standing at the customs gate, and when I reach him, he will lower his face to mine. We will kiss in front of everyone, not caring, like Americans, then pull back, look each other in the eye, and smile.

But suddenly, as I am thinking this, I realize I cannot recall Somesh's face. I try and try until my head hurts, but I can only visualize the black emptiness swirling outside the plane, the air too thin for breathing. My own breath grows ragged with panic as I think of it and my mouth fills with sour fluid the way it does just before I throw up.

I grope for something to hold on to, something beautiful and talismanic from my old life. And then I remember. Somewhere down under me, low in the belly of the plane, inside my new brown case which is stacked in the dark with a hundred others, are my saris. Thick Kanjeepuram silks in solid purples and golden yellows, the thin hand-woven cottons of the Bengal countryside, green as a young banana plant, grey as the women's lake on a cloudy monsoon day. Already I can feel my shoulders loosening up, my breath steadying. My wedding Benarasi, flame orange, with a wide *palloo* of gold-embroidered dancing peacocks. Fold upon fold of Dhakai saris so fine they can be pulled through a ring. Into each fold my mother has tucked a small sachet of sandalwood powder to protect the saris from the unknown insects of America. Little silk sachets, made from *her* old saris—I can smell their calm fragrance as I watch the American air hostess wheeling the dinner cart toward my seat. It is the smell of my mother's hands.

I know then that everything will be all right. And when the air hostess bends her curly golden head to ask me what I would like to eat, I understand every word in spite of her strange accent and answer her without stumbling even once over the unfamiliar English phrases.

Late at night I stand in front of our bedroom mirror trying on the clothes Somesh has bought for me and smuggled in past his parents. I model each one for him, walking back and forth, clasping my hands behind my head, lips pouted, left hip thrust out just like the models on TV, while he whispers applause. I'm breathless with suppressed laughter (Father and Mother Sen must not hear us) and my cheeks are hot with the delicious excitement of conspiracy. We've stuffed a towel at the bottom of the door so no light will shine through.

I'm wearing a pair of jeans now, marveling at the curve of my hips and thighs, which have always been hidden under the flowing lines of my saris. I love the color, the same pale blue as the *nayantara* flower. The solid comforting weight. the jeans come with a close-fitting T-shirt which outlines my breasts in a way that makes me shy, unable to look at Somesh. He shouldn't have been so extravagant, I tell him. We can't afford it. He just smiles.

The T-shirt is sunrise-orange—the color, I decide, of joy, of my new American life. Across its middle, in large black letters, is written *Great America*. I was sure they referred to the country, but Somesh told me it is the name on an amusement park, a place people go to have fun. I think it a wonderful, novel concept. Above the letters is the picture of a train. Only it's not a train, Somesh tells me, it's a roller coaster. He tries to explain how it moves, the insane speed, the dizzy ground falling away, then gives up. "I'll take you there, Mita sweetheart," he says, "as soon as we move into our own place."

That's our dream (mine more than his, I suspect)—moving out of this two-room apartment where it seems to me if we all breathed in at once, there would be no air left. Where I must cover my head with the edge of my Japan nylon sari (my expensive Indian ones are to be saved for special occasions—trips to the temple, Bengali New Year) and serve tea to the old women that come to visit Mother Sen, where like a good Indian wife I must never address my husband by his name. Where even in our bedroom we kiss guiltily, uneasily, listening for the giveaway creak of bedsprings. Sometimes I laugh to myself, thinking how ironic it is that after all my fears my American life turned out to be no different from Deepali's or Radha's. But at other times I feel caught inside a miniature world. A world where everything is frozen in place like a scene inside a glass paperweight. It is a world so small that if I were to stretch out my arms, I would touch its cold unyielding edges. I stand inside this glass world, watching helplessly as America rushes by, wanting to scream.

Then I'm ashamed. Mita, I tell myself, you're growing westernized. Back home you'd never have felt this way.

We must be patient. I know that. Tactful, loving children. That is our Indian way. We don't want to hurt the parents, make them feel unwanted. "I'm their life," says Somesh, and he's not boasting, merely stating a fact. "They've always been there when I needed them. I could never send them off to some old people's home." For a moment I'm angry. Then I remember my own parents, Mother's hands cool on my sweat-drenched body through nights of fever, Father teaching me to read, his finger moving along the crisp black angles of the alphabet, transforming them magically into things I knew, *water, dog, mango tree*. I beat back my unreasonable desire and nod agreement, knowing that Somesh is, as always, right.

Somesh has bought me a cream-colored blouse with a long brown skirt. They match beautifully, like the inside and outside of an almond. "For when you begin working," he says. But first he wants me to start college. Get a degree, perhaps in teaching. I picture myself in front of a classroom of girls with blond pigtails and blue uniforms, like a scene out of an English movie I saw long ago in Calcutta. They raise their hands respectfully when I ask a question. "Do you really think I can?" I ask. "Of course," he replies.

I am gratified he has such confidence in me. But I have another plan, a secret that I will divulge to him once we move. What I really want is to work in the store. I want to stand behind the counter in the cream and brown skirt set (color of earth, color of seeds) and ring up purchases. The register drawer will glide open. Confidently, I will count out green dollars and silver quarters. Gleaming copper pennies. I will dust the jars of gilt-wrapped chocolates on the counter. Will straighten, on the far wall, the posters of smiling young men in jackets holding foaming beer mugs and scantily clad redheads with huge spiky eyelashes. (I have never visited the store—my in-laws don't think it proper for a wife—but of course I know exactly what it looks like). I will charm the customers with my smile, so that they will return again and again just to hear me telling them to have a nice day.

Meanwhile, I will the store to make money for us. Quickly. Because when we move, we'll be paying for two households. But so far it hasn't worked. They're losing money steadily, Somesh has told me. They had to let the hired help go. This means most nights Somesh has to take the graveyard shift (that horrible word, like a cold hand up my spine) because his partner refuses to.

"The bastard!" Somesh spat out once. "Just because he put in more money he thinks he can order me around. I'll show him!" I was frightened by the vicious twist of his mouth. Somehow I'd never thought he could be so angry.

Often Somesh leaves right after dinner and doesn't get back till after I've made morning tea for Father and Mother Sen. I lie mostly awake those nights, picturing masked intruders crouching in the shadowed back of the store, like I've seen on the police shows that Father Sen sometimes watches. But Somesh insists there's nothing to worry about, they have bars on the windows and a burglar alarm. "And remember," he says, "the extra cash will help us move that much quicker."

I'm wearing a nightie now, my very first one. It's black and lacy, with a bit of a shine to it, and it glides over my hips to stop outrageously at mid-thigh. My mouth is an o of surprise in the mirror, my legs long and pale and sleek from the hair remover I asked Somesh to buy me last week. The legs of a movie star. Somesh laughs at the look on my face, then says, "You're beautiful." His voice starts a flutter low in my belly. "Do you really think so?" I ask, mostly because I want to hear him say it again. No one has called me beautiful before. My father would have thought it inappropriate, my mother that it would make me vain.

Somesh draws me close. "Very beautiful," he whispers. "The most beautiful woman in the whole world." His eyes are not joking as they usually are. I want to turn off the light, but "Please," he says, "I want to keep seeing your face." His fingers are taking the pins from my hair, undoing my braids. The escaped strands fall on his face like dark rain. We have already decided where we will hide my new American clothes—the jeans and T-shirt camouflaged on a hanger among Somesh's pants, the skirt set and nightie at the bottom of my suitcase, a sandalwood sachet tucked between them, waiting.

I stand in the middle of our empty bedroom, my hair still wet from the purification bath, my back to the stripped bed I can't bear to look at. I hold in my hands the plain white sari I'm supposed to wear. I must hurry. Any minute now there'll be a knock at the door. They are afraid to leave me alone too long, afraid I might do something to myself.

The sari, a thick voile that will bunch around the waist when worn, is borrowed. White. Widow's color, color of endings. I try to tuck the sari into the top of the petticoat, but my fingers are numb, disobedient. The sari spills through them and there are waves and waves of white around my feet. I kick out in sudden rage, but the sari is too soft, it gives too easily. I grab up an edge, clamp down with my teeth and pull, feeling a fierce, bitter satisfaction when I hear it rip.

There's a cut, still stinging, on the side of my right arm, halfway to the elbow. It is from the bangle-breaking ceremony. Old Mrs. Mukherjee performed the ritual, since she's a widow, too. She took my hands in hers and brought them down hard on the bedpost, so that the glass bangles I was wearing shattered and multicolored shards flew out in every direction. Some landed on the body that was on the bed, covered with a sheet. I can't call it Somesh. He was gone already. She took an edge of the sheet and rubbed the red marriage mark off my forehead. She was crying. All the women in the room were crying. Except me. I watched them as though from the other end of a long tunnel. Their flared nostrils, their red-veined eyes, the runnels of tears, salt-corrosive, down their cheeks.

It happened last night. He was at the store. Every other night it was his turn. It isn't too bad, he would say, not too many customers. I can put up my feet and watch MTV all night. I can sing along with Michael Jackson as loud as I want. He had a good voice, Somesh. Sometimes he would sing softly at night, lying in bed, holding me. Hindi songs of love, *Mere Sapnon Ki Rani*, queen of my dreams. (He would not sing American songs at home out of respect for his parents, who didn't care for such things). I would feel his warm breath on my hair as I fell asleep.

Someone came into the store last night. He took all the money, even the little rolls of pennies I had helped Somesh make up. Before he left he emptied the bullets from his gun into my husband's chest.

Only thing is, Somesh would say about the night shifts, I

really miss you. I sit there and think of you asleep in bed. Do you know that when you sleep you make your hands into fists, like a small child? When we move out, will you come along some nights to keep me company?

My in-laws are good people, kind. They made sure the body was covered before they let me into the room. When someone asked if my hair should be cut off, as they often do with widows back home, they said no. They said I could stay back at the apartment with Mrs. Mukherjee if I felt that I couldn't face the crematorium. They asked Dr. Das to give me something to calm me down when I couldn't stop shivering. They didn't say, even once, as people would have in the village, that it was my bad luck that brought death to their son so soon after his marriage.

They will probably go back to India now. There's nothing here for them any more. They will want me to go with them. You're like our daughter, they will say. Your home is with us, for as long as you want. For the rest of your life. *The rest of my life.* I can't think about that yet. It makes me dizzy. Fragments are flying about my head, multicolored and piercing-sharp like bits of bangle glass.

I want you to go to college. Choose a career. I stand in front of a classroom of smiling children who love me in my cream and brown American dress. A faceless parade straggles across my eyelids: all those customers at the store that I will never meet. The lace nightie, fragrant with sandalwood, waiting in its blackness inside my suitcase. The savings book where we have $3605.33. *Four thousand and we can move out, maybe next month.* The name of the pantyhose I'd asked him to buy me next week: sheer golden-beige. His lips, unexpectedly soft, woman-smooth. Elegant-necked wine bottles swept off shelves, shattering on the floor.

I know Somesh would not have tried to stop the gunman. I can picture his silhouette against the lighted Dewar's sign, hands raised. He is trying to find the right expression to put on his face, calm, reassuring, reasonable. *O.K., take the money. No, no, I won't call the police.* His hands tremble just a little. The disbelief in his eyes as his fingers touch his chest and come away wet.

I yanked away the cover. I had to see. *Great America, a*

place people go to have fun. My breath rollercoasting through my body, my unlived life gathering itself into a scream. I'd expected blood, a lot of blood, the deep red-black of it crusting his chest. But they must have cleaned him up at the hospital. He was dressed in his silk wedding kurta. Against its warm ivory his face appeared pale, remote, stern. Not his face at all. The musky aroma of his aftershave lotion. Someone must have sprinkled it on the body. It didn't quite hide that other smell, thin, sour, metallic. The smell of death. The floor shifts under me, tilting like a wave.

I'm lying on the floor now, on the spilled white sari. I feel sleepy. Or perhaps it is some other feeling I don't have a word for. The sari is seductive-soft, drawing me into its folds.

Sometimes, bathing at the lake, I would move away from my friends, their endless chatter. I'd swim toward the middle of the water with a lazy backstroke, gazing at the sky, its enormous blueness drawing me up until I felt weightless-dizzy. Once in a while there would be a plane, a small silver needle drawn through the clouds, in and out, until it disappeared. Sometimes the thought came to me, as I floated in the middle of the lake with the sun beating down on my closed eyelids, that it would be so easy to let go, to allow the water to pull me down into the dim brown underwater world of mud, of waterweeds as fine as hair.

Once I almost did it. I curled my body inward, tight as a fist, and felt it start to sink. The sun grew pale and shapeless; the water, suddenly cold, licked at the insides of my ears in welcome. But in the end I couldn't.

They are knocking on the door now, calling my name. I push myself off the floor, my body almost too heavy to lift up, as when one climbs out of water after a long swim. I'm surprised at how vividly it comes to me, this memory I haven't called up in years: the desperate flailing of arms and legs as I fought my way upward, the press of the water on me, heavy as terror, the wild animal trapped inside my chest, clawing at my lungs. The day returning to me as searing air, the way I drew it in, in, in, as though I would never have enough of it.

That's when I know I cannot go back. I don't know yet how I'll manage, here in this new, dangerous land where the edges of things melt into each other. I only know I must. Because all over India, at this very moment, widows in white saris are bowing their veiled heads, serving tea to in-laws. Doves with cut-off wings.

I am standing in front of the mirror now, gathering up the sari. I tuck in the ripped end so it lies next to my skin, reminding me. My secret. I think of the store, although it hurts: inside the refrigerated unit, blue milk cartons neatly lined up by Somesh' hands. The exotic smell of Hills Brothers coffee brewed black and strong, the glisten of sugar-glazed donuts nestled in tissue. The neon Budweiser emblem winking on and off like a risky invitation.

I straighten my shoulders and stand taller, take a deep breath. Air fills me—the same air, I think, that traveled through Somesh' lungs a little while ago. The thought is like an unexpected, intimate gift. I tilt up my chin, readying myself for the arguments of the coming weeks, the remonstrations. In the mirror a woman holds my gaze, her eyes apprehensive yet steady. She wears a blouse and skirt the color of almonds.

Chitra Divakaruni lives in the San Francisco Area with her husband Murthy and two children. She teaches English at Foothill College and is the coordinator for a helpline for South Asian Women. She has 3 books of poetry; the latest is BLACK CANDLE (Calyx). Her first fiction collection will soon be appearing (ARRANGED MARRIAGE, Doubleday). Her work has been published in Ms., Chicago Review, Chelsea, Zyzzyva, Beloit Poetry Journal, etc., and has been widely anthologized.

Part II

Islands

Sylvia Watanabe

A CONVERSATION WITH DARRELL LUM AND ERIC CHOCK

Long before "multiculturalism," Darrell Lum and Eric Chock founded *Bamboo Ridge, The Hawaii Writers' Quarterly* and its associated literary press in order to foster the growth of Hawaii's multi-ethnic literary tradition. Since that beginning in 1978, the journal has provided a vehicle for a wide range of voices and subjects. Special issues have been devoted to Native Hawaiian rights and traditional legends, the *tanka* of Hawaii's *issei* interned during World War II, and the writing of Hawaii's Chinese immigrants. In 1984, the press published the screenplay of Wayne Wang's *Chan is Missing*. Major local authors whose books have been brought out by the press include Lum, Chock, Susan Nunes, Wing Tek Lum, Juliet S. Kono, Rodney Morales, Gary Pak, Lois-Ann Yamanaka, and most recently, Marie Hara.

Now in its 17th year, *Bamboo Ridge* can be counted among the longest-running multi-ethnic publications in the country, as well as a major forum for Asian and Pacific regional writing.

Among the honors received by the journal and press is a General Electric Editors' Award from the Coordinating Council of Literary Magazines.

The following interview was compiled from a series of 1994 phone calls and written exchanges with Lum and Chock.

Let's begin at the beginning. What do you remember of your childhoods?

D.L.: I was born in Honolulu—in Alewa Heights—spent my whole childhood in the same house. The things I remember have mostly to do with growing up the kid brother. I have one brother, six years older than me, and at the time, I considered it my job to follow him around and he considered it his job to yell at me and tell me to go home.

E.C.: I grew up a couple of miles *mauka* [toward the mountains] of downtown Honolulu in Nuuanu Valley.

Not that far from Darrell's neighborhood—

E.C.: Yeah. The area where we lived was next to three cemeteries—Oahu Cemetery, Nuuanu Memorial Park, and another cemetery, much of which was still waiting for its occupants. I remember a small town pastoral childhood. Always barefoot. On the way to our house, there was a dirt lane, vegetable gardens, a watercress farm, fields of California grass, and streams in the back. A large fish pond to one side. No house next door. We had horseshoes under our house from the horsefield which had been there before. And pieces of old Hawaiian poi pounders.

As you talk, I get the same sense that I do from your poetry, where these sorts of images powerfully evoke a sense of place. What was daily life like? Were there particular family rituals?

E.C.: I led a fairly sheltered childhood. We had no allowance, so it was painful to visit the mom and pop stores down the street with neighbor kids who had spending money. Besides visiting relatives, we didn't go out much—to restaurants, to movies, or to the homes of our parents' friends. We weren't allowed to watch television, except for a few carefully chosen programs. When I was little, my mother took me to see

"Lady and the Tramp" at the Liliha Theater, but my parents never took me to any other movie. Oh yeah, there was one time I remember that my father gave me a dollar to see a movie with a classmate after Sunday school—I think I was in sixth grade. I remember going to Ala Moana Beach in the summers. I always had to beg my father all day Sunday, and then he wouldn't take us till it was late in the afternoon so the traffic would be less. We seemed to have stayed home endlessly, doing homework and chores. I didn't really have a very well-developed view of where I lived. It was probably myopic. Inwardly focused.

D.L.: I remember on Sundays my father used to take my brother and me to meet his buddy at Waikiki Beach, which seemed to have more sand then. This was in the late '50's. We parked two or three blocks from where the sea wall is now and carried our inner tubes to the beach. At the time I used to think we parked far away so we wouldn't have to put money in the meter—you know, part of that old Chinese Man Mentality—but it was Sunday, and looking back now, I realize we didn't have to do that. Anyway, my father had all these requirements about where to park the car, and then we'd go meet his friend who belonged to the same Chinese men's club. On Saturdays my parents dropped me off at the library while they went marketing, and we went to lunch afterward. I always wanted to eat at Kress, and they always wanted to go to the chop suey house.

You mentioned your dad belonging to a Chinese men's club—
    D.L.: It was made up of him and his high school buddies, loosely organized around basketball—
    E.C: You remember your dad playing basketball?
    D.L.: Well, no. They just continued meeting as they got older, and I'd have these weird images of these guys playing because they were all short and fat.

Is your dad first generation?
    D.L. Yeah, he was born in Southern China—I don't know exactly where—and he came to Hawaii as a small child of five or six, so he has almost no memory of China. He and my mom

once took a trip to Hong Kong and to China, and when I asked if he'd look up his ancestors and his family village, he said, Oh no, I don't want to do that; they're only going to ask for money. He and his family came to Hawaii when my grandfather was called here to be a schoolteacher—the community in Honolulu had asked for a teacher of Chinese language. In China, he'd been a provincial government official. He came out here first to see what things were like, then sent for his family. The school was in Honolulu, in the Kaimuki area, but my grandfather and his family lived in Liliha—not far from where my father ended up buying his own home, the house where I grew up. My grandfather eventually became a butcher because he couldn't earn a living as a Chinese school teacher.

When you say that it was the community who sent for him, was it some sort of provincial or village association?

D.L.: Maybe a branch of his church or his village society. One of the first things that immigrants from the same village did when they came here was to start a name society, which was both geographic and name-based. Some were made up of people with the same surname and some were made up of people from the same village or area. Lum Sai Ho Tong. This was our name society, which collected money for funerals, wrote letters, provided a place to stay for recent immigrants. I remember my grandfather belonging to this group and also my father. When my father was elected president, he never really enjoyed it because the president was required to sell tickets to the annual banquet, which meant that he had to buy tickets for a couple of tables. And the other thing was he had to get up and make a speech in Chinese. Though he spoke Chinese at home, he didn't feel comfortable with formal Chinese, so one of his buddies from his Chinese men's club had to write the speech, and my dad would call up his friends to practice over the telephone, and when he gave the speech, he never knew what he was saying. So it caused him a lot of anxiety.

What sort of work did your dad do?

D.L.: He worked for Hawaiian Electric as an appliance salesman. My mom was mostly a housewife, though she worked for a brief period, before she was married, at Woolworth.

And your mother's family?

D.L.: Her mother came here when she was very young—she was the third daughter—and she worked as a housegirl. It always seemed to me that her notion of home *was* Hawaii. She associated with older Chinese women who had been here for several generations and whose notions of the old country were already pretty attenuated. Maybe for older immigrants who arrived as adults, home was China, but for others, like my grandmother, the sense of home was formed here.

Was it important to your parents that you keep in touch with the family "cultural" roots—say, in terms of learning the language—

D.L.: The summer after sixth grade, I finally consented to go to Chinese language school, but I was put in the first grade class with real first graders. The oldest kid was a ninth grade girl. If the rest of us didn't want to be there, she *really* didn't want to be there.

Did you feel you were much improved in your language skills at the end of that summer?

D.L.: No, but I remember that I used to get a few cents to buy ice cake at the school store, and there was recess, and there were kung fu lessons, and we were next door to a mortuary, so it was really exciting when they brought out a coffin.

Eric, what of your memories of family?

E.C.: Let's just say that a lot of the images of my family can be gotten from reading my poems. What I have written about my family is largely, though not completely, true.

The two of you grew up in neighborhoods that were fairly close to each other. When did you meet?

D.L.: First grade.

E.C.: We were classmates from 1st through 12th grade.

Were you friends from the beginning?

D.L.: We weren't immediately friends, but we were tracked into the same classes.

E.C.: Later, at the University, we spent a lot of time playing cards and drinking beer together, and I got to see what he had written in his creative writing classes, and he got to see what I wrote in my attempts to be a lyricist—

Was that how you got started in poetry?

E.C.: Even before that, when I was growing up, my mother helped to form my sense of language. She always listened to the way my sisters and I used words; she made us read. Every month she took us to the Edna Allen Reading Room for children at the library downtown, and we borrowed books. If we came across words we didn't know, she made us go and look them up. And later, when I was in high school, she gave me books—ones she'd given my older sister—and told me to read them. I remember she gave me *The Great Gatsby* twice.

She must have really liked Gatsby.

E.C.: I think she just forgot. Anyway, around that time, in the 60's, I began wanting to be a singer/songwriter—like John Lennon, Paul Simon, Bob Dylan, Judy Collins, James Taylor. By high school, I had already handwritten a collection of my favorite pop song lyrics in a big book, and started writing my own lyrics for fun, to sing at night with the guitar, when my friends and I went to Ala Moana Beach. My favorite classes were Symphonic Band and English.

When I left Hawaii to attend the University of Pennsylvania, I had a friend back home who wanted words for his music, and after a while I wrote lyrics that didn't rhyme, and finally started writing poetry.

Darrell, can you also trace your start in fiction to such particular experiences or sources of inspiration?

D.L.: I was always around story telling. My father was a pretty good storyteller, and I eavesdropped while he talked to friends from his Chinese men's club on the telephone. My mother used to tell stories too, but they were usually in Chinese to my grandmother, and I always wondered what she was saying. I figured she was talking in secrets because she was talking in Chinese.

I guess I started writing in earnest when I went away to college—

Where?

D.L.: Case Institute of Technology, now Case Western, in Cleveland. I was terribly homesick and realized that in order to get letters, you've got to write letters. I transferred back to Hawaii after my freshman year and started taking creative writing classes.

What were your first stories like?

D.L.: They took place in the Midwest. The characters had names like Smith and Jones. Then I submitted one of these stories, which took place in Chicago, to my writing teacher, and he said, "Have you ever been to Chicago?" I said, "No." And he said, "I don't want to see anymore of this shit." Later I wrote a story for him, set in Hawaii, which was still pretty much written in standard English, but I also used some pidgin in it. Though I didn't know it then, I guess that's when I started finding my voice.

Eric, did you find your workshop leaders at the University to be helpful in a similar way—that is, in directing you toward your own cultural roots, so to speak, to find your voice and a poetic language?

E.C.: In my four years of hanging around poetry workshops, it was never emphasized that an ethnic viewpoint could affect the interpretation of an image in a poem, which after all is of the human spirit, whatever the race. But the one example where a cultural image came into question stands out clearly in my mind. A bearded *haole* student had written a poem about suddenly seeing a beautiful white crane in a field, in a sort of Americanized version of a Buddhist vision. A local Japanese student, who I found out later was the son of a priest, and who was from a part of the island not far from the rural setting of the poem, was offended that someone would try to take a common cattle egret and pass it off as the white crane of Buddhist literature and art. He couldn't understand why no one cared

about the difference, as we muddled over the image trying to
make it work.

*It sounds, then, as if you are suggesting that there might be a
way of defining an Asian Hawaiian or Asian American aesthetic—*

E.C.: In Hawaii, "Asian American" is a term we learned as
adults, not one we grew up with. We used specific ethnic labels—Hawaiian, Japanese, Chinese, Portuguese, Korean, Filipino, or "haole"—a generic term for all Caucasians. Or we just
thought of ourselves as local people, a mixture of the various
groups that grew up here.

For me, the term, "Asian American" began to make sense
when I became involved with the planning of the 1978 Talk
Story Conference. I was finishing my M.A. in English at the
University of Hawaii. All the writers we had studied were
white, all the teachers were white, almost all the visiting poets
were white. Unlike many universities on the mainland, we had
no ethnic literature classes here, unless you mean those in
Asian Studies. So we organized Talk Story as an academic conference to study the writing of ethnic American writers. One of
our goals was to discover ways of talking about alternatives to
the aesthetic we'd all been trained in.

D.L.: The full title of the conference was something like,
"Talk Story, Our Voices in Literature and Song: Hawaii's Ethnic American Writers' Conference."

Who were some of the other organizers?

E.C.: Stephen Sumida, Marie M. Hara, and Arnold T. Hiura
were the main ones, and almost two hundred Asian Americans
from the mainland, as well as hundreds of local people, attended. With Maxine Kingston's help—she was living here at
the time—the event was covered by the press in L. A. and New
York. It put us on the literary map. It placed us in the context
of an ongoing ethnic American literary tradition. And given
that the majority of our population is Asian/Pacific, I think it is
fair to say that Talk Story altered the perception and direction
of literature in Hawaii. It certainly changed my perspective as
a writer.

In what ways?

E.C.: With Talk Story, we created a new vision of ourselves. For local writers trained on white mainstream culture, it was a kind of literary, "I'm OK, You're OK," laying of the groundwork to explore local topics in our work, which, especially in poetry, had not been done very much before.

In that respect the motto of the conference, "Words bind, and words set free," seems to have been very apt.

E.C.: Yes. In my work with the Poets in the Schools program, I began realizing the importance of providing students with models of poets who had voices sounding like their own—with their various cultural backgrounds being the very guts of their poems, rather than a hindrance to their verbal achievements. I began to see how important it was to provide that sense of multiculturalism so that all writers could feel comfortable in using their most natural voices, instead of trying to conform to some standardized ideal, which changes over time, anyway.

This goes back to the controversy over the use of the "pidgin" vernacular which we broached earlier. John Reinecke, who wrote the first study of pidgin in the 30's was known for his progressive, left-wing politics, but even he believed that pidgin could not be, as he put it, the language of serious literature.

D.L.: Some of the most adamant opponents of pidgin are the most fluent pidgin speakers. If you read the letters to the Editor in the local papers, you'll see all kinds of letters from native speakers who are deadset against pidgin, who then go on to say, But I use it and I am able to use it appropriately in the right situations.

Where is this prejudice coming from?

D.L.: I suppose it is a response to the view of Hawaii as a colonial outpost. According to this view, pidgin, in and of itself, is a symptom of our supposed primitivism. Being able to speak "proper English" is supposed to mean that we have progressed to a more civilized state; that it is a measure of success to be able to speak standard. Opponents of pidgin see it as the primary impediment to the realization of the American Dream; as a handicap to be overcome—

E.C.: Perhaps a lingering effect of the colonial attitude is the continuing criticism of pidgin speakers as inferior people. So-called "legitimate literature," written in standard English, ignored a lot of voices.

D.L.: Many people here say they have to go to the mainland to overcome their linguistic handicap. In an interview with *Ka Leo* [the student newspaper at the University of Hawaii], our present governor, Ben Cayetano, who is a pidgin speaker and whose constituency is composed of native speakers of pidgin, says that when he went to the mainland to college he felt handicapped because of his speech, and to this day he continues to feel this way. He still studies speech improvement tapes. He even claims that pidgin has no place in schools except as a historic artifact and should be studied only as such.

But you both grew up using pidgin as well as standard.

D.L.: My parents didn't approve of pidgin. I've written a little about how my father would always point out whenever there was an "oriental" on t.v. or something, who we should emulate: "Eh, dat kid talk like one *haole.*"

But yeah, we had fluency in both. By fifth grade, we were adept at standard. We had oratory contests in school where you had to give speeches in standard English. Standard was the language of the classroom. Pidgin was for outside of school. I never believed that fulfilling the "American Dream" was necessarily connected to the language you spoke.

The language issue seems very much rooted in the sense of place one finds in both your work, as well as in the work of other writers of Hawaii. Where does this identification with place come from?

D.L.: Partly from an identification with native Hawaiian ways of defining oneself.

E.C.: Many Hawaiian names for places, trees, or fish still are used. Both standard English, as it is used by people here, and pidgin include Hawaiian terms. The Hawaiian language itself is making a comeback. Hawaiian religious blessings are commonly part of ceremonial occasions.

D.L.: I also think the sense of place here goes back to the native Hawaiian ways of locating oneself—the idea, at least according to my understanding of the tradition, that part of one's identity was where one comes from. According to old Hawaiian custom, when you first met someone, you'd say, "I am so and so, my parents are so and so, and my grandparents are so and so, of a specific place in a particular region." You see a form of this tradition being carried on even today when local people get together and one of the first questions they ask each other—if they've never met before—is what school they went to. Everyone understands that what is meant is what *high school*, which places a person in a particular geography. The second question after this is, Do you know my cousin who went to that school when you were there? I think that the connection to the land has been so internalized that it comes through even in this present-day ritual of introduction.

E.C.: Yes, and Hawaiian traditions have been overlaid with American and Asian influences which are part of the fabric of everyday life. The old feeling of being local was strongly rooted in this idea, of being part of a cultural mix. Of contributing to it and sharing in it. Of respecting differences and getting along. Intermarriage is so much more prevalent here than on the mainland. Of course the main sense of ethnic division used to be between locals and *haoles* because of the economic structure of the American system. But that division has become confused, as economic power shifts and the demographics change.

How do you see the relationship between place and ethnicity in Asian American writing from the mainland?

E.C.: I think that mainland Asian Americans find it much more difficult—partly because of sheer population percentages—to feel that their customs are woven into the general fabric of the life around them.

D.L.: Things get filtered differently here. I told you about my mother's mother whose notion of home was *this place*. She spoke Hawaiian pidgin and she already had a pidginized identity. To illustrate: you know, there's a kind of Chinese gelatin, called grass jelly, and there's a way you have of making it out of these long grassy-looking leaves that you can get at the Chinese market. And you eat the gel with a special sort of sugar syrup, which, after a while, everybody here replaced with log cabin syrup. Then the grass jelly started being sold in cans. The ritual of opening the can, taking the gel out, and pouring log cabin syrup on it was taught to me as something Chinese, and the person who taught me this was my mother's mother. I said, "Wait a minute, the only thing Chinese about this is the label on the can!"

Do you think of yourselves as Asian American and/or Chinese American writers?

E.C.: While I was helping to organize the *Talk Story Anthology*, the book that came out of the conference, I met Wing Tek Lum for the first time, over lunch in Chinatown, and he called me a "pake," the local term for Chinese in Hawaii. Being only half Chinese, I think of myself as "local." But when I told him so, he said, "You're a *pake* poet, you wrote 'Manoa Cemetery.'" He saw ethnicity in the voice of the poem, which is about my Chinese grandmother's funeral. It was a way of relating I hadn't considered.

What about you, Darrell?

D.L.: Well yes...I consider myself both an Asian American and a Chinese American writer. But my identity is primarily local. When I do write about things that are more specifically Chinese, I feel a connection to some of the issues that, say, Larry Yep writes about.

Such as—

D.L.: Like when he writes about relationships within the family or certain kinds of scenes, like around the dinner table or cooking. His preoccupation with things having to do with food— the best chicken, the best cabbage—which seems to me more Chinese American, somehow, than it is local. Subjects dealing with relationships outside the family seem more local—say when a kid steps outside his house and gets with his contemporaries. Then that kid seems less concerned with his ethnicity.

E.C.: Perhaps the most obvious significance of the term, "local writer," is that it helps to distinguish ourselves in the same way that other "ethnic American writers" distinguish themselves from the white mainstream.

D.L.: Part of identifying oneself as a local writer is acknowledging a common history shared by many residents of the islands—an immigrant past, a plantation history. One of the stories of Hawaii is a common sort of settler/sojourner story, which shares characteristics with settler/sojourner stories from the mainland, but is also unique to this place. The author who calls herself or himself "local" identifies with this narrative, even though it is not necessarily what he or she writes.

But what about the notion that being bound to a particular locality is a limiting way of identifying oneself? What happens to the notion of the universal order of art?

E.C.: I agree with William Stafford in his piece, "On Being Local," in *The Best of Bamboo Ridge.* He says, everyone is local somewhere. Not that universal themes will not be shared, but that they will be manifested in different forms. The voices will be different, even if they carry the same message. Or the message will be distorted through the prism of culture. But at the same time, I do not think that we should emphasize the differences at the expense of the commonalities—the common human qualities we all share.

From our conversation it seems that you both share a kind of inclusive vision which embraces a diversity of literary voices and styles. You mentioned earlier having known each other for a very long time, but how did you come together to found Bamboo Ridge?

E.C.: Our first real literary project was working on the *Talk Story Anthology* together. Seeing how big the Talk Story Conference was going to be, Darrell hatched the idea of creating a literary review which we would sell subscriptions for at the conference. It was the perfect time to hit our audience. We thought that we would start a regularly published review with a local slant which would provide a showcase for the local talent that usually dried up and died after college writing classes.

We wanted to encourage the development of a local literature.

And you've been pretty successful, to look at the some of the awards garnered over the years by the Press and the writers as-

sociated with it: the GE CCLM Editors Award, Pushcarts, Discovery and Before Columbus Foundation awards, as well as many honors from the Association for Asian American Studies.

D.L.: I feel we've been pretty successful, though in some ways we are battling the same battles. Even now, after almost 20 years, we still have the need to explain ourselves. I think I've learned over the years that it is not a reasonable expectation, as successful as we've been, that we will ever get beyond the need to explain what we do and what local literature is.

Why the name, Bamboo Ridge?

E.C.: One of Darrell's students, Tony Lee, came up with it.

D.L.: Bamboo Ridge is a fishing spot on some rocky cliffs right over the ocean, and a lot of old guys go after *ulua* there. Tony Lee had a friend who liked to hang out with these guys, so Tony met them, and he learned their special fishing technique, called the slide bait method.

Ulua like to go by the rocks where there is a lot of wave action, and they can get up to 80 or 90 pounds. So you need a very long pole—which used to be made from bamboo, but nowadays is made from fiber glass—so you can cast your line way out beyond the rocks. *Ulua's* favorite bait is *tako* [octopus], which they like to eat whole. But if you use a whole *tako*, with that long pole, you could never throw it out very far. So the idea is that you throw out a sinker attached to a barbed hook without any bait and snag it on a rock. Then you get the *tako* and slide it down the line, and you do it in such a manner that when the fish bite, you can unsnag the sinker and bring in the fish. Some of those old guys had never caught a fish for a long time, but they were still out there, doing it. So it seemed right—you know—it seemed like the right name for our magazine.

Lois-Ann Yamanaka

DOMINATE AND RECESSID JEANS

From *Wild Meat and The Bully Burgers*

FOR MONA LEI

THIS IS WHAT I have seen: The smoky sac with a puffy eyed bunny inside plop onto the bed of hair my rabbit, Lani, pulled from her chest. Then Lani eating away the sac so a blunt nosed, no ears, pink and black baby can breathe.

This what I have also seen: Hokulani, Lani's daughter, in her first hutch, bite the sac, but bite the baby too who wiggles wildly, but Hokulani keeps biting anyway, eating the baby who dies covered with fur from her mother's chest.

This is what I have heard: On a night darker than ink. The high shrill cry of the babies, babies being stepped on by their mother on a night too black for even rabbit eyes. And I pull closer to Calhoon who holds her blanket under her chin in deep sleep.

My father gave all of the rabbits to me. For me to feed pellets and water. For me to clean the cages. For me to dry and mulch the rabbit shit for fertilizer. For me to mate and breed, then sell to the pet store or put in the classified ads. For me to make lots of money to buy a bicycle with a white seat full of flowers and a white basket in front with matching plastic flowers. He promised to special order this bike from the Sears catalogue.

And I learned from my father who teaches me everything I know about dominate and recessid jeans. How pea flowers that are red and white make red flowers. Or white flowers. Sometimes pink. I consider this when I breed my Dutch bunnies.

Lani is black and white. Hokulani is brown and white. Clyde is black and white. It's important to make a chart of each mating to see who dominates. My babies are white, black and white, brown and white, buff and white and the best, the best of all, a rare gray and white.

The gray and whites, I don't sell. I give them to only special people who love bunnies as much as I do. One to Uncle Ed's son, Ernest. One to Jerry's cousin Ingrid who trained her gray and white to use the bathroom in kitty litter. And the rest, I'll build cages for to keep and breed.

And I bring them into the house to feed them snacks like lettuce or cucumber peelings, carrot peelings or celery tops. To their mothers, I feed the ti-leaf center shoots or milkweeds, pink thistles, milky sap, and all. But my babies, my beautiful babies, I bring them in the house so they get tame and don't buck or scratch when carried.

Calhoon starts a nervous twitch. She wiggles her nose and lips into a ball and moves it in a circular motion. My mother says stop bringing the bunnies into the house. Calhoon imitates the bunnies, her new twitch, a very bad habit. People will think she's retarded. I tell my mother it's because of some recessid jeans in our family history. On whose side is there a retard? She tells me to shut my stupid mouth.

Now Calhoon and me play with the bunnies on the grassy

hill next to the cages. And when we see 'io circling overhead, we gather up our babies and hide under the lychee tree.

Cal just learned to ride her bike without her training wheels. I see her at the top of the hill and I hold my gray and white close to my face. I see her bolt down the hill. "No. NO! Brake! My rabbit cages!" I see her hit the cage and fly over the totan roofs and rabbit shit sprays out in all directions like a million flies. Calhoon lands on a rabbit shit pile and when she gets up, the round little balls are all flattened.

This is what I hear: It's a Sunday morning. My father feeds my rabbits. "Hello Lani. Hello Hokulani. Hello Clyde." He doesn't know I'm watching and listening. I copy him by talking to the rabbits when I feed them in the same gentle voice.

This is what I have seen: My father puts Clyde into Lani's cage for the breeding. He tells me that Clyde will mate Lani and now I'll have plenty new babies. Maybe a gray and white that I can put in the new cage. "Now go into the house already," he says. I walk around the garage once and go back to the cages. My father pulls the long green hose toward his anthuriums on the other side of the yard.

I see Clyde on Lani's back. Her eyes pull out of her head. His claws dig into her side. Her ears pull back and her head too as Clyde moves up and down. Clyde dominates. Lani recessids. When he's through, Lani runs to the corner of her cage very scared. She breathes hard in and out with flaring nostrils. Clyde sits there and rubs his face with his paws. *Never, never let someone dominate.*

I do not see or hear: wild dogs late that dark night rob into my yard and kill all of my rabbits. In the morning, bodies are splayed all over the yard, stretched out rabbit bodies, broken necks and blood.

Hokulani, her eyelids transluscent blue and thin, over her purple blind looking eyes. Clyde, his mouth open. I *didn't hear them* cry. And babies all over the yard covered with purple fat black flies, the sound of buzzing. Lani, her fur bloodied and wet. The totan roofs are scattered and the wire cages torn open. "Can you imagine," my father says, "dog teeth tore open those wire cages."

No, I cannot imagine it.

My father says not to worry. That he'll buy for me Netherland Dwarfs which are better rabbits than Dutch bunnies. I can start my business over again and make it better. Calhoon says she'll kill those dogs with my father's .22.

My father takes us inside. He says he'll show home movies tonight to make me feel better since I love them so much. And even though the screen he bought from Kino's Second Hand Furniture Store broke, the screen that made us glitter on its diamond sandpaper surface, we can watch on the refrigerator door. He'll even buy us buttered Jiffy Pop for Cal and me to make over the gas stove.

Tonight my father sets up his 8 millimeter camera projector. The little reels scatter on the countertop. They're dated with pieces of masking tape. This is what I see:

Calhoon doing cartwheels on the grassy hill. Her friend Yvette Benevidez doing the splits. Jerry cartwheels to the camera and does a hoing very close to the camera. The shot cuts off. I remember my father chasing Jerry for getting silly and hitting him on the head with the camera.

When the movie continues, I'm standing over Lani's cage. I lift the rusty totan roof. Count four bunnies there. I feed them milkweeds and honohono grass.

Then I hold a gray and white. Calhoon comes running over. I see her saying, "Gimme it, gimme it," reaching her arms up to me. But I don't give it to her. She walks toward the camera, points at me saying, though we can't hear her, *Daddy look at Lovey.*

Look at Lovey.

This is what I hear:

The end of a film. The last shot of me holding the gray and white to my face. The white dots like white bunnies running across me, and the sad, sad sound of celluloid hitting the end reel again and again.

Lisa Asagi writes, "It is impossible to ban the sound of one's memory. The language of childhood and adolescence is uncensored and unaware of its own importance. It records for a later time. It waits for an opportunity to understand the predicament of its existence in order to survive."

Lois-Ann Yamanaka's second book WILD MEAT AND THE BULLY BURGERS, forthcoming from Farrar Straus Giroux, uses the voice of Lovey to tell the story of growing up in Hilo, Hawai'i. Yamanaka grew up on the Big Island of Hawai'i in Waiakea in the Hilo District, Pahala in the Ka'u District and Keauhou in the Kona District. She was born in Ho'olehua, Moloka'i. Yamanaka is the author of SATURDAY NIGHT AT THE PAHALA THEATRE (Bamboo Ridge Press, 1993). She lives in Honolulu with her husband and son.

Keeley Lake

R. Zamora Linmark

OUR LADY OF KALIHI

YOU DON'T HAVE TO BE from Kalihi Valley to know that the Virgin Mary lives at the top of Monte Street right below King Kamehameha School. You can be riding the skyslide in front of Gibson's department store, getting stung by a jellyfish at Bellows, going on a Buddha hunt at Camp Erdman, or climbing the thirteen deadly steps near Morgan's Corner, but the millisecond you turn towards Kalihi Valley or even think it, you see her. A woman walking out of a mountain carrying a baby in her left hand and a crystal ball in the other.

The first thing you notice is that she's not like the other Virgins. She doesn't have a fancy name like Regina Cleri or Medjugorje for she was simply crowned as Our Lady of the Mount. Not Our Lady of the Valley or Queen of Kalihi. But strictly Our Lady of the Mount. She doesn't talk to children like Queen of Fatima had spoken to Francesco, Jacinta, and Lucia because her mouth is veiled with asbestos. She doesn't dance when you blast the car stereo while the headlights are glimmering on her like Mary in Diamond Head Cemetery because her feet are bounded by a fat green snake with a pitch-fork tongue. She doesn't even look Asian like La Naval whose almond-shaped face, high-set cheekbones, slanty-eyes, and flawless gown got her to travel around the world.

And she doesn't heal the sick like Our Lady of Lourdes or perform miraculous feats like Our Lady of Mediatrix of All Grace who showered the earth with roses because Hurricane Iwa stormed into the island and turned it into a trash com-pactor. The buffeted winds jolted everyone and everything, in-cluding Our Lady of the Mount whose tin-foiled tiara and head were flung out into the Pacific Ocean.

For months, Our Lady of the Mount stood headless on the top of the hill until Father Simone collected enough donations and bought a disaster-proof head. It was so expensive it came with a free crown and a fully made-up face: baby-doll eyes, arched brows, protruding cheekbones, ruby-painted lips. But gone were her simple immaculate aura and melancholy eyes, always half-opened, always looking down like sad drapes on a stormy night.

Each time you visit her, you cannot help but wonder if she's still the same mother you saw the first time you grappled with the hike up Monte Street and collapsed in front of her snake-sandaled feet—a bouquet of roses in your hand. You cannot help but stare at her for a long time and search for the face that once spoke to you like a dream after you had woken up from the fainting spell and recited the Angelus. You convince yourself that behind those bright baby-doll eyes lies the gaze that used to make you feel safe and warm all over like a mother's sigh.

And each time you long for her beautiful sad eyes that had shed a sea of tears for your joys and pains, you see nothing but cold stone. You feel nothing but a weight of clouds suddenly pushing you down on your knees—a ritual which, you begin to realize and accept, is no longer out of devotion, but obligation. So you kneel and mutter words, not stopping to savor the last breath of each prayer, not waiting for answers, miracles, or ap-paritions. Or even the simplest: a mother's love.

MAMA'S BOY

YOU KNEW he was staring. You knew what those hypo-thyroid eyes meant. But you twitched your ass and made him feel like he was rainbow. Mr. Potato head with whiteheads the size of Rice Krispies. You twitched your ass once more and got mad because he pretended like it was nothing. Like he was not interested. Like all he cared about was watering his Santa Claus belly with a six-pack of Primo beer or bending over to wax his yellow car or waiting for his mother to call him for supper. You got mad so you started pulling the ends of your shorts high and played Bee Gees in your head. He raised his eyes, took his fat fingers off the rag, and grinned. I told you, *Stop it, Edgar, he's staring and his mother might see you*. But you went on dancing and twirling until you were dizzy in your shorts that looked like a bikini.

Mr. Softee truck turned into our street and drove up the hill, cranking carousel songs from a warped cassette. He flashed you a five-dollar bill and pointed to the toolshed. You told me I could buy anything I wanted if I waited. You told me,

Just watch for the door and his mother. I was scared but you came out after a minute and made like it was nothing. Like you went in to watch cartoons and got bored. I asked you if he hurt you and all you said was, *He didn't do anything, his eyes didn't even fall off.* And you laughed because he told you, *Your friend, call him. That's not funny*, I said, but you said, *He'll give us twenty.*

He came out of the toolshed, stuck his greasy hands in his pocket and drew out an Andrew Jackson. He snapped the bill loud and stared at me, his eyes lit. He stood there victorious like a giant pinball machine that couldn't be tilted. You told me, *Go ahead, he's a mama's boy and mama's boy only wants to touch, hurry, before the ice cream truck leaves.* You made it sound so easy. Like TV dinners ready in ten minutes. You said, *Don't worry, I'll be here. You better.* I said, and ran to the toolshed.

He closed the door, whistling. *Don't be scared*, he said, *you my little birdie, my Filipino birdie.* He rubbed his waxy hands all over me. Like I was his yellow car. He took my hand, spat on my palm, and used it as a wet cloth to wipe off his rash-red face and neck. *Edgar, Edgar*, I yelled. But you didn't answer. *Shhhh*, he whispered, pulling me closer to him. He drew out the money and tucked it in my shorts. *Why don't you dance?* he asked. But I didn't dance. I spun and spun and spun until I got so dizzy I didn't hear the melting tunes of Mr. Softee driving down the hill and out of the valley.

DREAMHOUSE

I SAW STEVE JOHNSON'S house for the first time last week. Florante, Mai-Lan, and Loata were helping me sell Jewel chocolate-covered almonds, the kind that came in a box with a two-dollar coupon from Pizza Hut wrapped around it. I needed to sell sixty boxes so I could go to Camp Erdman and participate in the Junior Police Officer's annual get-together.

After we nearly covered the entire valley and got the same response of sorry-just-bought-one, I told them I'd try once more before calling it quits. I walked to the nearest house and knocked. A fat lady wearing glasses so thick, they made her eyes look twenty-times bigger than the actual size, answered the door. I pulled out a box of Jewel's and was about to ask her if she wanted to buy some when she interrupted, "Too late. Just bought a case the other day. Too late."

We did an about-face and started to head back to my house when Mai-Lan came up with the idea of going to the far end of the valley where people like Steve Johnson live. "I'm sure we can sell everything in less than a minute," she said. "Yeah,"

Florante said, "maybe you might even win an AM-FM headset."

It took us almost an hour's walk to reach the road that became narrower and narrower as the houses got bigger and bigger. The first doors we knocked on were all owned by Filipinos like Nelson Ariola's and Alan Vicente's families. We sold over twenty boxes in less than thirty minutes.

We ran excitedly through the next couple blocks where the houses began to look more like a dream than wooden structures. Like Judy-Ann Kunishige's tea house in the middle of a lighted lily pond. Or Mr. and Mrs. Bernard Chun's indoor swimming pool with a jacuzzi. We sold only ten boxes and it took us more than an hour's wait for them to decide. Only the Chuns didn't hesitate because we are always spending our allowance in their store.

Mai-Lan counted the number of boxes sold. "Fifty-seven," she said. "Three more to go," Florante subtracted. "And one house left," I added. "That's o.k. We still have a chance," Loata said pointing across the field to the biggest house in the valley. It seemed so far from us that it didn't look like a part of the valley. Or the valley didn't belong to it.

With the sweltering heat on our backs, we trudged across the field littered by gravel, broken bottles, and thorny weeds. We stopped in front of the gate and read the wooden sign drilled through the iron bars. Stenciled in fancy letterings were "No Trespassing" next to "Visitors, Please Ring Buzzer."

Loata rang the buzzer and we waited while Mai-Lan and Florante pressed their faces against the bars that barricaded the house. "It's so beautiful and so quiet like a museum," she said. "Miniature rolling hills and Hollywood cars," he said. "A fountain of Cupid in the center of a pool," she said. "A walkway that unfolds like a wedding gown," he said. "It's a dreamhouse," she said. Loata pushed the button once more and did not let go. "Like Iolani Palace with department store windows," he said.

"It looks like Dillingham Prison," Loata blurted, finally releasing his finger off the buzzer. "I don't think anyone's home," I said. "But his parents' cars are there," he argued, "there's gotta be someone home." "Maybe they don't want to buy any chocolate," I said.

I did an about-face and started to walk back home when Florante shouted, "Look, there's Steve and his mom and dad." I turned around and saw the three of them standing behind the giant window. Like breathing mannequins on display. Steve and his mother smiling blankly, and his father blowing out smoke from the cigarette clipped between his fingers. Loata pressed the buzzer and we waited, our faces pushing against the bars.

But not one of them budged. They stood there posing like a Sears family portrait. We continued watching them until Steve's mother walked out of the picture and all we saw were bodies disappearing behind closing drapes. We stood there for I don't know how long, staring at the dreamhouse that was as far away as the hour it took us to get there and see them pretend that we were never there.

"Our Lady of Kalihi," "Dreamhouse," and "Mama's Boy" are taken from my first book Rolling The R's, a collection of short-short stories and poems set in Kalihi, a district in Honolulu predominantly populated by Filipinos—both immigrants and locally-born and raised. It is scheduled for a Spring '95 release by Kaya Productions.

I was born in Manila twenty-six years ago and moved to Hawai'i when disco was the craze and John Travolta was the polyester god of night fevers. I received my B.A. in English at the University of Hawai'i at Manoa, where I am currently completing a Master's Degree in Literature.

I never knew "writing" would end up as something I could be passionately involved with until I enrolled in a Creative Writing class taught by Detroit-poet Faye Kicknosway. From her, I received my very first voice lessons and valuable lessons too long to list down (e.g. When you get stricken by writer's block, hop on a bus, and write about the people).

When I was young, in the Philippines, I was an altar boy (believe it or not), and once had the desire to become a priest (like Father Mendoza), but things change, as passion tends to. I plan to write for as long as I can. And hope this passion will never leave me.

Darrell Lum

GIVING TANKS

THE BROWN AND ORANGE crayons always run out at Tanksgiving time. You gotta use um up for color da turkeys and da Indian feathers la dat. Yellow run out fast too. My teacher, Mrs. Perry, used to tell us dat we supposed to use dose colors cause ass da autumn colors. Supposed to be when all the leaves on da trees turn color, like da orange and brown crayons or da funny kine brown one in da big crayon box: burnt someting. I couldn't see how if da leaves turn color was pretty. For us, dat jes means dat da tree going die, or maybe stay dead awready. Or maybe like our lychee tree in da back yard, when da leaves turn color, they fall off and Daddy tell me I gotta go rake before I can go play.

Tanksgiving was when you gotta learn about da Pilgrims and all dat. Ass when da Indians and da Pilgrims went get together, eat turkey or someting. Kinda hard to believe though, yeah. Me, I like da Indians mo bettah den da Pilgrims. Da Indians had da kine leather pants wit da fringes and da small kine beads and dey fight wit bow and arrow la dat. Da Pilgrims had to wear da black suits, even da small kids, and da funny kine hat. Dey even had funny kine gun dat was fat at da end. My brother told me dat was one blundahbuss, dat da olden days guys wanted da bullets to spread all over so da gun was funny kine. He said da gun couldn't shoot straight though. Ass why da Indians mo bettah, I betchu arrows could shoot mo straight den dat.

Da teacha told me I had to do one report on da Pilgrims and draw one cornucopia. I nevah know what dat was. Even aftah I saw da picture I still couldn't figure out what dat was.

"Ass one horn of plenty," Louise went tell me. She smart, so she oughta know. "Stay like one basket fo put fruits inside, fo show you rich, dat you get food."

"Well how come always stay falling down and all da fruits spilling out?" I went ask her. "Funny kine basket, eh?" I not so dumb. So when I went home, I went try draw one horn of plenty but I couldn't figure out what was fo. Look more like my brother's trombone den one basket. And you no can play music wit one horn of plenty. Ho, sometimes da teacher make us do crazy stuffs.

In school we always do the same old ting. You know, make one turkey out of one paper plate: da plate is the body and you paste on the head and the tail and the legs. Sometimes we make one napkin holder turkey: you staple half a paper plate to your turkey so get one place fo put da napkins. Den you paste da neck and da head and da feet like you stay looking at um from da front. And you gotta color dat too . . . brown and orange and yellow. Den you fold up da paper napkins and put um inside da plate and if you use color koa napkins, look like da turkey tail. Mama really went like that one. She went hang um up on da wall and fill um up with napkins and put away da regular napkin holder until came all had-it and da head went fall off.

Everybody like go to Auntie Jennie's and Uncle Jim's house fo Tanksgiving dinner cause Mama said Auntie's turkey always come out moist. Me, I only like eat skin and gravy . . . Auntie Jennie make good gravy. And I like the cranberry sauce da best. I no like da stuffing cause I think they hide all da ugly stuff from inside da turkey in dere.

Auntie Jennie's house was nice. Her kitchen table had real cloth kine tablecloth not da plastic kine on top and she no put sheets on top her couch and had anykine knitted stuff, like those hat things that cover the extra toilet paper on top the toilet tank. And get anykine neat stuff all around her house . . . anykine souvenirs from all over da world, da places they went go visit. J'like everyplace they went, she went buy one salt and pepper shaker. Fo collect. Some look like animals and look like one house or one car or one famous building. Some you couldn't even figure out where da salt or da pepper come out!

Uncle Jim had this teeny tiny collection of knives. Wasn't real, was imitation; each one was about one inch long or maybe two inches long. Was anykine knives, like bolo knife and swords from all over the world and put on one piece of wood, j'like one shield. Maybe he went collect knives from everyplace he went.

Uncle Jim was da fire chief so always had firemen at his house. And he park his car right in front his house, one big red station wagon. Da license plate says "HFD 1," Honolulu Fire Department One. Dat means he da chief. Uncle Jim was tall and skinny and bolohead. Errybody call him "chief" and I know he da *fire* chief but he remind me of one Indian chief, tall and old and plenny wrinkles on his face. I betchu he get one Indian knife someplace, wit one leather holder.

My grandma, Ah Po Lee, was always dere too, sitting down on the couch in her plain stay-at-home clothes talking Chinese to my Auntie. I think she get nice clothes, one time I seen one silk *cheong sam* hanging up on her door with the plastic from the dry clean man but I nevah seen her wear um. And she wear one wide cloth headband dat make her look like one old Indian lady: all small and bent ovah, plain blue khaki jacket and black Chinese pants and fancy cloth slippahs wit small beads making one dragon and anykine wrinkles and spots on her face. Look j'like warpaint.

So ass what we did Tanksgiving time. Go Auntie Jennie's house and eat turkey and make paper turkeys and try fo figgah out what one cornucopia was. And in school, I kept tinking when we going learn about one Indian holiday. Would be neat if could, yeah? We could dance around . . . whoa, whoa, whoa, whoa! Anyways, all dat was jes one fairy tale. Like wrestling at da Civic Auditorium, fake. Same like da uddah tings in da books and da National School Broadcast, all fairy tales. Ah Po told me one time dat real Tanksgiving stay everyday. Ass why everyday she pray fo my grandfahdah. No miss. She burn incense and pour tea and whiskey fo him outside on da porch where get da bowl wit sand fo stick da red candles and da skinny kine incense. Sometimes I watch da ashes curl up, hanging on, hanging on. Da ting can go long time before it fall off.

I no can remembah my Ah Goong, my grandfahdah, except fo da big picture on da wall in da living room. But even my bruddah Russo said dat he nevah look like dat. He said he look mo old. Da picture stay one young guy. I guess ass one fairy tale too. Ah Goong was old, Russo said. Tall and skinny and old. So Ah Po burn candles and incense and pour whiskey and tea fo dis tall, skinny, old guy and I watch da ashes curling up and da smoke going up like smoke signals. Once, I went ask Ah Po how come she pray so much and she tell me she pray dat Ah Goong stay okay, she pray dat us guys, Russo and me be good boys, she pray "tank you" she get rice to eat. She tell me she get lots to pray about.

Everytime get sale, she go buy one bag rice. Could tell she felt rich when she had one bag rice extra in the closet. And toilet paper. Lots of toilet paper. And Spam and vienna sausages and Campbell's soup and can corned beef. Nevah mind she kept fixing and fixing her stay-home dress ovah and ovah, cause was stay-home anyways. Nevah mind dat she had one old washing machine you had to crank da clothes through da roller stuffs. Nevah mind sometimes she went eat *hahm gnee*, salt fish, and rice fo dinner fo three days when me and Russo went sleep her house and we wanted to eat plain meat and not all mixed up wit vegetables kine.

And I seen her finish eating da little bit meat off da bone from my piece of meat and how hardly had any slop for da slop man and how she went look in her button bottle for two quarters fo wrap up in red paper fo give us *lee-see* fo buy ice cream from da ice cream man. Ass how I knew dat my cornucopia wasn't one basket wit fruits and vegetables spilling out. Wasn't Indians and Pilgrims sitting down fo eat turkey. Was Russo and me sitting down at da table while Ah Po put her oily black frying pan on da stove and turned da fire up high until da oil smoke and she put noodles and carrots and a little bit oyster sauce and three, maybe four pieces of green onion cut big, so that we could see um and pick um out of our plates. She nevah used to have one big fat turkey fo Tanksgiving.

"Lucky," she used to say anyways. "Lucky da ice cream man come," even though he always pass by about three-thirty every Thursday. "Lucky you get *lee-see* to spend. Lucky. Lucky you come visit Ah Po," she would say and we would tink about what if we nevah come and miss out on noodles and quarters and ice cream.

I guess we was lucky, yeah?

Darrell Lum was born and raised in the Alewa Heights area of Honolulu and attended Maemae Elementary, Kawananakoa Intermediate, and McKinley High School. His father's father was a Chinese schoolteacher and a butcher and wrote poetry. His father sold appliances, wore bowties and had an elegant, flowing signature.

His mother's mother raised seven children by herself after her husband, a rice mill manager, died. She saved waxed paper bread wrappers, string, and foil; eggshells to dig into the soil of her garden and water saved from rinsing the rice. She spoke Chinese, a little Hawaiian, and pidgin. Lum's mother was the youngest of the seven and according to her older brother they were so poor she was nearly given up for adoption. Others deny this story.

Lum is grateful to his family, his wife, Mae, and his children, Lisa and Daniel for their stories.

Marie Hara

YOU IN THERE

YOU LIE THERE as if you were already dead. Your eyes don't focus on mine. They don't open up big to let the irises take in my image. So far today the only sign you give that you recognize my presence comes just briefly with the slight pressure of your grip in mine. But the rest of you works along with the respirator, which is breathing for you, because you can't.

They did a tracheotomy to help you breathe. The emphysema is fairly widespread, the doctor said. He compared your trying to breathe to a person drowning, because the lungs no longer process the air.

You have no voice. The deep resonance of your talking is in my imagination now, but I hear it as what I think you are thinking. You have shriveled. Always the biggest person in any room, the one who generated all the energy and noise and laughter in a given space, you suck on the air you take in and diminish in size by the hour.

The spooky feeling we used to laugh about when we visited

this hospital remains in this place. Fears circle me. This is going to be your last room if you don't hurry to protest the way this feels. It's not like you to keep so still. You need me to bolster you, to talk you up and out of here. You need to connect to my energy. But first you must come back from wherever you are floating.

The soap opera on the overhead television screen is the last one that will play during your lunch, but you don't care to follow the plot that you have talked about for years. You don't watch or listen. You don't care what's on or who's in here with you.

Something about you now is out of focus. You look fuzzy at your edges. I hang on to your fingers, stroking the smooth hand, shaping the oval fingernails, hoping for some kind of response to my being here. I no longer notice the difference in the color of our hands side by side; what I care about is that you are not there in feeling, that the balance between our natures, your being so heavy and my being so light, is not reflected right in this place we occupy now.

The room where you are is pastel green mostly, with yellow and orange flowered vinyl wallpaper on only one wall, the one behind your head. Looks like they tried to erase the institutional look with that one bright touch. It's the kind of hospital room that you worked in for years, and the ward outside is warm and busy with soft-spoken nurses bustling around. If you would pay attention, you would enjoy talking with them the way you always question people about their work. The techniques are different, and they're using new, time-saving machines as they go around from patient to patient.

You don't care about the computerized thermometer the nurse tries to tell you she's going to put into your mouth. You don't say "Ahh . . ." or make any face at all. Your being passive is so unlike you that I look at you again.

But later when you seem to be more awake, you are nervous. You avoid looking at the doctor, the occasional nurses, the visitors who deposit flower arrangements, get well money, a *bento* plate on the bedside table. Your eyes don't stay on anything very long. You don't want to look at me.

Everyone who enters the room is prepared to do something for you. Everyone wants a response or some kind of sign from you. Some try to say upbeat, encouraging things to you. One old lady says, too loudly, "Bumbye come betta, *ki-yo tsukete!*" You would have said that heartily to any one of your friends before. You make no sign of hearing. The people who come in here go out carefully.

Your oldest living sister arrives before anyone else in the family. The nurses laugh about her later. "You rememba da one yesterday? She wen' ask at the section desk for Mrs. Duffland," they report to me confidentially.

"When she came inside hea, she look and look at yo' mother. She call her name, 'Kikuko! Katie!', and then run outside, back to the duty nurses. She says, 'It's not my sister!' J'like dat. Screaming at us. We had to go check the patient i.d. number, l'dat. She cannot believe her own eyes, and she's scolding us j'-like we did something to yo' mother. Maybe we hiding her. Something else, yeah?"

Auntie Ritsi would be able to find something wrong with the hospital staff, that's her way. She's the one who always takes care of herself and keeps up with all the latest diets and health trends. She rarely goes out of her way to see you and always corrects your English. She speaks only standard English herself. It must have scared "the pee out of her"—your words—to see you so sick. Everybody calls Ritsi Minami the extra tight one. You used to call her Mrs. *Mina-Mina*, remember? Since a gift was placed on the counter by your glasses, a pair of fuzzy lavender stretch booties, she must have believed finally that it was her sister in there.

Lono and Ellen come in to see you and talk in whispers. Ellen places your crystal bead rosary in your hand and says she'll call the temple priest to pray for you. Lono strokes your forehead and says, "Auntie? Auntie, come home, okay? I like you get well and cook for me, alright?"

The other family members telephone each other, but it's the neighborhood who comes to see you. They bring kids. One ties a red heart balloon to the foot of your electronic bed.

Betty brings you an orchid plant. "Too bad she cannot see good, yeah? Wait until she's better. *Kawi-sona.*" Betty blows her nose. Your eyes are open but not in focus.

The owner of the Arirang Bar hands me a bottle of home-made *kim ch'i* for when you get better.

They ask me who found you after your collapse.

One lady keeps asking, "Is that so? Really?"

Her husband says "Yeah?" to everything.

They are curious about details. They keep looking shocked.

They listen patiently to the story of how many times you had tried to quit smoking before they told you it was emphysema. I explain again how luckily Betty came over extra early with the morning newspaper and found you slumped over the kitchen table, how the ambulance took so long but was packed with all the equipment you needed to keep breathing once they got you onto the stretcher, how we were so relieved that you're okay even though you're not yourself yet. You look peaceful while we stare at your face and continue to talk about you softly.

The early evening is the best time for them to visit. The hospital corridors are filled and noisy with people who look for their patient's room. Except for family, nobody stays very long, though. Maybe it's the way the rooms are like dark cocoons with only a flicker of ongoing TV light, a slow motion aquarium illumination, and the flooring tile everywhere holding on to an undefinable, persistent smell. Or how bursts of sound from people talking seem to get very loud and animated then fade in quick spurts into all the other regular noises which flow on when the talkers decide to quiet themselves and whisper again.

Nobody minds when you don't recognize them. They greet each other, as if that were all they needed to maintain a pleasant, working face. The landlord of the next-door apartment building is surprised when you decide to smile at him. I am, too. We both try to talk with you, but you aren't really interested.

I talk about medication and therapy with your doctors. You would be very interested in what they say. They will get a psychiatrist to you, they promise, to encourage your will to fight. They warn me not to have false expectations as they talk above your blanketed form. Not even when Dr. Kaneshiro's takes your pulse—you always judged doctors by how they did it—do you pay attention.

You don't care at all about anything like that. When we are alone, I talk and talk to you. You show no sign of hearing. You groan and make small ah ah sounds that frighten me, and then you subside into breathing.

You jerk suddenly as if in an animated dream, and the rosary falls to the floor breaking the string and scattering the shiny beads. Groping on my hands and knees, I search all over the floor and under the bed to find each one in order to string them up later. I pray for you with each bead I find. "Let her live. Let her live." I alternate it, out of breath but hopeful, with "Namandabutsu-Namandabutsu-Namandabutsu." I am too superstitious. It's not really an omen, I say to myself.

You stir and act alert, as if you are yourself again after an afternoon nap. I quickly take the opportunity. Because your eyes are yours again, I can talk to you.

"You can't just give up now, because only you remember O-Baban so well—maybe five or six people now living knew her at all—but no one as close as you, Mama, and if you go, all the true memories will go with you. All the important things about what she did and how she was will fade away from all of us." I add firmly, "You're not ready to join her yet," in answer to the thought I know you have just had when I mentioned your mother.

"And anyway, how do you know if there really is any life afterwards?" I go on, knowing I have you thinking.

Then you give me the sullen, mean-eye look. It's how you answer my comment. In that way you remind me that you will have me remember you do believe that dead people can communicate from that time after they pass on. I don't argue. I am so happy that you are yourself again.

I try for another run. What do I have to lose?

"O-Baban lived to 95. You are so young yet." You close your eyes.

I stand by the window and look down at the back of the hospital where an old wooden building is all that's left of the former hospital plant. I remember to remind you how long ago we once took O-Baban there to visit an old man who was dying in the care-home wing.

"Funny, yeah, how when we got to him, he said he knew that we would be there before he died?" That story doesn't register for you. But it's the kind of story you loved to tell.

Outside, down there, the sunlight is intense and very different from the fluorescent light in the room. I tell you about how Baban liked to peer out of the windows of the old Kohala house to look at the garden. You nod. Or is it an uncontrolled quiver. No matter, I am so happy I am tempted to open the glass door to the small *lanai* outside to let in some real air.

But I should stick close to your bedside and hold your hand or wait for some word that you might want to write on the pad of paper waiting on the swivel table top. I am afraid you will write D-I-E again like the first time we tried to get you to communicate when they moved you in here.

I yelled, "No, no, no," to you, but you pretended not to hear me. You were sly in your denial. I took the pencil and put it away.

You are much better now, I tell you again. I should brush the false teeth in the plastic container marked with your name so that they will be ready to wear when you feel up to it. I should tell you encouraging things about how you will get better and be able to sit out on the little concrete *lanai* in the sunshine, just like being on the porch at home.

You don't talk with your body or your eyes. I don't talk. Like you, I make no sign when nurses come in and out to do things and make cheerful comments.

Your face has no expression no matter what is said, whoever says it. You take in liquids and food and medicine by gurgling tubes. The places on your arms and neck and side where tubes are inserted look like reddened, irritating entrances into your pain. The white-wrapped cut in the center of your neck is mysterious in the way its tube dangles, inactive.

I get afraid and squeeze your hand, hoping to find the safety of your telling me what you want me to do. And harder. I try to fix your attention on me, the most comfortable way to be with you. But you can't respond from where you are. Your hand wants only to pull away from any more pain, that's all. You drift in and out of sleep.

On the third day, you are up very early like a regular day. You look ready. You search my face, and I know what you are thinking.

"Now why is she here?"

I don't know why either.

When you die, you seem very relaxed at first. You have let

me know with a hand squeeze that you understand me as I tell you that I love you so, and I want you to live. You tell me a clear *No* with your half-closed eyes and your shaking head. You ignore my anger. You sleep a while. Then you do open your eyes and slowly take me all in, and that does make me happy. But you crumple back inward by degrees, and I want you to rest. Your breathing sounds good.

An hour later I sit in your tiny bathroom preparing lots more of the Yes reasons. I practice how to say them:

You have to go on a "once in a lifetime trip"—your words—with me to Las Vegas and San Francisco and Tokyo, and you have to wear a big white orchid to my wedding, which will be someday very soon, and you have to stay alive to see your future grandchildren and you have to come home and sit on the porch and tell everybody what happened in the hospital . . . and you just have to. Because. That's the only way it can be.

When I go back to hold your hand, you are gone.

Born during World War II in a territory of the United States, Marie Hara has witnessed Hawai'i welcome statehood and anticipate sovereignty. A writer, editor and teacher, Marie Hara lives with her husband and two children in Honolulu. She also teaches handicapped students as a substitute teacher at Pohukaina School. With Nora Okja Cobb-Keller, she is at work on an anthology of prose and poetry by mixed race women writers titled *Intersecting Circles*.

Mayumi C. Hara

Cedric Yamanaka

THE LEMON TREE BILLIARDS HOUSE

THE LEMON TREE Billiards House is on the first floor of an old
concrete building on King Street, between Aloha Electronics
and Uncle Phil's Flowers. The building is old and the pool hall
isn't very large—just nine tables, a ceiling fan and a soda machine. No one seems to know how the place got its name. Some
say it used to be a Korean Bar. Others say it was a funeral
home. But all seem to agree that it has a lousy name for a pool
hall. At one point, someone circulated a petition requesting the
name be changed. But Mr. Kong, the proud owner, wouldn't
budge. He said his pool hall would always be called the Lemon
Tree Billiards House.

Mr. Kong keeps his rates very reasonable. For two dollars
an hour, you can hit all of the balls you want. One day, I was in
there playing eight ball with a 68-year-old parking attendant.
The guy played pretty well—I was squeezing for a while—but
he missed a tough slice and left me enough openings to clear
the table and sink the eight ball. I won twenty bucks.

Another guy walked up to me. He had a moustache, base-ball cap and a flannel shirt.

"My name Hamilton," he said. "I ain't too good—but what—you like play?"

I ain't too good. *Sure.*

"My name's Mitch," I said. "Let's play."

We agreed on fifty bucks. Hamilton racked the balls. I broke. It was a good one. The sound of the balls cracking against each other was like a hundred glass jars exploding.

As three striped balls—the nine, twelve, and fifteen—shot into three different pockets, I noticed a goodlooking girl in a black dress sitting on a stool in the corner. I don't know if I was imagining it or not but I thought I caught her looking my way. I missed an easy shot on the side pocket. I'd burned my finger cooking *saimin* and couldn't get a good grip on the cue stick.

"Oh, too bad," said Hamilton. "Hard luck! I tot you had me deah . . " He was what I call 'a talker.' The kind of guy who can't keep his mouth shut. The kind of guy who treats a game of pool like a radio call in show.

Anyway, Hamilton hit four balls in but stalled on the fifth. I eventually won the game.

Afterwards, the girl in the black dress walked up to me.

"Hi," she said, smiling.

"Hello," I said.

"You're pretty good," she said.

"Thanks."

"You wanna play my dad?"

"Who's your dad?"

"You wanna play or not?"

"Who is he?"

"He'll give you five hundred bucks if you beat him . . ."

"Let's go."

I'm a pool hustler and the Lemon Tree Billiards House is my turf. You see, I've been playing pool all my life. It's the only thing I know how to do. My dad taught me the game before they threw him in jail. I dropped out of school, left home, and travelled around the country challenging other pool players. I've played the best. Now I'm home.

All right, all right. I'm not a pool hustler. I'm a freshman at the University of Hawaii. And my dad's not in jail. He's an accountant. And I never challenged players around the country. I did play a game in Waipahu once.

I have been playing pool for awhile, though. Sometimes I do real well. Sometimes, I don't. That's how the game is for me. Four things can happen when I pick up a cue stick. One, sometimes I feel like I'll win and I win. Two, sometimes I feel like I'll win and I lose. Three, sometimes, I feel like I'll lose and I'll lose. Four sometimes I feel like I'll lose and I win.

I'll tell you one thing, though. I could've been a better pool player if I hadn't been cursed. Yes, cursed.

It all happened back when I was seven years old. My dad had taken me to a beach house. I'm not sure where it was. Somewhere near Malaekahana, maybe. I remember walking along the beach and seeing some large boulders. I began climbing on the rocks, trying to get a good look at the ocean and the crashing waves. The view was stunning. The water was so blue. And off shore, I thought I spotted some whales playing in the surf.

All of a sudden, my father came running down the beach. "Mitch!" he said. "Get off da rocks! Da rocks sacred! No climb up deah! No good!"

Ever since that day, I've lived with a curse. One day in the eighth grade, I dropped a touchdown pass and we lost a big intramural football game. I smashed my first car three minutes after I drove it off the lot. My first girlfriend left me for a guy in prison she read about in the papers. I'm the kind of guy who will throw down four queens in a poker game, only to watch helplessly as some clown tosses down four kings. If I buy something at the market, it'll go on sale the next day.

It hasn't been easy. The only thing I do okay is play eight ball. But I could've been better. If it just weren't for this curse.

I don't know why I agreed to play pool with this strange girl's father. Maybe it was because she was so beautiful. The best looking woman I've ever seen. Six feet, two hundred pounds, hairy legs, moustache. Okay. Okay. So she wasn't *that* beautiful. Let's just say she was kind of average.

Anyway, we got into her car and she drove towards the Wa-ianae coast. She had one of those big, black Cadillacs you saw in the seventies. The kind Jack Lord used to drive to Iolani Palace. In about a half hour or so, we wound up at a large beach house with watermills and bronze buddhas in the yard. Everywhere you looked, you saw trees. Mango, avocado, papaya, banana.

"My dad likes to plant things," the girl explained.

We walked past a rock garden and a *koi* pond and she led me into a room with a pool table. There were dozens of cues lined up neatly on the wall, just like at the Lemon Tree Billiards House.

"You can grab a stick," the girl said. "I'll go get my dad."

In a few minutes, I realized why she didn't want to tell me who her father was. I was standing face to face with Locust Cordero. *The* Locust Cordero. All 6–5, 265 pounds of him. Wearing of all things, a purple tuxedo and a red carnation in his lapel. Locust Cordero, who stood trial for the murder-for-hire deaths of three Salt Lake gamblers several years back. I was about to play eight-ball with a hitman.

"Howzit," he said. "Mahalos fo coming. My name Locust."

What should I say? I know who you are? I've heard of you? I've seen your mug shots on T.V.? Congratulations on your recent acquittal? Nice tuxedo?

"Nice to meet you, sir," I said, settling on the conservative. "I'm Mitch."

We shook hands. He wore a huge jade ring on his finger.

"My daughter says you pretty good . . ."

"I try, sir."

"How you like my tuxedo?" he said.

"Nice," I said.

"Shaka, ah?" he said, running his hands over the material. "Silk, brah. Jus bought 'em. What size you?"

"What?"

"What size you?" he repeated, opening up a closet. I was stunned. There must have been two dozen tuxedos in there. All sizes. All colors. Black, white, maroon, blue, red, pink. "Heah," said Locust, handing me a gold one. "Try put dis beauty on . . ."

"Uh," I said. "How about the black one?"

Again, I was leaning towards the conservative.

"Whatevahs," said Locust, shrugging.

I changed in the bathroom. It took me a while because I'd never worn a tuxedo before. When I walked out, Locust smiled.

"Sharp," he said. "Look at us. Now we really look like pool players . . ."

Locust chalked his cue stick. He was so big, the stick looked like a tooth pick in his hands.

"Break 'em, Mitch."

"Yes, sir."

I walked to the table and broke. I did it real fast. I don't like to think about my shots too long. That always messes me up. *Crack!* Not bad. Two solid balls shot into the right corner pocket.

"Das too bad," said Locust, shaking his head.

"Why's that, sir?" I asked.

"Cause," said Locust. "I hate to lose."

One day, not too long before, I'd visited an exorcist. To get rid of my curse. He was an old Hawaiian man in his late forties or early fifties, recommended to me by a friend. When I called for an appointment, he said he couldn't fit me in. There were a lot of folks out there with problems, I guessed. I told him it was an emergency.

"Okay, come ovah," he said. "But hurry up."

I drove to his house. He lived in Palolo Valley. I was very scared. What would happen? I could see it now. As soon as I walked into the room, the man would scream and run away from me. He'd tell me he saw death and destruction written all over my face. The wind would blow papers all over his room and I'd be speaking weird languages I had never heard before and blood and mucous would pour out my mouth.

But nothing like that happened. I walked into his house, expecting to see him chanting or praying. Instead, he was sitting behind a *koa* desk in a Munsingwear shirt and green polyester pants.

"Dis bettah be good," he said. "I went cancel my tee time at da Ala Wai fo you . . ."

I smiled. I told him my plight. I started from the beginning—telling him about the day I climbed on the rocks and the bad luck I've had ever since.

"You ain't cursed," the man said. He bent down to pick something up from the floor. What was it? An ancient amulet? A charm? None of the above. It was a golf club. An eight iron. "Da mind is one very powerful ting," he said, waving the right iron around like a magician waving a wand. "It can make simple tings difficult and difficult tings simple."

"What about the rocks?" I said.

"Tink positive," the man said. "You one negative buggah. Da only curse is in yo mind."

That's it? No reading scripture. No chanting?

"I tell you one ting, brah," the Hawaiian man said. "One day, you going encountah one challenge. If you beat em, da curse going to *pau*. But, if you lose, da rest of yo life going shrivel up like one slug aftah you pour salt on top . . ."

"Anything else?" I said.

"Yeah," said the Hawaiian man. "You owe me twenty bucks."

Locust and I had played ten games. We'd agreed on eleven. I'd won five, he'd won five. In between, his daughter brought us fruit punch and smoked marlin. It was already dark. I had an Oceanography test the next day.

On the final game, I hit an incredible shot—the cue ball jumping over Locust's ball like a fullback leaping over a tackler and hitting the seven into the side pocket. This seemed to piss Locust off. He came right back with a beauty of his own—a masse I couldn't believe. In a masse, the cue ball does bizarre things on the table after being hit—like weaving between balls as if it has a mind of its own. Those are the trick shots you see on T.V. Anyway, Locust hit a masse, where the cue ball hit not one, not two, not three, but four of his balls into four different holes. *Come on!* I was convinced Locust could make the cue ball spell his name across the green velvet sky of the pool table.

Pretty soon, it was just me, Locust and the eight ball. I looked at Locust, real fast, and he stared at me like a starving man sizing up a Diner's chicken *katsu* plate lunch. I took a shot but my arm felt like a lead pipe and I missed everything. Locust took a deep breath, blew his shot, and swore in three different languages. It was my turn.

And then I realized it. This was the moment that would make or break me. The challenge the exorcist guy was talking about. I had to win.

I measured the table, paused, and said the words that would change my life and save me from shrivelling up like a slug with salt poured on it.

"Eight ball. Corner pocket."

I would have to be careful. Gentle. It was a tough slice to the right corner pocket. If I hit the cue ball too hard, it could fall into the wrong pocket. That would be a scratch. I would lose.

I took a deep breath, cocked my stick, and aimed. I hit the cue ball softly. From here, everything seemd to move in slow motion. The cue ball tapped the eight ball and the eight ball seemed to take hours to roll towards the hole. Out of the corner of my eye, I saw Locust's daughter standing up from her seat, her hands covering her mouth.

Clack. *Plop.*

The ball fell into the hole. The curse was lifted. I had won. I would have been a happy man if I hadn't been so damned scared.

Locust walked up to me, shaking his head. He reached into his pocket. Oh, no. Here it comes. He was gonna take out his gun, shoot me, and bury my body at some deserted beach. Goodbye, cruel world. Thanks for the memories . . .

"I no can remembah da last time I wen lose," he said, pulling out his wallet and handing me five crispy one hundred dollar bills. "Mahalos fo da game."

Locust asked me to stay and talk for awhile. We sat on straw chairs next to the pool table. The place was dark except for several gas-lit torches, hissing like leaky tires. Hanging on the walls were fishing nets and dried, preserved fish, lobsters, and turtles.

"You must be wond'ring why we wearing dese tuxedos," said Locust.

"Yeah," I said.

"Well, dis whole night, it's kinda one big deal fo me." Locust leaned towards me. "You see, brah, I nevah leave my house in five years . . ."

"Why?" I said. I couldn't believe it.

"All my life, evry'body been scared of me," said Locust, sighing. "Ev'rywheah I go, people look at me funny. Dey whispah behind my back . . ."

"But . . ."

"Lemme tell you someting," he continued. "Dey went try me fo murder coupla times. Both times, da jury said I was innocent. Still, people no like Locust around. Dey no like see me. And das why, I never step foot outta dis place."

"Forgive me for saying so, sir," I said. "But that's kinda sad. That's no way to live . . ."

"Oh, it ain't dat bad," said Locust. "I play pool. I go in da ocean, spear *uhu*. I trow net fo mullet. Once in a while, I go in da mountains behind da house and shoot one pig . . ."

"But don't you ever miss getting out and walking around the city. Experiencing life?"

I was getting nervous again. I mean, here I was, giving advice on how to live to Locust Cordero. After I had just beaten the guy at eight ball.

"Whasso great about walking around da streets of da city?" said Locust, after awhile. "People shooting and stabbing each othah. Talking stink about each othah. Stealing each othah's husbands and wives. Breaking each othah's hearts . . ."

"You scared?" I said, pressing my luck.

"Yeah," said Locust, looking me straight in the eye. "I guess I am."

We didn't say anything for awhile. I could hear the waves of the ocean breaking on the beach.

"So," said Locust, shifting in his seat. "Where you went learn fo shoot pool?"

"The Lemon Tree Billiards House," I said.

"Da Lemon Tree Billards House?" Locust said, shaking his head. "What kine name dat? Sound like one funeral home . . ."

"Sir," I said. "I'm sorry. Can I say something?"

"Sure."

"You're living your life like a prisoner. You might as well have been convicted of murder and locked in jail."

Yeah, sometimes it seems I just don't know when to shut up.

"Evah since I was one kid, I had hard luck," said Locust, moving closer to me and whispering. "You see, I'm cursed . . ."

"You're what?" I said, surprised.

"I'm cursed," Locust repeated, raising his voice. "Jeez, fo one young kid, you get lousy nearing, ah? Must be all dat loud music you buggahs listen to nowadays."

"How'd you get cursed?" I said.

"One day, when I was one kid, I was climbing some rocks looking out at da ocean. Down Malaekahana side. All of a sudden, my bruddah start screaming, 'Get down from deah. No good. Da rocks sacred.'"

I couldn't believe it. Locust and I were cursed by the same rocks. We were curse brothers.

"Da ting's beat me," said Locust, shaking his head.

"You're talking like a loser."

"A what?" said Locust, getting out of his chair.

"Locust," I said, my voice cracking. "I lived with the same curse and I beat it . . ."

"How?" said Locust, sitting back down. "I tried everything. Hawaiian salt. *Tī* leaves. Da works . . ."

"You gotta believe in yourself."

"How you do dat?"

"With your mind," I said. "See, the first thing you gotta do is meet a challenge and beat it," I said. "Go outside. Walk the streets. Meet people . . ."

"You evah stop fo tink how dangerous da world is?" said Locust. "Tink about it. How many things out deah are ready, waiting, fo screw you up. Death, sickness, corruption, greed, old age . . ."

It was scary. Locust was starting to make sense.

"I don't know," I finally said.

"Tink about it," said Locust. "Tink about it."

One day, several weeks later, I was playing eight ball at the Lemon Tree Billiards House. Several people were arguing about the source of an unusual smell. Some said it came from a cardboard box filled with rotten *choy sum* outside on the sidewalk in front of the pool hall. Others said it was Kona winds blowing in the pungent smell of *taegu* from Yuni's Bar B-Q. Still others said the peculiar smell came from Old Man Rivera, who sat in a corner eating a lunch he had made at home. Too much *patis*—fish sauce—in his *sari sari*.

"If you like good smell," said Mr. Kong, the owner of the Lemon Tree Billiards House. "Go orchid farm. If you like play pool, come da Lemon Tree Billiards House."

I was on table number three with a young Japanese guy with short hair. He had dark glasses and wore a black suit. He looked like he was in the *yakuza*.

I had already beaten three guys. I was on a roll. It gets like that every now and then. When you know you can't miss.

The Yakuza guy never smiled. And everytime he missed a shot, he swore at himself. Pretty soon, he started to hit the balls very hard—thrusting his cue stick like a samurai spearing an opponent. He was off, though, and I eventually won the game.

"You saw how I beat the *Yakuza* guy?" I said to Mr. Kong, who was now on a stepladder unscrewing a burned out lightbulb.

"*Yakuza* guy?" said Mr. Kong. "What *yakuza* guy?"

"The Japanese guy in the suit . . ." I said.

"Oh," said Mr. Kong, laughing like crazy. "You talking about Yatsu! Das my neighbor. He ain't no *yakuza*. He one pre-school teachah . . ."

Just then, Locust Cordero walked into the Lemon Tree Billiards House. Mr. Kong stopped laughing. Everyone stopped their games. No one said a word. The only sound you heard was the ticking of a clock on the wall.

"Mitch," said Locust. "I went take yo advice. I no like live like one prisonah no moah . . ."

I was speechless.

"You know what dey say," said Locust. "Feel like one five hundred pound bait lifted from my shoulders . . ."

"Weight," I said.

"Fo what?" said Locust, obviously confused.

"No, no," I said. "Five hundred pound *weight*. Not bait . . ."

"Whatevahs," said Locust. "Da curse is gone . . ."

He walked over to one of Mr. Kong's finest tables, ran his thick fingers over the smooth wood, and looked into the deep pockets like a child staring down a mysterious well.

"Eight ball?" he asked, turning to me.

"Yeah," I said, smiling. "Yeah, sure."

As a kid growing up in Kalihi—a working class neighborhood in Honolulu—I had dreams of being the quarterback for the Dallas Cowboys or a drummer in a rock and roll band. I never had any real dreams of becoming a writer.

Somehow, someway, that all changed.

In 1986, I graduated from the University of Hawaii with a Bachelor of Arts in English. Here I won the Ernest Hemingway Memorial Award for Creative Writing.

A year later, in 1987, I was awarded the Helen Deutsch Fellowship for Creative Writing at Boston University. Between visits to Fenway Park and jogs along the Charles River, I received a Master of Arts in English with a Concentration in Creative Writing.

I returned to Hawaii where I worked first as a broadcast journalist in radio, and then as a television news reporter.

I am working on several writing projects, including a novel.

Garrett Hongo

SUNBIRD

IN VOLCANO, it was too expensive to keep a rental car for very long. Even at the lowest, "Kama'aina" rates—a scale of discounts given to island residents—the prices would've bankrupted my little store of savings within a few months. So I started hunting in the classifieds, speculating what it would be like to purchase one of the used vehicles of the island.

The run-of-the-mill island vehicle was like the one our neighbor Tony Billie used. He worked as a pilot of the air ambulance between the Big Island and O'ahu, transporting the sick and injured on emergencies over from Hilo Memorial Hospital to Queen's or Tripler on O'ahu. He kept a weekend house in Volcano and used a Honolulu condominium during the week. His car in Honolulu was a nice, late-model Buick Skylark—"an adequate, rust-free city ride" he said—but the one he kept at the airport in Hilo or in his garage in Volcano was a "beater"— an old, battered Volkswagen bug mostly the color of beans and melted cheese in a burrito made by a franchise taco stand. Its fenders rattled as if half-tracked over lava hummocks in our road, its bumper banged against the car's right front wheel, and the hood came unlatched at any speed over sixty.

"I don't need no speedometer," my neighbor said, "because, at 55, the hood just automatically flips up in front of my windshield, and I have to stop to put it down. It's perfect—I just don't get to go too fast. No speeding tickets, and no one in Volcano gives a damn my car is funky."

Tony took pride in his house and the little yard and garden of azaleas, birds-of-paradise, rose and impatiens bushes around it. He'd spend Saturdays weed-whacking the broomgrass and sedges down, pruning his bushes, and mowing the little hummucky lawn around his house. I'd walk over from our cabin to have a cup of coffee with him and talk story about his flying in Vietnam or about the latest Tom Clancy (he read *Argosy*-style novels), and I'd see him dressed in overalls or in polyester running sweats, weed-whacking with his protective goggles on, the little orange and brown runt of a car perched like a tubercular bantam rooster on the lava cinders of the curved driveway behind him.

Our other neighbors had cars like this too. Someone had a fly-green Chevrolet El Camino without side windows. It had been broken into, its windows smashed, and the owner simply patched the rider's side with black plastic from a Hefty bag. On the driver's side, to block the most intolerable highway wind, he'd string up an old real estate sign tied to the doorframe. The prettiest single woman in town—a neighbor three lots over—drove a hulking, fastbacked Chevy Nova that had lost its muffler to corrosion. When she fired it up to go to work in the mornings, or when she crept along our lava road returning from it, I could hear its engine roaring like the laughter of Jupiter. My best friends—a couple who lived in a treehouse—kept an old Ford Torino that was so wet and mildewed inside that I thought penicillin would grow on the dashboard. At the end of our road, the Carsons had an aluminum foil-colored Volkswagen squareback beater that was so rusted out under its cosmetic coating of silver spray-paint that it had to be held together with twisted clothes hangers and about a hundred yards of duct tape. Rust was such a major problem that, once a car started showing spots—small cavities and bubbles of corrosion pimpling under the factory paint—that would be the signal for its middle class owner to dump it on the used-car market.

A Volcano car, normally one of these used ones handed down across the islands and a generation or two of owners, would've started out with a delivery truck driver, a flight attendant, or a schoolteacher somewhere on Oʻahu—the biggest population center—and then gotten sold to the third son of a Japanese golfcourse groundskeeper in Kaneohe, who would've souped it up and painted flames on its fenders until he got bored or broke or sent off to the Mainland for college. Then, his father might've traded the customized vehicle—heavy-duty shocks, quad speakers, and all—for a new family vehicle. Knowing it was a crate, the dealer would mark it for exile, selling it off to a wholesaler who would then ship it off on inter-island barge over to Hilo where it would be stripped of its offending gew-gaws, its engine steam-cleaned, and its exterior and interior detailed out to sit in a commercial, used-car clip-joint.

Once over on the Big Island, it might go as a kind of "mother-in-law" car to the foreman of a macadamia nut processing plant who would drive it until the latches on its trunk started pronging through the crumbling-from-acres of rust car body, until its rocker panels started flaking away like the enamel off of decaying teeth. Over a 3-day weekend, the new owner might give up a fishing trip to Kona to stay home and give the old car a homemade paint job in competition orange for teenagers or bottle-cap silver for homeowners or absolute hospital white for generic suckers and leave it to dry in his garage a month, painstakingly performing the work of detailing, whipping out the whisk broom and Armor-All every day, shining up the freckled chrome, filling the tiny pits in the paint job with little morsels of putty coated over with even more paint, replacing the rear-view with something special from NAPA Auto Parts, vacuuming out all intermingled rust and beach sand from the trunk. He'd place a minimal ad in the *Hawaii Tribune-Herald* or even run a folksy spiel to be read by local, exclusively pidgin-speaking deejay "Braddah Waltah" on the Saturday Radio Trader. Thereupon the economy would bring him a likely mark in the form of a poor starving artist living on welfare and food stamps in Keaau, or a *pakalolo*-raising carpenter homesteading in Volcano, or a middle class weekender like my neighbor Tony, or a homeland-sick and peri-patetic sojourner like me.

Methodically checking into the used-car ads, I circled prob-ables like "Clean, 2-dr Civic, heavy miles," "Immaculate Diplo-mat, rental fleet," "3-dr Tercel, new paint," and "Auto Sentra, cherry." I'd call the numbers, have a short conversation with the owners or the sister of the owner or the child of the owner and try to make an appointment to see the vehicle if the price and specs were right. Often as not, the price would be good—a few thousand—but someone would say, "Yeah, dah paint fresh ass 'cause was in one head-on wreck lass mont'" I'd cross that off my list. Or, I'd drive out across roads carved on lava into a low forest of stunted 'ohia trees to get to a post-hippie A-frame cabin tucked back in the brush. In their early 40s, the guy might be from New Haven and his wife from Detroit. They would have been old Carlos Casteñeda devotees who had gone to the University of Michigan, traveled Europe by backpack and Eurail Pass, trekked through Nepal and the Himalayas on foot where they found powders and a crystal. This crystal would've told them to come to Hawai'i or to Phoenix. They chose the Big Island, bought land, found jobs, and had a kid. Now they needed a bigger car. The one they showed me had a timing belt that went out, its c.v. joints would need replacing, there might be rust near the hinges on the hatchback, and, when I drove it, I'd discover bad brakes with the left front al-ready metal to metal. With the struts completely out in the front end, they would still want thousands.

Or, I'd drive down from Volcano to Hilo for the appoint-ment—often in a sprawling apartment complex or at the one high-rise condominiums in town on the point along the beach-front just beside the outlet of the Wailuku River—and be met by a lower-level management type with Brylcreem hair who worked for C. Brewer or Ben Franklin or Safeway who said he was relocating to Phoenix or to Springfield, Illinois and needed to sell *fast*. He'd give me a good price if it was cash. He'd bought the car from the A-1 lot across from the Oldsmobile dealership in town, found it "cherry" except for a little rubber unraveling on the doorframes, except for the frayed seats showing cotton batting upholstery guts, except for the bubonic pustules of rust scatted all along its roof and rear. I'd get into it, drive a little along rain-soaked suburban asphalt roads and muddy and pot-holed plantation backroads, then ask him to park it so I could watch him go over the speed bumps in the parking lot. Often as not, when he hit one of the humps, I'd notice little flecks of compacted dirt and rust particles showering down over the tires from inside the wheel-wells. I'd nod and move on, shaking flaking paint from my rolled cuffs before I stepped back into the rental car.

I'd think about calling on my relatives that afternoon, giving in a little, needing help. But I didn't. I rallied. I called one more number in the classifieds that afternoon and got someone older and Japanese—perhaps heaven-sent.

"Hideo Hamada iss my name," he said on the phone.

He lived a couple blocks from my schoolteacher cousin. I drove down that evening. His place was one of those 50's Hilo lots off the beltline road built around the town then—deep and almost a half-acre. Hideo had several carports. In one was parked a new Cressida with the old Corolla he was selling parked beside it. In the back, beside the plants- and tools-cluttered garage, there was a Dodge Ram-Charger with a trailer and fishing cruiser behind it. Finally, way in the back beside a long hot-house where he was nurserying along with red anthuriums on cinder-beds of lava, there was an old Ford Bronco 4-wheeler up on metal lifters. I decided that the man was as completely local as could be, had his act together, and looked reliable—like he took care of his vehicles. I thought that maybe this was the score. The anthropologist in me said that we might match up well culturally—I could see he had his strong, materialistic Japanese values completely intact.

Hideo told me he knew my cousins and invited me inside his house "for watch the news, eat feesh I caught-em diss morning *good!*"

Traditional-looking, a tanned Nisei in his 60s, with bow legs and a beer-gut, wearing shorts and rubber beach sandals he took off at the door when we entered his home, Hideo ate his fish with lots of soy sauce and with his shirt off. I ate his fish—a *mempachi* reef-fish split neatly along its mercator lines, fried in rice powder sprinkled with sugar and seasoned with soy sauce—with my shirt on. The fish was delicious indeed, and I wondered if taking my own shirt off would've been some kind of sign of tacit assent to a deal. After this strangely deliberated preliminary, I finally got a look at the car, parked in the carport adjacent to the kitchen.

It was a mess. It had mildew stains and fresh mildew still growing on the cloth upholstery. I got in, opened the window on the driver's side, and a moisture puff of cloud escaped from its interior. He explained it had been parked for "tch'ree mont'" or more. He said I was the first to crack the door, that no one had been by before me, that there hadn't been a chance for it to dry out. He left me alone with it after that, and, instead of going through the entire ritual of driving it, taking it to the mechanic, and bringing it back to him, I just wrote out a polite note and left it under the windshield wiper. I could hear him whistling to a 40s, big-band tune from the radio as I shuffled along out of there. I thought it was Glen Miller's "Tuxedo Junction," but I know it was guilt that drove my imagination to melodies unheard that day.

I even tried going to a used-car lot. Soon after my non-negotiation with Hideo, I drove to Hilo absolutely set to buy something that day, tired of shopping, tired of missing second gears, cooked transmissions and dislocated suspensions, cynical about single-owner in Panaewa stories, jaded and disbelieving of repair records and the warm, local-boy handshakes, the offers of "free floor-mat t'chrown in." I wanted things to end. I wanted simplicity. I wanted to pay extra for a guarantee of no bullshit. I went to Hilo Harold's Hawaiian Used Cars.

The Nisei salesman, a smallish and deeply-tanned guy who carried himself as if, in another age, he would've worn zoot suits, two-tone shoes, and slouch hats in his incarnation as a Kalihi gambler with a swinging watch-chain, said that he knew one of my uncles. He gave me coffee, he then spread a broad, fish-market sized printed sheet on the formica-covered table that listed all the "new acquisitions" on the lot. He ran his finger in three quick, *samurai*-butcher strokes across the page, scoring the paper with his fingernail under a BMW, a Ford Galaxy, and a Pontiac Sunbird. Instantly, I knew he was trying to place me within a pattern across a tier of price ranges no matter that I'd told him what I was looking for. The BMW was "high-end" and fucked-up. Its once show-room splendid coppery gold paint-job had deteriorated and become patchy as the carpeting of moss on the forest floor around Kilauea-Iki where the ground still steamed and vented and wild pigs foraged on ferns, scoring the ground bare in ugly spots where their snouts had turned earth and ripped tree roots in search of worms to eat. The Galaxy was green as puke mixed with cat-doo. It was missing its gear-shift knob. The engine made huge, farting shots of black oil-smoke that jetted out of the corroded exhaust pipe when the salesman fired it up.

I took a large look at the Sunbird, though. It interested me. The paint job was original but still fresh and completely unblemished. I took a look into its trunk and found no rust dust or pimples burbling up under the trunk-lid. The tires had plenty of tread. The odometer showed an "honest" 66,000 miles for a car that was just over four years old. And its "setback" feature—that which made it cheap and available, still for sale, less than fully desirable on a friendship or family market where people traded their good cars cheaply to a small circle of intimates—was its bathroom powder blue and cigarette-burned interior plastic upholstery. I thought, "I can deal with that if the motor is good."

I took it for a spin around Hilo, gunning the engine, flooring the accelerator on light changes at intersections, taking what I figured to be its battered automatic transmission as harshly through passing gear as I could, slamming on the brakes and feathering them at stoplights, and generally driving like I was local-born Indy racer Danny Ungais transmuted into my body and sent home for ten minutes of low-stakes competition street-dragging with his old high school "braddahs." I took it up to Boiling Pots and the lowr *a'a* flows from Mauna Loa that ran along the Waimea River. I made the car climb from sea-level roads down around the used-car lot up to Hilo Heights a thousand feet higher where the sweltering tropic air cooled a little and doctors, lawyers, and other professionals had built homes styled after Nashville manor homes and French villas in New Orleans and Key West.

The Sunbird's engine did not chuff, its automatic gearshift slipped not once, and the suspension of sprung steel and pneumatic tubes behaved with complete obedience to the general laws of gravity and physics. I liked it, drove back to the lot, asked for papers and a payment schedule, and plunked my money down. Exhilarated, sensing that my trials were over, I gobbled a roadside, sunset meal of Chinese take-out and drove the Sunbird the 4,000 feet elevation-gain up Volcano Highway where, after a few miles of laboring after passing Glenwood and Ohia Estates, it broke down at the 26 Mile marker at the entrance of Mauna Loa Estates, its fuel-line somehow contaminated, its air-filter congested and asthmatic, its alternator made obdurate and inflexible, the micrometer-tuned pipette of its carburation completely clogged. In the midnight dark that evening, under a clear, violet bowl of winter sky flecked with pinpricks of stars and the broad belt of astral jewels around Orion's spackled waist, I tramped home dejected in worn-out beach flip-flops, cursing Detroit and Yokohama in one breath, shaking fists of abuse at all motorized, human-sold forms of transport, drowning in tears that were oily with rage.

Garrett Hongo is the author of two poetry collections—*Yellow Light* and *The River of Heaven*, which was awarded the Lamont Poetry Prize by the Academy of American Poets. A recipient of fellowships from the Guggenheim Foundation and the NEA, he has edited *Under Western Eyes: Personal Essays from Asian America*, *Songs My Mother Taught Me: Stories, Memoir, and Plays by Wakako Yamauchi*, and *The Open Boat: Poems from Asian America*. His latest book is *Volcano: A Memoir of Hawai'i*. He is Professor of English and Creative Writing at the University of Oregon.

Part III

Survival

Wakako Yamauchi

OTOKO

THIS IS THE SUMMER SOLSTICE, the longest day of the year. Tomorrow will be shorter, each day thereafter slipping away, taking along a measure of light. In December the cycle starts again; light grows stronger, longer, bringing spring back to us. But today is the turning point, and though the long lazy summer stretches before us, we know this is the beginning of the waning.

On this day, my brother Kiyo drops by. He brings three small boxes of berries from his in-law's farm. They work a few acres of raspberries in West Covina, maybe twenty miles east of Los Angeles and seventeen more from Gardena where I live. He shows me an album he found in a Japanese tape and record store there. He sets the berries in the sink and dusts the record with his sleeve. It's a re-issue of vintage Japanese songs. My mother sang them often. In those depression years the old Victrola was her trip home.

"Listen to this," he says.

Watashya ukiyo no watari dori (I'm a bird of passage in a floating world) . . .

I hear her now. I see her dancing. She is younger than I am
today.

"We've outlived them both, Kiyo," I say.

"Remember that old abandoned house in Westmorland?" he
asks.

It was a time like now. The bottom fell out of the stock market, they said. We didn't have stocks or money to lose but my
father did lose his job with the American Fruit Growers, a job
that included housing with salary. Until then life was all right;
there was good food, store bought clothes, a house with running water and a telephone on the wall. These are what I remember of life before our fall. Then the Great Depression descended. For us it was 1932.

There were lots of homeless people even in Westmorland, a
desert township near the Mexican border, even when a shelter
could be built with chaparral.

But a house of straw? The Japanese are proud. My father
took his family of four (Sachi was not yet born), borrowed an
old frame house from a friend of a friend, leased thirty acres,
moved the house on it and went into farming independently. If
you can call borrowing money from a produce company and
committing the entire harvest to them independent.

It was a struggle—too much rain, too little rain, frost. It
was the old "company store" syndrome: the loan, the high interest, the fixed prices. But the worst was yet to come.

The friend's friend reclaimed the house he'd loaned us. My
mother said no friend would do such a thing; my father said it
was a friend's friend. We had to find a place to stay until he decided what to do. He chose to remain in farming and he moved
us into this deserted house that stood by the dirt road we took
to town.

We passed it often. Kiyo and I used to throw stones at the
windows, called it the haunted house. We covered the broken
windows with cardboard, washed off the ancient feces left by
wandering (and prideless, my mother said) unfortunates and

moved in as squatters. It was summer; school was out and there was no need to explain this embarrassing situation to anyone. We hardly saw a person, much less a friend or a schoolmate. My mother said it wouldn't be for long.

My brother spent that summer working at a packing shed making boxes, hammering nails into wooden slats all day, his small fingers growing raw with tiny splinters. He was eleven or twelve. He gave all his pay to my father. He tells me now he's glad of that because it turned out that was all he'd ever do for him.

Kiyo's eyes swell with moisture. I see my brother with his hair turning white and thinning, almost crying over something that cannot be redone or even revised, and I too, almost cry.

Otoko wa iji, onna wa nasake (man is will, woman is mercy) ... The moisture dries before it falls.

Kiyo says he once drove with my father to Niland in the low desert, a place drier, sandier, more barren and wind-swept than our Westmorland. This was before car radios and air-conditioning. It was a hot and boring journey at thirty miles an hour, my father's usual highway speed. The friend my father went to see made a little money with early tomatoes that year. Our tomatoes were too late (as usual, my mother said) to cash in on the good price. Kiyo says now, he believes my father went to borrow money that day.

"They were rich. Radio—battery, of course. Console," he says. "Sofa in the parlor ... the works." He laughs and pats my couch. "I guess they turned him down because we left early and Pop didn't say anything all the way home. Twenty miles. Nothing. I remember that."

How do you ask for a loan? Do you wait 'til tea is served? Do you touch the sleek new console and say, "You did good this year, hunh?" Most likely the friend suspected the nature of the mission and immediately started talking poverty and my father left as soon as it was convenient. I can't picture him, cap in hand, rubbing the back of his neck, "My kids are hungry; we have no place to live."

"Maybe he didn't ask," I say.

"I don't know. The kids were showing me the new radio so I don't know. He was proud, all right," Kiyo says. "I wonder what he was thinking on that ride back. Well, we made it without their help." He takes a deep breath. "I guess he felt bad. Pop was proud."

"He." We talk about him as we would a stranger. "Pop." Calling him "Pop" after he's gone is a safe intimacy. He was a stranger. I suppose his life was a string of enduring humiliations like this one, rotating his failures and hanging in there drawing strength from beneath the silence, from his hope of one day returning to Japan. I heard it in the songs he sang when he drank.

I was a headstrong, impetuous and demanding child—the second of three: Kiyo, myself, and thirteen years below me, a sweet cross-eyed sister, Sachi. I was the only one of the bunch who was familiar with the knuckles of my father's hand. *"Onna no kuse,"* he said. That was an admonition to know my place as a woman.

I looked just like him: the long face, angular frame, the epicanthic fold. My mother was a beautiful woman and mercifully the others inherited her looks and my father's suppressed temperament. I was given the other combination: his looks and her tenacious nature.

The spring of the great Imperial Valley earthquake was the peak of my father's farming career—his grandest failure. One hundred and forty acres of lettuce nobody wanted.

I was fifteen. I was tired of hand-me-downs and recycled clothes and I went to Los Angeles to earn a few dollars to buy a coat of my own and some finery that might help me with the fellows. At that time the only jobs available to Japanese were in fruit stands, garages, and for women, domestic work. It was the summer of '39. In Europe World War II was already in progress.

I found a job in South Pasadena as a "school girl," a euphemism for inexperienced servant. I worked three months at twenty-five dollars a month plus room and board, washing, ironing, polishing furniture, vacuuming, and caring for two small girls. Not a lot of money even for those days. Of the seventy-five dollars I earned, I spent twenty-five, mostly for movies and restaurants on my days off. I bought a coral necklace and a pair of Gallen Kamp shoes with open toes. It was too warm to think about coats.

At the end of my stint, I was eager to come home. I missed my family while I was away living with white folks. I acquired a new appreciation for them along with the experience of truly being on the outside looking in. The grand piano with the velvet fringed scarf, mirrored bathrooms, red meat dinners with cloth napkins and sterling flatwear brought me closer to my family—my carping mother, silent father, quarrelsome brother and my sweet Sachi.

In the meantime my family had gone to Oceanside to work in the berry farms of Kumamoto-mura (Kumamoto Village), so named because most of the residents had immigrated from Kumamoto, Japan. It's now Camp Pendleton, a marine base. No doubt wild strawberries still stain the boots of bivouacking soldiers—a stubborn memory of the Japanese community that lived and farmed there.

In Oceanside I was appalled to find my family in a makeshift tent, using water from a communal faucet, washing, shaving, brushing teeth publicly. Other families from Imperial Valley were also there. It had been a disastrous year for a lot of us. In the three months I'd been away, my little sister's front teeth had rotted. She'd turned two and did not remember me.

Kiyo would not take the situation seriously: a few months camping in Oceanside, cool weather, a beach near-by, a few bucks, a kind of vacation. He laughed. My mother's lips grinned but her eyes did not smile.

I gave my remaining fifty dollars to her. "We'll buy a sweater for Father," she said, "and we'll give money to Kiyo to go to Los Angeles. There's no future for him here."

Kiyo left for L.A. He wrote later that he'd found a day job in a fruit stand and went to vocational school, nights.

And we didn't stay in the tent. A kindly bachelor who farmed a piece of land with a frame house on it offered us a room. "It's not right for a young girl to sleep on the ground," he said.

My mother said, "Michiko, remember this kindness."

"It's only for a short while," I said "We have to get back home. School will start in two weeks."

"We have nothing to go back to," she said.

The following week my mother was offered a job in town as a cook in a boarding house that accomodated Japanese migrant workers. The man who came was short and wiry. He wore boots laced to his calves. He said she would cook for thirty, forty men during peak seasons and off-season there would only be a few, say four or five, who chose not to move on.

"There're always some of them," Mr. Tano said. "They get tired of moving and if they don't have money to pay, well, I got to carry them. What can I do? They're Japanese too, eh? I'll give you a room for your family. Your husband can work out of the hotel like the rest of them. When farmers need help they come to me. I'll see that your husband always has work," Mr. Tano said.

My father went to bed that day. He had a stomach condition that plagued him off and on for years. He took a chalky white liquid for it.

My mother asked him, "What should I do? Should I take the job?"

His face was ashy. His lips were dry and cracked. On this hot day he pulled the blanket to his neck and turned away from us.

My mother persisted. "What should I do?"

He answered without turning. "Do what you want."

We moved to the city and lived in a room with a double bed and two cots and just enough space to move around them. With the money Mr. Tano gave her, my mother bought the supplies: rice, *shoyu*, *miso*, heart, liver, tripe—nether cuts. My father rode to work in a truck with the rest of the men and swallowed great quantities of chalky medicine. My mother bought me a herringbone tweed jacket with shoulder pads that made me look like a grown woman. I started my junior year at Oceanside Carlsbad Union High School. When the kids at school asked me where I lived, I said, "Out that way," and waved vaguely westward, too ashamed to say I lived in a hotel for transient men, afraid the down-cheeked youngsters would shrink from me, their mouths pursed.

Nokoru yume wo nanto shyo (what shall we do with the dreams that remain) . . . Kiyo flips the record.

Most of the men in the boarding house were over fifty. There were a few in their thirties—*Kibei*, men who were born in America, sent back to Japan for an education, and still seeking something they'd not found in Japan, they had returned— to join a legion of men who moved with harvests not their own. In this land of plenty, they bought the clothes in fashion which they kept in cleaners' bags, and went to movies together, wrote long letters to Japan, and visited neighboring farmers who had daughters. Sometimes in the evening some one would play a wistful Japanese melody on a harmonica or a wooden flute.

The older men were scruffy and bowed from years of scraping along on their knees picking strawberries (for tables not their own), and from bending over low grape vines. Their pants were caked with mud. They shook them out at night over the balcony. Conversations were colored with sexual reference and they responded with high-pitched laughter. They spent their free time playing *hana* (cards), or drinking *sake*, which my mother warmed and sold to them for ten cents a cup.

Once a man staggered off to the courtyard and passed out on the dirt, the ocean breeze cooling him, the sun warming him like the fruit he'd spent his youth harvesting. In the late afternoon he woke and walked away brushing himself off, without shame, as though it were his natural right as a man. Fruit of the land.

Within months the hotel was condemned by the Oceanside Department of Health. Not enough bathrooms; too many men in one room. The men scattered—tangling with the law was bad business. Some were illegal aliens. Mr. Tano also left. We stayed in the back house where Mr. Tano had lived, and waited for something to turn up. Again squatters.

The landlord came to check on his property and found us there. He saw my little sister with the rotten teeth and the lazy eye and me, haughty and cold. Sachi sang "Cielito Lindo" for him—a song she learned from the Mexican family next door. The landlord asked me to tell my mother that he was willing to remodel to meet health standards if she would run the hotel. He said he was through dealing with Tano.

My mother said to me, "You see? Someone is watching."

My father wasn't home that day; just my mother, Sachi—

smiling, showing her nubs of teeth, confident the world was safe and loving—and me, unrelenting.

By the time the hotel was habitable, it was winter and though a few men returned, most of the rooms were empty. I asked my mother if I could have one room for myself; I would give it up during the season, I promised. She said no. I begged and pleaded, sulked, slammed doors and cupboards, and banged dishes until she screamed, "All right! You can have a room!" She said I was a graceless brat—determined and self-centered. She said if I didn't change my ways I was in for a whole lot of trouble. "You'll find out!" she said.

Kiete kureruna, itsumade mo (don't fade, remain forever) . . .

It was the first time I had a room to myself, excluding the one in South Pasadena. It was on the second floor overlooking the courtyard. I dragged in a table and our two best chairs —in case I had company. I sewed dimity curtains for the window and pushed my cot against it so I could see the stars at night. I bought a vase in a second-hand store for a nickle.

The old men thought I was an upstart. Some devised ways of getting back at me: one used to wait until my mother left the room and then would rub his leg against mine and laugh at my indignation. One passed me on my way to the bathroom and cackled, "Three. Count them and see. Three holes. Count them." Sexuality was a man's birthright and nothing, no circumstance, no employer or landlord or upstart kid would deny them that. From cradle to grave, theirs. *Otoko* was the word that said it all: man, virility, courage, endurance.

Tsuki ga noboreba rantan keshite (as the moon rises, lanterns flicker out) . . .

My father went to work less and less. He found little jobs to do at home, sweeping the sidewalk, emptying ash trays, turning the *tsukemono* (pickles). In the evenings he joined the gambling and drinking; during the day he administered to his anxieties and griefs, silently, orally with chalk. My mother sucked in her breath and said, "He drinks *sake* and takes medicine.

Sake by night and medicine by day. What good does it do? *Sake* and medicine . . ."

I went to sleep to the sound of the cursing and laughing and reviling of the men gambling down the hall. My father was always there, taking the house cut and plowing it back into the games (my mother said)—grimly smiling, squandering the money that meant so much to her, fighting his last battleline: his manhood, his courage, his endurance.

Noda-san was among the group that drifted in from Fresno leaving the grape harvest early that year. He was about thirty, boyish and quiet. He didn't join the card games nor did he drink much. Sometimes if I was behind the counter, he'd ask for a cup of *sake*, counting the change in his palm slowly, flashing a shy smile with his white teeth.

One late night I was awakened by a gentle knock.

"Who is it?" I asked.

"*Boku yo. Noda. Chotto akete. Hanashi ga aruno.*" It's me, Noda. Let me in. I must talk to you.

I opened the door and he quickly slipped in. We faced each other in the dark.

"What do you want?"

"You," he said.

"Well, you can't have me," I said and switched on the light and made for the door. He turned off the light and barred the door with his arm.

"You ought not be here," I said, but his smile was so sad, so much in need, it was hard for me to hurt him. "You can't come in here like this," I said.

"But you let me in." He touched my face.

"You asked to come in." I pushed his hand away. "You ought to get out of here. You ought not be here."

"But you let me in."

This went on for a while until he got impatient and reached for me. He tried to kiss me. He stroked my struggling body. He maneuvered me to the cot, squirming and sliding in his arms.

We could hear the gamblers down the hall. "Let me go or I'll scream," I whispered.

"You won't do that."

"You can walk out of here. I won't tell anyone. Just let me go." I think I heard that in the movies.

His hands worked to calm me, to arouse me. "Shhh . . ."

"One more chance," I warned. Still he didn't stop.

I yelled, "Father!" He released me instantly. We heard footsteps thudding down the hall. He jumped away from me and we stood facing each other—in the dark—just the way he came in. The door opened. My father and two other men peered into the room.

"Oh," one of them said. No other word was spoken. The two men left, my father waited for Noda-san and followed him out, closing the door quietly behind him.

In the morning my father put a hook and eye on my door. And Noda-san smiled his sad boyish smile whenever he passed me at the counter.

Shina no yoru. Shina no yoru yo (China nights. O, China nights) . . . My brother says, "This was popular before the war. Remember Oceanside?"

Minato no akari, murasaki no yo ni (lights of the harbor against the purple sky) . . .

Hostilities, always present between America and Japan, worsened. The threat of war was constant. After a while you got used to it.

My brother returned to Oceanside. "You never know," he said. "We got to be together when whatever happens, happens." He found work as a truck driver in Vista, a few miles east of Oceanside. "Work days and study nights and still driving a truck," he complained.

I had gone to see "Sergeant York" that Sunday. When I came home my mother met me at the door. "America is at war with Japan," she said. Her face was white.

Within months, plans to incarcerate us were implemented—all of us: alien and citizen, rich and poor, sick and well. They herded us into ten isolated camps, 120,000 of us, and locked the gates. They said it was for national security even though there was no incidence of sabotage; they said it was for our own safety even though the guns on the guard towers were pointed at us. And one family, after all those years of struggle, lost the boarding house that was their ticket to the promised land.

Noboru janku no yume no fune (sailing upstream, the junk is a boat of dreams) . . .

"I wonder what happened to all those men at the boarding house," I say.

"Why, they went to concentration camps like the rest of us," Kiyo says.

"I mean now, Kiyo. What are they doing now?" I say.

"Why, they were old. They died, of course. Heh. Like our father and mother." He looks at his hands. "They never did get to Japan, did they?"

They never did.

My father died in camp after the war ended, just before camp closed. The government had been slowly dispersing the inmates over the past year and I was in Chicago and Kiyo in Tule Lake expecting deportation. His citizenship was revoked when he answered "no" to the questionaire that asked him to go to combat for the country that gave him the opportunity to wash fruit, study nights, and still drive trucks, took away every inch-by-inch gain in one swift stroke, incarcerated without due process, and gave him the choice to bear arms against the country of his ancestry or be deported.

My father had said to him, "*Kimi wa otoko da,*" you are a man, and had let his only son make his choice. I went to Chicago to work in a candy factory.

And so, only my mother and Sachi, who was eight, were with my father when he died.

Hiroshima ended the war. My mother said my father grew despondent after the bombing. By this time, the government had set a November deadline for closing the camps. She said she'd asked my father, "Where shall we go? What shall we do?" and he'd not answered. She said he began to vomit black beads of blood and at the end of October died without making that decision. She said, "I joined the last group of people going out. What could I do?" My mother and Sachi left their home of four years with my father's ashes. They had been there longer than they were in Oceanside.

The war ended and Kiyo, still in camp at Tule Lake was not deported. I left Chicago and Kiyo and I joined my mother and Sachi in San Diego. But my father died believing the nucleus of his small family was shattered.

Yume mo nuremasho; shiwo kaze, yo kaze (dreams may dampen; salt winds, night winds) . . .

Kiyo says, "These songs really get to me." He thumps his chest. "It's like going back to the past—to Japan. You ever want to go back, Michi?" he asks.

"Go back? Kiyo, we've never been there."

"Yeah. I guess we think of ourselves as them."

"Kiyo? What if there's no such place? What if it only existed in their minds? And we believed them?"

"There is no such place. It's Fantasy Island, Michi," he says.

The record spins silently before Kiyo turns it off. He tucks it in its jacket. "I better get going," he looks at his watch. "Mary's probably wondering what happened to me." He looks out my window. "Hey, I thought you planted agapanthas last year."

"I did. They didn't take," I say.

"Did you water them? They're supposed to be the hardiest plants around." He tucks the record under his arm. "Well, maybe next year, hunh?" He laughs.

And on the longest day of the year, he leaves me and hurries home.

I was born in the year of the Asian Exclusion Act in Imperial Valley, California where my father farmed during the years of the Great Depression—the landscape of most of my stories. In 1942 our family was sent to Poston, Arizona, one of 10 American concentration camps. My father died there in the last days of incarceration.

After the war I moved to Los Angeles to study painting. I married there and off and on during marriage, motherhood, and divorce, I wrote short stories of the Japanese in America. I wrote for the English section of Rafu Shimpo. Many years later one of my short stories found its way into AII-IEEEEE: AN ANTHOLOGY OF ASIAN AMERICAN WRITERS. Through this exposure, I was brought into playwriting. I owe my literary life to Asian American studies, educators and students and to Asian American theatre.

My fifteen minutes is encapsulated in SONGS MY MOTHER TAUGHT ME; STORIES, PLAYS, AND MEMOIRS, published by the Feminist Press and edited by Garrett K. Hongo.

*William P. Osborn and
Sylvia Watanabe*

A CONVERSATION WITH
WAKAKO YAMAUCHI

WAKAKO YAMAUCHI'S PARENTS emigrated from Japan to the Imperial Valley of southeastern California, where they became tenant farmers. Because the state's alien land laws restricted leases to the Japanese, the Nakamura family was required to pack up, move on, and begin a new homestead every few years. This forced itinerancy and the sense of dislocation it produced were to became major themes in Ms. Yamauchi's fiction.

Born into a home where only Japanese was spoken, Wakako and her older brother and sister acquired fluency in English after starting school. She grew to love books. She remembers fondly how reading filled the long hours on the isolated desert farms where she grew up. When her father's lettuce crop failed after the 1940 earthquake, she and her family moved to Oceanside, California, where they borrowed money to start a boarding house.

However, just as they came free of debt, the imperial government of Japan attacked Pearl Harbor and the Nakamuras were interned at Poston, Arizona. There, Wakako became friends with the writer Hisaye Yamamoto and worked as an artist on the *Poston Chronicle*. Her father died in camp, unable to make another beginning after learning of the U.S. bombing of Hiroshima.

Following the War, she attended art school in Los Angeles. She has painted since. She didn't begin writing until her thirties, after she'd raised a family of her own. Her earliest publications came in the Japanese American periodical, *Los Angeles Rafu Shimpo*, which has continued to feature her in its annual Holiday Supplement. Several pieces that first appeared there have been reprinted elsewhere. "And the Soul Shall Dance," for instance, has been republished eleven times since its first appearance in 1966.

In the mid-seventies, the author transformed that story into a play, which has not only seen publication half a dozen times itself, but production in almost every Asian American theater around the country, and national broadcast on PBS and A&E. Among other places, her prose has been anthologized in *Women of the Century: Thirty Modern Short Stories* (St. Martin's), *New Worlds of Literature* (Norton), *Staging Diversity: Plays and Practice in American Theater* (Kendall/Hunt), *Aiiieeeee!: an Anthology of Asian American Writers* (Howard University), and *Charlie Chan is Dead: An Anthology of Asian American Fiction* (Viking/Penguin). She is the recipient of playwrighting grants from the Rockefeller Foundation and the Mark Taper Forum.

The literary contexts into which she fits are many, and two deserve special mention. First, though Yamamoto has written longer, Yamauchi has ascended to a similar matriarchal role in the mainstream success of today's younger Asian American writers. She struggled for the words; she helped create the audience; she found the way to publication. Second, she has always been the clearest, most insistent voice among the Japanese Americans who experienced the internment, reminding us not only of the injustice of that ordeal, but of its larger significance—that once the constitutional rights of one group of people have been nullified, there is nothing to prevent the same from happening to others.

What follows is a compendium derived from a series of

1994 letters and phone calls between Grand Rapids, Michigan, and Ms. Yamauchi's home in Gardena, California, plus a late September meeting in Chicago, where she had come to promote her new book, *Songs My Mother Taught Me* (Feminist Press)—prose from a writing career of nearly four decades. The reading took place at the bookstore, Women and Children First. As she read "And the Soul Shall Dance"—her speaking timbre low, the page delivered almost as one might read aloud to oneself—we were enthralled. At the end of the story comes a song, which she sang rather than spoke, and this quite charmed us all.

We'd like to begin with beginnings. Can you tell us something of your early sources of inspiration?

I suppose it began with *The Book of Knowledge*. My father could not resist a traveling salesman, and he bought the twenty volumes even before most of us could read. I loved the epic poems of Scott and Longfellow. Also the western stories of Zane Grey, because I knew that lonely dust-and-sage territory. I used to read Thomas Wolfe for his enormous passion. After I was pressed to write plays, I read Tennessee Williams. Even his stage directions are beautiful.

When did you start writing, and in which genre?

I think I have always wanted to write but I didn't dare, because I knew it took enormous knowledge, education, and courage, none of which I had or have. I started writing very short stories in my mid-thirties, years after my mother died. I didn't want her forgotten. "And the Soul Shall Dance" was one of my first. I thought it was pretty good and sent it out to mainstream magazines. When it was rejected I decided I was doing something wrong, so I took a correspondence course in short story writing from U.C. Berkeley. I tried to fit that story into all the exercises my teacher, Ms. Bartholomew, gave to us. Then I submitted it for my final paper. She loved it. I took a second course from the same teacher and submitted three stories. One of them, "The Sensei," about camp life, made her very angry. She wrote novels for adolescents, and this probably had a lot to do with her critique. She didn't want the narrator, who starts as a rather moral woman, to end up so cynical. She wanted the American pie finish, not a criticism of the Japanese American internment camps in World War II. But the story was my husband's and I had to tell it the way it happened. I realized then that an acceptable philosophical and political point of view was important to mainstream publication, so I stopped trying for white publications and wrote for *Rafu Shimpo*, a local Japanese paper with an English section. They knew what I was saying.

What was your first national publication?

Aiiieeeee!, and it's meant everything. For the first time, people outside of the Los Angeles *Nisei* community read my story. After I entered an *Amerasia Journal* short story competition, they published me too, and Asian American academics began to use my stories in their classes. That's how it started.

How did the editors of Aiiieeeee! *find out about your work?*

Si Yamamoto told me about Frank Chin, Jeffrey Chan, Lawson Inada, and Shawn Wong putting together an anthology for the Asian American courses they taught. She advised me to send them five stories. I did, but they didn't seem to care. By this time, I'd grown used to rejection and it didn't bother me much. Then one day Shawn wrote. They were interested in "Soul." He loved my stories and promised to make me famous. It was great news, but my marriage was unraveling and the joy was tempered.

Was Aiiieeeee! *where Mako first read "Soul"?*

Yes. In 1976 he was the artistic director of East West Players in Los Angeles. He gave me a playwright-in-residence grant funded by the Rockefeller Foundation to adapt it for the stage. The play was produced and was surprisingly successful. I think that launched my career, because *Soul* did in a couple of months of performance what I couldn't do in years of writing short stories. After that I fancied myself a playwright.

Could you describe the process of adapting "Soul" for the stage?

I'd never written a play, didn't even like to read plays, but I'd worked out the plot years before, and only had to transfer the mood through dialogue—which was kind of tricky, because there's very little dialogue in the short story. Much of what happens is in the characters' heads, and I had to get it on paper.

What gets you writing? What do you try to accomplish?

I cannot sit and pound out a story. I must first have a need to tell it. I must know how I feel and what I want my reader to feel. A very important teacher in my painting life once told me: "You must make a statement: the sun is warm; the petal is thin; the earth is barren. Do not clutter your painting with too many statements." He always said less is more and more is less. This works for me in writing too.

Some writers can unchain their minds and soar with the power and fluency of a Momoko Iko or Frank Chin—let a story run, the characters taking the initiative. But I'm always reining in my plots and people. This has to do with my upbringing during the Great Depression.

A lot of us *Nisei* are unsure and inarticulate, having grown up in a racist America, bound to our parents' *enryo* syndrome. *Enryo* means self-restraint—retreating from your space and your due. If somebody makes a statement that your heart rebels against, you don't say anything. *Enryo* is also giving up food. If somebody says, "Would you like some tea," you say "Oh no, no, no. Don't trouble yourself." "How about a cookie?" "I'm not really hungry." You are hungry, but not enough to forget your manners.

Because of these influences on my development, I'm filled with self doubt. That's why my stories stay close to home, with people I know. I have to overcome a lot before I set down the first word for the first idea. I am in denial; I still don't truly believe I am a writer. A writer has responsibilities. A writer stands by her words. I'm not sure I can.

Yet here is this new book of yours. Under the pressures you're talking about, how did you continue?

I didn't continue. I wrote when I had a story to tell—two or three stories a year, at most. Well if you work at it long enough, you know, you get a little pile.

I never wanted all my stories in one place. That would just be like putting all the bullshit in one barn. I thought the sameness—the landscape, the attitudes, the style—would be boring. But Garrett carried me away on his energy and faith.

Yes, Garrett Hongo was responsible for bringing your book to press. Could you tell us how that happened?

Garrett's mother lives in Gardena, so Lawson Inada suggested that while Garrett was out this way he come and visit.

He did and read some of my stories. Later he said he would try to get a book of them together. He never gave up, and *Songs My Mother Taught Me* is his great gift to me.

Though the "Country Stories," as they are called in your collection, contain some physical descriptions of the desert, one also senses its presence in the way that it shapes the lives of your characters—that those lives would not be possible in another locale. What are your memories of growing up in that landscape?

In Westmorland, homesteads were separated by large areas of desert, because you had to farm near a canal to get your water. There were a few businesses and a two-room school on the highway that ran through town. My school's name was Trifolium, and it was about ninety percent Japanese. Most of our parents were farmers—quite a number from Okinawa. We got our groceries and went to the Buddhist church nine or ten miles away in the town of Brawley, where there were maybe twelve thousand people. Westmorland wasn't half that size. I disliked the barrenness of the land and the grim, close-mouthed, unyielding people who lived on it. We were so widely separated out on our farms that we didn't even have mail service. We picked up the mail every few days at the post office. But we didn't get much, you know.

No Bean's catalog?

You know what? My father used to subscribe to almost all the magazines. I guess he felt sorry for the traveling salesman trekking through the desert to sell subscriptions. I used to look through these women's journals and send for every free brochure and sample, no matter what it was, so that I could get some mail. It was like throwing bottles out to sea. They would send back catalogs, carpet samples, pictures of gas ranges.

Most of your public elementary teachers must have been white.

All of them were. When I first went to school I couldn't pronounce the R and L sounds, and I remember my teacher drilling me. Now, if a teacher spent all that time drilling, it wasn't meanness, it was trying to get me to learn. So they must have had some compassion.

When I was in third grade, I had a very much loved music teacher. All the kids wanted to hold her hand. We'd follow her around. Well, we had a Maypole dance. We were asked to contribute ten cents for the crepe paper, so every girl contributed ten cents. And when the Maypole dance was over the white girls got the leftover crepe paper, and none of the Japanese girls got anything. So I wrote a letter to the teacher. I wrote that we all put in our ten cents, so how come we didn't get crepe paper also? I accused her of playing favorites. Soon after, she yanked me off the see-saw and threatened to expel me. I was nine.

That's pretty feisty.
I know, but I was a spoiled, outspoken brat.

How did the desert of your California childhood compare with the desert in Poston, Arizona?
The terrain was similar, but camp life was different. It was hotter, dustier. There were thousands of people, and rows and rows of barracks.

In "The Boatmen on Toneh River," Kimi says she has "found something here in this arid desert that is gentle and sweet too." What do you think she finds?
The experience of unexpected beauty, the sense of possibility you get from that. In camp I used to enjoy the mornings, because every one was like a renewal. The early part of the day was clear, cool, bright, and physical, and it just felt like something good was going to happen. Sometimes you could get that same feeling from the elusive contact with people who never said anything to you.

Like the boy Kimi sees riding by on his bicycle. Has that landscape also shaped your work as a visual artist?
Yes, its spareness, People don't like to pay a lot of money for a painting of a pot with a dead-looking flower. The teacher who influenced me most told me if you are going to paint a picture of a checkered tablecloth, you don't have to say "Checkers, checkers, checkers." All you need to do is say checkers once. I think that's also true with my writing.

It seems the Japanese Buddhist aesthetic—the thing not said, the little brush stroke, the transience of things—might also affect your work.
My mother and father were Buddhists, and I went to the

Buddhist church, so I'm sure it does. But more, I think it was the stories my mother used to tell me of unrequited love, the bleak and doomed destinies of Japanese lovers. And American movies I saw, such as *Camille*, which had a mood of yearning unfulfilled.

I was the last among three kids and I was left at home while the other two went to school, so my mother used to talk to me a lot. I always felt that as long as she was there, we'd make it. I never got to know my father like I knew my mother. It wasn't because he wasn't strong, it's just that he was a very quiet man. About the time I started school, he worked as a supervisor for American Food Growers, so it was my mother who had the leisure to sing songs and tell me stories. After the depression hit, he had to farm for himself, and my mother went out into the fields. I was eight or nine.

That must have been a few years before you began looking at Zane Grey and the other writers you've mentioned. As you began to read more, were you aware of any work being produced by Japanese American writers?

My father used to buy tons of old newspapers to use as brush-covers for the seedlings. I remember sitting against the sunny side of the tool shed at the beginning of the cold season, reading the *Kashu Mainichi* and coming across an article by a writer called Napoleon. I had been looking for a spiritual friend since I was a little girl and it seemed I'd found that person in Napoleon—who I thought was male.

When I was fifteen, we moved to Oceanside and I met some girls from Kumamoto Mura, a cooperative of Japanese farmers. In trying to establish common ground with them, I mentioned that I liked to read, and that Napoleon was a writer I admired. I was surprised to hear them say, "Oh, *she* lives in Kumamoto Mura and nobody likes *her* because *she's* always writing about us." I think the same people told me about Napoleon being Si Yamamoto.

When I finally ran into Si at a Mura meeting, I was thrilled but she was cool and distant. I think we met only two or three times in that period, She claims she played tic-tac-toe with me at one of those meetings, but I have no recollection of that. I felt a drawing away. I sensed she knew she was an intellectual superior and didn't want much to do with me. I didn't realize this was part of her nature. There weren't that many effusive *Nisei* girls like me.

When was it that you actually became friends?

We made friends later, in camp, at the office of the *Poston Chronicle*. I don't know how. I think it was my persistence. Or maybe I drew back enough for her to trust me. Maybe she was overwhelmed by my admiration. Anyway, I learned a lot from her. She was in touch with the Japanese American writers of the time—Sam Hori, Kate Tateishi, and the poet Toyo Suyemoto. This was long before I dreamed of being a writer myself.

Critics often link your names, even your work.

Si and I have a common rural depression-era background, both of us coming from the families of immigrant tenant farmers. And although she is more secretive than I, through the years we have also shared personal stories. People have come to think of us as twin writers, but that's not right. I am not so self-effacing, and I am not an intellectual. I am more physical—a feeler—more earthy. I think in some ways I'm more apt to cut myself open and let it bleed. Si has a keen mind. She is more refined. And she had been writing a long time before I even dared to dream of it.

Aside from your friendship with Hisaye, the internment seems to have exerted a great pull on your writing. It is your subject matter and it shapes the lives of your characters.

Every valid story reflects its economic and political times; however subtle. Even fictional characters don't live in vacuums. They're shaped by cultural and political attitudes and fashions; they come from a particular social class. They walk, ride a donkey or horse, take a train or a plane. They drink water from goblets, cheese glasses, open spigots, or goatskin bags.

I don't think you can write about the Nisei and not include the internment experience in some way. It would be like writing about Black Americans and ignoring slavery and the Civil War, about European Jews and denying the Holocaust. The incarceration profoundly dominated *Nisei* lives.

Many well-meaning white Americans don't see what the experience has to do with them—or that it was that bad. What do you say to people who minimize the internment by saying something like, "It wasn't as awful as slavery or the genocide of the Jews."

Years ago I went to a party at which I was the only nonwhite. A psychiatrist asked me why we Japanese called the American evacuation centers "concentration camps." They were nothing like the German concentration camps for the Jews, didn't I agree?

I would like to have replied, "Concentration means concentration and camp means camp. What's the problem? We are Americans, and to us, all those history and civics lessons turned out to be nothing but lies." But my mind went blank, I choked up, my voice cracked, and tears welled in my eyes. I said, "I guess you had to be there to understand that one." I was ashamed of myself, but a faltering voice and teary eyes are all a good psychiatrist needs.

In the relative scheme of things, of course slavery and genocide are "worse," but the Japanese American internment was motivated by a similar logic. And when one loss occurs, others can follow. When we turn our backs on the first offense, and we don't understand that what diminishes one, diminishes all, then the finest cathedrals and pulpits will not save us.

What about people who say it's time to move on?

I believe people choose to remember or forget, either to affirm their lives or salt their wounds—whatever it takes to cope. Extreme trauma may force us to block out or deny, but the imprint of an experience remains, whether we know it or not.

It's hard to understand how 120,000 Japanese would comply so readily with the order for their own incarceration, Did the ethic of enryo, which you mentioned earlier, have anything to do with that?

I don't think we complied because we were meek. The *Issei* had a lot of vim and vigor. They took cases up to the Supreme Court!

What happened was, the authorities took all the leaders of our community away until there was nothing left but people willing to comply. Those that objected were silenced or separated. The median age of the Nisei was seventeen. We were led by the only national organization still allowed to exist, the Japanese American Citizens' League. Politically speaking, we were right off the turnip truck.

It must have been a frightening and bewildering time.

Especially for the *Issei*. Everything they had worked for was taken away, and they still had to provide leadership, at least in their families.

Though I am often moved to tears by heroic acts of individual patriotism, I came to believe that nationalism is plain dumb. Yesterday's enemies are today's accomplices, Nations make peace or war according to economics and trade or territorial advantages. The rest of us are tossed about like leaves in the wind.

There are only a few stories that I've ever wanted to tell. I wanted to record our lives so they wouldn't be lost. I didn't realize what a responsibility that was. I only wanted to put down a few footprints of our sojourn here, at this time, in this place.

Jeanne Wakatsuki Houston

O FURO
(THE BATH)

SNOW FELL IN SHEETS OF LACE, a translucent curtain swirling and fluttering with the wind. Through the barracks window, Yuki watched in wonderment. She had not seen snow for forty years, not since leaving Japan. Unused to the glare, she blinked, hoping it was not cataracts that caused her eyes to sting. Many elders in camp had developed cataracts, invisible films that grew over the dark part of the eye. She didn't want any veil to soften her view of the desert's harsh landscape.

The room felt cold. She turned up the oil heater and set a pan of water on top. It was still too early to retire. The thought of bundling up in blankets and sleeping the day away was tempting. But Dixon would soon be bringing dinner. She sat down and rubbed her cold stockinged feet. Should she worry about frostbite?

How good a *furo* would feel. She had not taken a hot bath

since coming to internment camp a year ago. The communal showers and toilets were one of the more distasteful necessities she had to endure in this crowded settlement of strangers. When she first arrived, she had refused to shower in the dark cement room where a dozen metal nozzles sprayed water over huddled figures, who covered their privates with a towel in one hand, and with the other—and another towel—washed themselves. Such humiliation! Wasn't it bad enough for one family to live all in one small room! But to bathe with strangers—and not even in a tub—was too much to expect. Now she showered in the middle of the night when others slept.

Yuki was seventy-three. She was proud of her youthful looks. Most people were surprised she was over sixty and often asked what she did to stay so young. "Dance and sing a lot," she'd say, "and take *o furo* every night." She would like to say, "and please yourself as much as you can." But that sounded selfish, especially from an elder, a grandmother who should reflect ideals of martyrdom and self-sacrifice.

Remembering her warm apartment in East Los Angeles, the large three rooms above Nishio's Shoe Store, Yuki often wondered what bad karma she had earned to end up in such a place. Dust, tumbleweeds, wind and heat! She welcomed the snow, how it blanketed the bleakness with white, giving an illusion of space, so that when she looked out, she could imagine herself back in Japan, back in the farmhouse surrounded by fields, large fields that spread up to pine forests bordering the land. She didn't think of Japan often. There were years when it seemed she never had lived there. She did play the *shamisen* and also taught dancing and singing. But sometimes it seemed she had created the art herself in America.

Yuki contemplated the snow. Did it have meaning? Her first thought was its purity. Its cleansing and purifying powers. But she also could look at the truth. She could accept the fact that winter had arrived, and she was now in the winter of her life, the time when tree limbs turned barren, just as her own limbs felt stripped of flesh. She had not seen snow for so many years. Was this a sign? An omen? Was she to die in this camp? What calamity! To die in an infertile desert, where she had not seen one bright flower! Even the rocks looked tired and jagged, chipped away by tumbleweeds smashing against them. No, she would not die here. Instead, she read it to be a gift from the snow-god, a gentle covering of ugliness, a reminder of beauty and innocence.

As the snow had transformed the desert, Yuki realized she too must transform her spirit. With this illumination, she felt a lightness in her heart she had not felt since the war began. It somehow gave meaning to the true purpose of her imprisonment. She now had a goal, a reason to create new rituals and ceremonies. Singing and playing the *shamisen* were not enough.

When Dixon brought dinner from the messhall, she ate with rare gusto. Even the dry rice and rubbery Vienna sausages seemed tasty. Noticing his grandmother's new zest, Dixon asked, "What's up, Ba-chan?"

The chopsticks gently gripping a sausage stopped midair. Yuki looked at him with mock startled eyes. "What you mean?"

"Come on, Ba-chan, I know you. What's cooking?"

She studied his face before biting the sausage. She liked the square jawline and swarthy complexion, double-lidded eyes beneath feathery eyebrows that lifted at the outer corners like eagle wings. Her own complexion was pale, with pink-tinged cheeks, a complexion coveted by both men and women in Japan. Lucky she was born into a family of Niigata, a Japanese province known for its ivory-skinned women. Dixon had inherited dark skin from his mother whose parents came from Kagoshima, the southernmost part of Kyushu. Yuki knew her grandson was intelligent, a fact revealed by his high forehead and steady gaze. He sensed things, felt thoughts . . . especially hers.

Yuki wisely had chosen him early, the middle son, a quiet, gentle child lost in the shuffle of a hectic brood. A widow such as herself would need a devoted grandchild to champion her causes, a defender and willing helper to depend upon in old age. She had raised Dixon to fit that role. He was her favorite and, even though the special treatment brought cruel teasing from his siblings and a coolness from his mother, he seemed to love *obachan* despite it all.

Yuki and Dixon now lived by themselves away from the family. It had been hard living with noisy teenagers, and she never had approved of her daughter-in-law, Rosie, either. Too much like the *hakujin*, not teaching the children Japanese ways and letting them run wild like coyotes.

A few months earlier, Yuki's senses had been bombarded to the flash point. Clifford's clarinet whined in concert with the grating voices of Dolly, Frances and Mary as they attempted to imitate a singing trio called The Andrews Sisters. She had crawled under one of the iron cots, refusing to talk to anyone— even Dixon, who tried coaxing her with food and promises of walks by the creek outside the barbed wire. But she remained silent, curled like an old cat taking refuge from a pack of savage dogs.

After three days, her son and Rosie became concerned, worried they might have to report this strange behavior. What would the authorities do to someone gone crazy? The whole family tried to cajole her, lying on their stomachs, baby-talking and patting her like she was a petulant pet. But she withdrew further, hiding her head under the army blanket Dixon draped over her.

On the fourth day, when Dixon brought food, she accepted it.

"Why are you doing this?" he whispered as he shoved the tray of rice and stew toward her.

"So we have place alone," she whispered back.

"Oh . . .," his eyes round, finally understanding her antics. "But there aren't any empties on the block. They're all full, Grandma."

She smiled, eyes crinkling into slits of light beaming from the dark lair. "Go to other block! Think big, Dixie-chan." Her voice was strong. "Tell papa *ba-chan* crazy because too much people. You me live someplace away. Okay?"

"*Obachan* is not used to so much noise, Pop," Dixon said. "Shouldn't we find another place for her?"

"Is that what she wants?" His father was surprised. Why hadn't she just asked? he thought. "But there aren't any empty rooms in this block."

Dixon answered quickly . . . too quickly. "There's one small room in the next block . . . block 30. I can stay with her."

"Oh, you've already checked?"

"No . . . I didn't check with anyone. I just noticed one of the end compartments was empty. When I was over at Lincoln Takata's place."

His father mulled the situation. Dixon had spent most of his life at his mother's apartment in Japantown. It would not seem odd for the two to stay together in the next block. In fact, it was logical, he rationalized.

Feeling a tinge of guilt for the relief he knew his wife and other children would savor with his mother's departure, he, nevertheless, agreed to talk to the next block's manager and request the empty room for medical reasons.

The new cubicle was located at the end of a barrack, smaller than others, but with the advantage of double doors. They could be swung open, allowing air and light into the dark interior of rough-hewn boards, shaggy and knot-holed and smelling of tar.

Yuki had kept the room stark and sparsely furnished. Even the iron cots were missing. With extra army blankets procured by Dixon, she had fashioned some thick futons upon which they slept at night and rolled up during the day. She stored her clothes—mostly kimonos—folded in the wicker trunk she had brought from home. Dixon's were stacked in an upended wooden box that served as a closet, its opening covered by a maroon curtain splashed with pink and white flowers. A shrine rested on a low shelf along with a picture of her deceased husband, Jun, and an incense burner and small plate for food.

Dixon asked his grandmother again, "*Ba-chan*, what are you thinking about?"

"No know yet, Dixie. I thinking too much. But, no worry. I not going to die this place."

"Ba-chan! What are you doing thinking about dying!" Wasn't her act about going crazy enough? What was this about dying!

"The snow, Dixie-chan. The snow. Something tells me. Soon I know."

Dixon gathered up the dishes to return to the messhall. It sobered him to think of Obachan dying. He knew it would happen someday, but he pushed those thoughts away, clinging to the hope that when that time came, he would be a grown man and blessed with the love of another woman.

That night Yuki meditated and chanted before the picture of her long-deceased husband. She lit the last of the incense she had brought from Los Angeles. She prayed to the *kamisama* of the desert, of the rocks, of the mountains, and even of the tumbleweeds. When she finally lay down to sleep, her last conscious image was herself as a child in Japan, walking in snow, her bare feet elevated by tall *getas* (wooden clogs). Gliding like a skater on ice, she seemed to float skimming the snow to a destination she did not yet know.

She awoke at dawn. Her last thoughts before sleep had continued into a dream she remembered in clear detail. Instead of being a child, she was a young girl of fifteen. Dressed in a cotton *yukata* (kimono) and no longer wearing *getas*, she trudged up a narrow rocky path on the side of a mountain. It was winter, cold and windy, and her bare feet ached against the steely granite. Still she persevered, knowing there was a purposeful end to her journey. She rounded a bend. On the side of the mountain, a grotto appeared. It seemed carved into the rocks. Inside, steam hissed over a bubbling pool. It was a hot spring.

She knew the dream's meaning. Gratefully, she prayed an extra strong mantra and left more food than usual before the shrine.

"Dixie! Dixie-chan, get up." She shook her sleeping grandson.

His eyes snapped open. He was beginning to wonder if Ba-chan really had suffered a nervous breakdown or stroke. Her actions were so strange lately.

"We make *o furo*. Real kind. Japan style."

"*O furo*? What's that?"

"Bath . . . bath. Lots hot water."

"What's the matter with the showers?"

"Not same same, Dixie. Ba-chan have to clean heart, spirit." She pointed to her chest. "Just like snow. That's why we have snow in desert."

"Can't you take a pail or bucket into the latrines? I see other ladies doing that."

She was filled with a sense of urgency and felt impatient with Dixon's lack of enthusiasm.

"No." She almost shouted. "I teach you make *furo*. Help Ba-chan, OK?"

Dixon sat up and yawned. He saw his grandmother wrinkle her nose and wave a hand in front of her face.

"Phew . . . bad smell, Dixie. You need clean soul, too."

The first thing to decide was where to put it. The space between barracks was too public, so the only choice was in front of their apartment, beyond the double doors. It meant they would have to extend a fenced-in area that would jut out past the other barracks. Yuki disregarded what the neighbors might think of this. She was tired of thinking of others. After all, her age entitled her to some self-indulgence.

Dixon scavenged some posts and plywood boards from the edge of camp where new barracks were under construction. He built a square fence about six feet high. Inside the enclosure, Yuki shoveled snow away and raked the sand underneath. She instructed Dixon to dig a shallow hole and place around it large flat boulders he had retrieved from the creek. But the most important item was missing. The tub. It was impossible to build a water-tight tub of wood. And no metal could be found for flooring, which had to withstand the heat of a fire underneath.

For several days, Yuki was depressed. Like her mood, the weather became ominously darker. The wind howled, tearing at the new fence and rattling windows. It was a blizzard, a fierce storm that brought cold she could not remember, even in the long winters of her childhood in northern Japan.

She knelt beside the oil stove, playing *shamisen* and singing old love ballads. Perhaps the gods heard and enjoyed her plaintive songs, for it was during an especially intense rendition that she thought of the solution. Or maybe it was the smell of burning oil. Suddenly she saw her *o furo* . . . an oil drum! The perfect tub!

"Dixie!" she shouted. "Tomorrow we go find empty drum! We make *o furo* from oil drum!"

Fortunately the storm passed enabling Yuki and Dixon to search the maintenance area, where stacks of grey barrels, some streaked with tar, were mounded behind a large warehouse. Brushing away snow, he searched the pile until he found one that had contained laundry detergent. About the size of a large wine cask, it was shiny and clean and smelled sweetly of pine. A perfect tub, too narrow for one to recline in, but wide enough for someone Yuki's size to comfortably sit on a stool.

They waited until dusk to build a fire. Yuki estimated the water would be hot enough by nightfall and hoped darkness would discourage nosey neighbors from peering into the yard. Already gossipy Ikeda and self-appointed block security officer Goto had paid uninvited visits, bringing *omiyage* (gifts) of old Japanese magazines and raisins. She knew they only wanted to see what she was up to and was smugly amused at their questioning eyes scanning the stark space cleared of snow with only a shallow pit surrounded by rocks.

"Dixie-chan and I are making a wishing pool," she had said in Japanese.

Their faces stony, they bowed stiffly, uncertain how they should assess the situation. Yuki knew they thought her strange. She had heard gossip she "wasn't all there," that the camp had driven her mad.

"Gentlemen! Tell me your wishes and I will ask the water-god for you when our pool is finished!" she shouted as they left the yard.

Dixon had fashioned a wooden stool from scrap lumber and also had made a platform of slatted wood to set on the metal bottom for protection from the heat. He put them in the tub, raising the water level up to three-fourths full. Outside, he had piled three boxes—like stairs—so Yuki could climb in. He was anxious, worried she might fall or even be boiled. The tub looked like a witch's cauldron to him. But his grandmother was shuffling around the yard, a busy pigeon checking the temperature and stoking the fire. He knew she, more than anybody, could take care of herself.

"*O furo* ready, Dixie-chan. Go now. I take bath."

Yuki took off the *yukata* and hung it on a peg attached to the fence. The air cut into her naked body. Sucking in her breath, she quickly discarded the *getas* and stepped up on the boxes, grasping the tub's metal edge. She swung one leg over the rim and felt for the stool with her foot. Finding it stable, she stepped down and brought the other leg into the tub, raising the water level to her breasts, barely reaching the nipples. Gingerly she seated herself on the stool and slid her feet across the slatted raft. The water was hot, very hot and in the seated position reached up to her neck. Already she felt pimples of perspiration erupting on her forehead and upper lip.

Her head rested below the rim. She was encased in blackness and savored the solitude, a canopy of blinking diamonds overhead the only source of light. The stars seemed to hang so close, she felt she could pluck them like cherries from a tree. Not even the steamy wooden *o furo* of her childhood in Japan could match this.

Yuki stroked her arms under water, softly massaging her bony elbows and hairless armpits. She rolled the flesh of her narrow haunches and thighs, noticing how easily she could grasp a handful of skin. Even the flat breasts, once taut and round with desire and then milk, felt like deflated balloons. Heart twinging at the remembrance of her sensuality, the succulence of youth, she closed her eyes.

Her first bath in America came to mind. It was her wedding night, the first night she would sleep with her husband, a stranger she had met only a few days before. She had been a picture bride, married by proxy to Shimizu Jun, youngest son of a stone cutter from a neighboring village. Already immigrated to America seven years earlier, he had earned enough money to pay for a bride's passage.

He had met her at the dock in San Francisco, and after a day of travel by wagon, they finally had arrived at the compound of bachelors in San Jose where he had been living. She had worn a kimono for the entire trip, arriving grimy and exhausted and grateful for the *o furo* the bachelors had fired up. They had anticipated the newlyweds would appreciate a hot soak.

Yuki recalled the bath ritual. While Jun poured buckets of boiling water into a large wooden tub partially filled with cold water, she washed her face, scrubbing away white rice powder. He removed his cotton *yukata* and began soaping himself. She had kept eyes downcast, trying not to look directly at him. He was her husband but still a stranger. She had scarcely seen his face, and now she would be sharing *o furo* with him.

Steam and smoke clouded the night air. He sat down on a small wooden stool to wash his feet. Hesitantly, she had moved next to him and washed his back with a cotton cloth. His muscled, yet smooth back, felt hard. With a small basin, she scooped water from the tub and poured it over him, rinsing away the soap.

They didn't speak. He stood up and stepped into the tub, his cool body sending hisses of steam as he sat down in the hot water. He beckoned for Yuki to join him. She took off her *yukata* and sat on the stool he had just left and scrubbed herself with a strong smelling yellow soap and cloth. She was shivering.

Water spilled over the sides and onto pebbles covering the ground as she slipped into the tub. She sat down, facing him with legs bent. Their legs pressed against each other, and she could feel his taut calves and hairless skin. Through the mist, she saw sweat roll down his cheeks and drip into the water. Her own sweat slipped down her forehead and stung her eyes. Afraid and excited, she felt her heart thumping. She wondered if Jun could feel its throb through the water.

A cool wind whistled into the drum. Her eyes snapped open. Slightly embarrassed by the sensual reminiscence, she stood up and peered over the edge into the yard. Where was Dixon? Another gust forced her to sit down again. Gathering clouds had not yet covered the moon, but the stars had lost their brilliance. She stared at the milky disc, imagining its rays stroking her body like a masseuse's hand. The light engulfed her whole body . . . the tub . . . then the yard and barracks. She saw it envelop the block, the fire-break, the camp . . . the country . . . even the world!

Softly and quietly, snow began falling. Delicate flakes floated from the now dark sky. Yuki studied an intricate flake as it descended, following the wafer of ice—so full of its own life and beauty, so unaware of the imminent end when its free-falling journey from heaven would finish in a metal drum filled with hot water. She watched the flake flutter close to her face. It seemed to dance and jump, almost mischievously. Then it fell into the water near her breasts.

"*Obachan!*" Dixon shouted through the open door. "Are you Okay?"

"Me Okay," she shouted back. "I get out. Your turn *o furo*. This bath number one bath, Dixie-chan. Best *o furo* in camp."

Dixon closed the door, allowing privacy for his tiny grandmother, who was rising up through the steam.

———

Jeanne Wakatsuki Houston is the co-author of the book and screenplay, FAREWELL TO MANZANAR, based upon her family's experience during and after the World War II interment of Japanese Americans. Ms. Wakatsuki views herself as "late-comer" to a writing career—a rehabilitated survivor of a 1950's mentality and a Japanese cultural background which valued the silent and domestic woman. She writes mainly about Asian American experience and is now working on short stories spinning out of the internment and a novel spanning three generations of Japanese American women. Married to writer James D. Houston, they live in Santa Cruz, California, and are parents to three children—Corinne, oldest daughter and twins Joshua and Gabrielle.

Howard Ikemoto

Hisaye Yamamoto

EJU-KEI-SHUNG!
EJU-KEI-SHUNG!

A Memoir

> *Ching Chong Chinaman*
> *Sitting on a fence*
> *Trying to make a*
>   *dollar*
> *Chop-chop all day.*
> *"Eju-kei-shung! Eju-*
>   *kei-shung!"*
> *That's what they*
>   *say . . .*
>   *–Lawson Inada, "Chink"*

EDUCATION WAS emphasized by Issei parents, too, but I only know this from hearsay.

Our own parents were not all that insistent about bettering

one's lot through book learning—in fact, I gathered that my father didn't see any necessity of higher education for women. But they did point out that my first two brothers, who came three and five years after me, were given the Japanese names of Tsuyoshi and Tsutomu, which together can also be read as *benkyo*, or study. Kyo was born before Ben, however, so the interpretation must have been in afterthought.

Besides, they were never called Tsuyoshi and Tsutomu except at Japanese school. Ordinarily they went by John and James, or Johnny and Jemo were what friends and family called them. (John and James, identified as the fishermen sons of Zebedee, were the names of Biblical brothers, too. In fact, Christ Himself gave the two disciples together the name Boanerges, meaning "sons of thunder," but I don't know whether He ever explained why. Perhaps because Zebedee's wife sought special favors for her boys, like having them sit to His right and left when He came into His Kingdom, so He considered her a thunderous woman? But another source says the fellows came right out and asked for this privilege themselves.)

But even without any propaganda to propel me, I loved school and on occasion did pretty well. Valedictorian here, salutatorian there, skip a grade here and skip a grade there, I was a sixteen-year-old with huge learning gaps when I enrolled at Compton Junior College for the equivalent of my first college year. But I see now that reading, writing, and arithmetic, revelation though they were, were only the plain backdrop into which the incidentals were woven in rich detail and living color. These were the more valuable lessons in being a human being, and these lessons seem to have found me an obtuse pupil, going through life in a semi-conscious state, unaware of the context of actions.

One morning in kindergarten, a boy comes in late. It is not the first time. He holds in his hand a fistful of white Jesus' breath and proffers it to the teacher. But she is angry. She shakes him slightly. "Where did you pick these flowers?" He admits he got them from the schoolyard. This angers her even more, and she sends him home, telling him not to come back without his mother.

Then, strange to say, a girl comes in late the following day with a similar bunch of flowers, which she freely confesses as being from the school garden also. I don't recall the teacher getting angry, or even paying that much attention, but I was aghast at the girl's daring. Perhaps her case, more complicated, was taken care of privately in the principal's office, but after a while she disappeared from our school for a year or so. When she came back, she seemed to be a half-grade above the rest of us, lining up with somewhat older children. We asked her how she had managed this coup and she grinned in triumph. She gave all the credit to her mother, who seemed to be her only parent.

But she was a person who had already learned wisdom. Her name was Myrtle and she was plump. We would tease her, calling her Fatty Arbuckle. "Sure," she would agree happily, "thanks a lot." And she seemed to mean it; she was truly content to be compared to the famous comedian. So we weren't able to make her squirm at all.

In kindergarten, another significant event occurred when a Japanese friend named Sumi brought her little sister to school one day. I, who only had little brothers around at home, was enchanted with this life-size, walking-talking Japanese doll. At recess, I carried her off to the patio and held her on my lap, delighting in the way she looked and the way she talked. Suddenly, she rocked backwards and fell from my lap over onto the concrete of the patio. I was sure I heard her head break.

She began to scream bloody murder. I was never so frightened in my life. Her sister came running. The teacher came running. Probably the whole school came running. I was afraid I had killed her, but she kept up the awful screaming, and I didn't know the English to convey to the teacher what had happened.

I don't remember what happened after that, but I carried a burden of guilt around with me for years, and I would never, never, hold anybody's baby if I could possibly avoid it. Finally relief came about a dozen years later when I happened to read that a girl of the same name, from the same locality, was taking part in a student fashion show at Bullock's. I only happened to notice the information in the newspaper because a friend of mine, staying overnight, was going to be mistress-of-ceremonies for the program the next day. The girl in the paper had made the dress she was modeling. She was lovely enough to be in a fashion show! I had not caused irreparable damage, after all: she was alive and well, not an addlepated mess.

It was in kindergarten, too, that one of my outstanding traits, physical cowardice, began to surface. At five I was tiny and never very good on the school playground equipment. The teeter-totter was pretty safe, but the monkey rings were too difficult, likewise the parallel ladder. I envied the others who gracefully swung from ring to ring or traversed the ladder in jig time, with large callouses on their palms where I would only blister. The swing was not too bad. I would carefully back up with the swing seat as far as I could go, then swing forward, but I never bothered to pump very high. One day one of the Sawai sisters, the younger one, came over to the swing to give me a good ride. She really put her heart into it and I began to go higher and higher, getting more and more terrified. Finally when I could stand the altitude no longer, I turned loose and jumped off.

Luckily, I only skinned my nose slightly on the gritty playground surface, but my friend was mystified. After school, when we all got off the bus together, I ran ahead to avoid her questions. But I could hear her voice pursuing me from a distance, "Why did you jump like that? Don't you know you could break your neck? What made you jump . . . ?" But I turned around and laughed, then ran for home, refusing to admit my cowardice, not realizing that my fear had driven me to a far more dangerous feat than swinging high.

In the first grade I began to learn how to read and write English and my parents were very proud. As soon as I was able to write passably, after many sessions of writing dense up-and-down bars and connected circles, off went painstakingly composed letters to the two sets of grandparents in Japan: "Dear Grandfather and Grandmother: How are you? I am fine. Yours truly."

And for years, Mama and Papa were able to quote verbatim the first story I ever read in English: "Zah dah seh narai. Zah kyah seh narai . . ." And the little red hen, time after time, said she would do the job herself then, and she did, even to eating up all the bread she had baked. A very satisfying tale, I thought, with the dog and cat and those other lazies going hungry just as they damn well deserved.

For some reason, part of the first grade was spent in another school, and I remember the last day there. In the excitement we rush pell-mell through the long closet to grab our sweaters and lunchpails on the way out. In the mad scramble, my hip collides sharply with the corner of a stored desk. The pain makes me stop and cry. The summoned teacher is moved to pick me up and carry me back into the classroom. She sits down in one of the children's seats, cradles me on her lap and cuddles me. "Ah," she explains to the children who are gathering around us in curiosity. "The poor dear, she's crying because it's the last day of school!" Her own inner bruise transferred to me, she rocks me tenderly. She gives me a picture book to take home for my very own, such sweet consolation.

It was not outright fraud, you know. I do not think my English at six was flexible enough to go into the details of the situation. But there is more than one lesson connected with that incident. The value of dissembling? The value of silence? The realization that there were some teachers who truly loved teaching, for whom the prospect of school vacation was a desolation? Or maybe only the side benefits of being wounded.

It was at this same school that I spent the longest day of my whole life. I think it was Memorial Day and the bus must have come to pick us up in the morning because I don't know how else I would have gotten to school. The project was for the whole student body to walk over to the ocean with flowers, in order to pay tribute to those who had died at sea. I straggled along with the others all right and got to the pier, from where we threw our posies to float on the water. But somehow, as I made my way back to school, everyone else seemed to drop away, one by one, and I arrived back at school all by myself. And the school building was locked.

It gradually came to me that there was to be no school that day, that there would be no bus coming to take me home, that I was marooned with no help in sight. I must not have understood the entire announcement the previous day. So I remained there the rest of the afternoon, maybe changing my seat occasionally from one side of the cement stairs to the other, maybe playing hopscotch on the sidewalk from time to time, maybe going up to the school entrance and peering in. I don't recall anyone passing by. But eventually my father came in the car, looking for me, and I was rescued at last.

It was in the cafeteria of this same school that I saw an older dark-haired girl praying before and after she ate, making some odd gestures in front of her face, then holding her hands together, then making the same gestures again. Because of this ritual, she even seemed to eat reverently, and out of the corner of my eye I watched her slow mastication with great admiration, stowing any questions about her irregular behavior in that pigeonhole in the back of my mind.

I think it was about the third grade, back at South School, that I first encountered the joy of being read to. *Dr. Doolittle* and *The Wizard of Oz* burst into my consciousness in this way, and even now I can't distinguish between the excitement of hearing these stories read aloud and the sheer rapture of anticipating the next chapter.

Meanwhile, I was also learning other things from the anger of my teachers. Once, during an art session, I was distracted by some old mucilage that had been left to dry on my desk by a previous occupant. I tried to remove the dried flakes of paste, ever so gingerly lifting at them with the tip of my scissors. Engrossed in this delicate task, I suddenly became aware that the teacher was standing right over me. There was fire in her eye. In front of the class I was held up as an example of the worst kind of vandal, a destroyer of school property, and made to sit alone off to one corner of the room. I still did not trust my English enough to explain the reason for my seeming criminality. But I did not weep, however. Taking a leaf from Myrtle, I clowned, making faces for the enjoyment of my classmates when they looked toward the seat of my disgrace. After awhile, the teacher reluctantly allowed me to resume my regular seat. I sensed that she did not think I was taking my punishment seriously. But deep down, I was thoroughly humiliated and never attempted to clean school property again.

I remember most clearly the anger of Miss Spring, the white-haired principal who was also our teacher. Her passion was a total surprise because she was a small fine-boned creature who could have posed for anybody's sweet lavender-and-lace grandmother. I no longer remember the cause of the commotion. Maybe the boy named Billy was tardy, but whatever his lapse, she grabbed him bodily in order to convey the extent of her wrath. She shook him mightily, with such energy that as he attempted to wrest free of the indignity, they both toppled over onto the floor.

She was even angrier, if that was possible, after she picked herself up. Billy was put outside to stand in the hall, but her fury had not entirely abated. She passed out scratch paper, so figuring that it must be for the next project in our arithmetic book, I set to folding it as the book instructed, feeling a bit proud that I was ahead of her next requirement. Never would she have reason to wrestle with *me* and shake *my* teeth loose.

Oh, woe! *She* had meant the paper for writing and here I had gone ahead and folded it in small squares! I timidly asked for another piece of paper. And the waves of her leftover wrath splashed over me, wretched gun-jumper that I was.

There were also lessons to be learned in the school cafeteria—heavenly smells of vegetable soup, scalloped potatoes, roast beef hash with gravy!—where the teachers seemed to be on duty as helpers. The first time I bought lunch I asked for *charge*, as I had been instructed to bring money back home, and the teacher at the cash register corrected me with a laugh. I had a harder time explaining what I didn't want to be served. I had noticed several students before me coming away from the counter with a green onion shoot decorating their trays, and it was inconceivable that I eat a raw green onion. I only knew it by the name, *negi*, so it was hard to explain that I didn't want one put on my tray. I think what I said was, "I don't want *negi*. So I held up the line for quite awhile before the teacher understood about my distaste for onion. As it turned out, green onions were entirely optional and it had been unnecessary for me to go through all the sign language and contortions, not to mention the anxiety, to get out of having a scallion with my lunch.

Once a boy by mistake grabbed my lunch, instead of his own, in the cloakroom and I was distressed by this first-time complication. The teacher took me down to the cafeteria and we found this boy wolfing down my sandwich of homemade strawberry jam and peanut butter. Obviously he thought his mother had given him a treat. It was no treat to me, just plain everyday lunch, but when the teacher had the happy solution

of me eating the boy's lunch, I understood why he was so delighted with mine. His sandwich, cut in four, was spread with a
thin amber jelly which had a queer taste, slightly tart. For all I
know now, this may have been a gourmet jelly, guava maybe,
but at the time I felt sorry that *hakujin* kids had such pallid
fare to look forward to every day.

To the east of the school was a hill which in Spring would
be covered with bright California poppies, Indian paintbrush
with its pink velvety ermines, purple lupines, yellow cinque-
foil. One day the whole school gathered in the yard facing the
hill to watch an eclipse of the sun. A few of the kids had strips
of film negative through which to watch the phenomenom, but
most of us looked skyward with naked eye, as I remember. I
don't know whether we had been warned about the danger of
observing an eclipse of the sun without proper protection, but
with my limited English I probably wouldn't have understood
anyway. The sun gradually became a crescent and less, then
disappeared for a second, during which the whole day grew
eerily dark, but it was over instantly, as though it had never
happened at all. I can't say I was impressed.

All this time I had also been going to Japanese school on
Saturdays, earnestly reciting *a-i-u-e-o, ka-ki-ku-ke-ku, sa-shi-
su-se-so,* along with the rest of the syllabery. There was a white
girl who studied with us and her name was Genevieve Wells.
An amiable girl, she once told us she had an aunt whose last
name was Bell, so she made fun of the combination, calling
herself Genevieve Wells Bells. It seems to me her younger
brother also attended our language classes. At the time, we accepted her without question, but in later years I wondered
whether she had ever made use of the Japanese, whether she
had pursued it farther, or whether she had put it away with
the rest of her childhood, to take out now and then to examine
as a curious relic.

One Christmas at Japanese school stands out. The Christmas program always meant for us a large tree and red mesh
stockings filled with oranges, apples, nuts, hard candy of every
kind and color—striped, corrugated, plumply filled, curlicued,
as well as those little tubular ones that had a tiny flower im-
printed in the middle. Each of us took part in the program,
reciting, singing, or dancing in Japanese kimonos.

On this particular program, the older students were going to put on a dramatization of the legend of the fisherman who comes upon a goddess taking a dip in the stream. She leaves her gossamer gown hung on a tree, and he holds it for ransom, refusing to return it unless she will grant him a boon. The Japanese school version had a goddess with a bevy of companions, all dressed in soft gowns of pastel blue, pink, yellow, green and mauve, with their stockings of the same color.

Do they wear wings? That detail is not clear. Maybe, half their age, I observe and admire as they ready for the play. A kind of radiance and warmth seems to envelop them as they flit about like many-colored butterflies, laughing, giggling, chatting, one or two bending over to pull on the silk stockings that match the sheer dresses of floating voile.

My mind's eye holds the picture yet, likening it to one of bridesmaids before a wedding or to a painting by Degas after another visit backstage at the ballet. Lovely nubile girls, full of joy and anticipation, aquiver on the threshold of womanhood. I envy them, even though I know that I will arrive at their age soon enough, that adolescence will come accompanied by its own peculiar pain and madness.

Joy Yamanchi

This spring has been pretty special because we became grandparents for the third time and great-grandparents for the first time. So we've been busy getting in some quality cuddle time. Both babies, a boy and a girl, are multi-cultural (between them, they're Japanese, Chinese, Norwegian, English, French, Mexican and that's just to start with). No doubt they'll be marking the Other box when required to state their ancestry, although I hope such distinctions will have become obsolete by the time they reach school. Wishful thinking? The future is shaped by our desires and aspirations.

My last published piece was "Peacocks" for *Hokubei Mainichi's* 1994 New Year issue, and I'm scribbling from time to time on a few more ideas, none of which seem very important alongside the two new babies.

William P. Osborn and
Sylvia Watanabe

A CONVERSATION WITH
HISAYE YAMAMOTO

FOR OVER FORTY YEARS, Hisaye Yamamoto has been publishing
stories in major literary and mass circulation periodicals like
the *Partisan-* and *Kenyon Reviews, Carleton Miscellany*, and
Harper's Bazaar, as well as in periodicals whose audience is
more specifically Asian American, like *Rafu Shimpo, Hokkubei
Mainichi*, and *Pacific Citizen*. She has been well anthologized,
among many other places in the *Heath Anthology of American
Literature* and Greenfield Review Press's recent *Home to Stay:
Stories by Asian American Women*, and has been noted several
times in the annual lists of the best American fiction; "Yoneko's
Earthquake" appeared in *Best American Short Stories, 1952*.
That story and "Seventeen Syllables" were combined in a re-
cent American Playhouse presentation entitled *Hot Summer
Winds*. Among her many awards are a John Hay Whitney
Foundation Opportunity Fellowship and the American Book
Award for Lifetime Achievement from the Before Columbus
Foundation.

In 1988, her most substantial short works were gathered in *Seventeen Syllables and Other Stories* (Kitchen Table: Women of Color Press). Some of the pieces in this collection represent experience that is specifically ethnic. There are views of life in a World War II Japanese American internment camp, for instance, and of the anti-Asian sentiment currently on the increase in American cities. Other pieces don't depend so much for their tension on the ethnic makeup of the central character as they do on the fact that she is female. How does a wife with children come to an accord with a husband who suddenly begins to gamble? How can a woman transmit to her teenage daughter her fear that the daughter will repeat the mother's mistakes? Binding these two thematic trends are the relations of these women with men whose behavior they seem barely able to comprehend: many of these stories are about the relations between the sexes.

Hisaye Yamamoto was born in Redondo Beach, California, in 1921. Her parents were Japanese immigrants, and the family was interned in the concentration camp at Poston, Arizona, in 1942. In 1944, she and two brothers were relocated to Massachusetts, but were brought back to Poston when another brother was killed in combat in Italy. She is married to Anthony DeSoto and resides in Los Angeles.

Though some material has been added through an exchange of letters after 1992 engagements at Yale and the University of California at Santa Barbara, most of the conversation that follows took place in March, 1991, in Grand Rapids. Ms. Yamamoto, a devout non-flyer, was on a tour of Michigan by train that included readings and conversations with students and faculty at the University of Michigan in Ann Arbor and Grand Valley State University in Allendale. She speaks in a low register, her sentences measured—there are pauses between phrases; her laughter is contagious and delightful.

In a recent issue of The Northwest Nikkei Review, *you responded pretty vigorously to the question, "Do publishers discriminate against Asian American males."*

Well, I don't think that the implicit charge was valid at all. David Mura and Garrett Hongo are being published, you know, and Frank Chin has several books coming out in a row. I guess what they mean is the best sellers like Amy Tan and Maxine Hong Kingston—that there hasn't been an Asian American male writer who's got the same acclaim, yeah? Hm. Well, I guess they should just wait. Their turn will come. Because they all write well, the ones who've been published.

Is this kind of direct response usual for you? That is, when you write fiction, do you often say to yourself something like, Well, I'm aiming for this particular audience? What do you think of the stand taken by some other Asian American writers, that priority must be given to developing an Asian American readership?

I guess I'm just writing to please myself, express myself, just trying to put down whatever is stuck in my craw as best I can. You know, get it out of my system. I've never thought of writing for anybody. I don't think you can write aiming at a specifically Asian American audience if you want to write freely. No, you just express yourself without thinking of that angle. I think more and more Asian American writers will be doing that, you know—like this sansei generation. Cynthia Kadohata—the fact that she's sansei doesn't figure that importantly. She might mention the Asian American background in passing but that's not the main thrust of her work.

That seems related to the point made by Bharati Mukherjee at a recent reading at the University of Michigan. She said that though she writes from her experience as an Asian American, she would like to be thought of as an American writer. How do you see yourself—how would you like to be seen?

I don't even bother to tell people I'm Japanese American anymore, because that's not what they want to know. I just say I'm Japanese. Not pridefully or anything, just a statement of fact. Of course I don't care for generalizations about any race. I know there will always be those who see the Asian in me first. But I go to the supermarket, the dentist, the malls, the museums, etc., without thinking about others' attitudes about me, and so far haven't felt any particular hostility. But yeah, I think any writer would like to be generally accepted, and not just on his or her own ethnic background. People don't say of Saul Bellow or Philip Roth, I'm going to read this Jewish writer, you know. So, well, I think it's okay to want to be generally accepted. But it's the general public that decides. Some will read my work because they consider it a valid part of American literature, or some will read it because it's about a specific ethnic background. Look at Amy Tan—wasn't she thirty-some weeks on the best-seller list? And it wasn't just Chinese Americans reading her. Everybody was. She will be studied as an ethnic writer, but some obviously won't be bound by that.

Salman Rushdie says that he's really interested in the question of how you bring anything new into the world—in literature and also in culture. And he says of his own work that he sees that newness is being brought into the world with the mixing of cultures.

It's the same newness that comes from intermarriages, right? There's a new person, a new literature, new kind of person, new kind of literature. But only if a new human being evolves—and there's not much chance of that—will racism disappear. So I guess we're stuck with the knowledge that there will always be people who will find us different and menacing and sub-human. Or quaint, at best. But there will be some who will accept us as fellow human beings, right? Maybe eventually, if the planet survives, everybody will be a product of this blending of races. Well, like Hawaii, you know—everybody gets along pretty well, except for the ordinary human controversies.

At your Grand Valley reading of "Yoneko's Earthquake," I was aware that this process seems to be exemplified in the character of Marpo, the Hosoumes' hired hand.

Well, no such person existed and I really laid it on. I gave him all kinds of attributes that probably no one person would have, but I think he's the product of all the influences that he was exposed to. And being a bright person, he absorbed a lot of different cultural attributes. If he sang Irish songs it was because he felt some affinity for them. And he was intent on developing himself physically to the fullest. Anyway, if he had been wealthy and could have endorsed all these things, then who knows what kind of superman he might have been. Even there he's a kind of superman. Maybe the future will fill up with these Super Men and Women (laughs). Isn't that what Nietzsche wrote about (laughs)? But he didn't mean it that way!

But do you see yourself as being part of this creation of something new, having been shaped by different traditions?

I guess I'm a product of every influence that I was exposed to. Of course some things I was more interested in than others. I don't think I've put half of that down yet in writing. Like when I encountered the French language, I was just smitten, you know—I loved this. I expanded that interest as much as I could—going to French movies and singing French songs, buying French records. That was way in the past, but I guess I still retain some of that, and I thought that was my language—which it isn't; I can't speak it. And, oh, I loved all the languages. Every language just fascinated me. The residue is that I believe I understand English words better than most people—from having studied all these various things. The roots of the words. That's nothing to brag about (laughs).

What we're getting into now raises the issue of when an openness to or embracing of other cultures becomes a form of appropriation. In Home to Stay *we included a story by Marnie Mueller, who isn't Japanese, but whose father had worked in a camp and who knew a lot of the Japanese families. A number of critics asked why we had included that story. They felt she was trying to appropriate the camp experience without having gone through it. The sense was that only Japanese Americans who lived through that time should write about it.*

Oh no no, she lived through it. I mean, it's part of her experience—obviously a very traumatic part of it—so she should write about it. Nobody should tell her, You can't write about it because you're not Japanese. No, she's perfectly entitled.

I guess the question we're asking you is, When is it permissible to cross that limit, for a white woman to write about the Japanese camp experience, for instance, or for a movie like Come See the Paradise *to use the internment experience as a vehicle for a hero who is white?*

Well, the impression I get from all the reviews in the Japanese American newspapers is that it's thumbs down on that movie because it's told from a white viewpoint. I haven't seen it yet. But I don't think any writer has to get permission from anybody. Just write about what *you* know and what is important to you. Nobody's going to write so that there's no criticism, so you just plunge ahead and put down what you want to put down. I mean, you don't need a license to write about the Japanese if that's what you want to write about. Anybody can write about anything they want. That's what the freedoms guarantee.

When Sakarauchi, the Japanese government official, first came out with his remark about the laziness and illiteracy of American workers, Michigan Senator Donald Riegle said, The arrogance of that remark is the same as the arrogance that led to the bombing of Pearl Harbor. A couple of days later, the prime minister of Japan said something about the U.S. lacking what it takes to compete in the international market. Then, Senator Hollings told workers in his home state of South Carolina that they should draw a map of Japan with a mushroom cloud over it, and label it, Made in America by lazy and illiterate workers; tested in Japan. What do you make of this?

For all the good it will do, the Japanese American Citizens' League and other Japanese American groups have taken note of the increased anti-Japanese and anti-Asian activity and issued statements about it. I don't think the message gets to the perpetrators. When I gave a talk at Yale, quite a few students made reference to the increased hostility towards Asians. I didn't hear any specific references to Japan-bashing, but then I was there for the 50th year observance of the internment, so I was kind of insulated, I guess, from non-Japanese attitudes. When I was at UC Santa Barbara in February, some of the students and staff spoke of their apprehension when going out in public, because of the Japan bashing and the increase in anti-Asian incidents generally. The U.S. has a long way to go in its treatment of minorities, including the descendants of the original inhabitants, and so does Japan. I believe the Japanese leaders are ignorant; Japan has a long-standing tradition of treating outsiders—Koreans, for instance—badly. And when you get an Iacocca blaming the Japanese for the failure of the auto industry here, it just adds fuel to the racist embers that have been smoldering all along.

(At this point we stopped for coffee and Ms. Yamamoto had a cigarette. When we began again, we talked about her fiction and working methods.)

"Yoneko's Earthquake," happens to be my favorite story in your collection. Do you have one you like best?

I really have no favorites. Because they're all in my past, you know. And if I didn't like best the one I was working on now, I wouldn't bother with it. But once *it's* done, it's not going to be my favorite either. No, I really have no favorites.

Could you say something, then, about process—about how you work?

I write with pen on paper—yellow, white, whatever's available. When the kids kept me busy, I would just scribble anywhere. I've got scraps of paper right now that I've got little things written on that maybe I can use. I like the Write Brothers, the fine point. It's a cheap pen that I can buy by the box. The best one I ever had I inherited from my cousin in Japan who died of tuberculosis at the age of eighteen. When she died just after the war, her parents distributed some of her things to her cousins in Japan and the United States, and I got this beautiful Pilot pen, which was perfect. Usually with ballpoints, they control you instead of you controlling them, but this pen wrote just the way I wanted to write. Then when I got Paul, one day he was playing with it and he banged it down on the wooden chair, and that was the end of my perfect pen. I've never had one as good. But I don't mind the Write Brothers fine point.

Anyway, when I've got a draft pretty well written down, I go to the typewriter. And then that probably goes through lots of versions and rewritings. When I was young I used to just dash a story off, you know—maybe even the first copy was good enough. I think when you're young you've got this over-confidence, exuberance or whatever, and when you get older you begin to doubt yourself a lot more and know that you know less and less. So you try to be a lot more careful, I believe. Funny thing is that these stories that I dashed off are the ones that are being reprinted. People don't pay much attention to the recent stuff. So either I wrote better then, or people want to look at examples of Pioneer Japanese American Writing.

"Seventeen Syllables" and "Yoneko's Earthquake"—these are stories that you dashed off! How long did they take you to write?

Not very long. Like "Brown House," I don't even know if I even retyped it. Could've been a first draft. I mean it was *fast,* you know. Maybe I was full of stuff I wanted to write down, too. I had a lot more to write about.

I'm thinking that because of the title and the fact that the Black man gets in the car with the family and is driven off, "The Brown House" might have something underlying it that was part of that material you had so much of early on—something to do with race.

Well, I was asked to write something for the holiday issue of *The Pacific Citizen,* so I dashed it off. And then when I reread it, it seemed like, well, this is not too bad. So I sent it to *Harper's Bazaar* and they sent me $300 for it, and that was, way back then, you know, lots of money. So I didn't particularly think about it being ethnic at the time—just a story. But I don't know, there must have been an actual brown house. Yeah, there was, but there was no gambling there . . . that I know of. Was there (laughs)? I wonder where I got that.

Where do your ideas for stories come from? How does a story come into being?

Well, I guess the germ of the idea for a piece starts maybe years and years back, and then it stays in the back of your mind, and then one day it seems ready to put down. I don't understand the process myself. I can't say it's inspiration. It's unconscious . . . although you can't really say that because you're writing deliberately.

If you have more than one idea competing for your writing time and energy, how do you choose the one to go to work on next?

I guess you pick the idea that seems to have kind of jelled—

that seems kind of ready to put down. I suppose that's the way it works.

Does this mean that you have the story partly in mind by the time you start writing it?

Oh yeah, uh-huh. Well, at least a vague outline of it, you know. My friend Wakako Yamauchi said that once I told her, get a good beginning and a good ending and fill in the middle. And maybe that's what I used to do. I could have been just kidding (laughs)! But I work over every bit of it now. Right now I have this story that I'm writing called "Florentine Gardens," which is kind of a play on words, because there is a Florentine Gardens in Hollywood—a nightspot. But it doesn't refer to that at all. And I have a quotation picked out already from Mary McCarthy, which is, "To spend May in Florence is the foreigner's dream." And then the whole story kind of substantiates that and also refutes it at the same time. I haven't written it in order, but I've got most of it written. The problem is how to put it together, because it's gotten so long. And then despite myself, it involves quite a bit of Japanese American history. I don't know if it's going to be unwieldy like "Las Vegas Charlie," which people have said is badly constructed.

There was a conjunction between the nightclub and the epigraph. Was the history part of the mix too?

No, not at all, but as I wrote it I found out I was writing about the camps and prewar. I don't know if I can include all that, because all that about the camps has been pretty well written about. But as it affected this one family that I'm writing about, maybe it's a little different.

It sounds as if your outline doesn't bind you.

No, no, no. New things creep in, you know. As you try to write down one idea, others occur to you and you start adding them. And this one—if I include everything that I've already written down—is going to be more of a novella (laughs). So I'll either have to leave it that way or really prune it. And I haven't made up my mind which I'm going to do yet.

I'd like to return to the question of process. Where do you write, and when?

I usually write in my chair, the same chair that I watch TV from, and sometimes I'm watching TV as I write. Well, my husband's watching something and he likes to comment on it. You know, you have to keep track of what's going on. And meanwhile, I'm scribbling in between.

Sounds like evening.

Or during the day, when I have to sit down. Maybe something occurs to me while I'm washing dishes or putting clothes in the washer. Then I go over there and scribble a little bit and go back to my chores.

And revision—do you have an office where the typewriter is, or is that out in the middle of things as well?

Well, the electronic typewriter is on the desk and it doesn't work. I just don't get along good with electronic stuff. I never could work that electronic typewriter. I never felt comfortable with it. So I got this manual, which I have in the bedroom, and that's relatively new. I've written one story on it I guess. It's open too, and it's collecting dust. I don't know if it's going to work when I get down to using it again.

How do you know when you have a story?

I guess it must be some kind of instinct. Oh, it's just like cooking food. You have a pretty good idea of when it's ready to serve, right? After you mix everything in and put it on the stove, you don't want to overcook it. But you don't really know *until* it's finished how it's going to come out, because the events and people you write about seem to take the story away from you and proceed on their own. When you finish, sometimes you're surprised at the way things turned out. A lot of times, an ending turns out so bleak, you know, or kind of suspended. And I really want to make people laugh, if anything. Evidently, something in me wants to acknowledge that at bottom, life is pretty grim.

You've said that you're not especially interested in the long

*form, but you do write poetry. What can you accomplish in po-
etry that you can't in fiction?*

Well, I think poetry is *the* highest form of expression— literary expression, I should say, since I find music maybe even
better. But that's what I would really like to write—poetry. I
understand William Faulkner said that too, but I don't know if
I've read any poems that he's written. I prefer the traditional. I
was just totally taken with this Vikram Seth—his novel in son-
net form called *The Golden Gate*. That's absolutely my most favorite Asian American work. It has a sansei heroine who is really appealing. But in poetry, I think you can express truth in a
few words. Like that section in Matthew Arnold, that says,
*Ah, love, let us be true/To one another! for the world, which
seems* . . . Oh, I can't even say it anymore. It's just that certain
poems have impressed me as the perfect way of saying something—that that's it and there's no more to be said about it.
With fiction you take a lot more words and you don't know
whether it's understood or not. People say, What are you driving at? They don't always get it, whereas in those few words
in a poem, it's all there. I remember, during the war, in camp,
memorizing John Donne—that section that begins, *Never ask
for whom the bell tolls.* I'd walk to work memorizing it and it
seemed the perfect expression of *that* idea. I guess it had been
made popular because of the Hemingway novel, but that's
when I first became aware of it. Elizabeth Bishop is my favorite poet. I've read and reread her. She had this inimitable
way of expressing herself that nobody else approached. She's
the only one you can go to for that way of saying that particular thing.

*You just mentioned music as a means of expression. Is there a
relationship between music and writing?*

Well, I'm a very rudimentary musician. I tried to play the
violin when I was in high school and I tried to teach myself
how to play the piano, but I never got very far. A friend noted
that I didn't usually go for the whole piece. The parts that I
would play over and over were the lyrical passages and I guess
that's the way I would like to write. You know, lyrically, although the subjects I choose you can't always write lyrically.

A moment ago you also connected writing with cooking.

Oh, I've done so much cooking over the years, you know, with five kids and with my mother dying early. I did a lot of cooking for my father and my brothers, and so I guess it's natural that I compare writing to cooking. I usually enjoy it, but my daughter tells her friends that I am not a good cook. When they invite their friends over for Christmas or Thanksgiving (laughs), they tell them, There'll be food, but don't expect much, you know, because she never knows how it's going to turn out.

We know you have a beautiful garden. What you say about cooking sounds a little like gardening, doesn't it?

Well, like a further part of gardening, I guess, is just going out there and grubbing around in the ground. I like it several days after a rain when the weeds will come out easy. It's so delightful to just be able to pull the weeds.

THE INTERVIEWERS:

William P. Osborn's fiction is published in *ACM, Carolina Quarterly, Gettysburg Review, Mississippi Review, Western Humanities Review,* and other literary magazines. He is the former fiction editor of *Mid-American Review* and is now an associate professor of English at Grand Valley State University in Allendale, Michigan.

Sylvia A. Watanabe co-edited *Home to Stay: Stories by Asian American Women.* Her fiction has appeared in numerous journals, and "Talking to the Dead" was selected for *The O. Henry Awards: Prize Stories 1991.* Her collection of the same name was a finalist for the PEN Faulkner Award.

Ruth Shigezawa

THREE STEPS A MINUTE

YOU SANSEI: coddled, soft. Listen to this. Think of rising at five, stumbling out the tent, the barracks, the boxcars. Those strawberry fields, stretch for miles, can't see no end. There you be, alone in section—picking, picking. Bend down, snap stems, put fruit in basket: gently, gently. No pay if you mash. Over and over. How long you think you could last, eh, kid? Eight hours? Hah, not hours, not even one. *You*—soft kid like you—I say two minutes. Then go nuts, that's what I say. You try it, come on, right now. Bend down, pick strawberries from floor, put in basket, search next plant. No pick green, no pay. No pick bug-eaten, bird-eaten ones. No pay. Pick-pick-pick. Come on, you! This foreman yelling at you—work faster. Eh! Not even thirty seconds. Eh, you squish one, no pay. You put inside basket too rough, mess up five berries underneath. No pay. This not salary job, you know. Piecework, pay by the basket. You never going earn your wages. How you going buy food? I timing you. How about that? Two minutes and you straighten up. Pretty smart, eh, for old man? No, I not laughing. (Two minutes, hee,

hee). No, not laughing! Hey, packing your stuff? You going? Guess kid is mad, don't like old man show him up. Ok ok ok! Try wait. I polite now. I answer questions. Yes, be serious. Yes, serious job, your book. Oh, that's it—doc-to-ral disser-tation. That mouthful sound like two-day meal of bad air. Ok, ok. Deadline when? Next year? Hooo, that a long time away. I know, I know. You told me, plenty times. Yeah, yeah, June 1970 you wanna graduate. Ok, ok! From now on—you ask, I answer. Sure, I wanna help. You gonna stay for dinner or something? I got tuna fish catfood to share—want some?

Your machine still on? Yeah? Ok. I serious now. Japanese name? Don't remember. You speak any Japanese? Too bad. I talk better in *Nihongo*. What for you study history then if you don't know language? Ok, ok, no need get pissed. Ben Inaba— that's all I gone by these last fifty-sixty years. Why so surprised? Don't remember my real name, nothing wrong with that. What's to be ashamed? Ben is good name. Short, sweet, something boss can say. See, there you go again. What the hell is wrong with having a name other people can say? It gets you jobs. Ok, next question.

What do I think about? What a question! Is that all you *sansei* college kids do, ask stupid questions? By time you *sansei*, third generation, come around, your mind soft. Ok, ok, I answer! I don't think about nothing. Now, don't go sour on me, I just joking around. You college kids don't know how to laugh either. Too busy protesting, growing long hair, wearing beads, waving flowers. Ah hah! You wonder how old man knows all about that. 1969, hoo, don't think I know that? You something else. You think I stick to this stinking room, all day, all night? I get around, I watch tv in stores on Broadway Avee-noo. Hear people talk. No, don't read English good. I hear people talk, ok? If you listen more, maybe you learn something.

Ok. What I think about? Think about walking. Yeah, how fast I walk. Used to be, I walk ten miles for nothing. I just do it. Used to be, I one strong sonuvabitch. Now, I use cane and walk slow, maybe three steps a minute, seems like. People huff behind me, brush past—I know what they thinking. See it in their backs. "Old man, get off sidewalk. Let us by, old man. We going places, there things to do. You finished. Done with, old man. We t'row you out."

Seem like forever to cross road out there. Car come around corner, maybe going knock me down, then in middle of the road, cars making left turn, scream at crosswalk and roar like animal. Stoplight always turn green for them when I halfway across street. I time myself by it. Three steps a minute. Old people take their lives casual when they cross streets.

You want facts, huh? Just facts. You sound like tv show. No, no tv now. Friend did once. In this place, even. We watch long time. "Let's Make a Deal," "Dragnet," "Dr. Kildare." Beats crossing streets.

Yeah, right. I know kids like you spit on tv—why I watch it then? What a question. To pass time. I deserve it. I passed time picking strawberries, picking peaches, picking grapes. In my old age, I deserve to sit and laugh a little.

Sour, today, aren't you? You always this sour? Professor don't like you? What he do? Give you B–? What so bad, it better than F, isn't it? Oh, graduate school different, ok. Professor treat you bad? Yeah, plenty things like that happen to me, all the time. What else happen? Oh . . . staring at you in street— high school kids make fun? What? "Ching, Chong, Chinaman, sitting on a fence." Heee, heee! That pretty funny! They can't tell apart Chinese and Japanese. What else? Yeah, that an old one, can you see anything outta those slanty eyes? All that happen to me, too. And more. Kids not the only ones who did it, that the problem. Me? Listen to this.

Japanese kicked in the balls in bars. Japanese run out of town. Ever hear of Turlock up north? Japanese cheated out of their pay. Herded to desert during war. Oh, you know about that? You study it? Ching, chong, Chinaman, nothing. You go to college, you study "ethnic studies," you have chances to make good. Why you complain? They don't give you respect? You gotta give it to yourself. Can't sit back and wait for them to give to you. They give you nothing and you going wait forever.

Spoiled, you *sansei* are. You have nerve asking why we *issei* didn't fight back at the camps? Some did. They got Tule Lake and then shipped back to Japan after the war. What that solve? Think they had an easy time of it, going back home, place they hadn't seen for years, wartime mess? If you lived back then, raised with same tough life, you only roll over and die.

Say something. You make me nervous. You want me to keep on with this, don't sit there like sack of rice. You and that puckered face. Tighter than a virgin's hole—that's you. Listen, have an idea. Ok, ok, listen minute. You teach me how run this machine and leave it. I tell stories my own way. Can't think when you tell me alla time speak in this pipe and ask stupid questions. Ok, ok. Teach me run this machine and I do it. Take it or leave it.

Hello, hello? Good, machine running smooth. Anything to get that kid off my back. Damn, he gonna hear that. Ok, so, no matter. Fill up tape, yeah, fill up tape. Talk about what? Too many things to do today. No time for foolishness. Bye, kid.

Hello, hello? Kid's on my back to fill up this tape. Ok, kid, I do it.

In *Nihongo*—Japanese. If you cannot understand me, you can find a translator. But you did want me to fill this tape fast and I can't do it fast enough in English. I'm very sorry. But I'm sure you'll find someone to tell you what I'm saying.

Today was the memorial service for my best friend, Takada-san. He had no family here, so we old men chipped in for an urn. One of the others will dump the ashes and all into the ocean, off the pier. My friends are all dead now, what do you think of that, kid? Anyway, all are dead. I remember this friend of mine, when he was young, he'd say, "Inaba-san, someday we shall go back to Japan so rich, we'll have all we want to eat, we'll eat 'til we're sick and then we'll have girls, too." We did have a good time when we could eat all we wanted. We were making twelve to fifteen dollars a day. That was good money at that time. We thought the money would last forever. We were young, strong, willing to work. We didn't think about tomorrow. The Big Time—that's all we wanted—make lots of money, spend lots of money.

They're all gone now. Only friend I have now is The Tube, that cat, toilet-water gray, comes in here every once in awhile, shares what I eat, pet food and tuna fish, share and share alike. You've seen him, I'm sure. No one else. My faucet drips, my lights dim brown in summertime. The hot plate shorts out. The management would take my hot plate away if they knew I had it: fire hazard. It's better not to eat in summer anyway, when it's hot like this.

I remember, my friend and I, not eating for days when we were young. Not because of the heat, but because we had no money. For days, we wouldn't eat. We'd cinch our belts and bend our backs and we'd pick that lettuce, the strawberries, the tomatoes. We'd even eat a few bug-eaten berries when no one was looking. We worked winters for railroads—Montana, Wyoming, Colorado. Summers in California, picking crops. I'll wager you didn't know I went to college, too. Sure, kid, four years, I studied in the winter, picked crops in the summer. I studied to be a CPA. Graduated, too. Then no accounting firm would hire me, so it was back to following the crops.

I looked around today, all around this hotel, and, for the first time, I've begun to see it the way you do, kid. Sweaty lobby downstairs and old Rick asleep at the front desk. Torn flowers in the carpet on the stairs, threads hanging out at the center of each step. The hall smells like burnt toast—hotplates working until they short out—and the whole place smells like sour bodies and piss. Real dim out there, that hall. Naked light bulbs jut out from the ceiling like an old whore's tits, burnt out, useless. Garbage sits in corners and flies buzz around oily dog food cans. Ripped up shopping bags filled with green wine bottles, tuna fish cans, bread wrappers. Yeah, it looks like Ben Inaba has seen better days.

Sometimes, here in my room, I can reach out, I can touch the opposite walls from where I sit. Once I slept on a bunk no wider than a shelf. In snow country. With a single blanket. In a bunkhouse where the snow flurries blew in. Thinking about that, this place is luxury. I don't feel so bad now, remembering those days.

Oii, kid? Want to hear something funny? Probably not. But I'll tell you anyway. I'm a year younger in America than in Japan. When a baby's born in Japan, we celebrate the new baby's birthday once on the day of birth and once on the next New Year's day. I was born in the twelfth month, December.

When January came around, I became one year old. Now in America, I shed that year, because Americans like to keep young. I used to tell employers in the city, as I got older, that I was a year younger in America than Japan and I would joke about it, "America keeps me young." They'd laugh and say, "Ben Inaba, you're a card," and give me gardening work. I was shedding years like winter clothing to get work. Younger and younger until one day it didn't work anymore—I was sixty-five and looked it. The years stuck to me after that like flaking dry skin I couldn't brush off me. I just couldn't peel anymore layers.

Now is the time in my life that I should go back to Japan. They honor the old people there. But too late. My home's here. I feel funny talking to spinning wheels, to a humming machine. No one answers me.

Kid, I'll tell you another story. I was riding a bus once: all the way to the beach and back. Hooo, that Santa Monica is nice: green, cool, blue. I wanted to get out of this place. It took a long time to ride out there and back, but I liked the bus ride. The air became cooler the closer we came to the beach. At the end of the line, at the beach highway, I got off to breathe a little and it was ten degrees cooler than downtown. If I had a room in one of those old apartments near the pier—things would be better if I had a room at the beach. Well, maybe, maybe not.

Anyway, before I got off the bus, I was sitting in front of this woman who talked about her entire life at the top of her voice. Nothing was secret with this woman. NOISY. It seemed everyone was getting off a stop earlier if only to get away from her noise. She was loud but no one heard her. I stayed on the bus. I know how it is to talk and no one hears you. She was still sitting there when I got off finally. I sneaked a look at her through the bus window. But she caught me looking and started to get off the bus, too. I can't walk fast, but I hustled. She plumped down again in a different seat by another window and I saw her from the sidewalk before the bus drove away. Through the window, her mouth still moving, she was staring at me. No one was hearing her, not even me.

More questions. On list this time. Notice I speaking English now? Pretty good, eh, two languages? More languages than you. And you have nerve telling me what I been saying not useful. Maybe you got da kine wax in your ears—cannot hear me good. So! Can't find interpreter in that college of yours? Shoot, must be around somewhere. And you have nerve: "What about dinner?" you say. "Of course, I'll pay," you say. Why not? I asking myself. Know damn well why not. Ben Inaba, you paying price for all this. Spill guts, old man. Kid paying this meal. Dance to kid's tune. But, what the hell, I go with you. Tired of tunafish. Good steak hits the spot.

You college kids, wear crummy clothes, you. T-shirt with holes size of quarters, sleeves ripped up. Blue jeans, no, white jeans, only junk sandals, no socks. But you wear good-looking wristwatch and all those beads. How can people take you serious? I pick out college kids on Hill Street downtown every time.

"Read the questions on the tape and answer." What this gonna win me, third curtain on TV show? Apartment at beach?

"1. In your opinion, what was the impact upon your life of the Immigration Act of 1924, namely, the Exclusion of 'Aliens Ineligible for Citizenship,' or specifically Japanese immigrants to the U.S.? How did this law affect your ability to find a wife? What other instances of prejudice can you name?"

Holy Jeezus. Can't even figure the question let alone answer. What this, eh, kid?

"2. In which internment camp were you situated during World War II? How long were you forced to remain there? What feelings of bitterness did you harbor upon release? Do you believe there should be restitution and if so what kind?

"3. Please answer the questions in the space below to the best of your knowledge. I reiterate that your answers will be kept strictly confidential."

Hear me, kid? I reading these questions over your machine so you know I read them. Hear this? List of questions squashed up, thrown out. That my answer. What jobs you have? Where you live? Answer, old man, answer! Talk about your sex life, old man. Count the times you been to whore houses. How many kids you got, you who not married? Ever bang a white girl? A black girl? Hell, I'm not a man to you, I'm a damn sta-tis-tic. Who needs it?

Last time I talking with you, kid. Sorry, no dinner. No worry, old Rick downstairs watching your machine after I leave. Evicted, kid. They tearing down this building. Condemned. Simple as that. No fussing about it. No asking me to stay in your apartment. No feeding me. I take care myself. I been in pretty tight spots. It wasn't all women and good food, you know. But I got through. I going look for room in Santa Monica, small one, maybe share. No worry, I always get through.

Got something for you. Call it going-away present. I answer one question on your list. How I came this country. I tell you that.

Some friends—remember Takada-san, who had funeral? He was one and there were two others. We landed in Mexico from Japan, this after 1924, Maybe that Exclusion Act you talking about. We couldn't land in America. We headed for border and plan to cross desert then sneak over to California. We hike by night, sleep by day, sleep in shade by tumbleweed. Hoo, hot enough to fry your brains and then some. Mountains we had to climb, the land rolling, rolling forever, heat melting the air. We wanted to see better living than at home, and that made us take one more step and one more.

Stupid. We so stupid. Didn't bring enough water or food. We got weak 'til one of us collapsed. Leave him or carry him? Draw straws to see who do the job if we leave him. Someone got to kill him so no suffering. Other friend say, "He can suck a piece of cactus." He lived. We crawl over border, dead night, tired out, dried out. After that, we so grateful to be in America, we say we make good, we make lots of money, work hard, go home rich.

What happened? Yeah, we make lots of money. We got rich, all right. But we spent all, then later no jobs. After that, we struggle just to get by. You know, I never done anything I didn't want to do. Everything came to me like I ask for. What can I tell you, kid? You feel sorry for old Ben, living here, eating cat food, riding buses to the sea. Don't. You don't know what kind of life I was headed for at home, in my village, nose in the dung, rice prices way down. A farmer's life no better.

The days we work hard, nights we whore it up. Maybe the other one still at it. Maybe. Or maybe he dead, too.

What the— Oh, just the cat, he jump up on your machine. No worry, not breaking anything.

Gotta go, kid. Listen, don't believe everything you hear. I can take care myself. I walk slow, sure, but I still walking.

Listen, take care my cat, will you? I hear landlords no like pets in Santa Monica.

Ruth Shigezawa, author of *Celeste*, a children's fable (Candlelight Press), plays flute in a concert band and two flute choirs. She grew up in Southern California and earned an MFA at the University of California, Irvine and an undergraduate degree in English from the University of Southern California. Her parents were both born and raised in Hawaii, her father on a Kona coffee farm, her mother on Kahuku pineapple plantation. Her parents were both the first from their families to graduate from college.

She has written extensively about the *Issei*, first generation Japanese, in short stories (several published in *Amelia*) and two unpublished novels. A novel excerpt about photo brides was published in *Hawaii Pacific Review*, and a short story won the third annual American Japanese National Literary Award, a short story contest established by James Clavell. Other short stories have appeared in *Outerbridge, Pulpsmith, and* a woman's science fiction collection (Crossing Press), *The Women Who Walk Through Fire*. She and her husband Gordon, both *Yonsei*, fourth generation, first visited Japan in 1993 and enjoyed Culture Day (November 3) at the Meiji Shrine, watching horseback archery and eating barbecued squid-on-a-stick.

Sesshu Foster

from *City Terrace Field Manual*

CITY TERRACE FIELD MANUAL, from which these pieces are excerpted, attempts to locate the essential life of one place where I grew up using stories and voices of people I knew as radar.

I remember getting kicked out of the Boy Scouts after leading my (all-Chicano) squad, our little gang of friends from the neighborhood, up onto the mountainside at a regional camp-out and as the scouts tried to sing around the campfire, we shouted down into the valley. "Who——who——who are we? We are vatos from CT!" Unlike many whites or Japanese, Chicanos never had a problem with my mixed blood background, perhaps because of their own heritage of mestizaje: Indian, Spanish, and black.

My family came off the road in the sixties to East L.A. battered, a bit bloody, dirt poor and at the end of a rope. Our neighbors in the community treated us better than family and made us at home. As 'happa' (an Amerasian) who grew up in the bilingual Chicano barrio, negotiating three or sometimes four cultures daily, I am interested in the cross-cultural, class, multicultural and personal dialectic which is the history of my experience.

In 1911 I was brought from Veracruz in a bundle, but was erased by measles. In 1921 I returned by way of Mazatlan and was removed by tuberculosis in a back room. In 1924 I staged a comeback and rerouted through Yuma, then was scalded by gas mains. In 1936 I managed to crawl up from Boyle Heights, only to be buried in an underground cave-in during construction of sewer lines. I appeared briefly in 1938, but got pot-shot by a security guard near the railroad tracks. I revived on Bunker Hill in 1949, in a state so enfeebled by age I died in a furnished room of natural causes. I gave up immigration for the time being, and did not affix my name to any papers.

America is in the Heart and we are in the canebrake, we do not want to see St. Quentin again, John Fante and Raymond Chandler meet across from Pershing Square to make know-nothing commentary on jazz joints down Central Avenue, we pack flour into sacks and stack them on trucks to remain in white while our families perish in the epidemic and they are burning down Chinatown to rid the city of slavery and disease who knows what sort of man was hanging in the tree because he didn't have any skin left on him, the locomotive scared the horses off Main Street, steam boiled up on us in the dark with the clanging of the trolley car while across the park behind the fruit stalls they sell little bottles of sex odors and maybe I need one maybe I need a new name an American name and I could be one of thousands getting up early to take the trolley to San Pedro and take the exam for the shipyard . . .

. . . the japanese man would not appear riding a horse above the telephone pole like the marlboro man the japanese man strode above the endive kale and parsley weeding the glendale truck garden his life was not picturesque like a hiroshige block print or a flight of golden cranes across a kimono though his cotton clothing absorbed his sweat like the pages of a book ab-

sorb the ink of meaning and desire itself formed in his mind
something long and cool as his woman a piece of iced celery
when he heard a shout in english stood upright and saw the
labor contractor standing on the flatbed of the white man's
truck waving him over this morning what did it mean? after
seeing the billboard in town NO JAPS WANTED THIS IS A
WHITE NEIGHBORHOOD/ the old issei sat in the cluttered
livingroom in the boyle heights bungalow with his cigarette in
the tin ashtray cradled in the linen napkin his wife always
placed on the arm of the couch for him and the marlboro commercial projected from the tv into the stale smoke as the old
man lifted the cigarette in his freckled knobby fingers and took
a long drag . . .

I was bleeding through the gauze I'd wrapped around my palm
in the usual half-assed way, but I couldn't wipe it off the slippery steering wheel because Jimi Hendrix was playing *the Star
Spangled Banner*, and, 20 years dead, Hendrix is still my favorite so I have to sing along and then slam on the breaks, the
kids' bikes in the back of the van crashing into each other, the
kids screech as I spun out of the lane to avoid some jerk doing
45, craning my neck back, "where the hell did you learn how to
drive, China?" but it was some beautiful girl putting on her
false eyelashes and driving with one hand just like me, as I noticed in the mirror all my papers flying around in the back,
"Hey kids, that's my Steering Committee Report. I was supposed to turn that in," and my wife is confiscating one of my
books they're whacking at each other with, and all of a sudden
the van is all over the freeway, we're weaving back and forth
fighting over the book, "Just lemme see it!" I'm whining, but
she wins the tug of war (the neighbor kids will be telling their
parents about it) and flicks the book past my nose, out the window ("Damn!"), "NO POETRY ON THE FREEWAY!" she yells,
"AND TURN THAT DAMN MUSIC DOWN SO I CAN
THINK!" Neruda goes flapping down the freeway behind us
like a sad bird and I'm wiping blood off the steering wheel with
my sleeve and cranking the steering wheel with the other hand
'cause we're gonna miss the exit if I don't jump that divider
that's all of a sudden come up on us.

Say. Tell me they add up to not dying, days we cut brush off the hillside, burred and stickered by a dusty sun, that they too are days of life's lust, breaking concrete sidewalks with sledgehammers and digging out mangled edges, tell me they will develop and grow tender, stay, night hours washing dishes in front of steamy windows, of dust-mopping long halls, disinfecting restrooms, scrubbing toilets, vacant urinals, say gleaming porcelain music stays more than memories of bone thrust, no ammonia grimace, downturned mouth sour, no, say so, the splinters jammed in your hand through the glove from a dried out shovel, a mattock whose head keeps wobbling off, sweat dripping into a widening cut of earth, tell me minutes huffing and puffing, catching your breath in an unreflecting eye of sun, pipes, shrill dry torn linoleum and rotten plywood pulled up, a ragged scraping of dragged two-by-fours pronged with nails caught, heaved up onto a high gray pile, that not all of it was like black snot from dirt or smoke snorted onto the ground, or wiped on pantsleg, that ants don't get it all, it too lives beside us, parallel to each day, moments and undelivered quarter hours and half hours waiting at a bench for a call, for interview or an envelope or nothing, sitting on a concrete step talking about our chances, our money, that does not ride our shoulders into the ground and kill us, down inside our foot steps, still it comes and breathes in us every hard time left.

These are the jails of the future, economized. Privatized. They will be constructed in basements of private homes, run for fun and profit. Cells will range from remodeled shopping carts wired together and cardboard boxes with duct tape, or bedframes in tin sheds out by Palmdale-Lancaster. Inmates will be kept one or two to a cell, nude and bound, often hooded for 24 hours a day. Body parts can be removed for benefits of interrogation or medical science.. Physical condition will tend to deteriorate, but females will receive extra attention from guards. Guards often come to work on their days off. Jails of this model have proven effective in reducing social recidivism in Argentina, Chile, El Savador, Guatemala, Indonesia, Brazil, Israel and elsewhere. The Rand Corporation's feasibility studies in the local area indicate the outlook is good for desert regions.

HOW TO GET THERE: downhill from the jail (where deputies run in training formation, stragglers stagger back up) past the school where we played (Dad showed up drunk on the lawn, grinning) down the avenue (behind Plaza market, "The Wall That Cracked Open" Willie Herron painted faces of the afflicted breaking through walls of oppression after Johnny—his brother, in my class—was beaten by gangbangers) the intersection (where I crashed April's car into a truck that ran the red light, the little Honda jumping into the air like a poodle, spraying out an arc of glass, rubber stripping and chrome fittings) where the library was turned into a laundromat, past the gas station (not there any more), apartments dusty narrow shops (bulldozed, replaced by St. Lucy's), across the freeway overpass (the motorcycle cop hides out there in the morning), make a right at the onramp down into the factory district (where I walked with my torn hand wrapped up in my T-shirt, through the heat-waves on the railroad tracks) in the flat hot smoggy sun of all those years: AND WHERE ARE YOU?

I was the needle in the rain. I fell through years like a character in the Mayan calendar. I was the Chinese woman a floor below the street, bent over her machine in the dusty half-dark. I was the only white guy on the Mexican railroad crew, I was the breed who caught it from three sides. I was the one always on the out. I was the government worker piling slash after the logging company had gone, knowing I was laid off when the job was done. I was the unknown artist sweating out images in the neighborhood garage. I was the guy whose only call came to sweep up at the factory, and I hurried to take it. I listened to the radio in the boarding house when everyone slept, and heard a seagull calling in the middle of the night. At noon, I was the spots I saw high in the sun over the telephone poles.

Marina Foster

My parents were art students on the G.I. bill, painters, married in a Zen ceremony in Santa Barbara in the fifties, and my dad had us living in drunken Buddhist poverty, on the road, up and down California until my mother divorced him. I grew up in the Chicanos barrios of East L.A., where I still live, work and raise a family. My aesthetic is the mestizaje of Marxism, Zen & Chicanismo.

Joseph Won

OVER HERE IS WHERE I AM

FOR A YEAR NOW they have been meeting on the second Sunday of every month. In the beginning they tried to formulate an acronym for their group, an acronym that would carry a message of independent significance or even vision—like M.A.D.D. or E.R.A.—but the consonants, like the seven of themselves, tended to bunch up in awkward configurations. The closest they came to a consensus was S.P.A.M. (Society for the Prevention of AIDS Misunderstandings). They ended up referring to themselves as "the Group."

They grew up together in a small town in Hawaii, where they assumed they would spend their adult lives, but the intervening years brought university educations, a desire for adventure, and an eight hundred percent increase in the price of Hawaiian real estate. So here they are, exiles reunited in Seattle, the new frontier.

This evening's meeting place, a sprawling Tudor-style house in the Roanoake section of town, belongs to Faith and Byron Soo. Faith, a media psychologist, and Byron, an investment banker, have been married for five years. The other regular members of the Group include Tibor Yokoyama and Ringo Yap, Christopher Chan and Guy Yano, and Mira Fung, who has brought a guest without the prior consent of the others. Mr. Ho is from Hong Kong, where he plans to stay after the Communists take over.

"Come visit me in Hong Kong in the year 2000, okay?" says Mr. Ho. "Bring food."

Everyone laughs. Christopher notices that Mr. Ho's teeth are small and widely spaced.

"You may also visit me in Vancouver, British Columbia, where I have purchased a modest bungalow," Mr. Ho continues. "Four bedrooms and four baths, just in case the Communists and I do not get along."

Dinner is nearly over and there has been no sustained discussion of any pertinent topics. Christopher, an attorney, raps his water glass with his index finger. He feels an urge to take control of the conversation. Guy beams a palliative smile at Christopher from across the table. Christopher scowls.

Faith and Byron are comfortable with disorder and imprecision, which are everywhere: in the meandering chit-chat; in the dining room windows that leak rain onto the hardwood floors; in the untrimmed spirea plants that tower over the front walk like shrubs that grow by highways. It gives Faith and Byron great pleasure letting things go, a habit that drove Christopher to distraction when he shared a house with them during senior year in college. The memory of that year still rankles.

"Please eat more," says Faith, circulating the platter of braised tongue, her contribution to the meal. "Enjoy, enjoy. Who wants more?"

"Your tongue is as usual superb," says Mira. She hands the platter to Ringo, then pokes at her serving with her fork.

"Beware the woman who speaks with forked tongue." Ringo warns, helping himself.

"Bite your tongue," Mira replies.

"We've never served tongue at 'Ciao Fun'," says Tibor, who, with Ringo, has run the small Wallingford eaterie for the past five years. "Mammalian facial parts have never been a big hit with our progressive clientele."

"Only one kangaroo can be king," announces Mr. Ho, who has helped himself to a huge slice of tongue. There is a stunned lull in the conversation. Mira, pouring herself more wine, bangs the bottle hard against her glass.

"That's bizarre," she says. "I thought I heard you say 'kangaroo'."

"Perhaps he was speaking tongue in cheek," says Ringo.

"Or in his native tongue," Tibor whispers to Christopher.

"Ah yes," says Mr. Ho, working the tongue with his steak knife. He excises what appears to be a lump of gristle. "An explanation is in order, okay? Kangaroos are those animals from Australia. I suggest you view them from a distance."

Christopher, sensing an opening, looks at his watch. Do it now, he thinks. If only Faith or Byron will take control, the Group can be led into a pertinent discussion. But before either Faith or Byron can speak, Ringo pipes up.

"We entered the fajita contest at the Evergreen Sea Fair," he says. "We won the open pork competition."

Christopher signs heavily. Another opportunity lost. More time wasted.

Now Faith is talking to Mr. Ho about goddess worship. "You are pagan," says Mr. Ho.

"Yes," says Faith. "It's quite satisfying."

Mr. Ho rummages for a pen in his suit pocket. "Here," he says, moving his chair closer to Faith. "Eternal life equals ten thousand years to infinity." He takes a napkin and writes it like an equation, complete with the infinity sign. "'Happiness now' is a good goal, okay?" he adds. "Also 'joy unspeakable'."

Faith motions for Mr. Ho to examine her rose quartz necklace. "You've got to come close to feel its aura," she explains.

"You are free for lunch tomorrow?" says Mr. Ho. "Perhaps I can feel its aura then."

"I'm doing polarity therapy for a friend who gave me a psychic reading last month," says Faith.

"Well then perhaps dinner," says Mr. Ho.

At the other end of the table Byron and Tibor have initiated a conversation about game shows.

"In my opinion," says Byron, "Jeopardy is a matter of timing. It all depends on how fast you push the dinger."

"Some people have faster dingers than others," Tibor agrees.

"Here's a humdinger," says Mira. "My neighbor's discovered a new thrusting technique that allows him to sustain near peak orgasm for over five minutes. It makes his toes curl."

"He told you this?" asks Ringo.

"I catch his cordless phone transmissions on my television," says Mira. "Channel 63."

At last the clasp disengages and Faith hands her necklace to Mr. Ho. "As I was mentioning," she says, "my friend's Jeep began to drive itself while she was exploring ancient ruins near Cuzco, but everything returned to normal as soon as she remembered about Gaia and the power of the crystal."

"Most interesting," says Mr. Ho.

"I was at a retreat last weekend, and they reported that the Shining Path and psychotelekinesis are big problems around Cuzco," says Faith. "Wait a second and I'll get you a picture of the Jeep." She stands and walks toward the living room.

Mr. Ho turns to Guy. "Ancient ruins near Costco?" he says.

"I think she meant 'Cuzco,'" Guy replies. "Cuzco, Peru."

"If it's *Jeopardy* you want to play, I've got an easy one," says Mira. "The category is 'People who are, like their initials, a whole lot of *B.S.*' The answer is, 'He didn't bother to call even though he knew two weeks prior that he couldn't make it'."

Tibor and Ringo exchange perplexed looks.

"Okay, let me make it easier," says Mira. "*Double Jeopardy*. The answer is, 'He was a lot more honest in the old days.' Or how about this one. 'He didn't used to be such an asshole'." She begins to hum the theme from *Final Jeopardy*. "What's the matter, Byron Soo: cat got your tongue?"

Byron leans toward Mira and whispers, "Do you want to talk about last weekend?"

"I *am* talking about last weekend," she says.

Faith returns with the photograph. "Could you feel it?" she says, taking her crystal from Mr. Ho.

"Very stimulating," says Mr. Ho. "I feel I know you."

"Quartz is really something, isn't it?" says Faith. "And it's quite reasonable if you buy it in bulk."

Christopher rubs his forehead and realizes that he is frowning. Perhaps he should drink wine. He reaches for the wine bottle, but Guy's hand touches his wrist. Christopher settles for potato salad, Mira's contribution to the meal. He bites down and misses, clamping his teeth on his fork.

"We have bored Christopher to death," says Ringo.

Christopher looks up in surprise.

"Correction, he's alive."

Christopher's jaw is vibrating, resplendent in the taste and feel of metal.

"I'll start Group discussion," says Mira. She is a junior faculty member at the university, where she is rumored to be a shoo-in for tenure. "My question is: What sort of educational programs should we promote in our communities? The question is also: Who are 'we'?"

"The lumpen proletariat," says Tibor.

"I have an allergic reaction to the perpetuation of high culture-low culture dichotomies," says Mira.

Christopher, too, feels an allergic reaction coming. He sneezes.

"Oh Lord bless us all," says Ringo.

"We need political activist intervention to close any gaps that exist," Mira continues. "But where are our role models? I'll tell you where they are. They're selling out. They're becoming investment bankers and the like." She finishes her wine in one gulp.

"Excuse me," says Christopher. He stands and walks to the kitchen. Behind him the door swings shut but not before he hears Faith begin a sentence, "The flux between energy poles . . ."

Christopher runs the hot water. Pans are soaking. He scours them clean and places them upside-down on the dish rack. He looks for a dish towel but cannot find one, so he wipes his hands on his pants. The printing on the side of a box of Wheaties attracts his attention. Rules for a Super Bowl giveaway: contest entries are due by the end of the year.

On the window sill above the sink is an old mayonnaise jar filled with parched philodendron cuttings. Christopher clears out the dead leaves and fills the jar with cool tap water. Out the window the backyard is very green. Gently disordered but surprising in its grace, it, too, is a reflection of Faith and Byron. Plantain and oxalis mix with and in some places overwhelm the grass. Camellias hide what would be a spectacular view of the lake. There are two colors of camellia: pink and white. Many years ago on a family trip to Maui he saw camellias in front of a house on the road to the summit of Haleakala. *Do* things always work out, he wonders.

There is a voice. Christopher can barely hear it. It seems to come from a great distance, tenderly, *Over here is where I am.*

"Who's there?" says Christopher, leaning toward the window.

A neighbor's daughter is playing her flute. She goes flat and then sharp, fast and then slow. It takes Christopher several moments to recognize the theme from *Cats*. He imagines a fifth grade band. Who are the girl's parents? Why, he wonders, does he think it is a girl?

Dementia. What did that mean? The losing of one's mind. Possible AIDS dementia. "The progressive loss of neural coordination, sometimes irreversible," the internist had said. "I can't become demented," Christopher had said, "I'm a lawyer." "Alcohol is contraindicated for consumption with your medications," the internist had said. "The side effects are unpredictable."

Alcohol-is-contraindicated-for-consumption-dementia, Christopher thinks. Side-effects-are-unpredictable-dementia. He wipes a little drool from the side of his mouth.

Outside it begins to rain. Twilight is fading into night.

Guy walks into the kitchen. He hugs Christopher from behind. They watch the rain together.

"Tibor is running out of *Jeopardy* facts," Guy says. "Did you know that the largest man-made structure in the world is no longer the Great Wall of China, but the mound of garbage on Staten Island?"

Christopher leans back into Guy. The day had started out clear. When had the clouds appeared?

Tibor comes into the kitchen. He is carrying a stack of dishes. "Do you think we hurt Faith's feelings with those tongue jokes?" he says.

"She's lucky she didn't cook brains," says Christopher.

Ringo enters. In a low voice he says, "Did anyone else get sick from the tongue?"

"Didn't eat any," comes the unanimous reply.

"Cowards," says Ringo. "My stomach feels awful. I need something to get the taste out of my mouth." He opens the refrigerator. "Cocktail onions. Yuck."

"How about Wheaties?" says Christopher.

"What about salted nuts?" says Tibor, opening one of the cabinets. "They've got bridge mix and macadamias. The honey-roasted kind."

"Give me some bridge mix," says Ringo. "Quick." Tibor shakes a handful of nuts into Ringo's hand. A filbert hits the floor and rolls under the refrigerator.

"Mr. Ho ate two servings of tongue," says Christopher. "Why not ask him whether he feels sick."

"He's in a deep discussion with Faith," says Ringo. "I didn't want to interrupt."

"I never noticed it before," says Tibor, touching Ringo's head, "but you've got two cowlicks."

"At least I've got hair," Ringo replies, munching nuts.

"Get a load of that cat," says Guy, looking out the window. "It's huge." He removes the philodendron cuttings from the sill for a better view.

"Here kitty kitty," says Tibor. A large calico cat, sitting not more than six feet from the kitchen window, arches its back and hisses before it abruptly turns and runs toward the camellias. Christopher thinks: right, yes, perhaps I'll call my father.

Mira and Byron, carrying the empty wine glasses, appear in the kitchen. "It seems like it's your life's goal to make me miserable," Byron mutters, his jaw clenched.

"Don't flatter yourself," says Mira.

Mr. Ho follows them in. He swings the kitchen door open for Faith and her platter of tongue.

"Yes indeed," says Faith, "there are a lot of things you won't find in university books. I was once a doubter. But then I accepted things. You will, too." She smiles at Mira.

There is a lot Mira cannot accept. Faith, for one thing. The fact that Byron will never leave Faith. The fact that he likes to buy, likes to settle, loves his wife, loves his life. Christopher is tired of it, the pettiness and squabbling. Maybe one day there will be an argument after which none of them will ever speak to each other again.

"I flew home last week," says Christopher. "My dad is very happy in the *Pau Hana* Home. He says Waimanalo hasn't changed much. He says to say hello."

"Your dad in Waimanalo," says Byron.

"Waimanalo," says Mira.

The voices change.

Makapuu, Moomami, Maunalani. Sharpness, accusation and fatigue are gone. Hauula, Kaaawa, Pupukea. They laugh. The time with Christopher's father in the taro patch; the twenty-two waterfalls of the *pali:* Waimanalo. They know it all, and the sound of the words transport them to that place. They think of home, not of unrequited desire and disappointed expectations, not of harsh politics and the murderous economics of disease, but of finer times. Their eyes are children's eyes: Waimanalo.

"Where is this Waimanalo place?" says Mr. Ho.

"You wouldn't understand," says Mira.

Back in their own home, Christopher and Guy are in the shower. From behind, Guy wraps his arms around Christopher in a bear hug.

"Murphy shitted in the draecena," says Christopher.

"What draecena?" says Guy.

"In the extra bedroom. I think he wants his kitty litter changed."

Guy runs his fingers across Christopher's lips.

"Are you okay?" Christopher asks. He knows how Guy will answer. Guy has been an optimist all the years they have known each other, and he remains an optimist despite the fact that every working day in the South Rainier Valley Social Service Center he sees the accumulated problems of the part of the city left behind by the prosperous eighties. Last week it was another gang flare-up: Flocco, the fifteen year old alleged driver of the car; and nine year old Reepo, the confessed trigger man. "I only have room for optimism," Guy likes to say. It frightens Christopher to think that Guy actually believes this. Such things are not humanly possible. People did not have limitless strength, and in spite of Guy's words to the contrary, Christopher has seen the fatigue overtake Guy, sometimes unexpectedly and always deeply.

"I'm fine, says Guy. "And I think you should call your father and tell him that the symptoms are beginning."

"Not now, not today," says Christopher. He sighs.

"Maybe we should tell the others in the Group," says Guy.

Let's not talk about it," says Christopher.

Guy shrugs. "Don't do anything in your life and not expect to feel pain," he says. Christopher gets the words in his ear like kisses.

Guy moves away, out of the shower. Christopher considers the time difference between Seattle and Waimanalo. The clocks are running on daylight savings time. Fall back, spring ahead. His father will probably be at church. The *Pau Hana* Home has a van service that takes people to church, to temple, to the mall.

Shutting off the shower, Christopher steps onto the bath mat. Murphy, the neutered gray tiger cat, jumps into the warm, drained tub and sits there.

"Hey Murphy, are you cold?" says Christopher, wrapping himself in his robe. "Today we saw a calico cousin of yours." Murphy turns his head with jerking motions, the way cats do when they lick their shoulders.

In the bedroom the television is on. It offers a preview of *Oprah*. There is a rap group on stage, then a cutaway to Oprah dancing with the rap group. Christopher switches the set off by remote control.

Outside the rain continues. It is a downpour and not the usual Seattle drizzle. The sound enters through the windows and bounces off the far wall so that the rain seems to be falling inside. Christopher shuts the windows. The geraniums in the window box bob up and down in the pelting rain.

In his bathrobe at his desk, Christopher does law work, mostly reading, mostly quiet. The yellow pad is soon filled with thoughts, remarks, reminders. He outlines three different arguments, all oblique, all unlikely. They are connected by the thin black line of a Pentel rolling writer. He considers a motion to exclude certain testimony from evidence. He thinks of the probable appeal if the judge does not understand his invocation of the extrinsic evidence rule, not a rule of evidence but a substantive rule of law, appealable even without objection. He thinks farther ahead to a possible retrial, to nuclei of evidence and slippery slopes. It may take years.

Then he thinks, believes that he is hearing it again even before he hears it.

"Is that you?" Christopher says.

He turns toward the bedroom door. The hallway is still.

"Is that you?" he stands up. "Who's there? Is that you?"

Faintly, like a song from far away, *Over here is where I am.*

"Who's there? Who are you?"

Christopher finds Guy in the extra bedroom. Still in his bathrobe, with his hand still grasping the empty bag of Jonny-cat, Guy has fallen asleep on the guest bed. Gathering up a comforter from the closet, Christopher unfolds and billows it over Guy, who does not awaken even as it settles on him. Then Christopher slips under the covers, too.

There is the sound of Guy's heavy, regular breaths. Christopher stares at the ceiling. There are the sounds of rain and wind, too. He notices the wind and then he stops noticing it. He is thinking about the time he flew to Minneapolis on the red-eye. It was a business trip, depositions on a fraud case. As they neared Minneapolis, the pilot announced a problem with one of the runways. Landing would be delayed, a minor inconvenience. Loved ones, like connecting flights, would wait. With the cabin lights gently dimmed, Christopher looked out the window and saw it for the first time, just like in books and on film. It was how he knew which direction must be north.

Thinking *At least I have seen the aurora borealis*, Christopher feels his body pick up and accelerate backward into sleep.

I haven't always lived in Hawaii. Before that it was Michigan,and before that Washington, New Jersey and North Carolina. I never owned a house in any of these places even when it was the financially smart thing to do.

I haven't always lived in a sense of Asian American community. Before that I lived in communities of lawyers, academics and Queers—to name a few such places—all of which seemed as separate and unlikely as states of the union. Several years ago, when a friend and writing mentor suggested that I forget about plot, I thought his advice referred to my fiction as written and not my life as lived, but now I'm not so sure.

Marianne Villanueva

BAD THING

FOR WEEKS, she had expected something to happen. She'd be driving along when suddenly she'd feel sick, as though she anticipated hitting a car or a road barrier. She could see the collision in her mind, almost hear the thud of something hitting her bumper.

She would be driving her six-year-old to school, and this feeling would make her slow down and look furtively right and left. When they arrived at the school without mishap, she would be surprised and thankful. Though she didn't know who she should be thankful to. She wasn't the praying sort. Still, she'd ease her unsteady legs out of the car, and call to her son with some measure of confidence, and push herself through the rest of the day. Like that.

And then, on the 17th of November, after months and months of her expecting something to happen, the man on a bicycle crashed into the front passenger side of her shiny red Corolla, and scraped both his forearms. Her son was not with her this time, thankfully. She was in unfamiliar surroundings, in Berkeley, where everything was a lot dirtier than down where she worked, at Stanford; where paper wrappers blew around in the street; where the students sat on the sidewalks on Telegraph Avenue as though completely unconcerned about germs and hygiene; where people bumped into her as she wandered on the sidewalk asking directions, causing her to remember her purse. So.

She heard the thud before she turned and saw him. When she turned, she saw a man's face, grimacing, pressed against the window. She was out of the car immediately, and grabbed the handlebars of his bike. Are you all right? All right? I'm so sorry. How stupid! She'd never even seen him. He'd been biking on the sidewalk. She'd been aiming for the entrance of a parking garage, but had been momentarily distracted by a sign that said: Sorry, Lot is Temporarily Full. And, staring at this sign in disbelief—disbelief because it was still so early in the morning—she'd found herself asking: What sort of crazy place is this?

Earlier, she thought she'd found a parking place, in a two-level garage on another street. But, just to be sure, because nothing about this place made her feel sure, she asked a couple of students if you had to pay to park there, they said, yes, and when she asked where they said you had to get a little ticket from a metal dispenser up by the entrance. And walking to the entrance, she suddenly saw a big sign that she'd not seen earlier. It said: This Lot Reserved Parking for Students Only, M-F, 7 AM-5 PM. And it was 10 AM, so she could not park there. Thank goodness she had thought to ask the students! The sign warned that "Violators will be Towed Away". And she didn't want that to happen, not in her current fragile state anyway, not with her feeling as though any unexpected occurrence would find her chipping and cracking, like the paint on an old wooden doll.

So. She was standing on the sidewalk, all five foot two inches of her, and the young man, who was very tall, who was at least six feet, and who had the pale, pinched look of an ascetic, was still bent over, inhaling deeply, though he refused all her offers: Shall I take you to a clinic? No? But your arm, look at your arm. Just in the few short moments they'd been standing there, she could already discern black and blue around the edges of the scrape, a telltale swelling. And another spot, on his hand, that was red and raw. She felt terrible!

She grasped the handlebars. Let me fix your bike. Let me take you to work. We can put the bike in the truck on my car, and I'll drive you. But the young man, whose name, she found out later, was Henrik, said simply: "Just watch out for bikers next time, OK?" Yes, yes, oh yes! But how could she tell him— I've known this would happen for months, but I didn't know when or how. And then, another thought: what if she were to go forward now, forgetting about that old feeling, thinking the bad thing she felt sure was about to happen had happened, and suddenly, something even worse, the real Bad Thing, came along?

It was like that with what happened to her sister. All the years they were growing up, and even until the time they were married and having children, and had both moved to the States, her sister was the Bad Thing. Anything her sister did made her ill. Her sister got a promotion at work. Oh, how happy it made her mother to tell her. Her sister's husband got a million dollar bonus for Christmas. Her mother told all the relatives.

But she, Teresa, would lock herself in the garage, smoking furiously. After a while, people noticed. Where is Teresa? What is she doing in the garage? Come out of there! What do you think you are doing—?

Maybe some of this feeling finally communicated itself to her sister, because in the last year, she had not called. No, not even to let her know that she was pregnant with her third child. Teresa found out from her mother, a month before her sister was due.

And then, six months after the baby was born, six months after Christopher, her sister died. Streptococcal pneumonia was the cause, though the autopsy report stated "sepsis." She had caught the flu, and it just dragged on and on, and like any typical thirty-year-old woman, her sister continued to go to work, in the big bank in Manhattan, and she had continued to go out for dinner with her husband and his friends, doubtless coughing all the while. And then, a few days later, she died. Just like that. No one could explain it.

And she thought her sister was the Bad Thing! Her sister's

death was even worse! Now she saw her sister everywhere! It was like the old woman had said—the clairvoyant, who lived in a *nipa* hut behind her aunt's house in Bacolod.

"You have a twin," the old woman said. "But she is of the spirit world. You and she look alike, and she follows you wherever you go. Turn your head quickly and you might see her, at the corner of your eye."

The old woman had given her an ointment for rubbing on her belly. For facilitating—what? She'd wanted another child after her son, but she and her husband just hadn't been able to manage it. Funny, she'd taken the ointment with her to the hospital in New York, those last few days before her sister passed away. What could she have been thinking? Was she going to rub it on her sister's belly—her sister, who by the time of her death already had three children? Stupid woman, she berated herself—you've gone daft, finally. She hid the ointment in her bag and told no one. Though later, looking at her sister in the hospital bed, looking at how bloated she'd become, she was tempted to lift the edge of her sister's hospital gown and rub the ointment on her stomach. Just in case. Just to try anything. Because nothing the doctors did seemed to help—not the antibiotics, not the hydrocortisone, not the ventilator, not the Pavulon, so perhaps this? This ointment from an old woman in Bacolod, from the other side of the world.

Hadn't the old woman decorated her one-room nipa hut with images of the Santo Nino and the Sacred Heart of Jesus? All those bleeding crucifixes and stigmata and curly-headed white saints. The bottle was filled with a sweet-smelling clear liquid and stalks of what looked like, must be, seaweed, and something else—a long sliver of hard white bone that she'd once crazily imagined had come from someone's finger. Hadn't the old woman breathed three times on the vial and clenched Teresa's hands tightly between her own and said the ointment was good, good, good?

She did not give the ointment to her sister. Perhaps that was why, later in the week, her sister died. Her sister died, and not even with anyone around her that she knew. She passed away in the elevator, while they were bringing her up to the operating room for a tracheotomy. Teresa can imagine the scene in the elevator—the panic, the pandemonium. Could they get a heart machine in there? Were they giving her EKG shocks right in there? Later, when they were all at the hospital, her sister was already in a winding sheet, her hands—poor hands! Still with the mauve nail polish—already tied together. The sight of the tied hands made Teresa unaccountably angry. The bruises on her dead sister's wrists and ankles were reminders of the times they had to strap her down to the bed because she was thrashing around, like a drowning person. Oxygen starvation, was what they called it. And the terror of drowning and of being tied down—! Tears would come to Teresa's eyes at the thought.

So this Bad Thing, her sister, was not really the Bad Thing she had thought it was. The real Bad Thing was the hospital, the indifferent nurses and doctors, the endless probing of her sister's helpless body, and, finally, the lonely death in an elevator. She would never forget that lesson.

She couldn't get the man out of her mind. Henrik. She saw him approaching the car, and suddenly her angle of *perception would shift and she* was him, riding blithely along on a fine red bike, on a fine morning that was warmer than you'd expect in November, and she suddenly saw herself in her red Corolla, flashing out of nowhere, and she knew without a doubt that the whole thing was her fault. Never mind what she told her husband later: that the man was obviously biking too fast, that he wasn't looking or he would have seen her, that he should have stopped before crossing the entrance to a parking garage, etc, etc.

Now her shiny red car, which was only two years old, had a dent on the front passenger side, and scraped paint. But what of Henrik? She'd given him her number, and extracted from him a promise that he would call to let her know how he was doing, but that night, though the phone rang and rang, it was always someone else. It was funny, they almost never got any calls, and suddenly last night there was a call from Mike Villacrucis way down in Los Angeles, whom they hadn't heard from in almost eight months, telling them how his father had a stroke after breaking the bank at Marapara; and then there was a call from her *Tita* Tessie, up in Daly City, telling them how out of the blue she'd gotten a call from *Manang* Jopay, who apparently had left her husband in the Philippines and come to the States on her own, and now needed a place to stay; and then a call from Dick, a friend of her husband's, talking about how his wife, who was six months pregnant with triplets, had suddenly contracted chicken pox. But no Henrik. Henrik had disappeared. Maybe he'd lost the scrap of paper on which she'd written her number. Maybe he'd taken it out of his jeans pocket later and found he couldn't read it—God knows her hand had been shaky enough as she'd begun writing her name. She'd written her name on a slip of lined paper torn off a page from a notebook—and even that was strange, because usually she carried a card with her, but that morning she couldn't find it, not anywhere in her handbag. It seemed to have disappeared into thin air. She'd written her name, Teresa Lardizabal, and writing it had felt her guilt weigh so palpably on her shoulders that she felt faint, almost as if she could sink to the ground and ask *him*, Henrik, to deliver her to the nearest clinic. Then her number. And, oh god, should she give her office number, in case this guy turned out to be a crank, one of those loony ones with friends who'd tell him to "sue the bitch for all she's worth"! She was glad her car was dirty—maybe Henrik would think she was just a student. She was glad she had found no card to give him, only a slip of torn paper. But she was sorry, too, about his forearms, and about the nasty shock she had given him. Would she ever be able to set foot in Berkeley again?

Sometimes she'd have crazy conversations with Henrik in her head. Why didn't you stop, she berated him, over and over. What if something really bad had happened and you got a concussion? Then your wife—or girlfriend, whatever the case may be—would be crying her eyes out right now!

So. For months, she realized, she had expected it to happen. Like the shedding of old clothes. The breaking apart of some outer skin. She'd be standing there on the sidewalk, her two feet in their scuffed, sensible black loafers planted firmly on the ground. She'd be standing there, like some acolyte waiting to be admitted to the feast. Why was she not more prepared? Why was her hair in a mess, flying about her shoulders? Why did she allow her belly, her breasts to sag? Why did her shoulders stoop, why did her eyes dart uneasily from side to side instead of staring straight ahead boldly, confidently?

Other people walked the ground without even paying attention to what they stepped on. It continued to hold them up. No problem. She walked gingerly, as though the earth had a skin one must be careful not to break through. As though there might be something underneath. And everything was fragile. The cup she held in her hand in the kitchen that morning found itself inexplicably on the white tiled floor, shattered into dozens of pieces. Her son, whom she loved and held close at every opportunity, told her stories of things that happened to him at school, stories that tugged at her heart and made her alternately angry, bitter, and sad. Her husband's body, too, seemed to be melting, losing form and definition, assuming a different shape entirely from the one she had grown used to. One evening she watched him working at his computer. He was thin, but his stomach hung loosely over his belt. Why was that? And his face had numerous tiny wrinkles at the corners of his eyes. Noticing this, she would run to the mirror in the bathroom and minutely examine her own face, wondering, wondering.

She made an appointment with the Help Center at work. If she thought the ground was in danger of cracking, she might as well talk to someone about it.

She didn't tell her husband. Once, during a fight, she called his mother in the Philippines, to make him stop shouting. Ever since then, he called her "sira-ulo"—broken head. She didn't want to give him any more opportunities. She might one day do the inconceivable and run away with her son. She imagined her husband might hire a lawyer. He would then mention that his wife, the broken-head, had once made an appointment to see a "counselor," which she believed was what those people in the Help Center were called.

She didn't know why it didn't make much difference to her that her husband called her such things. When she was growing up, her father often referred to her mother as Idiot Number 1. Her sister was Idiot Number 2, and she was Idiot Number 3. Back home, everyone thought this was wildly funny. Now, she imagined confiding in one of her American friends about this childhood experience. She can imagine the reaction: Pig! Perhaps the word "chauvinist" might precede it. But there you had it.

She made the appointment soon after the accident with the bicyclist. The appointment was with a Dr. Mary Chang. Dec. 3, 1:00. December! She hadn't known it would be that far away, and by then she'd be thinking of Christmas and who knows whether or not she might actually have been swallowed up by the earth by then. They'd find a few strings of her long black hair in the shower stall, and that would be it.

But she found she couldn't wait that long, and one day she cracked open the yellow pages of the phone book and called various toll-free numbers. At each one, the counselor would begin: Hi! (in that sincere, falsely bright American way) My name is ——! What's your name? And she would hang up.

Finally, there was one number. A place called the Bridge. A young man answered and didn't ask for her name. He sounded so young. She became suspicious and asked him, "Are you a student?" He admitted he was, and she almost laughed out loud. She, a 31-year-old woman, confiding in this *child!*

Mostly he listened to what she had to say, interspersing her narrative with a non-committal "ummm, ummm", and there were long stretches when he said nothing at all. After a while, she began to feel strange, as though the voice on the other end of the line was detaching itself slowly from the telephone. Thank you very much, she said abruptly, and hung up. She wondered if he'd been about to say "Ummm."

So she did nothing. And very soon Christmas was almost upon her, and the news that her brother-in-law, a small secretive man who had lived in New York the last five years, would be arriving in San Francisco on that Saturday, and wondered whether he might stay with them? Her husband grumbled— lazy, good-for-nothing was what he called his unnamed company, and he'd told them he owned a vacation home in the Poconos, though none of their other relatives on the East Coast had ever been invited there and doubted whether it actually existed. He rented a room from a Filipino family in Jersey City, and sometimes when Teresa called she heard the sound of clanging pots and pans and the hiss of something frying on a stove. She heard an old lady's voice shout her brother-in-law's name, and he would come to the phone out-of-breath, saying he'd been out back, barbecuing.

But. Still. She remembered the dark figure in the overcoat

who came to the hospital when she was in New York during her sister's dying. He'd come up the elevator to the intensive care ward, where she was sitting in rumpled clothes on a plastic-covered sofa, and later took her down to the hospital cafeteria where he bought her a hot dog and cocoa. She'd found herself staring with new interest at his face, which did not remind her at all of her husband's. The face that was now in front of her, partially obscured by lazy smoke from his cigarette, was soft all over and in some places pock-marked, and the hair was light brown and thinning at the forehead. They had sat across from one another at a vinyl-top table on some avocado green plastic chairs. Only moments earlier, in the intensive care ward, it had seemed to her that exhaustion would suck her down, down, right through the linoleum-tiled floor of the waiting lounge. But now she was here, in the cafeteria, her brother-in-law a solid presence, a dark figure in a heavy overcoat who sat silently nodding his head. He did not disappear—in fact, refused to be distressed by her tears. After a while, she began feeling better. As though the hot dog which had sunk like a stone to the pit of her stomach were the only cure she had ever needed. She'd stood up then, made a joke, and later observed how the snowflakes fell on the shoulders of his dark coat as he turned away, towards Lexington Avenue.

Later, back in California, she'd forgotten about him. Doubtless her husband called to let him know the news, but Teresa did not care. She lay all day on the bed, a pillow hugged to her stomach. Those days her mouth was stopped up with something vile and bitter that made it impossible for her to talk or even to cry. One day she thought she, too, might be dying, and dragged herself to the car. It was four in the morning. Her husband and son were still asleep. She drove herself the four miles to the nearest hospital, and by the time she reached the emergency room she was shaking uncontrollably.

"Tell me—is it pneumonia?" she whispered to the young doctor on duty. He'd laughed, then. "No, just the flu," he said. He gave her two Tylenol tablets and sent her home.

But she is alive! She does not know exactly how or when the mood of sadness slips from her. She only knows that now she refuses to be sucked under the ground and no longer fears to crack the surfaces of whatever it is she is walking on.

The earth begins to assume solidity. She presses gingerly with her toes on the damp ground. Because of the winter rains the ground is muddy and the mud cakes her boots. She happily tramps around in this mud, as though remembering once again what it was like to be six or seven years old. She grabs her son's hand firmly as they walk to the park. Sometimes, very occasionally, she will even sing. An old song from long ago.

"Leron, Leron sinta—" she will sing. She does not know where she finds the words. Or, at other times, "Bahay kubo, kahit munti—." Silly words, really. When her son asks what they mean, she can say only that they are songs she can remember clapping her hands to, in an old house covered with vines in Manila.

The next week, she is rear-ended while crossing an intersection along El Camino Real. The hit is hard—so hard she hits the car in front of her, which in turn hits the car in front of it. But when she gets out of the car to take a look, knees shaking, she sees only that the rear bumper is a little askew. Barely scratched, even. While the lady behind her, in the shiny maroon sedan, has a dented hood and a smashed left light. "It's a brand new car, too," the lady says mournfully. And Teresa wants to put her arm around her and hug her. But she does not. Instead, when the young policeman asks her if she wants to make a report, she shakes her head. Her heart is still beating painfully in her chest, but she forces herself back into her car, and pulls away from the curb without looking back.

Born and raised in Manila, I came to the United States at 21 to do my masters in East Asian Studies at Stanford University. I fully expected to return home after two years and teach at the Ateneo de Manila, my old university. Instead, when I graduated, my family urged me to stay, and after working briefly in New York I decided to apply to the Creative Writing Program at Stanford. I was accepted in 1983 and graduated in 1985 with a masters in English, concentration in Creative Writing.

I have published a collection of short stories, Ginsend and Other Tales from Manila, and have had works included in several anthologies, both here and in the Philippines. I have written for publications as diverse *Asiaweek*, *The Filipinas Journal*, *Filipinas*, and the *Stanford Daily*. I now live in Redwood City, California with my husband and son.

Carol Roh-Spaulding

PAGES FROM THE NOTEBOOK OF A EURASIAN

BE, SAY, EIGHT. Be swinging on the playground, your feet kicking free, as Joanie or Sarah or Jill, they're anonymous to you, now, swings next to you. Be the one who kicks higher, flies farther out, up into a clean sky. Kick higher still, when she shouts, "Are you Chinese?" Shake your head no, and remember your dreams at night of swinging so high you release yourself, effortlessly, into blue. When she shouts again, as though it were the only other possibility, "Are you JAPanese?", don't even bother with an answer. Try to continue in the reverie of swingsets. At night, fly from them, working your arms past rooftops and telephone wires, opening and shutting your mouth like a fish.

You know the next question. She's dragging her feet in the sand, slowing. She's stopped. Okay, slow down. Get it over with. She's twisting on the chain now. You both wind up, the rusty links twined above you, taut with potential motion. Now let go—whop whop whop. Whirl and stop, she's facing you. She makes a hat with her hands, her thumbs reaching down and pulling at the corners of her eyes—pulling so hard it hurts to watch. Now she looks like you. In exasperation, she asks, "Well, then, are you SIAMESE?" If you feel like it, give her the answer that never satisfies, that isn't even exactly true. You don't know what it means anymore than she does. Go ahead, tell her: "Korean." Say it. Already it's become, for you, a limp and roundish word that leaves you with a guilty mouth. She's never heard of it. None of the kids you know have heard of it, but it shuts them up for a while. All they want to know is how come you look like they do except for one thing—your slanty eyes.

Explain something. You're older, now. Why couldn't you have said it proudly—that you were part, half, Korean? Or why couldn't you have shot back *what's it to you* at the very least? Instead, you swallowed down the word with the slightly sick sensation you felt when you saw a man with no legs sitting down to a meal in a restaurant, or a dwarf buying her groceries at the market. Unusual people acting like everybody else. Pretending, it seemed. Like you. Sometimes. But you could also just forget you weren't white—easy enough, most of the time. Especially at home. You and your brothers plopped in front of the TV watching "I Dream of Jeannie," sharing peppery slivers of kim'chi from a huge jar and washing it down with glasses of Hi-C. You knew the Korean for "sponge" and "pajamas" and "crotch" and a few other simple words. But none of these marked you as different, as long as it didn't make it outside. It was like wearing those glasses that automatically darken in sunlight: inside was normal, outside was different. Still, most of the time you could forget, could just be a kid.

Don't forget about Miss McEachern, though. Be in sixth grade, now, at Manchester Elementary. Remember the teacher you all loved to hate because she *looked* so hateable with her pale, liver-spotted face and hands, her mouth lined and puckered around some permanent lemon. Her glassy eyes rimmed red with age. Her wiry violet curls wound so tight you could see the scalp, the color of a dog's belly, peeking through. At least

Miss (who would ever marry *her*?) McEachern she left you alone most of the time. You smacked the softball during recess and went in all sweaty, your blood still singing, to lick your math problems and pen your book reports. You had a light on inside.

One quiet afternoon Miss McEachern is at her desk in the back of the room. She calls for you. Set down your book about the Salem Witch Trials. Go to her. She's leaning back in the only comfortable chair, looking at you—staring unabashedly for the longest time, as though you've got something wrong with you that nothing can fix.

Finally—"Tell me how your parents met."

Hmmm. Tell her what you know, which isn't much. "They met at Berkeley. They were both in college."

"Where is your mother *from*?"

"Oakland." You see that this isn't what she wants.

"Your parents didn't meet during the war?"

"What war?"

You're making her tired. If you would only give her the right answers, you would get along fine. Miss McEachern sighs and looks away. "Is your mother American?"

This is like asking if your mother is a woman: You've never had reason to question the obvious. Answer her, "I think so." You're only eleven. When grade reports come out, you won't suspect that these little interviews have anything to do with the letter N ("not satisfactory") in a neat line, like little stabs, for handwriting. You have beautiful handwriting. Other girls, even grownups, envy your sleek letters, your curly but controlled cursive. Every other grade is an A. But you can't prove anything. Do you want to talk about discrimination? It's such a used-up word. At eleven, though, you haven't even gotten beyond confusion and hurt, to suspicion. Your mother opens the door to you after school, astonished at your tears. She soothes you with hugs and money for the ice cream truck, but she doesn't question the grades. You should tell her about it one day.

When you grow up, you don't look like the kid on the playgrounds or in the schools of your childhood. Somehow your round face narrows, your eyes even pass for Caucasian. Maybe you owe it to the hours and hours you spent, on your way to adulthood, plucking at your eyefolds, trying to make *lids* that you could smooth blue shadow on. Or maybe it's because you spent so many of those years denying the murky yellow half of you. You told your friends your *real* mother was French. Made up a name you thought sounded appropriate, along with an elaborate story about how you came to be living with this "Chinese" woman. You got it from that old movie *A Lady From Yesterday*. Funny that you thought this more acceptable than having an *American* mother of Korean descent. And whenever it was that you figured out your mother wasn't *white*, you wouldn't be seen with her nor wear the clothes she made for you. Once, she bought you a dress for a dance. She took the sash and tied it into a "Korean bow." You tied it back into what must have been an "American bow" as soon as you left the house. In those actions, you thought you were so different. You were just being a typical teenager, with your peculiar reasons for rejecting your mother.

Try being fifteen. Your father's left home, your parents have divorced. Dad finds another woman, Mom goes to work. This other woman is Filipino—fortyish, nice enough, never been married. An aunt on your father's side, who hasn't heard the news, gets it from you. Her mouth drops open. She claps the word back just in time—"Ohmigod, not another. . . ." Not fast enough for you, though. You know what she was about to say. She was about to say *Oriental*. That word, oriental, oriental, or-ee-ant-all is undulant and shameless as a snake. Winds into your ear and names you—or, names that part of you that's your mother's fault. Here's a list of what you could have said:

1. Or-ee-ant-all: just let her hear it, finish her sentence.
2. Answers, "Another what? They're both American."
3. Answer, "No, Aunty. She's Filipino. Mom's Korean.
4. At the very least, you could have asked, "What's it to you?"

But you still can't seem to manage that, can you? Nowadays, you can spot the ones with prejudices because they still use it—Oriental. They don't know it's *Asian* now. They probably also still say Eye-tal-yun. Nowadays there's words that didn't exist when you were eight or eleven or even fifteen: *diversity, multiculturalism, Amerasian*. Nifty words that give you a category to fit into, words that wouldn't have helped, anyway, in home room.

Be there. You know the boy you like, Rick Tallon. He wears leather jackets with no shirt on underneath when he can get away with it. You like him because he gets away with things and because he's so uncomplicatedly what he is. You're all sitting at shop tables in Mr. Snyder's first period. Angle drills and planers and other equipment line the walls. It seems so simple and solid and unambiguously American to know how to, say, make a desk. You're thinking about signing up for shop class next term—maybe you'll meet a boy that way. Rick Tallon is going on about his sub in math class, the Chinese bitch who gave him detention. He makes a hat of his hands, his thumbs pull at the corners of his eyes. Go ahead and laugh with them. It's protection.

But you're not quite covered, are you? It's your current best friend, Karen, who calls out. Her voice is like her nose—clean, pert, looking for trouble. The way she asks her question she could be Joanie, Sarah, Jill. She asks, "Hey, what's that teacher's name?" And Rick says your name, your father's solid, white American name, which your mother has kept. And Karen announces that the Chinese bitch is your mother. And they look at you. Rick looks at you. You could kill your mother for taking a sub job at your school.

How do you explain yourself? It wasn't as though you lived in poverty. It wasn't as though you were *black*.

Try saying something about your mother. How she grew up in downtown Oakland, just outside of Chinatown, the daughter of Korean immigrants. Methodists, just like your father's side. How she folded sheets and pressed shirts and trousers in her mother's laundry service. Cleaned the rooms of the few boarders they took in. Swept the gray or black snips of hair from the floor of the barbershop across the street where her father worked. How she got through her childhood was by having tremendous faith in Jesus Christ. That and saving up her small weekly allowance so that she could have things—fabric for dresses, shoes that never did fit, something for movies out and phosphates after the show with her girlfriends. She wanted to go to college, say that. The first in her family. Wanted to become a math teacher and almost did, when she met your father and dropped out of college to put him through law school and have babies. Just like so many women of her generation.

But go deeper. Tell how it felt to leave her family for the very first time, to go off into the world with a white man, no blessing from her parents. They cried, but they were not there when she exchanged her vows. Tell about her honeymoon night, when their nice Christian friends chased them through the Berkeley hills with tin cans tied to the back of their Buick and their carhorns blaring. How she thought there'd be so much to get used to, and how she thought, *I can do this, I can make it work.* And of later how her heart thumped at the realization that she had crossed an ocean without even leaving town. And of how her heart thumped that night because her wedding bed was an ocean, too, and she was being taken across it. No, stop. There's so much you never knew, still don't know.

You do know that your Korean grandparents softened when you were born. Then, just as all were reconciled, your family moved away from Oakland to a nice white community in the Central Valley. There, your mother made homemade aprons and curtains and baby clothes and four-course meals. Remember? Do you also remember how she dressed you up in the little Korean gown of green, rustling silk with shimmering rainbow sleeves and a parasol just like a bigger version of those mai-tai mixers? And what about those evenings when guests from the church would come and sit on the floor to eat bul'kogi and rice and kim'chi? How many pounds of kim'chi have you eaten in your life? Do you remember your Korean-American mother as only wanting to be white? Do you liken your shame to a shame she must have passed on to you? Be fair about the fact that she tried. Only, the way you're stuck with your own self-indulgence, your own inability to understand what you are if you aren't white.

You knew you never quite got the hang of things at *halmoneh's* place, when all the relatives gathered for New Year's and other holidays. When *halmoneh* sat at the head of the table, muttering her endless prayers in unintelligible Korean. Sometimes it was so funny, her going on and on as the steam rose from heaped plates, that you were afraid you would bust out with laughter. Even your mother didn't understand everything she said—it having to do with deceased she'd never heard of. At least everyone else *looked* Korean or at least some acceptable version of Oriental. You towered over even your boy cousins. But you didn't quite fit in your father's world either, riding in the golf cart with Grandpa in Palm Springs or looking out from his high-rise in downtown L.A. The way they disappeared on New Year's Eve to go have cocktails with friends, returning just before midnight, made you feel like an intruder into the lives of the elegant. Your grandpa's dirty jokes and *Playboys* laying around on the coffee table. Your mother's shyness and father's red-faced laughter.

You are so determined not to fit in anywhere at all.

You can't even write like an "ethnic." Where's the catalog of kitchen smells, the italicized language terms sprinkled throughout, the mention of little customs that authenticates your story? You make for a lousy Oriental, an even worse Asian. Why can't you just be white, if not yellow? Or try gray. No one wants to hear about race anymore, anyway. We're all ethnic now, isn't that right?

Try this one more thing, then. Be there at *halmoneh's* funeral just a couple of summers back. Stand before her casket at your mother's side. You and she have had years to work things out. Nowadays you say quite proudly, "I'm part Korean." People scrutinize you, looking for signs—both Asians and the whites do. They say, "You must mean you're one-quarter Korean." Smile to think that, years ago, this is what you wanted—not to bear the signs. Should you start pulling up your thumbs at the corners of your eyes?

Slide a carnation from the bunch and lay it carefully near your grandmother's papery hands. Hold your arm tightly around your mother. She's sobbing, but she'll be fine. Look carefully at this woman, with whom you never had a single substantial conversation. "You eat biiig," she would say. "You tall girl, now." And you'd nod, bending your cheek as she pulled you close for a kiss. Desire to know all of the stories that she died with—the girlhood in Pusan, the trip across the ocean, the births of eight children. Suffer that loss. Now turn around. See your mother and aunts and uncles and cousins and second cousins. Start with them. But don't stop there, because you are not yellow and never will be. And you are not white, and never were. Try gray. Or swing once more into a clean, high blue. Go on, work your arms. Fly a little.

Carol Roh-Spaulding was born and raised in California's Central Valley, the setting of the novel she is writing based on the lives of her maternal and paternal grandfathers, one a Korean immigrant laborer and the other an established Anglo-American businessman. Ms. Roh-Spaulding has published stories and poems in magazines such as the *Beloit Fiction Journal, Ploughshares, Amerasian Journal,* and *Korean Culture* and was awarded a Pushcart Prize in 1991. She is a Ph.D candidate and instructor of American literature at the University of Iowa, where she is writing a dissertation about the Amerasian authors Sui Sin Far, Onoto Watanna, Diana Chang, and Han Suyin. Ms. Roh-Spaulding lives surrounded by thriving cornfields just outside of Iowa City.

R. A. Sasaki

A DICTIONARY OF
JAPANESE-AMERICAN TERMS

Nihonjin [nē'hon'jē-n']

At the age of six, I thought "Americans" and "English" meant the same thing—"white people." After all, Americans spoke English. You have to understand, this was at an age when I also wondered why "onion" was spelled with an "o." It seemed to me that it should be spelled with a "u," except that would make it "union," which was a different word altogether.

I never thought about what I was. My parents referred to us as *"Nihonjin"*—Japanese. *"Nihonjin"* meant us. *"Hakujin"* (white people) meant them. Being *Nihonjin* meant having straight black hair and a certain kind of last name. The Chinese kids looked like us, but had one-syllable last names.

When I was in the first grade I got into a fight with Lucinda Lee because she claimed that she was American. "You're Chinese," I accused her. She started to cry. Later, I told my mother about the disagreement, and, to my outrage, she sided with Lucinda. It had never occurred to me that Lucinda was American. That I, too, was American. Other kids never asked me if I was American. It was always, "Are you Chinese or Japanese?"

That's how I found out that I was American—one kind of American. I still wasn't sure how I could be both American and *Nihonjin* (was I English, too? I wondered.)

Then a little girl who was REALLY *Nihonjin* moved in next door. Her father worked for a Japanese company, and the family had moved to San Francisco straight from Tokyo. Kimiko wore dresses all the time, even when she didn't have to. She covered her mouth with her hand when she laughed, and sounded like a little bird. When I stuck the nose of my wooden six-shooter in her back and called her a "low-down, dirty tinhorn," emulating my heroes on television westerns, my father, sitting in the next room, shot me a dark, warning look that made me quake in my boots. It was no good insulting Kimiko, anyway, because she wouldn't get mad and fight back. If Kimiko and I were both *Nihonjin*, well then, all I could say was that there must be different kinds of *Nihonjin*, too.

Jiichan [jē chăn]

I don't remember my grandfather.

Jiichan died when I was too young to remember him, but old enough to be afraid of death. He haunted my childhood by appearing in a nightmare so disturbing that I used to force myself to recall it every night before going to sleep so that I wouldn't dream it again. I believed that terrors could only get you when you were least expecting them.

In my dream, there was a large pile of laundry, mainly sheets, on the floor of the dining room in our house on 23rd Avenue. I was sifting through it with my sister, playing in the mountainous folds suddenly dropped into the midst of the usually neat order of my mother's house. We climbed the mountain; our feet sank into the soft mass. Suddenly I clutched a stiff hand. I screamed, and the dream ended abruptly; but I knew, without seeing the rest, that it was *Jiichan's* corpse in there.

My sisters, being older, had known *Jiichan* and did not have such dreams. They were not afraid of him. They remembered his quiet presence watching over them as they played in the back yard of the house on Pine Street. They remembered him tending his beloved cherry tree. I was the only one who needed to reconstruct him. I tried to do it by collecting facts—his name, for example, where he was born, that he had left Japan and come to San Francisco sometime around 1897.

But a part of me has always distrusted language, especially facts. We are so often deceived by them into thinking that we know something. Language is applied after the fact. It is a way of labeling an experience, and if we have never been to Wakayama, Japan, it means nothing that our grandfather was born there. Or if we were not alive in 1897, how can we understand what it meant to leave Japan at that time to come to America?

In 1975 I went to Japan to teach English. I didn't really know why I was going. Finding one's roots at that time was an expression which had been rendered meaningless by overuse. It was just that part of me that distrusts language, wanting to trade facts for knowing.

Other people don't seem to be haunted by the need to bring their grandfathers alive. Perhaps they remember their grandfathers, spoke the same language and heard their stories. If you know who you are and where you come from, or if you are accepted in American society at face value, you can forge ahead and never look back. My Asian face doesn't let me forget my origins. Everytime I start to forget, I will come upon that stiff hand, which will remind me. And if I don't know who my grandfather was, who I am, I will scream with terror. But if I know, then I will know that it is my grandfather's hand that I hold; and I need not be afraid.

osewa ni natta [o-sĕ'wă nē năt'tă]

I decided early on that it was hopeless; I would never be Japanese, so why try? There was too much to know, too much to be understood that could not be conveyed by the spoken English word. I would rather be forward-looking—American.

But much as I tried, I could never leave it behind. Someone would die. We always seemed most Japanese when someone died.

"We should go to the funeral," my mother would say. "Iwashita-san came to Pop's funeral." If someone had sent flowers, we would send flowers. If they had visited the house and brought food, we would do the same. *Koden*, funeral money, was carefully recorded and returned when the occasion arose. It seemed there was a giant ledger that existed in my mother's head that painstakingly noted every kindness ever rendered or received. How could I ever know or remember its contents? I couldn't keep track of my own life. A friend of mine was hurt once because I didn't remember staying at his sister's house in Minnesota. I felt awful about not remembering. It seems that there are whole periods of my life that have simply dropped from memory. Sensory overload. Am I busier than my mother was, or is there a Japanese gene that weakens in succeeding generations with increased Americanization?

Perhaps I was simply born too late. The youngest of four girls, I was the only one who didn't remember living in the old Victorian in Japantown where my mother grew up and my grandparents lived until they died. I was the only one who couldn't understand what my grandmother was saying, even when she was speaking English. When someone talked about what a family acquaintance had done for us, I was the only one who didn't know who the person was.

This record-keeping and reciprocation did not revolve only around death. My mother would tell me one day on the phone, "The Noguchis are coming up from Los Angeles. They want to take Kiyo and me out to lunch."

I had never heard of the Noguchis, but it turned out that sixty years before, *Bachan* (my grandmother) had let them stay at Pine for a month after Noguchi-san lost his job. Noguchi-san had recently undergone surgery for cancer. "*Osewa ni narimashita*," he had said. He had incurred debt. He wanted to repay it before it was too late.

The repayment of debt, then, apparently passes down from generation to generation. What will happen when my mother and my aunt Kiyo are no longer around? The ledger will be gone. How will I know to whom I am obligated, what debts to repay? One day in the future will I open the door to find a total stranger bringing me home-made sushi because of some kind act my grandmother did in 1946? Probably not. When I meet the grandsons and great-granddaughters of my grandparents' friends, who among us will know that our families were once connected? We will have lost the intricate web of obligation and reciprocation. The people who remember. This community.

Japanese-American [ja-pə-nēz′ ə-mĕ′-rĭ-kən]

A Japanese-American is someone who has been trained in the Japanese ways of ultimate courtesy, but who has a quite independent and secret American sensibility locked into that pleasant and self-effacing exterior—like a *bonsai*. A tree trying to grow, but forced, through clipped roots and wired branches, into an expected shape. Like *bonsai*, a Japanese-American can be considered warped or deformed, or an object of uncanny beauty.

A Japanese-American is someone who, after a lifetime of being asked if she's Japanese or Chinese, or how long she's been in the States, or where she learned her English, will laugh when some white guy who has taken two semesters of Beginning Japanese tells her that she's mispronouncing her own family name.

Being Japanese-American means being imbued with certain values treasured by Japanese culture—values such as consideration, loyalty, humility, restraint. Values which, when exercised by white Americans, seem civilized; but they make Japanese-Americans seem unassertive, not willing to take risks, lacking confidence and leadership qualities.

Some sansei are like brash young redwoods, so new and naive. It's so clear why the nisei didn't talk. The nisei, whose psyches were wired like Japanese baby pines by the internment. They wanted the third generation to grow up American, like redwoods. They wanted them to shoot for the sky, tall and straight, to walk ahead like gods. To free themselves of the past like a rocket that discards its used stages as it shoots into space. Let go of the past; if you carry your spent burden with you, you will never reach the moon.

the story of when I was born [thə sto'rē əv wĕn' ī wəz born']

When I was a little girl, and my mother put me to bed, she did not tell me stories about enchanted forests or beautiful princesses. I had seen "Sleeping Beauty." I knew "The Three Bears." These were not the stories I wanted to hear from my mother.

"Tell me the story of when I was born," I would say, mummified up to my chin by bedcovers. There were no magic wands or fairy godmothers in this story. No poisoned apples or pumpkins that turned into coaches. It was a simple story, a sequence of mundane events, barely connected and sparingly described, peopled not by bad wolves or evil stepmothers, but sisters, my father, my mother of course, and friends of the family. The reason I wanted to hear that story, the reason I liked it so much, was because I was in it. It was real.

Life for me began just eleven short years after the Japanese dropped bombs on Pearl Harbor, precipitating events that would inflict on my family a kind of willed amnesia that would last for forty years.

As soon as he could after the war, my father moved us out of Japantown, into an orderly and integrated neighborhood where we had an Armenian grocery, a Russian delicatessen, an Italian piano teacher, and kind *hakujin* neighbors named the Freemans. The Richmond District of San Francisco, where I grew up, was always foggy. The fog would come in off the Pacific during the night, and when I woke up, I would hear the mournful dialogue of fog horns warning ships in the Golden Gate. Sometimes the fog would burn off by noon, and we would get a glimpse of the blue sky that California is supposed to be so famous for. But often the fog remained all day, or came back in the afternoon, so thick and low that it seemed like a white smoke. If we went anywhere else in the city, we must have looked like foreigners, just come in from Siberia, in our sweaters and coats and knee-high socks. We probably had an intensity, too, that outside people, people who lived in the sun, lacked. A seriousness. An introspection, come from too many days spent inside the house reading, or a range of options that did not include barbecues and lying on the beach.

In school we learned about the explorers, the Mayflower, the American Revolution. When we studied California history, we learned about Father Junipero Serra and the California missions. History, it seemed, focused on the conquerors, never the conquered.

The first time I went to Japan, I was twenty-two. My plane lifted off from San Francisco International, gaining altitude as it banked over the Golden Gate. Down below I could see the Richmond District, the geometrical avenues where I had spent my childhood. Then the plane entered the fog, and for a few seconds there was nothing but whiteness outside my window. For a few seconds, there was no east or west, no time. No memory. Suddenly, we were through. Above the floor of clouds, the sky was blue. The wing of the plane reflected pure sunlight. It was like all the time I was growing up, I thought. We were down there, under the fog, going to school and church and piano lessons—and all that time there was this blue sky, this glorious sun. And suddenly I hated that fog. I'm out of it, I thought, my heart leaping. I'm on this side now.

Going to Japan was like that for me—like breaking through the fog and seeing, for the first time, in full light, where I had come from. What my grandparents had left behind. What they had intended to return to, until circumstances intervened and they ended up staying in America. Until I went to Japan, I was a person without a past; I looked into a mirror and saw no reflection. All I knew was the little white house on 23rd Avenue, in the Richmond District.

It wasn't until I was much older that I realized that the house my mother returned to from the hospital, after she had me, wasn't that house. The school where my sisters had a Halloween parade that day wasn't the school that was just up the hill from that house. All those years, I had imagined the story, my story, in the wrong place.

Living in that fog-shrouded world perhaps made it easier for my mother and father to forget the past—America's lack of faith, the internment, the shame. To forget a heritage that cast suspicion on their loyalty. I didn't have to forget—I never knew.

In wartime, one must choose sides. But the price for doing so can be paid for generations.

Rob Leri

Even as a child growing up in the Richmond District of San Francisco in the 1950's, I wanted to be a writer. I felt at an extreme disadvantage, coming from a happy family. "What am I going to write about?" I moaned. My imagination ranged far and wide, from Churchill Downs to the Battle of Lexington. This may have been an early manifestation of identity crisis. A musical play I wrote in high school featured an African-American queen, a Filipino-American king, a Russian witch, and a chorus of Asian-American princes and princesses. Only in the Richmond District could such a multicultural cast have been put to such bland use.

The "ethnic identity movement" in the early '70s made me realize that the most interesting story I could ever tell was the one that no one had ever told me: What it is like to be Japanese in America. First, I had to read about the history of Japanese in America, which I'd never been taught in school. Then I had to live in Japan to figure out what it meant to be Japanese. Gradually I uncovered my world, buried like a treasure, or a lost civilization.

History disappears if the stories are not told. So, in *The Loom and Other Stories*, I told them. Sometimes readers complain that I use Japanese words in my writing and don't explain them. "Fiction," I say, "is not a dictionary."

My stories have been published in *Story Magazine, Growing Up Asian-American, Pushcart Prize XVII, Growing Up Female, Making Waves*, and broadcast on NPR's "Selected Shorts."

Neela Sastry

TREMORS

IT WAS JUST AS Lupita Bravo absent-mindedly pushed the plug into the socket, that the booming and the rattling started. Straightening up—vertebra by vertebra, she paused. All was quiet. She shook her head and thanked the saints that it was finally Friday evening. Picking up the bulky canister vacuum, she moved to the stretch of dark brown carpeting that spilled over from the boss's room to the main office. Standing at the edge of the carpet, on the rusty-hued linoleum that graced the rest of the floor, she lifted her foot to push the starter when boom-boom-boom . . . boom-boom-boom. The oak-veneered partition that ran from ceiling to floor, separating the president's sanctum from the rest of the office, started to shake, accompanied by mini-explosions that created hollow reverberations round the room. *Ay, Dios mío!* She ducked behind the secretary's desk. *Ay, Dios mío!* She crossed herself and wriggled her buttocks under the desk just as she had wriggled into her coral pull-on pants this morning. A twinge in her back made her groan. It did occur to her—momentarily—that the Big One, if this indeed *was* the Big One, was affecting only one side of the room. Fear prevailed, and as they had so often advised on television, she decided to stay under the desk. The plastic-framed painting of a zebra fish with its mouth eternally open—finger-painted by one of the boss's children, looked ready to leap off the wooden partition. Boom-boom-boom . . . boom-boom-boom-boom.

Boom-boom-boom-boom . . . boom. Pause. Boom-boom-boom. Pause. Boom-boom-boom . . . boom. And then it stopped.

Lupita stayed put, longing for a drink of water. She waited for more aftershocks and remembered the telephone just a few inches above her head. The hand that reached out shook and she quickly withdrew it. Where were the sirens? The car alarms? Did no one else feel the earthquake, or whatever it was? She felt a desperate urge to be back in the overheated tightness of the apartment she shared with her husband and youngest son. Whatever it was, had stopped—at least for the time being, and she wasn't about to wait for a second round. Poking her head out, she was wriggling out on her knees and the heels of her palms when the boss's door swung open. She gazed at the wing-tipped shoes of the man who paid her to clean the office five evenings a week, and behind them, a pair of pale legs perched on red pumps.

Ashok turned his head to the right and sniffed at the traces of Tina's perfume in the interior of his car. If he closed his eyes, and didn't try too hard, it would come to him in a milk waft of musk and body warmth. A few minutes ago Tina's body had filled that empty space, curved against the fawn leather of the seat. He was still reeling from the last kiss she had pressed upon him before disappearing into her apartment complex. He was a child, in delirium after a visit to Disneyland. It was *his* secret. He thrilled at the thought of intrigue. The stolen kisses at traffic stops, the furtive fondling as they skipped the freeway and instead took the surface streets to Palms. Yes, it was *his* secret. His brow furrowed as he remembered Lupita. That damned woman. Of all the days to come in early. He'd told her time and again to only come in after seven-thirty. *Hope she keeps her mouth shut. That's all I need. Trouble!* He flicked his

palm in the air. He didn't care. It happened all the time—
bosses banging secretaries. That cleaning woman probably
didn't even know what had happened in there. It was perfectly
normal for Tina and himself to be working late. Nothing extra-
ordinary here. Or was it? Exactly how long had Lupita been in
the front office? *I wonder if she could have heard!*

For fifteen years, Ashok Gupta had been a loving family
man. He had built up an anodized aluminum business in part-
nership with his two older brothers. Now they managed the
factory, and he took care of the business part of it from a small
suite in downtown LA. He had given his aging parents a permanent home in his own four-bedroom-four-and-a-half bath
property in Westchester. His children went to expensive private schools. By the grace of Lord Ganesha, they were smart
girls. Maya, his wife, was a contented woman. She had never
lacked for anything from the day she had held hands with him
and walked seven times around the sacred fire. Her cheeks had
a permanent glow—or oily shine as it were, from keeping a full
kitchen, maintaining a houseful of guests for six months of the
year, and fulfilling the innumerable demands of a housewife,
besides keeping her husband and children satisfied. In return,
Ashok had given her this large home, their two children, count-
less trips to Artesia in her champagne Mercedes 300 E—to pick
up the latest in saree fashions from "home," and of course, the
inevitable monthly visit to the jewelry shops. She bought an
ounce of gold a month—solid security for the future—in her
opinion. Ashok had treated her fetish with amused indulgence.
Only Crédit Suissé or the Maple Leaf would do. Sometimes, as
they lay in the darkness, with his hand gently squeezing and
kneading her healthy belly, he'd ask her how close she was to
beating Fort Knox. He was a virgin when he married her and
had been faithful to her all their married life. Until today.

If Maya should ever get wind of it. . . . He shrugged his
shoulders. Unlikely. Even if she did, what was the worst that
could happen? She'd be upset, of course. Broken-hearted,
maybe. After all that she'd faithfully done for him. She'd cry.
Scream. Malign him to his family and hers. Go to her mother
in Bombay for a couple of months. And then return. *Don't they*

always? Besides, it's not as if I'm in love with Tina. Or Tina with him, for that matter. It wasn't something he had planned.

In fact, it was Tina who had made the first move. He had just succumbed to her demand for a raise. He couldn't say what prompted him to do that. He had certainly not made his money by squandering it. She had hugged him as she said thank you, and kissed his cheek, by the side of his mouth. It was no coincidence that their lips had met. He'd thanked his Sports Connection membership over and over again as her hand moved over his flat stomach. Thank goodness his wife had stopped using butter and *ghee* in her cooking! It was just lust on his part. And adventure. It was amazing—the kind of things his secretary could do, she was so . . . luscious. With Maya he'd never been at the receiving end. She was always quiet in bed. Suppliant. Merely supporting him physically through his exertions. Through the years he had learned to tell when *she* wanted sex. The signs were subtle . . . a snuggle under the covers, rubbing her feet on his. . . . But then, Maya had been conditioned that way—to behave like a decent, family woman. And he didn't think he wanted it any other way. What if Maya didn't return? *What if she took both the girls and her gold and left?*

Ashok waved goodbye to the last thought. Maya would never know. As he maneuvered the vehicle through traffic, his thoughts reverted to his evening of pure pleasure. He went over the event, moment by moment . . . from the first exploratory kisses to the last climactic thrusts, his body excited at the very thought of it. Tina was so . . . sensual. He could smell her perfume, her perspiration. Hear her quick breathing as she licked his ear-lobe. She was there in his car. He marveled at the near-tangible feeling he had of her presence. A sidelong glance to his right ridiculed his fanciful meanderings. Reality dragged him back as the driver behind him pulled up into the right lane, honked and jabbed a middle finger upwards. Behave yourself, Ashok told the swelling knot between his legs. No more for you today. And there she was again. His hands were on her, pushing her towards the wall. . . . This was getting out of hand. At this rate, Maya would definitely smell a rat. He should have stopped off at a health club for a quick shower. He could smell Tina on his clothes . . . his skin. He could smell himself. He hoped Maya wouldn't come to the door. It would be better if one of the girls did. Then he could say he was tired and head straight for the shower. There he could wash the smell off his body. And hopefully rinse his briefs out before his wife spotted them. Not that it was important. He could always tell her he was thinking of her when the accident happened. But she knew him too well for that. What if the kids were asleep, or in their rooms upstairs, watching television when he arrived? Maya would smell it right away when she took his jacket. Suddenly, he wasn't at all sure that she would treat this as a schoolboy's prank and forgive him.

Eight blocks from home Ashok guided his 380 ZX through a U-turn and pulling up alongside a phone booth, called Maya. *Don't wait up for me, I'm at a restaurant . . . yes, alone! I'm working a little late again . . . yes . . . alone!* Except for Lupita . . . if she was still there. Maya had never asked him that question before. He decided to go back to the office and wipe himself down with paper towels before he went back home. In future, he would keep a change of clothing at the office.

Ashok hoped Lupita wouldn't create any problems. A lot depended on Lupita. Maya sent her a gift every Christmas, and Lupita always reciprocated with a thank-you phone call. Some evenings, she had even picked up the phone when Maya called, and made conversation with her. Ashok thought it was hilarious. Lupita's broken English, matched by Maya's *poquito de español*. What if Lupita were to develop a sudden allegiance with Maya, woman to woman. One never knew. All it would take was one phone call . . . and his world would come to an end. He had to talk to Lupita. To reason with her. She must have a family, she would understand. He had to *make* her understand. There were too many lives involved besides his own. Maya. The children. Yes, he would appeal on behalf of the children. Would she want their innocent lives destroyed by a parental rift? Two innocent girls forced to grow up without the influence of a father. Ostracized by the narrow-minded Indian community. They would be lost. Adrift. Their mother would teach them to hate him. To hate all men. Maya would never be able to get them married. They'd end up wild, without morals, like . . . Tina.

And his own *parents*. Their faces—etched with sorrow—

rose before him. He saw them through the windshield—super-imposed over the city lights. His face contorted as tears coursed down their wrinkled faces. Son. My boy. What have you done? No, no, no. He couldn't let Lupita do this to them. He had to stop her from making that phone call. Oh God, if he ever got through this whole affair without incident, he'd make up for this ten times over. He'd fire Tina. He'd never do something stupid like this again. He'd build shrines in his home-town for every one of the family deities. He'd feed a hundred poor children. He wondered how many children Lupita had. A husband? If only he could get her to understand. He hoped that she'd still be at the office.

A cup of coffee and a few local phone calls were the only fringe benefits Lupita allowed herself at Señor Gupta's office. She considered herself to be honest and God-fearing. However, she had decided that at fifty-three, with her growing back problem, even the Lord would have to overlook some minor trespasses. She liked working here because there was no pres-sure. The bookkeeper and that witch—the secretary, usually left promptly at five. Señor Gupta himself stayed a little later, but not too long, so she could conduct her chores at her own pace. Héctor had been at her back for a while to ask her boss for a raise. Lupita hated talking about money, it embarrassed her acutely. Her sister Lea, who she would have to call in a few minutes, had emphasized time and again that sometimes Lupita would have to leave shame at home. She would have to walk right into Señor Gupta's office, look him straight in the face and ask for a raise. Lupita sighed as she put the coffee cup down on the secretary's table, unable to understand her own reticence. Señor Gupta was a nice enough man, not nice enough to *volunteer* a raise, but quite approachable. He was a family man after all, and might even empathize. He *had* dis-concerted her somewhat, earlier in the evening. She had re-mained speechless, balanced on all fours looking up at them. She shook her head at the image she must have presented. Not that they looked less foolish. He with his fly half open and that woman with her nylons dangling from her hand. Lupita had never met his wife, but she had spoken to her on the phone now and then, and at Christmas. She always sounded quite self-assured. Well, wait till she found out. It was bound to happen, sooner or later. Lupita shrugged and grimaced as pain snaked up her back again. She washed and put away the coffee cup. Sitting at the secretary's desk, she drew the phone towards her.

It was just as he had suspected. She was going to do it. Lupita was going to call Maya. Stepping out of the elevator, he had cat-footed it to the office, and with admirable dexterity, turned the key noiselessly in the lock. And there she was—grimly making that phone call which would annihilate him. Throwing the door fully open he rushed towards her, wondering in mid-flight whether to crush her skull or push her down the elevator shaft. The minutes ticked away as he tried to reach Lupita behind Tina's desk, but she had already dropped the receiver back into its cradle and jumped out of the chair, wincing as she moved. *Lupita! No . . . no! Nada . . . nada! Have you gone crazy? Are you trying to destroy me?* Ashok's eyes were wide open. His voice had risen.

Lupita stared at Ashok's shaking hand on the telephone and then at his face. *Ay!* All because she had tried to make *one* phone call. Maybe not one, exactly, but what was it to him? Peanuts! If she could afford it she would use her own phone at home. Yes, if she could *afford* it she wouldn't be working here, cleaning *his* office. Lupita put a hand on her chest, trying to quell the sudden resentment that she felt. She looked at him as he collapsed in the secretary's chair. There was something akin to fright in his face, but she ignored it. Taking a deep breath, she folded her arms. *Señor, I . . . want . . . more dinero. Necesito más dinero!* Señer Gupta didn't say anything. His eyes moved to the desk and rested on the phone. Lupita waited.

Ashok decided he wasn't going to react. He was going to stay calm and play for time. *Damn . . . the woman is actually blackmailing me!* He should have handled this better, being a businessman and all that. They should have gone to Tina's apartment. To a motel. Better still, he should never have gotten himself into this mess. *Think, brain, think.* How could he possibly think? With the woman standing before him—gloating.

Señor! You . . . hear Señor?

Necesito. She was challenging him. She was blackmailing him outright, and he didn't have a thing to say to her. *You want more dinero?*

Sí, más dinero. Lupita nodded. Her mouth had lost some of its tightness but her gaze was still steady.

Ashok held her dark eyes with his own. He could chance it and refuse to pay her. What if she called Maya? She *would* call Maya. There was something about that expression But if he buckled, she might take it as a sign of weakness and continue to blackmail him. Even as he considered the possibility, her eyes narrowed and she glanced at her black-faced watch. Well, he would just have to play this very carefully. Ashok reached within his jacket for his check-book. He wasn't going to let her dictate the amount, of that he was sure. He would offer five, maybe six hundred dollars. What if she were insulted? Better to start with a thousand and then haggle if she protested. He *had* to be strong. He would just write her a check for a fixed amount and be very firm about it. He felt Lupita watching him as he picked up a ball-point pen off Tina's desk and scribbled across a check. Detaching it, he pushed it casually towards her. Women . . . why did he have to complicate his life with women?

She was surprised that he hadn't protested. Or argued. Or even bothered to inform her how much of a raise he was giving her. Lupita reached across and picked up the check. One thousand dollars. *Dios mío!* She knew he was a good man at heart. But this. All she wanted was a raise and he had given her this. She wasn't going to question it.

As Lupita said *gracias* and left, Ashok rubbed the back of his neck vigorously and leaned back in Tina's chair. That took care of *this* one. She was easy. Maybe he should have offered her less, after all. What a day! Never again would he be so careless. To almost throw his life away for a little flutter on the side. His eyes rested on the zebra fish and he yawned. Maybe next time—if there was a next time—he would be a little more circumspect. Stretching, he heaved his body out of the chair to wash up. The phone rang. Maya . . . inquiring how late he was going to be! It was Tina. *Hi! I called your home . . . your wife said you were still at work. Wanna stop by . . . on your way home?*

The undergraduate college which I attended in southern India had separate staircases for men and women. Transgressors, especially female, *anglicized* ones, were treated to a public discourse meant to dissolve any traces of self-esteem that they might have salted away. It wasn't proper for a *decent girl* to vocalize her objections to societal norms. So I wrote instead—harmless satire—trying to make sense out of the nonsensical. I hear the staircase tradition continues even as the twenty-first century awaits its cue, and wonder if the lectures do.

My parents introduced me to books. What I loved best were the yarns my father spun for my sister and me. His geologist's mind led us through fantastic subterranean caves and hidden cities, and we explored for brilliant blue diamonds as big as our refrigerator. . . My mother's frenetic writing was inspiring; at fifty-five she wrote her first script for a successful TV series.

Almost a decade since I left my homeland and at times I still awaken expecting the inimitable aroma of hot Indian coffee. In Arizona I dream of an Indian monsoon while watching gila woodpeckers dart in and out of saguaros. Now I savor prickly pear punch and *nopalitos* as if I were raised on them.

Thanks to the incessant nagging of my husband, always the professor—*publish or perish*—I'm in the throes of putting together a collection of short fiction.

Shawn Wong

FEAR OF FLYING

from *American Knees*

BRENDA UMEKI SAYS she's disgusted every time she sees an Asian man with an ugly white woman. She's not saying all white women are ugly when they're with Asian men. She's not a racist. When she sees it, she just sees some pathetic Asian man so desperate to smack up skin to skin with a white girl, he'll pick anyone who'll have him. In the cases where the Asian man is actually pretty nice looking, he looks kind of guilty when she's staring at him.

Aurora says, "Maybe because it's the way your mouth gets all twisted up in that sneer."

"He's got this look like he's been caught in the headlights, and he doesn't know which way to run."

"That's fright, not guilt."

"For Asian boys there's no difference."

Brenda says for the handsome Asian men with the truly

gorgeous white girl, you know, some awesome Barbie babe with the blonde curly mane and legs and the tits, great beach material, those boys just stare her down or ignore her like "go ahead and hit me with your headlights, I'm indestructible." He's with the woman all men lust after. Brenda says she's the kind of girl she wanted to be when she was thumbing through the pages of *Seventeen*, harboring some self-contempt while Mom's telling her the advantages of straight black hair.

"What about the ugly nerd Asian boy and beautiful white girl?" Aurora asks.

"I don't mind. I'm not threatened. No love or lust there," Brenda says. "It's a charity case or more likely it's study hall time. She needs a passing grade in Calculus in order to stay on the cheerleading squad. Henry's there to help. He has his day in the sun. Then he melts, unless he's too rich to melt."

"Why do you care, Brenda?" Aurora asks. "You don't go out with Asian men."

Brenda says she's tried to but doesn't know how. She's *sansei* and never knew any Asian boys growing up in the suburbs, never went to school with them, never been around them except in college. She was in a sorority, and there weren't any Asian guys in the frats. She got invited to some Chinese Student Association dances but felt out of place. A lot of the Chinese girls froze her out because she was a sorority girl, she was Japanese, she was from the suburbs, Japan invaded China, hell, pick one of the above. Brenda went on a date with a Korean guy, but both sets of parents nearly went on full tilt just thinking about the Japanese-Korean thing. The stereotypical monumental and monolithic rudeness of Koreans and the invasion and occupation of Korea by the Japanese was too much to overcome. Brenda went out with a couple of black guys, but she couldn't handle the vicious backbiting and the looks among the black women she met. Some of the women would talk loud enough for both her and her date to hear, "Got hisself a yearning for high yellowness so high he got a chink." The chorus behind her voiced its uh-huhs. If you can't fight back, you can't survive in that environment. One time Brenda got so mad she said something about this black woman wanting to be Asian so bad she ironed and processed her black hair straight until it was a toxic waste dump of chemicals. Brenda's date had to step between them. Over his shoulder Brenda said something about the woman's mother and her pubic hair. Brenda's date got a blackeye.

The Korean and the black experiences even made Dad much easier to handle when she started dating white boys again. Brenda asks Aurora which was the lesser of the evils. Koreans and Japanese head the hate list dating back to Japan's invasion of Korea followed by their rudeness and abrupt manner. Japanese practice *enyro* and *gaman*. You know, nobody takes the last piece of chicken no matter what; let it go uneaten back to the kitchen, defer and be patient. Fight over the bill until you tear it in half. Send a thank-you card as soon as you get home. Next time make an excuse to go to the bathroom, and pay the bill secretly in the back. Chinese scrimp on things at home, clip out coupons, never buy retail; warehouse stores are made for Chinese shoppers, but they too will fight to the death over paying the restaurant bill. Gives them "big face." Chinese Americans and Japanese Americans have patched things up between them over the invasion of China. Chinese buy Japanese cars until they can afford a Mercedes. Ever see a Mercedes with clear plastic seat covers protecting the leather? Chinese and Japanese have been out of the Chinatowns and Japantowns a long time now, been neighbors in the suburbs together.

Korea invaded the black neighborhoods and took ownership of the corner grocery store, and an urban war started. Filipino boys in their leather jackets, tank tops, gold chains, and Monte Carlos with the tinted windows go hot and heavy for the tinted blondes. It's the American dream they've been reading about in their American textbooks and watching in the American movies and television back in the Philippines. Every Filipino boy wants to rescue Ginger from Gilligan's Island. But they marry Filipino girls in the end out of filial duty and Christian and familial guilt. Sometimes people can't figure out what they are and simply refer to them as "that Spanish kid."

Brenda says the Thai boys at the Thai Take Out are polite and have beautifully smooth skin. The mother of the family that runs the take out looks young enough to be the boys' sister. She wonders if they can dance.

Streetwise Vietnamese and other recent immigrant boys

are always staring at the Asian American women who shop in their grocery stores, coming up to them and saying, "Hi, how are you?" with an accent that begins with forming their mouths as if each word begins with an "O." Sometimes they walk up to Brenda dragging the heels of their shoes on the floor which drives Brenda crazy. She wants to yell, "Pick up your feet!" They want to know what you are to see if it's okay to go out with you. "Are you Chinese? I'm Vietnamese Chinese." Sometimes she tries to be friendly and joke with them, but they don't allow themselves to laugh properly, you know, the way Brenda's Japanese grandmother says she shouldn't. At the grocery store their family runs, they try too hard to make strained casual conversation out of what you buy, what you eat, what you drink, what magazines you read. Brenda buys aspirin and they want to know if she's "making a headache?" Brenda never buys tampons from them.

Brenda says Asian men have great bodies. She doesn't want to date them, or have sex with them, or marry them. Brenda says, "Let someone else marry them. We've been married to them for 4,000 years." She actually just likes the way they look: that hairless look, that Bruce Lee muscle tone. Brenda likes going to the kung-fu movies and the samurai movies, likes her Asian men to be virile and heroic and strong. Her support of them in this way has something to do with history and loyalty to the race. Privately to Aurora, Brenda will put Asian men down as mates, but in public she'll defend them when she hears a non-Asian say something racist about them. Too bad white guys can't have Asian bodies. Brenda hates chest hair and hairy backs. She's sometimes afraid she'll end up married to some white guy that'll wear his jeans too low and the crack of his hairy white ass will show when he bends down. Too bad Bruce Lee had that accent.

Aurora tells Brenda the men aren't the problem and that 75 percent of Japanese American women are marrying out of the race compared to 20 percent for the men. Aurora herself is the product of a statistic, the offspring of the rule rather than the exception. According to the statistic, the odds favor Brenda becoming one of those hyphenated women keeping their identity correct in their names—a Umeki-Miller, or a Umeki-Polanski, or a Umeki-Washington. Aurora tells Brenda about the time Raymond and his buddy, Jimmy Chan, were walking down the street and saw this Vietnamese guy, obviously fresh off the boat, walking hand in hand with a white girl. Raymond nudges Jimmy and says, "Look at that guy." Jimmy says, "Shit man, FOB's be stealin' our women."

"Umeki-Washington, now there's a thought, Ro." Aurora wonders if black men who have a thing for Asian women are less likely to be racists than the white men who have a thing for Asian women. Do they have to have that black hair down to the waist fantasy? Subservient, submissive, docile geisha?

Brenda says she likes black coffee, black silk, little black dresses, black tights, black shoes, black leather pants, over-sized black T-shirts, black bras, black cars, black linguini.

Brenda's aunt married a white man during the war when she was sprung from Minidolka Relocation Center to go back to school in Chicago. She says it's better for the kids so that the next time the country wants to round up the Japanese and haul them off to camp, they won't be able to recognize them, like the Germans and the Italians who got off easy during the war. Brenda's aunt says the sooner the Japanese all marry out the better. The whole country is going to be Hispanic in a few years; maybe we can pass for Hispanic in a generation of two, then pass for white after that, even change our names like the Jews and the Mexicans. "Buy American" means a whole bunch of things.

Brenda's aunt says the kids got it all wrong in the sixties with all that search for identity and self-determination crap. "What is it you kids don't know? Why do you want to draw attention to yourself? You kids didn't even know we were in camp until you read about it in your high school textbooks. Then you come home wearing black armbands wanting to know why we never told you about the camps. You never asked."

Brenda' aunt and uncle took their family to Disney World after they got their $20,000 redress money and an apology from the President for the internment and bought a new fishing boat and named it "Camp Harmony" after the first camp they were sent to during the war, or as the War Relocation Authority called it, "Assembly Center." Meanwhile the letters to the editors pages of every newspaper in America are filled with readers who can't tell the difference between Japanese Americans and Japanese. They want to know if redress will be paid to the "Americans" who died at Pearl Harbor.

Brenda says when she was growing up, she didn't want to be Japanese; she wanted to be like all the other kids. In the sixties "Orientals" suddenly became "Asian Americans" looking to establish ethnic studies classes, going into Chinatown clothing stores and buying *mee nahps*, taking judo and karate lessons, and spelling out ten nonnegotiable demands on a bullhorn.

Brenda has a very un-Asian body. Brenda says it's all natural. She's tall, long-legged, short-waisted, and has breasts. Her breasts she got from her mother, but otherwise her mother and father are short, bow-legged, and long-waisted. Vitamins and stretching her limbs, says Brenda's mother, are what did it. Brenda's mother says she pinched Brenda's nose when she was a little girl to make it thin. At birth Brenda's mother was relieved when she saw her daughter had all her limbs, and toes, and fingers, *and* double eyelids. She's an all-American girl.

"They shouldn't give Asian women large breasts because we have enough problems as it is," Brenda says to Aurora. "In American culture, the boobs become your identity. You know, 'Hey, she's got big tits,' instead of having an identity first. Even Asian women mention it. Men come up to me and actually point at my breasts and say, 'Oriental girls don't usually have those'."

Brenda says the best of both worlds would be to marry a white guy and have 100% Asian babies "because they're so cute." Brenda is a mass of contradictions. Aurora says that white girls who marry Asian men want 100% Asian babies too. White couples want little blond boys and want to adopt Korean girls. American society is a mass of contradictions.

Brenda went out with Glenn Tompkins once. Everybody in the Asian community calls Glenn Tompkins "Red." It's a real cliché because of his red hair, but then none of the kids growing up in Chinatown ever got to call anyone "Red." Glenn floats between Chinatown and Japantown, dabbling in things Chinese and Japanese because he likes Asian women. Red joins the Japanese Buddhist Church, volunteers to drive the Church van and takes the old timers out for their excursions, cooks for the bazaar potluck, buddies up to the *nisei* aunts who might introduce him to their daughters, tutors English down at the Chinatown community service center, and takes Chinese and Japanese language classes. Red is not some midwest sailor who, on R&R in Hong Kong first time away from the family farm, gets a taste of some Oriental poontang and a massage and signs himself on the waiting list back home. Red knows the difference between the stereotypical Hollywood image of an Asian woman and the real Asian American woman. He's more comfortable being a white guy immersed in a culture he can study and understand, instead of being what he is—part Scottish, Irish, French, and, as always, a sixteenth Cherokee. A lot of Asian women have gone out with him once, but he doesn't know that he falls into the same category as the other boys their aunts set them up with—a boring wimp, and in this case, a boring wimp who wants to talk about Asian culture.

Red is trying to be like the guys, hang with them, be polite so maybe some day one of the women will like him back and think of him as a brother because he's been hanging around so long. For a while some thought Glenn was gay and was cruising through the community in order to get hooked with some rice queen, as they call them. Asian men stayed away from Glenn and wouldn't even walk on the same side of the street. It's odd that when they found out he was after the women, they didn't mind his presence.

One time three gay guys, one white, one black, and one Asian came to a community fundraising dance put on by the younger members of several of the Asian organizations to "celebrate diversity" among the new Asian populations. After asking several Asian men to dance and being refused, they wondered out loud about the theme of "diversity" and how discrimination and homophobia seemed to be well protected by a double standard. Three of the women asked them to dance, saying that would be "celebrating diversity" for them.

In the movies Chinese men very rarely play real men: Hop Sing, Charlie Chan, Cain, Fu Manchu. They rule by proverb, not brawn. Most times in movies Chinese men can't even play themselves and have white actors in yellow face with latex slanted eyes stepping in for them. On *Bonanza* a white woman can be shy about showing her ankle to Hoss or Little Joe, but she can walk around Hop Sing's kitchen with her corset on without fear. Everyone knows nothing will happen to her. Hop Sing talks a line of excited jibberish, but he's no real man. Chinese men have been defined by these role models for decades. Raymond's friend Jimmy Chan, a writer for the Oakland Tribute, says that apes have made greater strides in self-determination in the movies than Chinese American men. Apes went from King Kong pounding on the gates of Skull Island to speaking and taking over the world in "Planet of the Apes." Meanwhile Chinese men have gone from Charlie Chan to Cain in the television series "Kung-fu," both proverb-spouting effeminate men played by whites in yellow face. Cain does fight, but it's artistic, not lethal. Asian men in the movies never have names like Bo or Max or Leroy or Scarface.

Jimmy Chan says, "Why is it every time I go to the bank to withdraw cash and I get an Asian woman teller, she's got to go in the back and check my signature and my bank balance? I've been banking at the same bank for years, and they've got two Asian women tellers. They know me. I give them a break and think maybe I've got an attitude. So I go up to the window of this one woman all friendly like and look at her name plate and call her by her name, 'Hey, Angela, how are you doing today?' She says, 'Fine,' like a robot, and before I can begin speaking again, she spins around and heads for the back again. She's fuckin' with me."

"You're being paranoid," Raymond says, even though he knows it's true. "Maybe she's got a crush on you. Likes to have you linger around. Wants to see if you got enough money to keep her happy!"

"I know what it is; they're prejudiced."

"Why is it," Raymond joins in, "every time I get on an airplane and walk down the jetway to the plane I see ten, twelve people walk by the flight attendant and she stops me and wants to see my boarding pass? Is it because I'm cute and she wants to make small talk? Is it because she thinks I can't read or speak English and I might be getting on the wrong damn plane, that I'm too stupid to match flight numbers! These days I make it a point of walking right up to them and getting all chatty, holding up the line, just so they won't ask, and I say,

'Howdy! (I never say howdy.) Howzit goin' today? Hope we'll have a humdinger (I never say humdinger) of a flight!' Do I look like I'm from Japan?"

Jimmy Chan says one time this white Moonie holding a flower out at the airport tries to stop him by speaking Japanese to him, and Jimmy stops and launches into a tirade on this poor sucker about how his family has been living in California for five generations, he's a writer for the Oakland Tribune, he's Chinese, and every Asian ain't a Japanese tourist and he better get his sorry Moonie pin cushion haircut back to the temple before he really gets mad.

"What's the worst thing about flying?" Jimmy asks.

Raymond says the worst is when he's given a seat next to another Asian. The flight attendant automatically think the two "Orientals" are together. If he or she is from Asia somewhere, neither Raymond nor they really care. Maybe he can even help them out with the English. It's a relief to them because Raymond can tell they would rather be sitting next to another Asian than not. Like the time Raymond and Jimmy were flying to New York and Jimmy tried to use his bad Cantonese on this woman about the choice in meals on the plane, one was beef, *nowyuk*, Jimmy pronounced it, and the other was shrimp, but Jimmy said the word for lobster instead. The woman chose lobster, but smiled when she got her shrimp because Jimmy meant well. It's why foreign-born Chinese call American-born Chinese *jook sing*, hollow bamboo; we look Chinese, but we're hollow inside, no substance. But if the other passenger is an Asian American woman, and it's the bank teller from Jimmy's bank, we're in big trouble. The flight attendant is going to come by and ask, "What would you two like to drink?" Everybody gets irritated by the assumption. It becomes a contest of body language that says, *I'm not with him, I don't know him, I speak English, I don't date Asian men because they're domineering wimps.* "No, I don't want tea. I'll have coffee—black."

"Then there's the Asian woman with the white husband who have been assigned the seats next to you," Jimmy adds. "They go through this dance thing where they're trying to figure out who is going to sit next to whom. What makes the best sense. We're all trying to be polite standing in the aisle while trying to suppress the fear in our eyes, trying to suppress the apologies for even considering what might look better, trying not to be racists about it all. Finally the woman sits by the window, I sit on the aisle and there's this oversized hairy white guy sitting between us like a human demilitarized zone. I'm looking to see if there's an empty seat nearby next to someone with a more reasonable color combination. It'll help settle the question as to whose wife she is in the flight attendant's mind. I want to tell her that I've got no problem with her marrying a white guy. I'm a nice guy. I want to make small talk with her husband about sports and regular guy stuff."

"It's like a black guy walking down the block at night behind a white woman carrying a bag of groceries. She turns from time to time and looks over her shoulder. The black guy sees she's kind of nervous about him being there, so he crosses the street and slows down a bit so she doesn't think he's a mugger even though he has to cross back across the street later to get home."

"Exactly," Jimmy sighs. "I look for another seat on the plane so no one feels ashamed, or guilty, or defensive."

Raymond talks about travelling with his old girlfriend, Gretchen, the one after ex-wife Darleen. She was an attorney he had met when he went back to work at the Orange County Department of Human Rights as a temporary replacement for a woman on maternity leave. Gretchen was blonde and has these looks people have seen somewhere before but can't place it—a magazine ad, a television commercial. Jimmy remembers her very well.

Men at airports and in hotels would come right up to Gretchen as if Raymond weren't there and start talking with her or offer to help her with her bags. They assumed Raymond was (a) not with her, (b) a business partner, (c) an employee of the hotel, (d) a driver delivering her to the airport, and/or (e) someone named Hop Sing. Get back to the kitchen. Those who didn't approach her would stare at her, openly flirt with her, or say something crude, and Raymond would either have to pretend he didn't hear them or have Gretchen restrain him. Gretchen would try and mollify Raymond's irritation by saying men do that to her all the time. She doesn't go to war over their ignorance; why should Raymond?

"I'm no threat to them," Raymond once said to her. "This thing between you and me couldn't be anything real. They've seen houseboys like me on television. By not standing up to them, I prove them right—Asian men are wimps."

"You don't have to prove anything to me. I know who you are. Believe me, Raymond, men's I.Q.s go way down when they see blond hair. It's not you."

"Yeah, like when they open the door for you and follow you through while I'm left on the outside."

"That's happened only six or seven times. You know I'm always holding your hand or being affectionate in public. It's not like I pretend I'm not with you. Plus don't you even notice that when I'm with you these white women think they can come up to you and start talking to you? They're racists too. They think I'm going to share my 'houseboy' with them. I've had friends as well as strangers ask me what it's like having a Chinese lover. You don't think I know something about racism because I'm white and Norwegian. I'm not one of those white girls you see in Chinatown walking around in those black kung-fu shoes, eating vegetables their midwest mothers never heard of, wearing silk Chinese jackets, and speaking Cantonese phrases to the store clerks. You Chinese boys should be ashamed of yourselves for chasing after and seducing those ninnies like your friend who memorized some phrases out of the *I Ching* and recited them over dinner at the Lotus Pod restaurant."

Gretchen says that Raymond is too sensitive. What she leaves unsaid is that part of his discourse on identity and Asian male masculinity is very much part of his conceit—that trying to prove something about how men react to her is also trying to prove something about dating a white woman in the first place. Gretchen knows Raymond takes real pride in being *able* to date her. He thinks other Asian men might be in awe of him or at least green with envy. She's used to it and doesn't really mind. She's not interested in going out with some white guy with a red Camaro wearing Blublockers and deck shoes.

Raymond remembers that Gretchen was right about her display of public affection and that he very rarely returned her affection in public, at least in the same enthusiastic way. He couldn't be affectionate toward her and vulnerable while at the same time steeling himself for the next racist affront. One time

Raymond and Gretchen were holding hands while walking down the street, and he saw an Asian woman walking toward them about a block away. Pretending he had an itch, Raymond drops Gretchen's hand, not out of guilt but to again steel himself against a racist affront, even a racist thought never spoken. Racists come in all forms. No one white guy has ever come up to Raymond and said, "Keep your slimy yellow paws off our women." And no one dressed in a white sheet has ever come up to Gretchen and called her a "Chink lover." In the end most of it was blown out of proportion in Raymond's mind, because Asians are generally accepted anywhere, and no one ever said an unkind word when he was with Gretchen. Only the Asian woman walking down the street who had seen Raymond drop his girlfriend's hand had said to herself as she passed them, *look up the word "double-standard" in the dictionary and there would be a picture of that jive dude.*

Guilty.

Shawn Wong's first novel, *Homebase* (Reed and Cannon, 1979; reprinted by Plume/New American Library, 1990), won both the Pacific Northwest Booksellers Award and the 15th Annual Governor's Writers Day Award of Washington. A German language edition of *Homebase* was published in 1982 by Nexus Verlag. He is also the co-editor and editor of several anthologies of Asian American literature including the widely acclaimed *Aiiieeeee! An Anthology of Asian American Writers* (Howard University Press, 1974; reprinted Mentor/New American Library, 1991) and, *The Big Aiiieeeee! An Anthology of Chinese America and Japanese America in Literature* (Meridian/New American Library, 1991). He is co-editor of *Before Columbus Foundation Fiction/Poetry Anthology: Selections from the American Book Awards, 1980–1990*, two volumes of contemporary American multicultural poetry and fiction (W. W. Norton, 1992). His second novel entitled *American Knees* will be published by Simon & Schuster in 1995.

In addition to the publication of his poetry, fiction, essays and reviews in periodicals and anthologies, Shawn Wong was also the recipient of a National Endowment for the Arts Creative Writing Fellowship.

Wong received his undergraduate degree in English at the University of California at Berkeley (1971) and a Master's Degree in Creative Writing at San Francisco State University (1974). Wong has taught at Mills College, University of California at Santa Cruz and San Francisco State University. He has served as Chairman of the Seattle Arts Committee, Coordinator of Seattle's Bumbershoot Festival Commission and as a consultant for public arts agencies, including National Endowment for the Arts. He is presently an associate professor of American Ethnic Studies at the University of Washington.

Shawn Wong's other pursuits include professional drag racing. He has been racing for fifteen years. In 1984 Wong won a prestigious National Hot Rod Association "Oscar," the highest award in drag racing, for his win in the National Hot Rod Association Northern Pacific Division finals. His 1970 Dodge Challenger is sponsored by several companies including, Fel-Pro, Edelbrock, Alliance Cams, Ghent Racing Engines, Taylor Spark Plug wires, and C&P Racing Converters.

Shawn Wong was born in Oakland and raised in Berkeley, California. He is married to Vicki Tsuchida and has lived in Seattle since 1976.

Shawn Wong

REFLECTIONS

IN THE SUMMER OF 1967 I wrote a poem, then another, and another, and then I started thinking about being a writer. I was eighteen and just about to enter San Francisco State University where I became a pre-med student and an English major. In between my chemistry classes I took a writing class from the Irish poet named James Liddy and another writing class from Kay Boyle. I was hooked. Kay Boyle became my mentor. It was under her supervision at the age of nineteen that I started writing the early parts of *Homebase* (1979).

Homebase started out as a poem. I re-wrote *Homebase* eight or nine times after I graduated from the Creative Writing Program at San Francisco State. Each time I kept taking things out of the story in order to make the language work harder and to make the reader slow their reading pace down. I wanted the reader to read, reflect, re-read, and remember. I call it a poetic memory that comes from a very deliberate repetition in the work, that is, there are places in *Homebase* where the reader has to remember something from an earlier part of the book. For example, there's a very unspecific, abstract reference at the end of Chapter Five, the chapter that takes place on Angel Island, in which Rainsford Chan says, "On days like today, I hear someone moving through the chain-link fence, something she's wearing strikes a note on the fence post and as the vibration fades away, she moves through." The reader is supposed to recall that sound is from Chapter Two is the sound Rainsford's mother's jade bracelet makes as she moves about the house.

I experimented with the first person narration in *Homebase* because I wanted to give voice to the three generations that came before Rainsford and whose history was lost and forgotten.

Kay Boyle once told me that writing is about belief. She said writing wasn't about doing a lot of "creative writing exercises" and learning this technique and that technique. If you have belief and commitment, then you will work on your writing until it reaches a level that is equal to that commitment and belief. That thing called belief is not only the political and personal, but also the belief that drives you to write. So that at *all* times in the writing of the novel you want every line, every paragraph to reflect exactly who you are. You find yourself looking at a piece of the writing and you can honestly tell yourself, about that piece of writing, "That is exactly what I meant to say and that is exactly how I feel in my heart and mind." YOU look at that writing and you tell yourself that you can't say it verbally any better, sing it any better, act it out any better, paint, dance, or anything any better than it is. YOU reach the point where you know that you can't write any better than what's on the page. There shouldn't be any places in the novel that you aren't completely committed to, that is, there shouldn't be places in the novel where you think it is just narrative explanation and a sort of transition to the next really important, heartfelt part. Of course there are places in the novel that may not be as momentous or important as far as the story goes, but the commitment to the writing at all times in the novel is at the same level from beginning to end. I labor over a character drinking a glass a water in the same way I labor over a character experiencing grief or love.

When I sit down to write I always feel that I can be a better writer than the day before. Most of us reach a plateau in our writing where we are competent and skilled. Do we know what it takes to be even better? How do we recognize when we are better? How do we recognize a piece of writing that says "this is exactly what I feel in my heart."

In my second novel, *American Knees* (Simon & Schuster, 1995), I wanted to write a novel that would make people laugh out loud, and cry in public, and be in love. I also had very specific things to say about gender and racial stereotyping and intra-Asian and interracial relationships. As I was working on it, I had this very deliberate idea that *American Knees* would be completely different from *Homebase*, but as I wrote I realized that the two novels were very much alike in the sense that they're both love stories. *American Knees* is a contemporary love story between a biracial Japanese and Irish woman and a Chinese American man and *Homebase* is a story about a son's love for his mother and father. While stylistically *American Knees* is not nearly as complex as *Homebase*, I think the passion and the belief match. Some readers say *American Knees* is more "accessible" than *Homebase*. I never thought *Homebase* was inaccessible or too literary. At the foundation of the classic search for identity in *Homebase* is a very basic tale of grief and love.

It's really a very simple act to see oneself on the page. We writers resist, we play games, we procrastinate, we sidestep the real issue, then at some point we write and we find our own heart at risk when we see how honest we've been. Somewhere in there lies the belief. And taking that risk is what we do.

I read novels written by good friends and I sometimes marvel at how honest they are about their most private selves, their pain, self-hatred, guilt, and all. It's almost like you want to read the novel behind a screen or read out of the side of your eye. But that doesn't mean a novel is confessional or therapy. It is far from it.

The common question I'm asked about *Homebase* is whether or not the story is autobiographical. It is and it isn't. Yes, I lived on Guam when I was six, and yes, my father died when I was seven and my mother died when I was fifteen, but the other facts are not true. I'm second generation, not fourth, and both my parents came to America from China as students. The Chinese American history in *Homebase* is not my family's history, but I felt I had to assume responsibility for it because I knew by the time *Homebase* was published it might very well be the only Chinese American novel in print. Depending on how you define what is a Chinese American novel, it was the only one of five Chinese American novels I knew of when it was published in 1979, two of them were out-of-print, Diana Chang's *The Frontiers of Love* (1956) and Louis Chu's *Eat a Bowl of Tea* (1961), and two of them were novels for children, Laurence Yep's *Dragonwings* (1975) and *Child of the Owl* (1977). There were at least ten Asian American sociological and autobiographical works in print. The irony here, of course, was that ten years ago I was the only Chinese American writer I knew and now in 1979 I was one of two Chinese American novelists in print in America. To add to this scenario very few people read *Homebase* until twelve years later when it was reissued by Penguin as part of their Plume Contemporary Fiction series in 1991.

I was twenty when I realized I was the only Asian American writer I knew (and I wasn't very good). Until then not one teacher in public school or college ever used a work of fiction or poetry by an American writer of Chinese descent or any Asian American writer or even mentioned one. As a comparison, I remember trying to imagine being an African American student and having no knowledge of African American writers, musicians, singers, actors, and painters. I knew no Chinese American painters, musicians, comedians, singers, and only a handful of actors I had seen on the screen playing the stereotyped roles of the soldier who dies, kung-fu expert, gardener, and houseboy. While enrolled at Cal I took it upon myself to continue three courses of study: my pre-med major, my standard English undergraduate major, a field of study within the university with specific requirements, and Asian American history and literature, a field of study that didn't exist on the campus. In my public school education, I never learned the Chinese built the Central Pacific Railroad over the Sierra Nevada Mountains, or that they were a major force in establishing California's agricultural industry, or survived years of exclusion and anti-Chinese legislation at all levels of government. Some of my Japanese American classmates didn't even know their parents had been incarcerated in Japanese American concentration camps during World War II. When they asked their parents why they were never told, they answered, "You never asked." I had to teach myself how to learn outside of the university, how to do research outside of the university libraries. I wanted to know who the writers were that preceded me, who described the Asian American sense of self the generation before me. The first step was learning how to ask the question.

In 1970, through Kay Boyle, I met my first Asian American writer, Jeffery Chan, who was teaching at San Francisco State in the Asian American Studies Department and had been a student of Kay's. He told me that another Chinese American writer lived just two blocks from me in Berkeley and he gave me his phone number and mentioned that this writer had just published a short story entitled "Food For All His Dead." The phone number belonged to Frank Chin. I called him that same evening. I remember the conversation going like this:

> "Hi. My name is Shawn Wong and I'm a student at Cal. Jeff Chan gave me your number and told me that you're a writer. I'm also a writer, or want to be a writer and I'm Chinese too."
> Frank said, "You Chinese?"
> "Yes. Jeff said you published a story."
> "What do you write?" Frank asked.
> "Poetry."
> "Meet me at the Med in fifteen minutes."
> I agreed and hung up, but forgot to ask what he looked like. I knew the Med, a coffee house on Telegraph Avenue, would have more than one Chinese guy sitting there. When I walked in I saw a tall, thin Chinese guy standing in line and he was wearing black jeans, black cowboy boots, a blue denim cowboy shirt, a necklace of beads, and had long hair and a scraggly, thin mustache. I went up to him and asked, "Are you Frank Chin?"
> "Do you want a cappuccino?" he asked.

I had no idea what a cappuccino was, but I said yes out of fear of not being hip. So, in one moment of literary history, I met my first published Chinese American writer and had my first cappuccino.

A few weeks later, Frank and I were in Cody's Bookstore on Telegraph Avenue and Frank found an anthology of Fresno poets entitled *Down at the Santa Fe Depot* (1970). Inside the anthology we found the poetry of Lawson Inada.We got his phone number from the publisher and called him at his home in Ashland, Oregon. The conversation pretty much went like my call to Frank: "We're Chinese American writers and we saw your poetry and we'd like to meet you." We found out Lawson was publishing his first collection of poetry, *Before the War* (1971). Frank invited Lawson to a publication party in Berkeley for an anthology entitled *19 Necromancers From Now* (1970) edited by Ishmael Reed. Lawson drove down from Oregon the next day and met us at the party.

I was extremely fortunate to have been in the right place at the right time. The writers I met that evening in 1970 were Ishmael Reed, Al Young, Victor Hernandez Cruz, Alex Haley, Richard Brautigan, and others. Without knowing it at the time, I had enrolled in an extended course outside of academia in American multicultural literature. By 1973 I had met Mei-mei Berssenbrugge, Leslie Silko, Simon Ortiz, Joseph Bruchac, Gary Soto, Ricardo Sanchez, and Jessica Hagedorn, before any of us had published a book.

Jeff, Frank, Lawson and I founded an organization we named the Combined Asian-American Resources Project (CARP) and started searching for other Asian American writers and we found them in used bookstores, in public libraries, and in attics and basements. We read their out-of-print books and did our literary research not in the university library, but in the telephone book. We wrote the authors letters, called them on the telephone, and visited them in their homes armed with a tape recorder. Many of our interviews are now housed at the Bancroft Library at U.C. Berkeley.

In 1970, we found Toshio Mori's collection of short stories, *Yokohama, California*, in a used bookstore for twenty-five cents. Inside the front cover someone had glued an old newspaper review from 1949, the year the book was published. At the end of the review, the writer mentioned that Mori lived in San Leandro, California. I remember Frank saying that we had to talk to this important writer. How were we going to find him? I was *born* in 1949. The task seemed impossible to me. Frank said, "Let's look in the phone book." I thought he was crazy, but there in phone book was Toshio Mori's name. We called him and asked him if he was "Toshio Mori, the writer." We invited ourselves over. To our amazement, not one Asian American writer or student or teacher had ever come to see "Toshio Mori, the writer" in the twenty-one years since the publication of his book, the first book of fiction ever published by an Asian American writer. For the next three days, we taped his interview, rummaged through his scrapbooks, read his unpublished manuscripts, and listened to his stories about writing and growing up in Oakland and San Leandro. Mori gave us names of other writers he remembered in camp from the 40's. Using our now refined tactic of literary investigation, we called them on the phone—Hisaye Yamamoto, Wakako Yamauchi, Diana Chang, Jade Snow Wong, Dorothy Okada, the widow of novelist John Okada, and dozens more who wrote the significant works, the stereotypical works, the racist works, the sociological works, and the historical works. A true literary history had to document the good, the bad, and the ugly.

In 1974 Howard University Press published *Aiiieeeee!* and it instantly became one of their best sellers. Out of the dozens of reviews from the *New York Times* to *The Rolling Stone* to *The New Yorker,* the only bad reviews we received were from the only two Asian Americans to review the book. One reviewer from Hawaii said there was no such thing as an Asian American sensibility in the literature while another took us to task for not including more than Japanese, Chinese, and Filipino American writers. The fact that the writer couldn't name any of the writers we were supposed to have excluded didn't seem to bother him.

In 1975 Jeff, Frank, Lawson, and I organized the first Asian American writers' conference which was held at the Oakland Museum. We brought together the older generation of writers with the new generation. *Every* Asian American writer we knew of was invited and *every* writer invited came to the conference: Hisaye Yamamoto, Toshio Mori, Wakako Yamauchi, Jade Snow Wong, Yoshiko Uchida, Janice Mirikitani, Ben Fee, Jeanne Wakatsuki Houston, Sam Tagatac, George Leong, Joaquin Legaspi, Alan Lau, Hiroshi Kashiwagi, Iwao Kawakami, Momoko Iko, Emily Cachapero, Oscar Penaranda,

Al Robles, Russell Leong, N.V.M. Gonzales, Kai-yu Hsu, Connie Young Yu, and at least a dozen others. In an award ceremony, we honored several pioneer writers—Hiroshi Kashiwagi, Louis Chu, Ben Fee, Toshio Mori, Joaquin Legaspi, N.V.M. Gonzales, Toyo Suyemoto, Wakako Yamauchi, Hisaye Yamamoto, and Iwao Kawakami—with this opening tribute read by Connie Young Yu:

> The greatest honor we can give any writer is to read his work through to the end and be forever changed. The members of CARP, if not most of Asian America have taken a long time to catch up with the writings of our Pioneers. But we feel we owe them much more. We feel we must try to make up for America's suppression of their voices. For a time some of our own people even denied the works of the Pioneer, and so, for this, we honor them. We ask the Pioneers to accept these awards as meaning more to us than to them. This is our promise to you. We've finally learned to read you, and we want to know everything you've written and everything you'll ever write.

Jeff, Frank, Lawson, and I took it upon ourselves to educate an audience to Asian American writing. If we were going to be writers and call ourselves Asian American writers, we wanted readers to understand the tradition of Asian American writing. The anthologies, all of them, *Aiiieeeee!*, *Yardbird Reader, Volume 3* (1975), and *The Big Aiiieeeee!* (1991) were designed to create and start a dialogue, define the community of writers, create a controversy, and name the canon.

After I graduated in English from Cal in 1971, I went back to San Francisco State to work with Kay Boyle and got my master's in Creative Writing in 1974, the same year *Aiiieeeee!* was published. An early version of *Homebase* was my master's thesis.

It took me awhile to get through graduate school because I was hired by Mills College in Oakland in 1972 while I was still enrolled in graduate school at San Francisco State University. I was twenty-two and had no teaching experience and no graduate degree. Mills College had just started an Ethnic Studies Department and when I was interviewed, I was asked what I could teach by the Dean of the Faculty. I said Asian American literature. "You're hired," the Dean said. And so I began an academic career by accident, teaching a subject I taught myself outside the university. At the time I knew of fourteen Asian American books of fiction and nonfiction. I remember looking at the semester schedule and noting that it was fourteen weeks long so I assigned all fourteen books to the class and because all of the books were out-of-print except *No-No Boy* by John Okada we had to get each book photocopied for each member of the class. *No-No Boy* was still available in its original 1957 hardcover edition published by Charles Tuttle Co. for three dollars. The 1957 print run of *No-No Boy* was only 1500 copies and fifteen years later it was still in print which translated to less than a hundred copies sold for each year it was in print. The poor sales figures of Okada's classic novel and the thirteen out-of-print books reminded that first class of mine how much Asian American literature had been neglected not only by the literary mainstream, but also by our own people. In 1972 I was certainly not laying any blame.

My education was like everyone's American education of the fifties and sixties even when I wasn't living in America. I attended the second grade in Taiwan. Given that I'm Chinese, this is perhaps not a startling revelation. What was startling about this experience was that I was born in Oakland, California and raised in Berkeley and spoke no Chinese. In Taiwan, I was enrolled in an all American U.S. Navy school. When my mother and I boarded the school bus on the first day of school, the children chanted, "No Chinese allowed! No Chinese allowed!" I thought they were referring to my mother. It was alright in America then to stop being Chinese, or stop being German, or Irish, or Norwegian, or Italian and just be part of what was then called "America's melting pot."

My elementary school education began in the fifties in Berkeley, California and scattered itself all over the Pacific Islands and California—eleven schools from kindergarten to the 12th grade—and at its most basic level my memory is dominated by my being the "new kid" followed by the question, "What are you?" I never thought I was much different from my classmates until that experience in Taiwan. A consistent monocultural education throughout the eleven schools that make up my public school education spoke to our common backgrounds, made us a homogeneous school population, but did not inform us about the kid sitting next to us.

When I was growing up the U.C. Berkeley of my childhood in the fifties was thrilling, a large part of the thrill had something to do with my father attending Cal as a graduate student in engineering and my mother as an art student. By the time I got to Cal in the late sixties, the university life I had looked forward to as a boy had disappeared. It was a different time and in many ways, I couldn't have picked a better time. U.C. Berkeley was in turmoil with demonstration after demonstration over the Vietnam War, the civil rights movement, and the creation of an ethnic studies department. Prior to coming to Cal I had spent two years at San Francisco State University during the tumultuous and controversial administration of university president S.I. Hayakawa. But in that era of strife and strikes, the first ethnic studies departments had been born on that campus and others. The first ethnic studies departments gave students the ability to ask the right questions, perhaps as basic as, "Are there any Asian American writers?"

Very few people know that Jeff, Frank, Lawson, and I worked very hard to bring all these classic out-of-print Asian American books back into print. When no one would republish *No-No Boy*, we, under the CARP name, re-issued the book in 1976 with money from our savings, from friends, and from John Okada's brothers. We did not want to be in the publishing business, but someone had to take the responsibility for the recovery of these classic literary works. With the success of re-issuing *No-No Boy*, we were able to convince the University of Washington Press to begin publishing out-of-print Asian American books and CARP's publishing business closed after one book. It's amazing to me that even today with the popularity of Asian American books, I still have to be very aggressive about getting publishers to publish historically important Asian American literary works and that I'm still being turned down. In 1994 the University of Washington stepped forward to re-issue Diana Chang's *The Frontiers of Love*. After nearly two years of trying to find a publisher for Violet de Cristoforo's important collection of *haiku*, *Shattered Dreams*, written in the Japanese American concentration camps by the first generation *issei*, I finally convinced Sun & Moon Press of Los Angeles to publish, in 1995, this one-of-kind book complete with photos of the *haiku* writing clubs and very literary journals produced in the camps.

It's also surprising to me how few of the younger Asian American writers are involved in the recovery of classic Asian American texts. Both Hisaye Yamamoto and Wakako Yamauchi were published in *Aiiieeeee!*, yet only recently has a publisher published them in book form; Yamamoto's *Seventeen Syllables and Other Stories* was published in 1988 and Yamauchi's *Songs My Mother Taught Me* was published in 1994, both by feminist presses. It's been twenty-one years since the publication of *Aiiieeeee!*; I feel I shouldn't have to be the one proposing, as I did a week ago, that the University of Washington Press publish the unpublished work of Carlos Bulosan housed in the University of Washington Library archives. We should know how to ask the question by now.

Shawn Wong
December 19, 1994

Part IV

Heartland

Usha Lee McFarling

COOKING LESSONS

THERE, ON THE STOVE. The cauldron my mother has used for eight years. I hate it. Milk burnt black on the bottom. Scratches, too many scratches from the knife. I hate it. I hate everything cooked in it. *Aloo, gobi, bindi, channa*, they all taste bitter.

My mother leads me to the cauldron, makes me pour lemon juice into the boiling milk. You are old enough to learn this, she says. The curds dry; I squeeze, drain, flatten, push. You know, I say, it's stupid to make this lumpy stuff when we can buy shiny orange cheese at the store.

My mother slaps me, but not hard.

Cheese, she says, is not something one buys.

Mother began teaching me to cook two weeks ago, the day after I came home from school and told her I was changing my name to Stephanie. I will be eating only hot dogs, corn from a can and chocolate chip ice cream, I said. When mother asked me what was wrong in Punjabi, I pretended not to understand a word.

We cook. *Chicken tikka masala*. Flat, round *roti*. I know these lessons are a punishment. I let one side of the bread burn on the griddle when time has come to turn it. Mother throws it in the garbage without speaking, hands me another ball of dough. I don't want to be surrounded by curried, ancient smells. I want perfect cheese slices wrapped in clear plastic. I want my mother to speak English with no accent.

Mother slides the mortar and pestle toward me. Push the cardamom from the green pod, she says, pull the seeds from the pomegranate. I'm grinding. Wood on wood, seeds into powder. I'm grinding as hard as I can. I want to destroy everything in this bowl, make it a dust that will leave no taste. Wait, mother says, you've left the husks whole.

Mother doesn't understand why cooking is so hard for me, why my bread is oddly shaped, why I can't decide when we have added enough turmeric. Mother never flips the bread too early, never adds spices a second time. Mother's cheese is always perfectly thick.

Mother's equations were always elegantly solved. She studied biochemistry in Wisconsin, getting a PhD, feeding her roommates all the while. She came here from a New Delhi August, my father said, opened her books and didn't put her sandals away until two months into the first winter.

Mornings she'd apply the red bindi to her dark forehead, glamorous in the midwest as any Monroe. Wrapped in her thickest sari, walking along the lake to the lab, she'd turn the heads of the strong-handed men studying agriculture, turn the head of my father. He says, when I saw her injecting those rats, wearing that blue sari . . .

Papaji sent eight children to America for schooling, and waited years for each to return. The two eldest sisters came home the day after their graduation, suitcases filled with lipsticks for the sisters and radios for Papaji, barely enough room for their fading saris.

Mother put off her return for two weeks, for four. She packed, then unpacked the blue jeans she'd bought. She wondered, in an aerogram to Papaji, if she could marry this American boy.

The question was incredible.

So impure, these Americans, so sloppy. No tradition, no religion, Papaji shouted. No American is worthy. Come home.

After one year, my father flew to Delhi. He left with no wife. He returned the next year, hair combed, names of the gurus memorized, American dollars falling from his pockets.

Now, Father is Papaji's favorite son-in-law. You are more Indian than those scoundrels, he says from Los Angeles where his five youngest children live. Each day he carefully wraps a grey turban around his head. Each day he slips on the Nike sneakers my father has given him.

My mother hands me the iron frying pan. I wait until the oil is hot, hot, hot. The mustard seed pops, the cumin seeds dance, the onions go sweet. Standing over the oven I close my eyes. I dream of someone who looks like me, a sister, to see if I truly belong. Oh, mother says, you've singed the coriander.

My mother lost eight babies before they were born, before I was born. One boy would kick, but only when mother said the word mango. One girl, still with wings, had a smile, my mother said, a smile. I grew somehow in the deadly womb. When they wanted me, I stuck out only one foot. They pulled but I would not follow. So they cut my mother's swollen belly with a knife and gasped when they saw the thick cord around my neck. A tug would have choked me. There are no accidents. There is only this: I made it past the one who keeps the babies. I am the first child. I am the ninth child. There never would have been a ninth child. There was no tenth.

Papaji named me Usha. Father's mother nodded and said, Usha, it sounds like Uschii. A good German name. I have a name in India. I have a name in Germany. But here, here no one can pronounce my name.

I do not look like my mother. I do not look like my father. I am exactly between their colors, golden-brown. But where do my eyes come from—brown, then green in the sun. Where do my lips, this much too wide, come from?

I wanted once to look like my mother, her red lips, longest hair, the silk that falls down her legs. But I can't wear a sari. This is North Dakota and I am too young. I wear a brown snow suit, underneath, jeans with an elastic waist. A snail embroidered on the back pocket. A matching shirt with stripes. Clothes my mother bought, waist too big, arms too short. Clothes that don't fit. American clothes. Every day I used to ask, mother may I wear a sari?

My North Dakota, arctic circle. These short winter days I wait for my school bus in the darkest morning, the little dipper just above. Snow, everything white, transformers turned to igloos. No break, no asphalt showing through, no mud. Yes, I wore shorts six months ago and even sweated, but I don't think of North Dakota in summer. I just think of the cold and the whiteness of it. Yes, the whiteness.

I don't know there is a Los Angeles, I don't know there is a New York. I don't know there are cities filled with Indians, people who don't look anything like this town's Kims and Desirees.

We have to live here. My father is designing a radar that can only be built in an empty field at the edge of America. Later will come, among the army of engineers, a Martinez, a Hiroko, people with accents and strange-smelling kitchens. But they will arrive months after we leave, headed for the next barren radar site.

Mother never says she wants to leave, to be near her sisters, to smell for once, someone else's curry. She sighs when she runs out of cumin. It will be weeks before her sisters will mail her more. She smiles when she opens the box of new saris that arrives from Delhi each December 1. She lets me touch the gold thread at the edges.

Mother decides to teach us, the Brownies, an Indian dance. A month later, at the annual Girl Scout banquet, me, DeAnn Goble, Arlene Peplow, and the rest of troop No. 276 walk across the stage. We dance to sitar music in our gingham saris. I look at nine other brownies dressed like Indians. I still don't look like them.

I don't look like the other contestants in the Little Miss Sweetheart of Demolay beauty pageant either. I see the mothers clustered backstage. Mrs. Goble is wearing peach stretchy pants too tight across her round stomach. Mrs. Peplow is wearing men's glasses. My mother, in a red sari, would win a mother's beauty contest. They announce the winners as I'm looking offstage. I don't win. DeAnn Goble does.

You think you're a beauty queen? Think you are? The tall boys from school circle me at recess. They call me monkey girl. They call me shit girl. They push me to the ground, push me to my knees to tie their shoes. The taste of dirt, the taste of blood dripping, the taste of the sharpest pebble. The taste of a kick.

I do not cry.

DeAnn and Arlene lift me up and we walk away quietly, scared the boys will follow us. I hear the boys shouting the name they have given me: Ooshit! Ooshit! I don't care about the blue eyes. I don't care about the yellow hair. Just give me please, please, please the pale skin. I know that I am almost brown and that if only I had pale skin I would one day wear red lipstick and make the tall boys cry.

Ooshit! I'm scared I will never stop hearing their voices.

I don't want to see my brown skin anymore. I stop looking in mirrors. But I can't help but see, at every moment, my own hands. When my mother says, what is wrong? I do not tell her. For she is browner than I.

I look at her. Hair thin at the ends, spots of mud where her sari dragged along the ground. My mother says, what is wrong? I say: From now on, I will eat only hot dogs, corn from a can and chocolate chip ice cream. You must call me Stephanie.

The cooking lessons continue, but I won't eat that food. Not even the spinach with the cheese I helped make this afternoon. Not even if it's my favorite.

My mother smiles. She says, How is your dinner, Stephanie?

I take a bite from the hot dog and bun on my plate. The bright yellow mustard is cold. The hot dog tastes bitter.

You can see my ancestry in my name: My first name, Usha, comes from India, my mother's land. It is the Sanskrit word for the first ray of light. My second name comes from Scotland, through Maine, perhaps, or Iowa, and eventually to South Dakota, where my father was raised. Such a melting pot name, probably as American as it gets.

I have lived all over this country: Maine, Texas, North Dakota and California. First, I moved along with my parents. Then I moved to take jobs at newspapers. Now, I live in Cambridge, Massachusetts. I write about science for the Boston Globe and about myself and my family for my fiction.

Mabelle Hsueh

A PLATTER OF
STEAMING DUMPLINGS

PROFESSOR LIU STOOD in the doorway of his apartment building
and watched the rain coming down hard on the sidewalk. He
rubbed his hands together—a gesture acquired from years of
teaching electrical engineering, when he'd spent hours at the
blackboard, getting his hands covered with powdery white
chalk. This habit had not been obvious to anyone, himself included, until his retirement from the university a year ago.

When the rain subsided a little, he stepped out onto
Thompson Street. He kept close to the buildings and cautiously
made his way to Shanghai Garden around the corner.

Jingma, the middle-aged woman who owned the little
restaurant, was waiting on a young man wearing dark glasses.
She wrote down his order and almost missed catching the
menu he tossed back at her.

Professor Liu entered the restaurant just as Jingma was
about to go into the kitchen. "Hello, Jingma," he said.

The woman turned around. "Long time no see, Professor Liu," she cried. "How you? Where you been for many days?"

"Nowhere," Professor Liu answered, embarrassed at the concern in her voice. "I was in my apartment."

"Where your umbrella? You wet and cold. I bring you hot tea."

It always amazed him that Jingma, hardly five feet tall, had such a deep, loud voice. It resonated with cheer and good-will. He walked over to his table nearest to the kitchen, took off his coat and dropped it on a chair. He saw that the booths along the wall were empty, but the four tables in the middle of the room were occupied. The air was pungent with the smell of ginger.

As soon as he sat down, Jingma was beside him with teapot and cup in one hand and chopsticks, bowl and plate in the other. "My cook sick today so I run around, here there, like that big wheel in circus," she said. "My sister took me to see when I first come to America. What that called?"

"The Ferris wheel?"

"Nah, that machine go slow." She shook her head. "Go wrong direction. Never mind, what you want for lunch?"

"Perhaps beef and broccoli?"

"Okay, okay, but I got something special. You wait." She turned to go, then added over her shoulder. "How your book coming along, Professor, about Chinese . . ." she hesitated, ". . . buildings."

"Chinese architecture," he said. "It's coming along just fine."

"Good, good." Jingma nodded and disappeared into the kitchen.

He poured the tea and took a sip, acutely disappointed that she had no time to chat leisurely with him. He wanted to tell her his book was not coming along just fine, especially since he had not written a word for days.

With the approaching of the lunar new year he had grown restless, unable to concentrate. He spent his waking hours in aimless reading and pacing around and around the apartment as if he wanted to measure the width and length of every room. The nights were disrupted by dreams of China, of the house with the shapely roofs built by his grandfather for all his descendants. He seldom remembered the details of these dreams when he awoke, but they always left him with a sense of loss and the desire to weep.

He drank more tea and the delicate flavor of jasmine pricked his nose and tongue. He recalled how his mother enjoyed adding a few fresh jasmine flowers to her tea whenever the plants in the garden were in bloom. Suddenly he noticed the young man with the dark glasses, who had been sitting at the table near the door, coming toward him.

"Professor Liu," the young man greeted him. "You don't remember me, but I took one of your classes several years ago."

Professor Liu peered at the young man: T-shirt and jeans, medium height, thin with an oversized head. A topheavy column in the Ancestral Hall, he thought to himself. Out loud he said, "I'm afraid my memory is as bad as my eyesight." He rubbed his hands. "What is your name, young man?"

"Tim Wilson. The word is merry-go-round." The young man picked up the professor's coat and carefully draped it on another chair before he sat down,

"I beg your pardon?" Professor Liu said.

"That woman was describing how busy she was. Like a merry-go-round."

"Oh, right. Jingma works so hard."

As though summoned, the woman came into the room bearing a trayful of food. She paused for a second, surprised to see the young man sitting with the professor. She put the broccoli and beef in front of the professor; the seafood noodles in front of the young man; and, with a great flourish, a platter of steaming dumplings between the two of them.

"Early this morning I make two hundred jiao-zi," Jingma said, waving two fingers in the air. "I thought if no one come to eat, I freeze them. But you have come and you can eat them fresh. That's best way. Now I am happy." She smiled broadly.

Professor Liu lowered his head and inhaled. "O! Jingma, I am happy too. Why, I haven't had jiao-zi for a long, long time."

"Taste one, taste one when hot." Jingma reached for Professor Liu's chopsticks, picked up a dumpling and put it on his plate.

Then she leaned toward the young man and peered into his dark glasses. "You are friend of our professor, huh? You like jiao-zi? Chinese New Year coming and jiao-zi New Year food, you know." She waved her hand over the dishes as if blessing them. "Eat, eat, you two. All food taste twice better when eat with friends." She pulled at her apron, tucked the tray under her arm and went over to the cash register where a customer waited.

Professor Liu bent forward and put the dumpling in the middle of his tongue. As the juice squirted out of the soft dough and filled his mouth, he closed his eyes and sighed with pleasure. "When I was a boy," he began, "my grandmother always made jiao-zi, along with other foods, on the twenty-third day of the last month of the Chinese year. They were offerings for the Kitchen God."

Using a spoon instead of chopsticks, the young man put a dumpling in his mouth and tasted it. "Delicious," he said.

"Every Chinese kitchen has a kitchen god, do you know that? And a very important celestial being he is because on the 23rd of December he makes his yearly journey to heaven to report on the conduct of all the members of his earthly family." Professor Liu paused to catch his breath.

"Ummmm . . ." the young man mumbled and picked up another dumpling. "So everybody shapes up," he said finally, "like kids for Santa." He cradled his spoon under another dumpling.

"Yes, yes," the professor agreed, delighted. "I've never thought of it in just that way." He put down his chopsticks and placed both arms on the table. "In fact, my grandmother habitually smeared honey on the picture, on the Kitchen God's mouth, so he would say nothing but sweet things about our family." He chuckled and ran his hand, like a washcloth, over his face. "Why, that was what I dreamed of a few nights ago, the honey on the picture!"

"The Kitchen God isn't a statue?" the young man asked and lifted another dumpling from the platter.

"Just a red and gold picture. Each year my grandmother would buy one from the market—you know, a man with a red face, wearing a red robe, sitting on a chair with legs apart—and paste it on the wall behind the stove. There was also a little altar on the wall, I remember, with a tiny incense burner and joss sticks in it."

He stopped, poured himself more tea after checking the

young man's full teacup. "Last night I dreamed of my mother coming into my room to dress me up for New Year. Somebody had laid out all my new clothes—a black cap, red vest, and yes, a pair of red cotton-padded shoes—on the dresser." He laughed aloud. "All my dreams are coming back to me now.

"Nice dreams." The young man spooned the last dumpling onto his plate.

Professor Liu was aware that the young man was not listening to him. But he could not stop talking for it seemed an avalanche rumbled inside his head. Bits and chunks of memory, shaken loose, came tumbling down and out of his mouth. He described the rustle of silk gowns and dresses worn by relatives; the aroma of sandlewood incense wafting up to the high ceiling and hanging on there for days; the elaborate ceremony of kowtowing and offering food and drink to the ancestors; and the explosion of the earsplitting firecrackers just before everybody sat down for the New Year feast. "Such happy times," he said. "So much easier to talk than to write, isn't it?"

The young man did not answer. He was eating the seafood noodles now, his eyes darting here and there like minnows in a stream. At last he said, "Professor Liu, you should have taught Chinese Civilization instead of Chinese Architecture."

"Oh my dear young fellow." The professor looked startled and rubbed his palms. "I became interested in Chinese architecture only after my retirement. Are you sure . . . ."

The young man choked and began to cough. Professor Liu was about to offer him some tea when the young man suddenly got to his feet, walked out the front door, and disappeared into the rain. The action was accomplished so quickly and quietly that none of the other diners noticed. Stunned, Professor Liu remained in his seat with one hand still grasping the teapot.

Jingma gave a big yell, "Hey wait, wait," and ran after the young man, flapping her apron in the air like a broken wing.

As he got up from the table, Professor Liu knocked over his cup of tea in his hurry to get to the front of the room. He posted himself next to the cash register. Many of the other customers had stopped eating and were craning to see out the window. Professor Liu began to rub his hands as if he could never get the chalk off.

Soon Jingma returned, gasping for breath, her hair matted

to her head and her face wet with rain and perspiration. "You see? He did not pay!"

I am so sorry," Professor Liu said. He unclasped his hands and put them behind his back.

"Oh, why he do this? But you know him?"

Professor Liu shook his head.

"Then I call police."

"No, don't do that." He reached out and touched Jingma's arm. "I'll pay for him."

"Why? Why you pay?" Jingma glared. "He is thief."

"No, he's my guest. He gave me a pleasant time."

Professor Liu went back to his table, picked up his coat and reached into the pocket. Then the other pocket. His money was gone.

"What is matter, Professor?"

"Jingma, put it on my account, please." He paused as a couple entered the restaurant. "Remember, don't stay on that merry-go-round too long."

Jingma smiled, uncertain what the last remark meant, and hurried away.

Professor Liu righted the teacup he had knocked over. For the first time he noticed the row of small red lanterns above the cash register and the bigger lanterns in the two doorways. They were bright red, the color of hope and joy. No doubt Jingma had hung them up for the coming Chinese New Year.

He dropped a few paper napkins in the puddle of spilled tea and wiped the table clean before he reached for his coat and pulled it on.

Now he was eager to leave. He wanted to get home, to look at his manuscript, to read the last page he had written seemingly so long ago, about the flying eaves. How fascinating those eaves were: shaped like swallows' tails, they cantilevered outward and upward like arms lifted in prayer.

I was born in the city of New York and my parents took me back to Fujian Province, in southern China, when they finished school—I was three months old. My grandmother was slightly disappointed that her first grandchild was a girl. Still, my colicky cries endeared me to her because, as she told all her neighbors, I cried just like an American baby.

I lived in China until I was old enough to come to the U. S. for college. I was terribly homesick and a professor at the University of Michigan encouraged me to write about growingup in China. These stories won a prize and that started my life-long interest and commitment. I have written stories set in both China and the U. S.

Ann Arbor, Michigan where I have lived for many years, is my favorite place.

Kiyoshi Young Najita

DOVETAILING

EACH TIME the phone rings, I know it will be about you, news about you, an update of your condition. Our mother will be on the phone, talking in waves, sound and information dovetailing. Today you're better, yesterday you were worse, tomorrow you may die. There are tubes in your arms, for you cannot eat; there are tubes in your mouth, for you cannot breathe. I make a picture of you, helpless and the recipient of pathos, but I know you did this to yourself. You brought this down on yourself.

I'm alone in the house, the house we grew up in. Neither of our rooms is intact. We left them so long ago that even our smells are nowhere to be found. Our posters, our books, our toys, our clothes, gone. I'm sleeping in our parents' bed because it's the most comfortable, and nearest the phone. Our parents are with you, probably by your side, maybe holding your hand. I'm here to take care of the house, water the plants, feed the old, fat cat you brought here. At work I can almost forget that our family is a tray of dishes flung in the air. At home my feet drag through the bones and ashes of our childhood to leave gritty footprints in the bed as I try to sleep. And each day I know the phone will ring. Each day our mother will give me the news, the details meaning so little under the weight of her voice, like the sea above a barnacled stone on its floor.

Each time the phone rings, I'm sure it will say you're gone. Two days ago; two days ago it nearly happened. Two days ago the machines stopped recording and registering. In a flutter of valves and surging fluids you might have seen the lips of infinity part and salivate. Our father said you were fearless and accepting. Were you? Do you accept the inevitability of this? Are you aware of how much time has passed since your body stopped functioning and started poisoning you? Or does your back on the bed only say that you've been sleeping? When the machines stopped, did you feel yourself lifted and rising, did you fly up from your bed of pain with tears of joy in your eyes? Or did you feel the floor fall away beneath the bed, did the walls and ceiling vanish above as you fell, our parents' hands reaching for you? These questions hammer at my skull like the clapper of a bell because you coaxed the machines back. The doctors were impressed. Our mother said you weren't ready to let go: she still thinks you can escape, but you and I know. You and I know.

I'm alone in the house, the house you left behind so long ago, when I was a child and didn't know why you were leaving, only that you were. I can see you walking out our back door, your things already packed into a friend's car. I sat at the top of the stairs and watched as you left these walls, for they had become like a vise on your shins. Our parents were stony and brave because they were so angry with you; when you announced you were planning to leave—leave school, leave friends, leave us—they agreed. After each argument with them, you expanded. Your unrest filled our house, and our parents knew you'd seen every crevice of every room. So up until the instant the door shut like the cover of a book, they were stony and brave; but when all that remained of you in this house was the painfully familiar back door and the fading warmth of your hands on her shoulders, our mother wailed. Our father held her, I stayed on my stair and we all began wondering, from that instant, when you would return.

Each time the phone rings, I know it will be about you, news about you, an update of your condition. Today you're better, yesterday you were worse, tomorrow you may die; sound and information dovetailing. Our mother asks me distracting questions about her house, my work. I answer her questions and realize that our words have become purely sonic; no matter what the topic, we're really discussing you—how you were found unconscious in a bus station far from where we thought you lived, your breathing almost extinguished, your skin the color of fish store ice, lightly tinted with blood. Our mother says how hot it is where you all are, but what I hear is: my daughter is dying, my first-born child is going to die. And I'm angry that no words can come up my throat without carrying your flavor with them. The doctors are preparing for their operation. Without it, you will die very quickly. If you survive the operation, you may not live long afterwards. Although our mother speaks about this like something that must be done, I wonder if it is what you truly want. I wonder if, as I am, you're beginning to envision yourself removed from your own body.

I'm alone in the house, our house, the house we were raised in. Standing on the living room rug in my bare feet I can feel years of Christmases woven into the shag, poking between my toes. If I put my ear to the carpet I can hear your voice, too loud for the morning, though your fingers open your gifts with care so as not to tear the wrapping. If I run my fingers over the carpet I can hear your laughter. Each twist of fabric is a seedling in a garden, the garden of our life together on this carpet, within these walls. For whatever reason, the phone isn't ringing tonight. I briefly entertain the possibility that you're gone, but I know our mother would call right away. No, this must be a good sign; sometime during the course of this day, this drastic situation defined its own norms. The slow process of your dying has been normal today.

Each time the phone rings, I'm sure it will say you're gone. Our parents' phone has an electronic ring, not an old-fashioned bell as I would prefer. It whines in the kitchen like a forlorn pet. Although sometimes I can barely hear it, I can never ignore it. Tonight, it's our father; his voice sounds like a swinging chain. He tells me you survived the operation: a massive blood clot was taken from your body, glistening black like an expired organ. He tells me your condition is stable enough for him to come home for a few days; there is work he must do. At first, I'm happy I won't be alone in our house anymore. Then I'm afraid, for while you are dying on the other end of this phone, he will bring the throb of the machines attached to you into the kitchen; he will bring the rasp of your breath into the shower; he will bring the clenching of your hands into my bed. We say good-bye, the phone goes dead, and I can already feel him and you coming home.

I'm alone in the house, the only house I can clearly remember as a child, though other homes appear as bursts of flashguns in darkened rooms, details fading almost as soon as they're discernible. Although I must be awake very early for work, I stay up very late at night. The remote of the television becomes a cybernetic extension of my hand with which I make the channels jump like frightened children. When I've sampled each station a dozen times, I turn to walking the floors of our house. Without the lights on, my eyes begin to detect iridescent residue of every foot to ever cross these floors. Amongst the movements of our parents are innumerable children's tracks, the smaller ones mine, the larger yours. They are different colors, and some glow more vividly than others. As I travel the rooms, stairways and halls, I watch our footprints growing— toddler to child to adolescent. Our tracks cross occasionally, but are most often separate; in your old room is a huge collection of your footprints, dancing in circles like fossil footprints in a cave. The feet gradually increase in size and brightness until, at a certain point, they grow no larger. Throughout the house, the dark spaces between the remaining trails widen from this point on.

Each time the phone rings, I know it will be about you. Our father is home now, but he's never answered the phone. When he walked through our door, he looked like he had traveled for years to reach it. He reminded me that you could go at any moment; the operation has only allowed you some more time. Our father's hands cupped his knees as though they were tiny skulls. I asked him if our mother would be all right by herself and he answered that he didn't know . . . and then he wept, the first time I'd ever seen our father's tears. A terror reached like a slender finger beneath my eyelid: your dying is so much more real to our parents then it is to me, or perhaps, even you. Our father is leaving tomorrow to return to you and our mother, and he asks me if I want to join him. Our parents have always given me choices that they never gave you; it would be so easy for him to demand, or simply suggest that I come with him. He does not do this, though. He advises me to think it over, and to make my decision based on my needs, not my obligations. I wait for a voice to tell me to go, but I hear nothing. If our parents had asked me on the phone to come to you, there would have been no dilemma; all I know is that you're waiting for us in a room that I can only imagine as white.

I'm alone in the house, the house on the corner across from the bookshop. Our father left this morning; I chose to stay. I told him I couldn't see you now, that I was too afraid. We embraced, and he tried to absolve my failure with his arms, his hands. He is already by your side, stroking your forehead, softly singing what he can remember of your favorite songs. What song was playing that day, the day men came looking for drugs you stole? What tune were you humming as you unwittingly answered your door to find a hand clamped over your mouth? What song fled from your mind as you watched the men sliding their knives, over and over into your lover's chest? Could you have heard any music as the men heaved his body through your window and ordered you to follow him? Was there any music left when you awoke in a dumpster atop his cold, wet body, knowing the men believed you dead, knowing you had survived, knowing you would have to hide all traces of this? How many millions of songs have filled your head, as you forced everything you could into your body that might help you to forget that day? How ever many, it was not enough: you never forgot, you are still living that day, over and over, even now, as you sink into your bed and our parents sing to you.

Today I told the people at work that you died last night. They are good people; they reacted quickly, compassionately and with strength. I could not take any of it from them. I envision the machine that drew a topography of your heartbeat—peaks and valleys etched green on black depicting the horizon, the vanishing point. I can only imagine what happened when your machines calmed and settled. There must have been a moment of silence, a silent moment that contained the first caught breath of every word ever uttered—and I can hear that silence. All that follows I must recreate from the infinite quiet of that instant when our parents looked at you, then at each other, and knew this ordeal was over. All that follows, and all that preceded, I must recreate from the walls and floors of our house, the glow of its lamps, the coolness of its doorknobs—for I was not there. I chose to stay in our house, and in so doing I have chosen these re-creations as my final images of you. Our mother said that the swelling from your poisoned blood changed you, that you became a plump, peaceful buddha, smiling as all life drained from you, smiling as your grip on our mother's hand softened and released, as the gentle jets of breath from your nostrils ceased.

Each time the
phone rings

I'm alone
in the house
we grew up
in.

I was born in Northfield, Minnesota in 1966. Had a freight train been passing on the tracks that divide the town, I would have arrived in the back seat of a VW.

My mother, a second-generation Korean, and my father, a second-generation Japanese, were both born and raised on the Big Island of Hawaii. I enjoy spending time at our second home in the small ranch town of Kamuela, surrounded by family and friends.

My wife, Gillian Gilman Culff, and I live in Chicago where I teach 5th grade at the University of Chicago Lab Schools. My short stories have appeared in *Nota Bene* and *Other Voices*. When I'm not writing, I play loud electric guitar in the band Anatomy of Hope.

Connie S. Chan

JOURNAL ENTRIES

Baby Log

FEBRUARY 9

CINDY IS PREGNANT! She called after receiving the lab results on the phone. I was so thrilled I wanted to shout and scream and call everyone I know to announce our great news. We have worked so hard to find this donor that we felt we really *deserved* to have it work. And it did! We are going to have a baby—I counted the forty weeks of pregnancy out on the calendar—in October. What a glorious day it is. I rode my bike to work, powered by our dreams.

At work, it was difficult to attend to meetings. I kept repeating to myself, "We're going to have a baby. We're going to have a *baby*."

Later that night, Cindy and I went to a Chinese New Year's celebration dinner. Still in the clouds, I whispered to our friends, a blend of gay and straight folks, "Cindy's pregnant and the baby is coming in October." They were all congratulatory; some were curious, and some were downright nosy, asking us, "How did you find an Asian donor?" "Have you been looking for a long time for the right one?" "How long did it take to get pregnant?"

"Would you like to have one for me, too?" asked a gay male friend of ours, only half-joking. "No thanks," we replied. The frustration we'd endured all those months dissolved rapidly, like a single drop on a sizzling grill, leaving us to dance with excitement that evening.

For the first time, it even felt possible to talk about the cultural issues that we had unexpectedly faced: how hard it had been to find an Asian sperm donor. In our year-long search for a donor, we discovered that Asian men tend to feel a stronger sense of ownership and responsibility for their sperm, and no one had been willing to donate "without strings attached." The only Asian men who were more open to being donors were gay, but with risky HIV-status. Finally, last month, we found an anonymous donor with a friend as our go-between. Our donor was a Chinese-American doctor, perhaps able to see the medical/scientific side of things rather than just the emotional/cultural view. We arranged the insemination, and joy of joys, glory of glories, it worked! Cindy is pregnant! We're going to have a baby. Today our efforts and patience have been rewarded—things are coming to fruition. This feels like the beginning of our life as a family.

SEPTEMBER 1

Cindy is now in her eighth month and doing well with her pregnancy. We have been busy with all the preparations for the new arrival. Only a few more weeks to go.

Yesterday I toured the friendly skies between D.C. and Chicago, returning for four hours to inseminate because it was the last chance to try for this month. I went straight from O'Hare to the doctor's office, and tried unsuccessfully to meditate as I lay on some kind of medical examining table, then cabbed it back to the airport for the return flight to D.C. Made it to the meeting room for my presentation with an hour to spare, and now as I write this, I'm on the plane heading to Chicago again. It seems crazy to spend so much time and money, but if I get pregnant this month, I'll have the baby at the end of May. That means I can take the summer months off to be with the baby. It's worth a try. We're more relaxed about my inseminations than we were with Cindy's. It was considerably easier to find white donors.

We have put so much thought into the timing of our babies, their racial blend, and our family dreams that we might have a hard time giving up our (supposed) sense of control once the kids do arrive. We've had to work so hard to make our family dreams come true that we do feel a sense of accomplishment already.

The impending arrival of the baby is forcing me to take care of long-avoided responsibilities. I finally wrote a letter to my family while I was on the plane after the insemination. What was I to tell them? My parents are extremely traditional in their views, seemingly unyielding in their expectations of their children. How can they understand that my relationship with Cindy is so strong and satisfying that we want to share it with children, to enrich our lives and theirs? I feel vulnerable, like a child again, each time I fantasize what my parents' reaction will be. I have struggled to make my life my own, without compromise. How can I help my parents to understand that my choosing to create a family of my own is really a testimony to them, that I am trying to write my unique chapter in our family's long history?

My choice to create a family is very much related to having grown up in a warm caring one. Because of my own family experiences, I *believe* in spending my time nurturing a new life, much as we kids were the center of our parents' lives. Why is it then, that I am filled with fear and apprehension, so palpable that it sits, solid and heavy, in my chest as I write. I fear that my parents will not accept my life, my decision to have a family in the manner that I have chosen, and that they will reject me after all these years.

This is a letter that I have written many times over in my mind. Today the words look back at me on paper and I feel satisfied. It represents me; it expresses what I feel in the only way I can tell them, in a way I hope they can understand:

> Dear Mom, Dad, Eric, and Adrienne (I decided to be un-Asian and to write to all four at once. That way there will be no secrets):
>
> I am writing to you because I need your love and support.
>
> After considerable thought and discussion, Cindy and I have decided to raise a family together. We are very happy and excited about our plans. We've decided to give birth to one child each and to raise the children as siblings. So that the children will be a blend of our own ancestry, we have decided to have "hapa" kids. Our children will be half-Chinese and half-white, a beautiful combination, we think.
>
> We are getting pregnant through "alternative insemination" of sperm from anonymous donors. Cindy became pregnant last January and the baby is due in October. Our days have been filled with anticipation and preparation for the baby as well as with great excitement. I inseminated last month, did not get pregnant, but am hopeful that this month's insemination will be successful.
>
> I realize that this may seem like an impulsive decision to you, but we have thought about this and planned this carefully for a very long time. We feel emotionally and financially ready to add children to our lives at this time. I hope you will join us in accepting two new little ones into our family soon.
>
> Love from Chicago

SEPTEMBER 4

These last couple of days have been filled with a mixture of anxiety and dread. Each time the phone rings I gather myself for an instant and wonder if it is my family. I have various fantasies about their reactions to my letter. Most of the fantasies are good ones but there are the nightmares, too.

It finally happened tonight. My brother was on the phone, sounding terrible. His voice was dragging, monotone, but with a nervous quality to it. He had received my letter, he said, and wanted to talk. Then he blurted that he and Adrienne and my parents were completely shocked and upset by my "irresponsible actions." So upset that Mom was practically speechless and unable to function. At this point she started screaming into the phone at me. Unknown to me, all of them had been on the line the entire time, though Eric was the only one who spoke at first. In spite of the desperateness of the conversation, I have to look back on this part as somewhat amusing. My mother always knew how to maximize the impact of her words, and on this occasion, her entrance was classic.

I was ruining my life, they said. Worse yet, I was ruining *their* lives. "It is a terrible thing to have children without being married. You are destroying our family by doing this. How could you do this to us? What are we going to tell our relatives and friends? Why didn't you tell us sooner so we could talk to you about it?" I answered that it was because I was afraid they would carry on like this and I didn't want to hear it. They just went on, "We want you to come home this weekend so we can talk some sense into you. What's wrong with you anyway? We are so ashamed!"

This call was close to one of my nightmare fantasies. My parents alternating between yelling and crying. My brother lecturing and whining. My sister silent. It was no use trying to reason with them. I began repeating, like a mantra, that I was proud of my decision and that I was proud of them for bringing me up to be a responsible person. I told them I loved them, but that I had to live my own life according to my own values. It felt very frustrating. It was a good thing that I had spent my last two therapy sessions preparing for this. What my friends and I have joked about all these years was proving to be true— that there *are* no limits to what Asian parents will say or do when it comes to controlling their children. They clearly could not recognize that I was now an adult and capable of making my own choices. My mother made an allusion to the fact that I was a disgrace to the family and even to my race, and how could I live with myself. "We live very well," I answered, "very well." I remember thinking that the old family dynamics were coming through again and I was being treated as the wayward, rebellious child.

We had been on the phone for an hour and the call only ended because I told them I'd had enough. They repeated their demand for me to come home the following weekend. "If you love us, you wouldn't do this to us," they pleaded, "if you love us, please come home now; if you love us, you'll stop this nonsense about having children." "I do love you," I answered, but promised nothing, and hung up.

Disillusioned, upset and drained, I was also saddened. Yet another family was unable to accept their "disobedient, deviant" daughter and I felt a great loss not only for myself but for my family. *Both* families—the one I came from and the one we were creating.

Cindy and I held each other and grieved for the loss of my dreams of an extended family, of grandparents waiting at the airport with open arms for their new grandchildren. I cried for myself, for my parents, for our children-to-be, for all daughters and sons who have lost their families upon finding themselves. And for the parents, sisters and brothers who have misunderstood us, turned away from us, and are missing our company. Later that evening, I cuddled up to Cindy and lovingly caressed her round, full belly. "You will be entering a hard world," I whispered to the roundness, "but we await you with love and the will to survive."

OCTOBER 12

4:30 a.m.: The phone's ring is incredibly loud and despite my attempts to will it silent, it does not stop. My head hurts, I don't know where I am; I only know that I *have* to stop the ringing. Groping around, I remember that this is a hotel room in D.C. I am feeling slightly nauseous. It's Cindy's voice, measured and calm, "Might be going into labor, I'm not sure. Have had cramping on and off all night." "Well, is it or isn't it?" I say. "I have a meeting today and I'm planning to be back by 7:00 tonight." As I become more conscious, I realize how callous that sounds. "I mean, I'll come home if you want. Do you really think the baby's coming today?" I try to soften my voice while all of me spins with the now-familiar "morning sickness" nausea. I am nine weeks pregnant.

"Yes," she answers definitely, "Could you come home? I want you to be here. Just in case."

7:30 a.m.: Flying this early in the morning is never comfortable; it is unbearable when you feel nauseous even *before* the flight takes off. Mercifully, it is a short flight, and not crowded on this Sunday during the long holiday weekend. Cindy is standing calmly at the gate as I deplane. I want to hiss at her for dragging me back so early, and hug her at the same time, because I'm glad to see her. At first glance, I am always a little surprised at how huge her belly has become, how very pregnant she is. I am also excited: we are *both* pregnant in this space and time; what anticipation we feel.

9:00 a.m.: On the drive home Cindy is apologetic, "Sorry, the baby must not be ready to come out yet." I nod and realize that I don't care anymore about the meeting I have just left—my only goal is to get home and into my bed. It is amazing how pregnancy has changed my priorities and tempered my goals for the day—all I want is to get through it with a minimum of discomfort. Forget about deadlines and other essentials.

1:00 p.m.: We wake from our naps feeling refreshed but famished. Fortunately, Cindy's best friend Tina is here to take care of us and make a big pot of oatmeal with apples. It's a little like a pajama party as all three of us cuddle in bed and laugh about Cindy's false signs of labor. She's feeling fine now, with no cramping anymore. I stretch out on the floor, relieved. I'm too tired to be able to deal with labor after such an early awakening. Still fatigued, Cindy goes back to bed and I read the Sunday paper downstairs.

2:00 p.m.: Cindy's moaning and whimpering as she sleeps, so I go upstairs to investigate. In a stupor, she complains of stabbing back pains and that she needs to go to the bathroom badly. Supporting her weight with my body, we maneuver into the bathroom. "It really hurts," she grimaces. "A lot. Feels like labor cramps."

Swinging into my labor coach role, I remember that we should start to time the contractions. Within ten minutes, while Cindy is sitting on the toilet, she has five contractions about two minutes apart. She's in a lot of pain, complaining that she can't possibly move when I try to get her up. My mind starts to race—this could be the start! I ask Tina to call our doctor's office to report the contractions. They tell us to get to the hospital as quickly as we can. All this time, I am counting out loud for Cindy *slowly* from one to four, just as we have practiced in childbirth class. Her eyes are shut as she screams at the onset of each contraction. I tell her that we have to go to the hospital. She looks terrified and shakes her head, "No way." She can't even move because of the intense pain. Tina yells back that the doctor's office has offered to send an ambulance. We accept. Everything feels like it is happening way too fast. This isn't the way we had rehearsed this little scenario. "Let's take it slow," I want to say, "hold on. Wait." The contractions are not waiting. I look up and there are two firemen in the house outside the bathroom door. Firemen! They stand there, like wooden soldiers, not knowing what to do. "The ambulance will be here soon," they stammer. "Help me get her downstairs," I direct them. At the bottom of the steps Cindy has to lean against the railing, seized by a sharp contraction. Almost continuous now, the contractions are getting stronger and stronger. By the time we reach the front door of our house, the EMTs have arrived and the firemen are relieved (pun intended). They help me get Cindy onto a stretcher and into the street. At the end of the courtyard there are two ambulances and a long red fire truck along with a crowd of people. "What a spectacle," I have time to think before we are whisked away into a sirening ambulance.

2:30 p.m.: I continue with the counting and the breathing exercises in the ambulance and Cindy starts to feel dizzy. As the ambulance weaves in and out of traffic, a quick swerve and a wave of nausea throw me onto the rubbery, smelly floormats of the ambulance. Breathing deeply, I try not to think about how badly I feel and that I might throw up. Cindy needs me to reassure her and to keep counting. (Who is going to reassure *me*?) The trip is tortuously slow. I make a promise to myself to always get out of the way for ambulance drivers in the future. It's not easy getting through traffic in this city.

3:00 p.m.: We are rushed into the emergency room. Cindy looks pale; her eyes are glassy, and she is desperately pleading for help from each new person she sees. The emergency room nurses quickly determine that the baby's head is not yet crowning and send her up to the labor and delivery room.

3:10 p.m.: The doctor and nurse meet us in the aisle as we zoom into a labor and delivery room. There is a great deal of activity and many questions as they put a fetal heart monitor onto Cindy's round belly. They want to know about contractions, waters breaking, what she has eaten, etc. Cindy's not answering, she's in too much pain, so I do the best I can between counting, reassurances, and the queasy feeling in my stomach. "You're fully dilated," the doctor announces. "You can begin pushing." Pushing! It was not supposed to happen this quickly. "I can see dark hair coming out," yells the doctor.

"Dark hair, yep, that's ours," I want to proclaim. But there's no time for talk, no time for anything but awe as the baby's head begins to emerge. As I see the head breaking through the stretched skin, I think to myself that it's a boy. I don't know how I know, but I do.

One more push and the baby slides out. "It's a boy!" they cry. I just stare, transfixed on the baby and on the fact that a real live human being has come out of Cindy's body. He's small but beautiful in an animal sort of way, with jerky movements. Compact, arms and legs tightly pulled against his chest.

"We have a son." I squeeze Cindy's hand and kiss her cheek. "We have a son," I repeat over and over in my mind. I like the way it feels. We have a son.

OCTOBER 15

Waking up early this morning, I lie in bed alone and reflect upon how this will be my last morning in such solitude. Cindy and the baby are coming home today—the start of a new life in this house. The two days since Robert Kawika's birth have been thrilling, fast-paced, and exhausting. I have been filled with wonder each time I've held our baby against my chest and kissed his head. There is so much warmth, tenderness and love when we touch him. My parents must have felt this way when they held my siblings and me: being a new parent makes me feel more connected to them. I want to call them and say, "I understand now what it must have been like to welcome us into the world. Thank you for loving me and taking care of me all those years." Even more, I want to share my good news with them, to let them know how my life has been enriched with this new child. I have called everyone who is important to me except my family, with whom I have not talked since that call in September. The impulse to call them now is strong and I glance at the phone, but my self-protection wins over. Wonderful news of a baby should not be met by silence or rejection. I cannot risk it.

Instead, I write a letter telling them of the birth, the boy, the changes in my life. I tell them that we are all well, that I miss them, and that I love them. By then, it's time to get dressed and go to pick up Cindy and Robert at the hospital. The baby is coming home with his mothers!

DECEMBER 25

Christmas in Hawaii. Just as I've enjoyed it for all these years but this time it is different. Cindy, Robert and I are in Hilo, as we had planned months ago, but we're not seeing my family as I had expected. My parents never responded to my request to visit with them, so we're at a friend's home. The sunlight and warmth are glorious today, a welcome relief form the dark Chicago winter. Looking out over the lanai, I can see the familiar landmarks of this city which will always be home in my heart. There is an ache in my chest and tears in my eyes when I think of my family. They, too, have expressed their sadness at our separation this Christmas. On the phone, my mother spoke of the pain she feels; sometimes at work she will remember that I won't be home this year, and why, and she goes to the bathroom to hide her tears. I understand, I told her. Sometimes I ride my bike to work and the pain finds me too, catching me during an unguarded moment. I told her it didn't have to be that way, that they could welcome all three of us this

Christmas. There was only silence and a request to see just me, "no other people." Robert and Cindy are not "other people." They are my family, the loves of my life, the smiles that greet me each day.

We celebrated Christmas local-style with our shoyu chicken, kim chee, and guava sherbet dinner after Robert went to sleep. Before I went to bed, I checked in on him, all curled up in his crib, and covered him up with his blanket. The moist Kona breezes were gently rustling the fern bushes at this house on Piilani Street, ten miles and two generations away from my parents' home. Robert is two-and-a-half-months old; I am four months pregnant.

JANUARY 11

Still in Hawaii. These three weeks have passed quickly. It is not difficult to get used to a daily routine of a leisurely breakfast, laps at the pool, nap time in the park, sunsets along the shore, fixing dinner at home. We've been lucky to house-sit at a vacationing friend's home so we've established a little family routine with Robert. He is mostly a delight, so sweet and cheerful, warming our hearts.

Our vacation ends today. Last night I saw my family for the fourth time on this trip—alone as they had insisted—and it was awkward again. We went out to dinner and studiously avoided all mention of my pregnancy or my life in Chicago. I felt as if I was with strangers, these strangers I've known all my life. When I could bear no more of the distance, and we said our farewells, they went through the familiar routine of giving me local foods and an orchid lei to take with me on the plane. I know they still care about me and I wanted to hug them, to plead with them to give my life and new family a chance, to meet my son, Robert. But I said nothing. I accepted their gifts, including a pregnancy Hawaiian blouse, held my tears, and cried on the way home. We'll fly back to reality and Chicago later today.

FEBRUARY 25

Six months pregnant with a four month old squirming on my lap, I'm packing for a business trip to the West Coast. I've just finished talking to my parents and need to be productive. While I'm glad we've resumed our weekly phone conversations again, this one was more upsetting than the usual superficial talk. I can't believe that my mother had the nerve to insist that I not go to San Francisco because "one of our relatives might see me." Her concern about what others might think is causing her shame and heartache. I refuse to behave like I have something to hide. Other conversations have left me sad; this time I'm angry.

MARCH 3

The baby's moving around inside me more and more. It's my favorite part of being pregnant, feeling the squirms and prods. I was dreading yet another confrontation with my mother on the phone, but she asked only about my trip out West and how did it go? What a relief. I am trying so hard with my family. In spite of their unreasonableness, I do want to work towards keeping them in my life and in our children's lives.

MAY 20

Today was my due date and nothing happened. I was sort of hoping to have had the baby out by now but I guess there's no rushing the baby if it's not ready to make its move. Spoke to my parents on the phone yesterday and told them nothing was happening yet. They sounded uncomfortable when I gave them the pregnancy update. My family has always operated on the principle that if you ignore something long enough, it might just go away. They must know, however, that this is never going to go away. Their first grandchild is about to be born. I wish I could share the birth with them, a birth that will transform me, in their eyes, from a daughter to a mother. It should be a joyous event that should be trumpeted rather than whispered. In my fatigued, large state today, I started to feel a little cheated by my parents' reaction. There may indeed be some truth in that old saying about a woman wanting *her* mother with her when she gives birth. My need *for* mothering is mixed in today with my need to *be* a mother to Robert and to the new baby. So many needs today. . . .

Some of my needs to be mothered have been met by Cindy and some by *her* mother. She arrived today from Seattle in hopes that the baby would be born and she could help us out. She's been a wonderful grandmother to Robert and seems to be ready to accept our next baby as her grandchild. I am very glad that our kids will have at least one doting grandmother. She would probably be even more motherly to me if I accepted it, but I'm resistant, still keeping the protective walls up. If I can't have my own mother here, I prefer self-indulgence, imagining myself as a motherless child. However, pregnancy and motherhood have their own relentless ways of wearing me down: I feel much more needy than usual. Fortunately, our friends and my work colleagues have been very supportive; I feel nurtured and cared for.

MAY 26

At 9:16 tonight, my 42-hour labor ended as the baby squirted out of my exhausted body. The intense pain stopped abruptly, as if bells that had been ringing for hours were suddenly stilled. My attention was focused on my body's relief and release; for a second, and for the last time in the weeks to come, the baby was an afterthought. I looked up in time to see tears in Cindy's eyes as the nurse shouted out, "It's a girl!" We have a daughter! A loud, wrinkled pink one. "Your name is Nina Leilani," I told her, "you have been long-awaited, and you are welcomed with much love." Cindy and I were able to cuddle her, kiss her, nurse her (both of us!) for over an hour after her birth. She is the result of our long labors *and* a small miracle.

The first person we called with the news was Cindy's mom,

who had returned to Seattle and missed the birth by two days. "My first granddaughter," she cooed, "you did well." I did, and I was appreciative of her approval as well as her acceptance of Nina and the significance of her name. (Nina was given Cindy's maternal grandmother's name in honor of Cindy's mother.)

My long travail in the labor and delivery room was finally coming to an end, and after Cindy accompanied the baby to the nursery, she headed home for some rest.

Alone for the first time in 48 hours, I felt drained, relieved, and oddly enough, alert. In my hospital room, I listened to the random sounds of footsteps, soft moans, snorts, light laughter from the nurses' station. I thought I could make out the sound of a newborn baby's sharp cry, but perhaps it was the sound-track from a movie in someone's room. I wanted to sleep but felt the urge to share my big news so I called Joe, and then Pam, long-distance. Then I decided I should really call my parents. I was a little scared but I knew that not only was it the right thing to do, I also wanted to tell them of their grand-daughter. They sounded calm when I told them the good news. My mother compared this birth with her own labor experiences with my siblings and me. It was good to hear these stories. It made me realize that Nina is the newest link in a long chain of children; one day she too will hear my story of her birth. In my exhausted state, I ended the call to my family without telling them the baby's name. No matter, I thought, before drifting off into delicious sleep, this grandchild of theirs, this welcomed child of two mothers, will make her own name in this world. It is only a matter of time. Time that will soothe the pain, time that will provide the challenge, and time that will see our families grow and flourish.

Connie S. Chan was born in Hong Kong and grew up in Honolulu, Hawaii. She is Associate Professor of Human Services and Co-Director of the Institute for Asian American Studies at the University of Massachusetts at Boston. As a psychologist, her work focuses upon the interaction of culture, gender and sexuality among Asians in America.

"My writing allows me to tell stories which explore the complexities of emotions and how we choose to hide or to expose them to ourselves and to others. I am particularly intrigued by cultural nuances and the ways in which families have become cross-cultural as well as inter-generational."

Part V

Full Circle

Alan Wald

INTRODUCTION TO
H.T. TSIANG

H.T. TSIANG is among the most innovative and idiosyncratic writers drawn to the United States Communist cultural movement of the Great Depression. Tsiang also ranks as one of the more productive Asian American authors of imaginative literature in English of the interwar period, perhaps matched only by fellow leftist Carlos Bulosan and the artistocratic Lin Yutang. In addition to editing a Bay Area magazine called *The Chinese Guide in America* in the late 1920s, Tsiang published *Poems of the Chinese Revolution* (1929), a book of verse; *China Red* (1931), an epistolary novel; *The Hanging on Union Square* (1935), an "American Epic" novel; *And China Has Hands* (1937), a novel of New York's Chinatown; and *China Marches On* (1938), a three-act play. A sixth volume, "Shanghai-New York-Moscow: An Odyssey of a Chinese Coolie," was announced in the late 1930s; a copy has not been located, but a manuscript may someday surface.

According to autobiographical information appearing on

covers of his various books and gleaned from a few letters in various archives, Tsiang was born in 1899 in the village of Chi-An in the Nantung District in the Province of Kiangsu. Although his family was impoverished and he was orphaned at age thirteen, Tsiang excelled at examinations that won him scholarships through the university level at Nanking where he received a B.A. in 1925. While in school he obtained a job as student secretary of the Nanking Y.M.C.A., and, after graduation, he was employed as a secretary to the Chinese revolutionary leader, Dr. Sun Yat-Sen.

Tsiang made his political debut as an elected alternate member of the Central Executive Committee of the right wing of the Chinese Nationalist Party, Kuomintang. When the left wing nationalist government in Canton issued an order for his arrest, he escaped to the United States where he undertook post-graduate work at Stanford University. To support himself, he was employed as the associate editor of the Chinese right-wing nationalist daily *Young China*, but he soon began moving leftward and started to publish *The Chinese Guide in America* to promote his views. By this time, the Chinese government in Nanking had switched from the left to the right, and began to pressure the U.S. immigration office to order Tsiang's deportation.

Tsiang was defended by both the Communist-led International Labor Defense and the American Civil Liberties Union, as well as by the prominent socialist novelist Upton Sinclair, eventually winning the right to remain in the United States. In 1928 he moved to New York City to study at Columbia University. However, his main activity was writing and producing his five books, most of which were issued by tiny publishing houses or by himself, often with ornate covers featuring Chinese lettering and designs. He hawked his books at political meetings and gathering places of leftists around the city, and he occasionally read at left-wing literary events such as the "Red Poets Night" sponsored by the Communist-led John Reed Clubs.

With the advent of World War II, Tsiang moved to Los Angeles to start a new career as a film actor, at first depicting Japanese villains. Among his film credits are "Behind the Rising Sun" (1943), "The Keys of the Kingdom" (1944), "The Purple Heart" (1944), "China Sky" (1945), "China's Little Devils" (1945), "Tokyo Rose" (1945), "In Old Sacramento" (1946), "Black Gold" (1947), "Singapore" (1947), "Chicken Every Sunday" (1948), "State Department—File 649" (1949), "Panic in the Streets" (1950), and "Smuggler's Island" (1951). According to notices in the Communist Party's West Coast *People's World*, Tsiang also gave public performances for leftwing audiences of *China Marches On* and a stage version of *The Hanging on Union Square*, starring himself, actress Ruth Krenkel, and a "Supporting Cast" of "Three chairs and One Candle."

After hundreds of actors, actresses, screen writers and other Hollywood employees were called before investigating bodies of the House Committee on Un-American activities Committee in 1951, Tsiang vanished from the scene into Los Angeles Chinatown. Nine years later he resurfaced to act in "Ocean's Eleven" (1960) and "Winter à Go-Go" (1965), before dying in 1971 at the age of seventy-two. Other than a few brief references, the only sustained scholarship on Tsiang is the analysis of the plots of *China Red* and *And China Has Hands* in William's Wu's excellent *The Yellow Peril: Chinese Americans in American Fiction*, 1850–1940 (Hamden, Conn.: The Shoestring Press, 1982).

In advertisements for his books, Tsiang frequently printed the statement of novelist Waldo Frank that *The Hanging on Union Square* is "a satiric allegory, a potpourri of narrative and song . . . [with] fanciful and often fantastic visions of the workers on Union Square and of the parasites in neighboring night clubs and office buildings . . ." It is the only one of Tsiang's five works in which all the characters are white, although there is a brief, satirical vignette of himself trying to sell his books in a New York cafeteria frequented by radicals.

In *China Red* and *And China Has Hands*, Tsiang recreates West Coast and East Coast Chinatown experiences, including laundries, restaurants, cafeterias, dance halls, gambling houses and brothels, as well as depicts an Afro-Chinese woman from the South. In contrast, *The Hanging on Union Square* features de-ethnicized Euro-Americans in New York City's Union Square vicinity. They are given symbolic names such as "Nut" (an unemployed worker lacking class consciousness), "Miss Stubborn" (a young revolutionary), "Mr. Wiseguy" (a phoney socialist), "Mr. System" (a capitalist), "Miss Digger" (an opportunist) and "Mr. Ratsky" (a gangster). Tsiang's style has surrealistic features, and also recalls the Marxist playwright Bertolt Brecht's use of "alienation" effects. However, his use of brief chapters, short paragraphs (sometimes one sentence), genre mixing, the blurring of history and fiction, and his over-all episodic construction may well be a consequence of his background in traditional Chinese literary forms, as well as the difficulty of writing in a second language, or perhaps translating mentally as he wrote.

The narrative of *Hanging* is organized around the frustrated love affair of Nut and Stubborn, presenting many sharp insights about the ways in which human relationships are deformed by the capitalist economic system. Although there are many odd aspects to Tsiang's treatment of sexuality, *Hanging* is somewhat unusual in its central depiction of a female as well as male worker, with the female more politically advanced and rarely rendered through maternal or other imagery emphasizing biological difference.

The following excerpt is from pp. 165–181, Chapters XXXII–XXXV, of the novel. Depicted is the penultimate stage of Nut's stumbling efforts to achieve class consciousness, and his still-unresolved love affair with the leather-jacketed Communist, Miss Stubborn. Characteristically, Tsiang repeats the same aphorism at the start of each episode in this segment. After confronting an *agent provocateur*, Nut gains new insights and continues on his fantastic adventures.

———————

Alan Wald is a Professor of English at The University of Michigan in Ann Arbor.

H.T. Tsiang

from *The Hanging on Union Square*

XXXII
A MAN WALKED ON HIS HANDS

"There is heat in the sun.
Vertically, at any time,
Horizontally, in any space,
Things must be done."

It was Mr. Nut philosophizing.

Half past six when the City Hall demonstration was over.
Nut came back to Union Square.

On the Square a fellow approached him.
"How did you like the demonstration?"

"What do you mean—'like the demonstration?' With two dead persons in front, do you think it was a picnic?"

"You are very revolutionary, I see! I'm sorry—I'm awfully sorry. Are you a communist? Are you a Party member? What unit do you belong to, comrade?" The fellow spoke to Nut in an intimate tone.

Nut looked at him; looked at him carefully.

The fellow wore a pair of old, wornout shoes and a pair of expensive socks, which could be seen underneath his raised trousers. And the suspicious eyes of that fellow's freshly-trimmed head, resting on a policeman's neck, looked at Mr. Nut attentively.

It was the same fellow who had been in the Cafeteria on Fourteenth Street last night. But when the fight had started, Nut had seen him talking with the police, and signalling with his eyes to some other fellows who had the same suspicious appearance.

While Nut was looking at him, the fellow spoke again: "What do you think of this?—you know, about two or three months ago, someone tried to shoot the President? Talkin' for myself, I'm awfully sorry the guy missed."

Nut still looked at him.

"If you're interested in my face," continued the fellow, "I've got to tell you I haven't shaved yet. In the capitalist system, the razors are fake too. You know we should kill all those capitalist guys." And the fellow smiled at Nut intimately, and he looked at Nut from head to foot.

"If you want to kill somebody," asked Nut, "why don't you go ahead? What do you have to tell me for?"

"You see, I saw you today in the Communist demonstration. I think I can call you my comrade." The fellow lifted his lower lip a little and turned it to the left of his mouth. By this, he meant to show that something must be done and that he was confident he had found a real friend in Nut.

"Look here—what did you tell the police, last night, in the cafeteria?" asked Nut.

"I say—do you think there'll be rain tonight?" The fellow swiftly changed the subject.

Nut kept on looking at him.

"I think," continued the fellow, "you must be very different from those so-called Communists! Parades! Demonstrations! Those guys are just a bunch of cowards. They're all yellow! Russia is no good, either. Why didn't it send a Red army here to crush the Capitalists—dammit—blow up Wall Street and kill all the guys down in Washington? Cowards, that's what they are. Yellow! They're yellow I tell you!"

"Is that what the police told you last night in the cafeteria?"

"Say, don't be so suspicious! If you're a coward and yellow, too, just say so. Don't throw mud at me." The fellow again looked at Nut from head to foot.

"Were you in the demonstration?" inquired Nut.

"Of course! I saw two dead bodies on the beds. I saw a girl stand on the platform. Beg your pardon!—she was just on a table. And I saw a boy on the City Hall porch waving a red flag. I saw you too. You were right after that leather-jacket girl—Heh?"

"Your shoes are rather clean—you must have walked on your hands," Nut observed. He was getting mad.

"Take it easy! I know you're a good Communist, fellow-worker—a good comrade!" The fellow took an even more intimate air with Nut. He patted him on the back.

"I'm not a Party member," said Nut. "But I don't like the way you discredit the Communists. You have a pair of clean shoes, so you haven't any right to kick."

"This is what I tell you—because those Communists are so damn yellow, I don't care to be mixed up here with them. I like action. I want to . . ." the fellow here made a gesture of chopping someone's head off.

"Is there anything else you've got to tell me?" asked Nut.

"Come here!"

"What is it? I can hear you," answered Nut.

"It's a secret!" the fellow whispered.

Nut got closer.

"If you want a weapon, I have it."

"Where is it?" asked Nut.

"Somewhere."

"Will you go with me?"

"That's why I talked to you, you see," the fellow replied with a hearty smile.

"Let's go," Nut whispered.

"You're a good guy. You're some guy." The fellow looked at Nut with a cold and artificial air of intimacy.

"What's that? What's that?" Nut suddenly exclaimed.

Nut had turned over the overcoat collar of the fellow, and a badge was revealed.

The fellow walked away. As he walked, he looked back at Nut and warned him: "If you hang around Union Square and mix up with those dirty Russian Reds, I'll get you some day." And after these words, he looked back at Nut once or twice more.

The plainclothesman finally disappeared from the scene.

But something remained in Nut's mind.

Nut was thinking.

Because the fellow was a plainclothesman, Nut did not join him.

But because of what the fellow told him, Nut got an idea. He would, by himself, kill somebody.

"Zangara! Only fifty-nine capitalists rule us!"

"Murder! Kill! Go!"

XXXIII
UNTIE THE TIE

"There is heat in the sun.
Vertically at any time,
Horizontally, in any space,
Things must be done."

A Negro, selling newspapers, came towards him, yelling:

"Daily Worker! The Only English Worker's Daily in America! Three cents a copy!"

Nut took a look at the headlines and asked the Negro: "What do you think of Zangara?"

"Because of him, capitalists tried to frame communists! We do not approve of individual terror! One capitalist is assassinated and another takes his place. We have to change the whole system!" the Negro answered Nut, and then walked on, to attend to his business of selling communist papers.

Nut began to worry about his plan.

"I don't care about my own life," said Nut to himself. "But if I give the capitalists the opportunity to frame communists, well . . . am I the communists' friend or enemy?"

Nut began blaming that leather-jacket girl, Stubborn. If he hadn't met her twice in the communist cafeteria, three months ago, once last night in the cafeteria and another time this morning in the eviction, Nut might not have been in the demonstration and therefore he might not be suspected by others of being a communist. Then he would be free to do whatever he liked. But now . . .

Nut had to give up the idea of assassination.

He was sitting on a park-bench. He took out his remaining pretzel and began biting it.

While biting the pretzel, he felt physically better.

But mentally, because plans were no longer occupying his mind, he felt restless.

Nut was again lovesick!

No.

He was not going to get into more trouble.

He thought how he could get rid of the trouble he already had.

He was trying to untie the tie.

He was trying to "de-hypnotize" the hypnotized.

For love was pain. At least to him. At least to him at this time.

This was the first stage of the situation.

A few moments later, he began to ask himself whether that leather-jacket girl, Stubborn, was worthy of his love.

He had greatly worshipped Stubborn for her heroism. But now he could not understand why it was that at the demonstration at City Hall, she had just stood on the platform and had not spoken—though she had not wept.

Had not her mother and father both been killed by the capitalist, Mr. System? Then why didn't she take advantage of the occasion and call upon the workers to revenge them?

Would it help any to stand tragically and poetically on a platform?

Nut was disappointed in Stubborn. He had found that Stubborn was not stubborn at all and was just "so-so." She was just one of those girls.

This was the second stage of the situation.

A few moments later he began to worry about the meaning of love.

If Stubborn had spoken at City Hall and had been heroic through and through, would it have been necessary for him to love her?

"Love is a nuisance," he thought.

Hadn't he once loved a certain girl and hadn't he, in the process of feeling mysteriously, thought that if the girls would not love him, he would kill himself? And hadn't he—because he met another girl later, gradually forgot about the first girl— and still kept on living?

"God is love," he had often heard.

"Love is God," he now believed.

"God and Love are the same nuisance and both are the inventions of the ruling class!" he concluded.

This was the third stage of his inward situation.

"Bolony, Nut, you don't really think that," he argued—with himself—a few moments later—"Love is something Nature has given us in order that the species may not be destroyed—that it may exist forever."

"God is no sense at all; Love has some sense!" Nut re-defined.

This was the fourth stage in the situation.

A few moments later he got mad with himself. He felt that the hesitation and lukewarmness of that leather-jacket girl, Stubborn, toward him, were evidences that she was not the least in love with him. And this one-sided, make-believe on his part, was stupid. "There is more than one fish in a brook!" Nut reminded himself.

This was the fifth stage in the situation.

While thinking, he looked at the other girls who were passing by on the Square. (Fishing?)

He could not appreciate them.

He felt that the leather-jacket girl, Stubborn, was still the only one.

And now he began to think that maybe Stubborn had been too bashful to say what she wanted to say.

He decided that he would ask her about this when he met her next time.

But he did not know where to find her.

And the question he wanted to ask her would be hard to ask even when he did see her again.

So he was rather miserable.

This was the sixth stage in the situation.

Then all the stages got mixed up.

Even as scientific a person as Nut couldn't be scientific any longer.

"Stop your self-hypnotism," Nut warned himself.

"Untie the tie!" Nut advised himself.

"De-hypnotizing" got him more hypnotized.

Untying tied the tie tighter.

XXXIV
IT AND SHE

"There is heat in the sun.
Vertically at any time,
Horizontally, in any space,
Things must be done."

The reason that Stubborn had not spoken at the City Hall demonstration was not a psychological one. It was physical.

She had fainted.

She was carried to the City Hospital and she could not even see the bodies of her parents buried.

"This girl is a Red," complained the Lady-Superintendent. "If she doesn't like this country, why doesn't she go to Russia? Now the city has to take care of her and it costs money."

"It will not cost her money, the old hag!" whispered one young nurse to another.

While Stubborn, semi-conscious, was lying on the hospital bed, her problems ran through her mind.

The landlord had killed her mother.

But her father was a suicide.

The father of a communist—a suicide!

She had not been able to convert her own father to Communism; how was she going to convert others?

Yet she thought she had convinced someone who was outside her family.

Even in her present very sad mood she could still remember that Nut had been at the demonstration.

In the midst of all these tragic and sorrowful events she felt, nevertheless, that there was at least one person who had been added to the communist ranks. And he would avenge her family in a definite way and work for the working class movement as a whole.

The demonstration had given many, many workers a chance to have their eyes opened.

And Nut was one of these workers!

Although Nut was only one of them, Nut was one.

A mighty river can grow from one drop of water and a mountainous building be started with one brick.

Because of the significance of the Whole, she had to give attention to this very One.

She had to be glad that Nut was in the demonstration.

Since Nut was only one of many, why was she bothered—even at this moment—when she thought about him?

She now recognized such an unreasonable feeling as Love.

Was there to be love in this world?

No. Since this world, she thought, was filled with hate as a whole, how was it that she, one atom of the whole, had the feeling opposite to hate for another atom?

Was there to be love in this world?

Yes. If love were banished altogether, when the new world arrived, where would the future love find its seed? And why should one worker die now for another, and what are revolutions made for?

As a revolutionist, and as a communist, Stubborn was of the opinion that there was love for the biological reason, for the artistic reason and for the political (revolutionary) reason.

As she was now in such a sad and tragic state, Stubborn had no mind to analyze clearly the reasons why she loved Nut. But she was sure of the fact that among all the reasons there was not, in the least, any buying and selling business.

Stubborn went back to when she had met Nut that morning, and found the cause of her uneasiness.

It was because of the tradition that made a woman "It" and not "She." As an "It," a girl had to be passive.

As a revolutionist and as a communist, Stubborn felt she must overthrow this tradition and stand up and become "She."

Being able to stand up and become "She" was a joy, a privilege and a human right.

To love whom she wanted to love and to express her love—express it openly—that was a revolution.

And to express what she did not love, and to express it openly, was also a revolution.

Stubborn decided that when she saw Nut the next time, she was going to tell him she loved him.

No.

She was not going to tell him.

Why—

Strategy?

No.
Since it was not a business transaction, strategy was not necessary.

No.
She was not going to tell him.

Why—
Time? (They had known each other only a short while.)
No.
Love was just a kind of experiment and time mattered very little.
No.
She was not going to tell him.

Because if the capitalists knew about it, they would say: "The communists use women to make men become Reds!"

Yes.
She was going to tell him.

For when Stubborn thought the matter over, she felt that if a girl was not governed by the ideas of a cheap movie and was not dreaming of marrying the boss for money, she was not so bad. Let the capitalists say whatever they liked right now. The workers would argue with them, after the revolution, if they could still be found.

XXXI
"MASSES FOR ASSES!"

"There is heat in the sun.
Vertically at any time,
Horizontally, in any space,
Things must be done."

Nut slowly and aimlessly circled the Square many times.
The night was getting on: it was growing deeper and quieter.

And the people on the Square were becoming fewer and fewer.

And because the night was silent now, he could hear clearly the talk of the few persons who remained on the Square.

Nut heard talk about the Masses. He heard many words, many phrases. Out of it all, his mind made this:

"Masses! Masses! New Masses; Old Masses!

"Nothing can be said that is new. Nothing can be said that is old. Masses are Asses in all ages.

"Stupid! Selfish! Contented! Short-sighted!

"One burden is taken away; another is put in its place.

"They are always expecting to be saved. But they can never be saved.

"There must be something on their backs.

"If there is nothing on their backs, there must be something around their necks.

"Those fakers know that the Masses are—the Asses. The fakers use beautiful phrases with which to crown them—'average man'—'forgotten man'—names used to get something from the Masses.

"The Communists know too, very well what the Masses really are; and yet they have to say everything good in their defense.

"Make the story short—there is no need to go back to long ago.

"Make the story short—there is no need to say anything about others.

"Just take myself—Nut—as an example.

"As a worker did I join the union? No. For I thought the union was a violation of my individual freedom.

"As a worker did I vote the Communist ticket in the last election? No. For I thought then that Communists were all Russians.

"As a worker did I read and support a worker's daily? No. Every day I spent money to buy capitalist papers and, by giving myself poison, help those papers' circulation and help the owners become Czars!

"If the workers had small cars or radios in their homes, then everything was O.K., and the world could go to hell!

"Mean. Cheap.

"Now these Asses cannot even have the little things they once had.

"With so many workers out of work, how many votes did the Communists get in the last elections?

"In one word, Masses are Asses!

"And I, Nut, as one of them, know it."

As Nut went around the Square, he was nervous, lonesome and miserable. He had lost all the enthusiam, courage and hope he had possessed while at the City Hall demonstration.

He was so nervous, lonesome and miserable that he slapped his face several times with his own hand. The Square was then so quiet and the slaps he gave himself were so vigorous, that the sound of every one of his strokes was sharply echoed back from the walls of the surrounding buildings.

Nut was not slapping at Nut himself. He was slapping at the Ass. He was slapping at the *Asses!*

Slapping at one. Slapping at many!

Since, during the last thirty-four hours, his face had been hit so often it did not feel pain any more.

So he stopped slapping and instead he started pulling his hair.

He could not see the blood coming out from his head, but he saw the red dew at the root of every hair pulled out.

Now he was full of pain.

Yet he was happy!

And was laughing.

"You Ass! You Asses! You Nuts!" Nut murmured, "This is a punishment for your stupidity. This is your punishment for not being class-conscious!"

Nut noticed the Flagpost in the center of the Square.

Silent.

Still.

Two ropes came down from the very top of the Flagpost to the ground.

At the bottom of the Flagpost was a brass tablet with the Declaration of Independence inscribed on it.

A brisk wind rattled the ropes of the Flagpost and the ropes called: "Come to me, you Nut! You would be a better Flag to hang up on me. You would be the Flag of Starvation Amid Plenty! You would be the Flag of So-Called Civilization."

Nut answered the call.

He crossed the iron wire-fence.

He held one rope in his hand.

He pulled the rope and made a test of it.

He made a knot.

He made a noose.

He took off his hat, put the noose over his head and measured the size of it.

He took the noose off his neck and examined it to see whether it would work properly.

He walked away from the Flagpost, for he had to find something to stand on. And something he could kick away and so have a free swing.

He picked up some stones from off the Square. He basketed the stones in his overcoat.

With the stones he re-crossed the iron fence.

He piled up the stones and made a stand.

He made the noose of the rope higher.

He tested the noose again.

Everything was ready.

No. Not quite ready.

He had read in the newspaper that when a person was alive he might be penniless, but that after his death, he would have twenty-five dollars, for a hospital would pay that much for the anatomical use of his body.

How should he dispose of the twenty five dollars?

He took out a pencil. He wrote on a piece of paper and willed that seventeen dollars of the twenty-five be given to his landlady as payment for the back rent of the furnished room he had had. And eight dollars he left as a contribution to the Communist paper to be used for revenging his death.

Nut put the rope around his neck and kicked away the stones from under his feet.

He was worriless—free from care; and rested.

It was twelve o'clock, Monday night.

Mr. Nut ended the story literarily, non-propagandizingly and publishably.

Adrienne Tien

TANGENTS

NOTHING COULD KEEP ME from my summer escape! And there I go right over the George Washington Bridge and baamm, I'm out. Hands on the wheel, head vibrating full of top forty songs from the summer of sixty-nine! The first New York man I dated couldn't drive. I couldn't believe it. Where my immigrant parents raised me up, birthplace of the American automobile, not being able to drive is like not being able to cook a fried egg! But lots of New Yorkers can't drive, maybe that's why they stay, maybe that's why they didn't feel like I did at the beginning of this summer—a fly on solar boil, caught between a screen and a window, the dead-weight heat all around like fresh tar on a closed-off street, and no way to get quiet for sleep at night, except by shutting the windows, and then, the skin puffs up soggy like a rotten tomato, oozes yellow sweat like one giant pustule. If I hadn't found someway to get out of the city this summer, I would have thrown myself out of my apartment window and landed on top of Tran Di Yuet.

"Where do you live?" I'm often asked. "Chinatown," I say,

and I want to add, 'but look it has nothing to do with the fact that I'm Chinese.' I just chanced on a loft space I could afford there. In fact, my father was disturbed when I made my move. Only FOB's live in Chinatown, the immigrants, the ones who can't speak English, the ones who still have to make it. To him, his daughter living in Chinatown means she's not making it. He doesn't understand, I got a loft!

And my mother tries continually, desperately to save me from myself. Checking the mail—of all the ironic things, she sends me a review of the best-selling *Joy Luck Club*, as if to say, can you do this? Her answer arrives in the form of catalogs from law schools across the nation. She's been using my name and forging my signature on dozens of letters requesting applications. To date, I've gotten twelve application booklets! Hers is a vote of no confidence, my father's of incomprehension.

Why go on about their thoughts? I haven't lived with my parents for more than a decade. Instead of relatives, I have housemates. My portion of our loft is at the front, with big windows facing the Manhattan Bridge and a convergence of streets. An enviable space, but I'm oppressed by a sense of guilt that originates in my brain and refracts up from the sidewalks. Every day, the trucks fart their way in and belch out crates of green vegetables, fruits, cans of soda, whole pigs and plastic bags full of bean sprouts. Come to think of it, I've never seen hairties or hairbands delivered. Perhaps those bins of colored do-bobbies, the Kudzu of New York, appear through spontaneous generation. I often see bones tumbling off handtrucks on to the street, I frequently pass the tourists sitting down to wonton soup, and I wonder do they taste the shoe leather?

I said I felt guilt. Yes, not only from the obvious source, but also when I compare my life to that of the immigrants around me. If I couldn't speak Chinese, perhaps I'd ignore them altogether and not feel anything, but when I buy milk, garlic, a bottle of oil or soy sauce, our lives touch like tangent circles. A few of the grocers and waiters now recognize and occasionally speak with me. Each one has asked and then keeps asking again and again, "What do you do?"

They see me on the street at all different hours of the day, all the days of the week. No pattern, no set schedule, no time put in at the shops, the stalls, the basement kitchens, no waiting tables, no baby strapped up in red embroidered carrier on my back.

"Writer," I said once. The grocer's face lit up, "Ah, yes, you must be very smart." No, no, I thought, I'm half crazy, or is it lazy. If I was smart I would be a dentist, a doctor, a lawyer, an MBA, anything but the half-baked writer that I am. If I was smart, I'd be a publicist, but I'm nothing but an oyster on the half-baked shell. *One of a million, wasting away, leave me alone, Ma . . . I can't do anything but this . . . and someday maybe . . . for a hobby okay, but you need to think of the future, a career . . .* so many like me, dreams mixing and floating with the carbon monoxide rolling up from the streets like bundles of black insulation, bumping in poofs against my windows. I gotta get outta here. A truck roars, the subway runs past full blast like a meat grinder on wheels. Down there in all of that, in her place almost under the bridge, she sits.

Tran Di Yuet.

One of my housemates, BB, a sculptor noticed her first. "Have you seen the woman that's selling her stuff outside our door? God, what a face she has, what life! What beauty!"

One day on the way home, I stopped. She sat outside our door on a little stool next to a wooden tub. Her face was strong and bright from country mornings, her tiny eyes jet black, and her cheeks red as ripe fall apples. She smiled at me. She waved her hand and as I stepped over, she lifted the slatted lid covering the wooden thermos tub. Inside, fresh, homemade cubes of ivory-white Do Fu were floating in clear, cool water. She held up one finger, one dollar.

"Thank you," I said in Chinese, "But I'm not cooking tonight."

She loved that! I could speak Chinese! She didn't care that I had laminated postage stamps hanging from my earlobes and lived with four men who weren't even Chinese. I explained about learning the language in college and living for awhile in China. "You're so smart," she said. "Really smart." No, I thought, no, but because she thought so, I felt it might be. Maybe I wasn't so worthless? *You're so thin . . . can't gain weight because of the pollution . . . living in a place like that, no steady job, with your education . . . Ma! Have I ever asked you for money . . .*

From then on, we always exchanged smiles. Sometimes, we'd chat for a few minutes. How many kids, how was life? I could only understand about 20 percent of what she said because of her dialect. As for what I said, I myself only understood 30 percent of that. What she understood, I don't know, but her enthusiasm in our conversations never flagged for a moment. She would call me over and cheerfully fire off a few sentences, nodding away at the elliptical phrases I returned. I found out she lived in a tiny apartment across from my loft with her husband and four children! After that I was careful to close my blinds at night. Had she seen me parading around in my lacy nighty (a birthday gift, I swear), going from work area, to phone area, to bedroom, to sitting area—my space three times what she and her family had for their six braided lives.

Tran Di Yuet was out there every morning, every as in seven days a week. She stayed there with the trucks blaring, the buses exhaling, the people squeezing past on the sidewalk, and the cars sidling up to the curb. She was there until the sun went down. Then her husband or sometimes her fourteen-year-old son would come over and help her carry the tub across the street and up the five flights to their apartment. When did she make the Do Fu? In her sleep?

Money, money, how to make money? How to make the green stuff? Tran Di Yuet's dough was ground soybeans, fermented with gypsum, squeezed dry, compressed into protein cakes. My way was temporary typing assignments in corporate offices. And there are so many days when I can't do what Tran does, I can't bear to go out and bring home the bacon. And some days I can't write and I just sit around reading a novel or yakking on the phone to my other underemployed friends. What a life! Great, until I'd start thinking I don't deserve to be so free. What if my mother saw me at home midday, midweek. What if Tran knew. Writer, whisper the grocers, writing stories. Do they believe it? Do I?

Once when I stopped to talk to Tran Di Yuet, she told me she came from the south of China. I told her my family's old home was Hupei, North of the Lake as in the opposite of Hunan, South of the Lake. Lake North, Lake South, Uptown, Downtown, Midtown, East Side, West Side, Wall Street? It's too damn hot to be hearing jackhammers! I commented on her hairdo. I didn't really like it but I said I did. She was losing some of her glow. Her cheeks were only a trace rosy, and now with this new haircut and tight perm, she looked like she was trying to look pretty when before she had been beautiful because she was without artifice. She admired my long hair and told me that back in China, she had worn her hair long to her waist and done it up in a bun. She smiled, a big smile, showing her square white teeth as she mimicked how she combed out that long shining black hair and looked at herself in the mirror.

"No time now. No time for combing long hair. Just one quick wash." She bent her head and mimed a one-two scrub. A waiting customer suppressed his impatience, eyes popping slightly. I said goodbye as she lifted the lid of her wooden tub and placed two squares of Do Fu into a plastic bag.

One Tuesday morning around ten-thirty, I came downstairs, heading to the library for some inspiration. I go there to see all the books and the people reading, and then I think: see people read, people are reading, writers do do something, you are meaningful, now go home and write. On this particular day, I came down and there was Tran Di Yuet, same happy face, but she was sitting behind a silver cart, with sliding glass windows, and a little gas tank attached on the side.

She grinned at me over a vat of bubbling grease. Sizzling away were pieces of green pepper and eggplant cut like little boats, holding some kind of stuffing.

"Come, I'm treating you."

With a wire mesh scooper, she lifted a couple of pepper and eggplant pieces from the pool of hot oil and set them on a paper tray. "Hot sauce?" She stuck a plastic fork in the little fried pieces and handed them to me.

"Hao Chi." I nodded, raising a green pepper to my lips. The fried pieces were good, like potato chips only even more satisfying because they were thicker, fresh cooked, and in spite of all the grease, still part virtuous vegetable. A line was forming at her cart. Old customers back for the Do Fu, now sold on the side, new ones curious for a taste of the fried delights. She worked so damn hard, out on the street even when it rained and now she had saved up and gotten a vending cart! If I had an iota of her energy, I'd have written several novels of epic proportions.

She'd had the cart for about a year passing through the winter months, the quick spring ones, and then as I began to tell you, the summer arrived. I was going to explode, I couldn't hear anything inside my head except the phone ringing, cars honking, the subway wheels screeching, beeping from my answering machine, beeping from other people's beepers, and then bleep into my head came the idea to rent a car and drive the hell out of the city until I got into green country, and I'd do this whenever I felt like it.

So there I was busting up the West Side Highway listening to jazz greats and singing "Hallelujah, I'm a Bum." Three times I did it, picking up a little blue Sunbird from Sunshine Rent-A-Car, shooting out over the GW bridge and up to some nameless place, occasionally, staying the night in a motel listening to the chirp of crickets. First time, I rented the car, I decided to swing back to my house and take care of my laundry. The only space I could find to pull up in was right in back of Tran Di Yuet. She turned from her frying vat with surprise. She nodded at the car with interest and I blurted out. "This isn't mind, it's a friend's." I was so embarrassed, caught midweek, not working and with a car. I hoped the grocers didn't see me. "I borrowed it for some errands," I added. Tran Di Yuet stared at my car. I realized she hadn't been looking so healthy lately. Her cheeks were gone white like the underside of a fish. Had she been ill? I wondered if something was wrong with her.

I ran upstairs and came back with my bags of laundry and hoisted them into the car. I wanted to get away before my shame at having a car and free time, made me sign up for the Army. Tran seemed about to ask me something important when a customer came up, and I quick seized the chance to jump in my car and cut out of there.

Heavy hot summer air got swept upside down and blown back cool as I cruised up ole Riverside Drive. I put on some sunglasses, took the curves smoothly and felt joy in my heart. I was born lucky. You dog, you lazy bitch. *Look Mom and Dad, one of these days . . . I'll make . . . I won't end up with nothing as nothing* . . . Stop it. You are different, going somewhere else, the place that you don't know you are going until you get there. Thoreau?

Yeah, right out of the city for now.

On my fourth trip out, I came down the stairs, thinking to buy one of Tran's treats for the road, but she wasn't there. Another guy was set up in her place selling butcher knives off the top of a cardboard box. In the last month, she'd been letting up on herself a little. I hoped her occasional absences meant her family circumstances were improving to the point that she could afford a day off now and then. I zipped on up the highway, going so fast and thinking about something so stupid that I ended up shooting past the bridge and found myself in Westchester County, flying along the green shady Sawmill River Parkway. What the hell! A different route. I decided to swing into one of the towns and see if there might be a cheap apartment for rent and maybe a part-time job posted up at the general store. I rode into Dobbs Ferry.

I came round and out near a path that led up from the commuter train station. Ahead, walking on the shoulder of the road, was a figure somehow familiar, yet impossible for me to take in as recognizable. I slowed my vehicle to a crawl as my mind constructed that, yes, it was

Tran!

What was she doing walking along the road in this small town so far from her spot next to the soot sneezing bridge? I thought of speeding up and rushing past. I couldn't have her thinking I owned a car. She'd never understand that I was renting and out for a leisurely drive, no destination in mind, no deliveries to make. She'd think I was rich, she'd never realize that I was just like her in urban America, barely keeping my head above the bills flowing out of my mailbox each day. I wasn't a good for nothing, got it all easy American-Born-Chinese, a hollow bamboo tube. I was working, I was writing, dammit, that is work too. What was she doing here? Of all the weird things! I could make a quick right and avoid her completely, but something was wrong. She was walking slowly with her head bent down like the crook of a cane. I pulled up alongside her, but even with the car rolling right next to her, she wouldn't look up. Why would she imagine anybody but a crazy person stopping for her. She stared straight ahead with tears running down her cheeks. I pulled over and jumped out of the car.

"Tran!" I called. "Tran!"

For an instant, she was horrified to see me, no doubt convinced I was a ghost, and then a wave of relief swept away her shocked disbelief. I pointed at the car. She nodded and followed me back and climbed in the front seat. She sat there like a child and didn't look at me. Cars whizzed past. I turned on my hazard flashers.

"What are you doing here?" I said in Chinese.

She shook her head and raised the back of her hand to each of her eyes.

I waited for her words to hit me like static from a radio, hoping there'd be one or two that rang clear. Nothing. No words.

"Where are you going?" I asked. "I'll take you there."

I looked at my sunglasses, discarded on the dashboard. I hoped Tran didn't think my shorts were underwear or notice that my top was a mere square of silk held up by straps that could be better described as strands. I didn't expect anyone to see me when I was wearing my wild, sexy driving attire. Tran Di Yuet had on her usual garb, blouse untucked, plain dark cotton pants, soft slip-on shoes.

"Where are you going?" I said again.

She reached into her pocket and pulled out a neatly folded page of paper. I unfolded it.

Our eyes met and she began to speak, "I already have four! I can't afford anymore. We're working for the ones we have. Can't afford . . . not enough money."

"I understand." I said. I wondered why she was coming all the way out here, who referred her, what the insurance deal was, but then it would have been too complicated to ask, and she might have only understood me saying, why, why, why as if I questioned what she was doing.

I parked the car. We approached the clinic and then my head went dizzy with fear and anger. Protesters came at us like rabid bats, waving signs and shouting. Placards swiping all around us like giant fly swatters. MURDERERS, KILLERS!

"What?" Tran said to me, horror scaling her face, twisting her mouth into a gaping expression.

Mine fell open, how to explain? Three men approached with a clipboard, momentarily thrown off by facing Asian women, our faces telling them of birth in the yellow river basin, centuries of famine, toil, coaxing green sprouts from mud, filling hollow bellies with grains of rice, leaves of trees, no-names and footbinding. They faltered, then started in. "You are about to commit a sin. Come pray with us. We'll help you. The heartbeat of a fetus . . ."

Tran hid her proud, worn face in her hands. One of the men was shaking his gory poster at her. I grabbed for it. Different people kept blocking our path. I marched towards the doors of the clinic, scared, my heart pounding. Tran's arm linked with mine. I shouted back at those that shouted at me and nothing was heard but the noise of human bellowing. We got inside and there was one protester, handcuffed to one of the chairs in the waiting room, stretching her arm out to make us take a pamphlet, her smile twisting wretchedly like a figure from Dante's Inferno.

I handed Tran's appointment paper through the window to a tired-looking nurse. Outside the protesters had begun a chant, "Stop the Murders, Stop the Murders."

"What are they saying?" Tran asked.

I looked down at Tran's hands, one on top of the other on her lap. I'd never seen them still. They worked so ceaselessly, dipping the mesh-spoon into the frying grease, squiring the hot sauce on, folding the wax paper bags, handing over the plastic forks, taking the dollars, quarters, dimes, and in quiet moments, wiping the smooth steel of her cart with a damp, battered rag. I reached and squeezed her tanned, wrinkled hands. They began to shake as the chanting of the protesters grew louder, angrier, more vehement, and I thought, I hope they don't smash the car, we need it to get back to the city.

"Tangents" was inspired by a certain woman and the richness of the street life I encountered daily when I lived in Chinatown. It came to me quickly in an intense burst of writing. I then edited it to half the original length.

Ironically, my husband and I have left the city, and moved to a town near the one mentioned in the story. We have a two-year-old. Until I had my son, I was ignorant of the world of children, now I am immersed in it. Everything else fits in after my life as a mother. I am working on a novel, an excerpt of which will appear in "Intersecting Circles," an anthology of writing by people of mixed race. I am part English and part Chinese—born in Philadelphia, grew up in Michigan.

In the past, I tried to write characters that had no race, but that inevitably became a problem. Maxine Hong Kingston first expressed this for me in "Tripmaster Monkey" when she wrote, "He whipped around and began to type like mad . . . And again whammed into the block question: Does he announce now that the author is Chinese? Or, rather, Chinese-American? And be forced into autobiographical confession. Stop the music—I have to butt in and introduce myself and my race . . ." Since I have become conscious of this block for myself, I normally decide upon a race for the story's narrator, state it plainly, or know it clearly in my own mind and then get on with it. The main challenge of every story is finding the particular voice. For me, that's where it begins.

Leslie Lum

SAM

from *Cat Country*

1.

We first met Sam soon after we moved to Greenwich, Connecticut from Manhattan. Sig Mon, my husband, was desperate for a place which would bring back the feeling of city, something crowded and bustling, full of ethnicity. This was impossible in Greenwich.

In Greenwich, the stores were lined up on two main streets which intersected each other. They were small storefronts with brightly colored woodwork and carefully lettered names on the windows, names that suggested serendipity, romance, elegance. Inside the windows, colorful crockery, English chintz tablecloths or French bedding were crowded together with sprays of lavender, tulips and azaleas in a busy display. Quaint restaurants showed a vast assortment of cheeses, baguettes, tarts topped with shiny orange apricots or bright red strawberries on stark white lacy doilies. There were art galleries, antique stores, decorating shops, all manned by polite, well dressed women who seemed to be running the shop as a form of recreation.

The next town, however, still had a large first generation Italian population and a supermarket to service it. It was huge, right off the highway sandwiched between the housing project and a cheap motel. There was nothing polished about it, no special lighting to enhance the vegetables, no complicated displays, no employees dressed as animals or clowns. It was simply a marketplace for the ethnics as we would have said in the office. Sig Mon was excited the first time we caught sight of it. It was so New York with the barbed wire fence circling the large parking lot. It was there that we met Sam behind the fish counter.

"Are you Chinese?" Sam asked waving one hand which was wearing a huge yellow rubber glove. He stood on the terra cotta tile floor in large rubber boots and a white cover-up cotton coat which came down to his knees.

"Cantonese," Sig Mon answered in Cantonese. He always relished the opportunity to show his facility in Cantonese. He was always egging me to practice more. "And you?"

"Cantonese also, from Vietnam," Sam answered. "How long have you been here?"

The encounter reminded me of my childhood days when people would meet my mother on the streets and induce exactly such an introduction. The key question was how long have you been here. It signified a lot of things. Maybe how much English you spoke, whether or not you had a good job, whether or not you had bought your own house yet, how many people you knew.

In the days when I first met Sam, I had discarded a lot of the habits of my mother, the way she used to run to seek out the Chinese clerks in a store, the way she would befriend them and ask for special favors based on their shared circumstances. Once she did this to a woman who was primly dressed like the teachers in school with British woolens and a white blouse. I remember how crisply the pleats on her skirt were pressed as if she never sat on them. She blushed, embarrassed with my mother, and said, "I'm sorry, I can't help you."

It was different nowadays. The new immigrants were able to look at the old ones and ascertain how long they had been here without saying a word. They were more perceptive, less naive, more aware. They would look at Sig Mon and notice he was tall, probably drank milk from a very young age, that though he was casually dressed, he was dressed well—expensive trousers with fabric which fell in one smooth cascade to the heel of his shoe, not too long and not too short, but giving no hint of being altered. They would notice the quality of the knit shirt, his leather jacket, how soft and supple the leather was even though they could not feel it. They would know by the way he cut his hair and the type of glasses he wore that he had attended a good college, perhaps even Ivy League, if they understood what Ivy League was. They would know that he had a good professional job, how high a level didn't matter because he was so obviously out of their reach. He had been here a long time.

"A long time," Sig Mon spoke with that sardonic curl to his lips. "How long have you been here?"

"One year," Sam answered in Cantonese. "I've been working here for two months. It's quite nice. They have a dormitory for us to stay in. I can save money."

"That's good," Sig Mon said distractedly. He surveyed the fish behind the glass counter and looked back at Sam. "What can you recommend for us? Something fresh."

"Of course." Sam jumped to attention, his rubber boots squeaking together. "How about some cod filets?" He said, pointing to a pile of carefully sliced white fish slabs.

Sig Mon wrinkled his nose. "Westerner food." He looked around the case again and his eyes glinted. "How about some squid?" He said looking up at Sam.

Sam smiled. He reached for the limpid purple and white masses to the side of the case. The legs wiggled as he lifted up each squid for inspection, selecting the meatiest and whitest ones. "Remember to clean it very well." He said pointing to the dark ink traces around the opening of the legs. "Use a sharp knife and score it into criss-crosses. Slice it into squares. Pan fry it with slices of chicken and snow peas. Little bit of oyster sauce. Good eating. Good eating."

2.

"I took my first driving lesson today," Sam said proudly to me when I arrived at the fish counter. "Funny, working here at the fish counter, my hands are usually ice cold, but as soon as I touched the steering wheel, I started to perspire." Sam stood behind the stainless steel row of sprays, scaling a large sea bass. "I'm almost finished here. Can you wait?"

"Don't worry, take your time," I said to him.

Two other fish clerks were leaning against the counter idly waiting for customers. They knew never to even try to wait on Sig Mon or myself. We always wanted Sam. Sam took care of us.

"It's a funny feeling sitting in the driver's seat," Sam continued in Cantonese as he briskly scraped the sea bass. "You push the seat front and you push the seat back and still it doesn't feel like it's the right distance for you to reach the pedals. Then you have to move the mirrors here and there, back and forth. Even after you've done all that, sitting there, you can't see right. There are pieces of car in the way, the frame that holds the glass in place, pieces of the hood, the stickers they have on the glass. You're expected to be aware, to see both front and back at the same time. Very difficult. Very difficult." Sam frustratedly slapped the sea bass on the cutting board and came to the glass counter.

"Just go slowly and it will come to you." I wanted to comfort him, remove his agitation. I wanted him to focus on the matter at hand. "What's fresh today?"

"You assume that the car is part of you, that when you turn on the engine that there will be a surge of power through you also." Sam absentmindedly picked up a lemon sole filet, inspected it and laid it down again. He picked up a piece of flounder. "You assume that the car becomes an extension of you and somehow you can feel where the front and back ends, feel where it goes." Sam's voice drifted slightly. "Flounder is on sale today. Very nice fish. You can take it, grind it up, add some water chestnuts, egg, scallions, ginger, soy sauce. Roll it into a ball for soup or in mushroom steamed . . ."

Without consulting me, Sam began to make a stack of flounder filets on a red and white checked paper boat. I didn't protest.

"Cars were useless in Vietnam. There, roads were bad. They were expensive to keep. Expensive to buy gas."

Sam weighed the flounder on the scale deducting a quarter pound for the weight of the paper boat. All the other fish clerks deducted a tenth of a pound.

"Only soldiers had cars. When you saw a car coming in your direction, you were afraid because you didn't know what it was going to do. It didn't matter who the enemy was. Anyone in uniform. All you could do was draw the car into the jungle and hope the jungle would eat it up." He wrapped the flounder carefully in ivory colored paper and sealed the package with the price sticker.

Sam looked over the counter directly at my face as he handed the package to me. It was the first moment that I was sure he realized who he was talking to. "Make a large bowlful and freeze it. So convenient, freezing things. Use it later on tofu or make it with wonton skins into soup dumplings."

"Thank you, Sam," I said in Cantonese. "Good-bye," I said in English.

3.

"Look what I have here." Sam signaled as I approached with my shopping cart. I followed him to the side of the glass counter as he held up a large white plastic bucket. "Salmon fish heads," he said with the hush that one saved for a precious piece of jewelry.

The sight of the fish heads made me think of the old kitchen, of the black cast iron skillet, of the gas burners that we had to light with matches. Inside the skillet five salmon fish heads stewed in black bean sauce. Close by, there was the turquoise formica kitchen table with brown flecks which sparkled. At the side of the table, there sat one or two of the old men who lived in the rooming houses in the neighborhood.

They always felt drawn to our house, maybe because we had been there so long. They would sit there for hours. When dinner time came, my mother would extend the obligatory invitation to join us. They always declined but still sat there rolling cigarettes or drinking tea. My parents would hold sporadic discussions with them as we ate, ask them about their families who were trapped in China or relatives who had come over.

I often told Sig Mon how much I hated having those men sit there watching us eat. Sig Mon said nothing when I first mentioned it. But everytime we set down roots in bigger and progressively uptown New York apartments and people began to drop by unannounced, Sig Mon would look at me and deadpan, "Pretty soon they'll be sitting here watching us eat."

"No," I said to Sam. "I don't know how to cook them." That was a pointed response. It meant that I didn't want them. It meant don't insist the way that you have to insist according to Confucian tradition. It meant this isn't going to be a two times no, third time yes proposition. It meant I am incurably stupid and could never in my lifetime learn to cook these fish heads.

"Look at how much meat there is still on the head." Sam pointed undauntedly to a fish head he picked up. "The head is the best part because it doesn't move. The meat is the tenderest."

I turned my head to signal no again.

"You can stew these fish heads, little bit of black bean sauce, garlic. It would be good eating."

"Really." I protested.

Sam paused for a minute. He searched my face, looking everywhere but never making eye contact. "Westerners are so funny," Sam said. "The more fish doesn't look like a fish, the more they like it. Look." Sam pointed to the fish steaks stacked in neat oval piles over ice. "Doesn't look like a fish. If it did they wouldn't buy it. We . . ." He accentuated the we. "Now, we wouldn't buy a fish unless we could see it swimming . . . know that it's fresh. Westerners are strange."

"I don't know how . . ." I protested feebly.

Sam stood with both rubber gloved hands on his hips. "I think your husband would want these fish heads." He said.

4.

"How is your husband?"

"Good. Thank you for asking." Sig Mon was busier now. He rarely ventured out for food shopping anymore. This Saturday he had gotten up early and gone back into Manhattan to work. I was hoping that he would not be too late for the dinner party we were giving tonight.

"Lobster is good today. You're Cantonese. You can cook it Cantonese style with ground pork, egg and scallions in a sauce with the innards of the lobster." Sam rattled over the glass counter. He seemed to be in a particularly good mood today.

"Let me take a look first," I said to him as I paced the glass counter peering at the array of seafood.

"No problem," Sam said in English.

"Driving lessons are going very good," he said falling back into Cantonese. "At first I thought this is crazy. I have to spend $50 a hour for driving lessons. I go to a special school run by a guy who came from Rumania. It takes me a day and a half to earn enough money for one hour of driving lessons after they take out this and that. How can I save to bring my family here?" He paused and looked at me. "How much did you pay to take driving lessons?"

"My brother taught me," I said thinking how amazing it was that one immigrant would take such advantage of another—$50 an hour. "How's the rock fish?" I said pointing to the pile of grouper.

"Too old," Sam said shaking his head. "How lucky. I have no family here." He shifted his position leaning against the glass counter. In his right hand he was holding one of the red and white checkered paper boats. "Americans, they grow up with cars. From the time they're babies, they ride in cars. Some of them start to drive when they are twelve years old. When they reach manhood, they get their license."

"What about the halibut?" I asked using the English word for halibut.

"Not bad," Sam said. "But it's $7.99 one pound, very expensive. Later on in the year they put it on sale for $5.99. Lobster is only $3.99 one pound. All over a pound and a half. I'll make sure you get only live ones. You know, America is the greatest car society in the world. There were never so many cars as there are in America."

I hated cars. They were a brutal primitive way of transporting people. Ever since the accident with the boys, I feared cars. I couldn't drive down the quietest streets now without thinking that stopped cars would bound out and hit me. I could feel that dull thump, losing control and falling into that terrifying spin. I turned my head to look at the boys in the back seat. Steven's two-year-old body jolted like a wooden mannequin. Justin was barely three months. I was praying, "Please let us get out of this alive."

They thought they had wiped out cholera, diphtheria, smallpox, reduced infant mortality, major wars and other forms of dread fatal disease and arbitrary death. But they had replaced it with traffic accidents. There was no epidemiological basis, a perfectly normal person could take the wheel of a car and for one accidental moment become wild-eyed. It was the worst of fates to die by car.

Sig Mon took the opposite view. "Thank god for the Volvo," he said. "Thank god for safety cages and air bags."

Sig Mon had always loved cars. Even now when he had so little time to do anything but work, he insisted on washing the cars himself. He would massage the body with slow wide strokes using the chamois cloth. Then he scrubbed the small areas with a toothbrush to catch the grease. There were special polishes which beaded up water like smooth round hemispheres on the hood. Heavy duty cleaners kept the wheels so shiny that they looked brand new. He would spend hours applying protectants to the dash and seats, rubbing carefully into each groove. "It's my way of bonding with the car," he said.

"Give me the lobsters," I said thinking about how great a pile of steamed lobsters would look on the new platter. "Make sure that they're alive," I stressed, waving my finger over the counter.

Sam saluted me with his paper boat.

5.

"I failed my driver's test today. I failed. I almost hit a car." Sam was speaking so quickly in Cantonese that I could barely understand what he was saying. I had never seen him so disheveled before, so out of control.

Sam began writing on a piece of wrapping paper. "I spent $1000 on driving lessons and $165 to rent the car. $1000 on driving lessons and $165 to rent the car from the school." He scribbled numbers pressing hard against the counter.

I gasped. It cost only $60 to rent a car from a car rental company, less than that with a corporate discount. Then I checked myself. Sam had no driver's license much less a corporate discount. How could he rent from a car rental company?

"The trouble was I took all my driving lessons in this town. I know the roads in this town. I know them well. They moved the testing station to another town. I wasn't familiar with the roads. There were hills. The hills changed the landscape. They made everything different."

Sam walked back and forth behind the counter, waving the wrapping paper with the numbers on it. "I was coming down the road and the man wanted me to merge into another lane. I wasn't familiar with it." He stood still and gestured the scene with his hands, slicing a path with one rubber glove while the other rubber glove collided into it.

"It cost me $165 to rent the car for the test." He stood still, looking past me as if at a train or boat which had just left. "How can I bring my family here? It will be like living in a prison if I can't drive."

"Sam," I called to him trying to put a snap in my voice. "Whey, Sam . . ."

Sam wadded up the wrapping paper and threw it disgustedly into the large garbage can.

"Sorry," he muttered. "Dragon's tongue." He continued in the same low tones. "Very fresh today. Coat it with egg and flour and deep fry," he said half heartedly. "Make a sauce with mushrooms, peas, ham and a little bit of cornstarch."

"You can take the test again," I said to him in equally half hearted tones.

"I can." Sam was using twice as much paper as necessary to wrap the fish, rolling it over and over again with the ivory paper. "I'll have to take more driving lessons. I could pay another $165 to rent the car." He handed me the package refusing to look me in the face. He bent his head down and started to write on the wrapping paper again, long trails of numbers. As I turned to leave, he was drawing a summation line with the same motion he used to slice off the head of a whiting.

"Sam failed his driving test," I told Sig Mon that evening at dinner. Sig Mon was sitting across the table holding Steven on his lap. The boy manipulated a pair of chopsticks picking at the food in Sig Mon's bowl. It was an annoying habit he had, allowing the children to eat from his bowl. The children usually ate before we did, but Sig Mon insisted on feeding them nonetheless. "Better than having them watch us eat," he had said once.

"Really," Sig Mon said. "See big boy use his chopsticks like an old China hand." He switched to Cantonese half speaking to the boy.

"He almost hit a car."

"Whew, no wonder they say Asians can't drive," Sig Mon said in English. "Look at that, big boy picked up a pea with the chopsticks." Steven smiled proudly dribbling pieces of grey sole down his chin.

"Don't feed him anymore," I said irritably to Sig Mon.

"Can I help it if my son likes Chinese food?" Sig Mon riposted as he gently lowered Steven to the floor.

"I was thinking . . ."

"What?" Sig Mon said as he efficiently shoveled his food into his mouth.

"Maybe we could lend him the car."

Sig Mon looked at me with his food sitting in a pile at the bottom of his open mouth. "You mean—the Volvo?"

"Yes, we don't use it that often. It costs him a lot of money . . ."

"Why are you so worried about his financial situation?" Sig Mon shouted back at me. When Sig Mon got upset, he always fell back to his bad habits, shouting like a waiter and talking with food in his mouth. "How many hits do you think the car can take?"

I could feel my face turning red. "He has no one to help him."

"What about the liability? Do you want to be responsible?"

"It was something I thought you might want to do," I said slowly looking straight into his shiny black eyes. Sig Mon had that glazed over look. He was not listening to me.

"Where do you think we are?" Sig Mon said shoveling more food into his mouth, "in Chinatown?"

I have come back to writing after a long hiatus. This return was made possible by the birth of my two children. Previous to this, I had published in Canada (a series of small literary journals and two short fiction anthologies). I currently work on my writing with the Asian American Writers' Workshop.

Thelma Seto

INSHALLAH

WE DRIVE INTO the mountains to have lunch with a Moslem farmer who is a friend of my father's. It is a clear, spring day. Beirut shimmers below us. In the harbor the Sixth Fleet sits motionless, as if anchored to a subterranean magnet.

After the usual dance of courtesies—the elaborate greetings, the kisses on both cheeks, we are escorted to a terrace cultivated with grapes a short distance from the tiny mud house. Tribal carpets are arranged on the rocky, early spring grass around a white, ironed tablecloth.

My brothers and I look at each other awkwardly. We are silent, having nothing to say to each other or anybody else. It seems we are always being dragged around to strange places to do odd things with people who are singular, unlike anyone else we have ever met or ever will, so that each experience which we stumble through, surviving only with considerable embarrassment and discomfort, is basically useless—except as good training in shyness. We are children, being educated for the future. Our job, my father says, is to keep our wits about us, pay close attention and learn from everything. Later we will need this information for our survival. But it seems nothing we learn will apply at that late date.

The farmer's wife, a silent stone-faced woman, baked sheets of bread before us over a hot fire. The motions of her hands are mesmerizing, flipping the paper-thin dough like pizza. As soon as the appetizing bread is baked, the large hands of the grown men grab it. On the tablecloth are little ceramic bowls of soft, tart goats' cheese, salted black olives whose wrinkled dry skins indicate they'd been cured a long time, home-made yogurt, freshly picked dill, mint, fenugreek, thyme, oregano. My stomach growls. We sit for what seems like several hours, crosslegged, around this tablecloth in a field. Small, black birds fly overhead, calling to each other in warning. The farmer and his five grown sons smile and rub their hands. There is a chilliness to the air, as if it might snow, though it is too late in the season for that.

The farmer and his sons make polite small talk with my father in Arabic. They do not address my brothers and I or the farmer's wife. The farmer's wife, my brothers and I say nothing. No one makes a move towards eating, to my dismay, except to nibble the fresh mountain bread, cheese, olives, and greens. We ignore our hunger, pretending no one's stomach is rumbling. It is a strong, healthy sound: Rumbling stomachs on a mountainside above the Mediterranean which shimmers below us like a tablecloth of coins.

At some point, when I am sure my stomach can stand it no longer, the farmer and his sons stand up and invite my father to see their orchard. He smiles expectantly and agrees. I am puzzled but there seems little point in clinging to the tablecloth. Perhaps the little bit of bread and olives is the lunch we'd driven two hours up the mountain to eat. Dad had said on the way up the twisting, mountain road that this family was poor, but all my parents' stories about their farm childhoods had an underlying moral to them, that farmers rarely went hungry. I am doubly confused but I am used to that.

The farmer gives my father a rifle. He offers one to my older brother but my father waves his hand in the air and says something under his breath in a mocking tone. My older brother scowls and my younger brother swears under his breath. All his life he has been fascinated by any and every implement of destruction. The farmer laughs a big belly laugh. His sons join in. They have very large, very white teeth, like horses. When they throw their heads back, their teeth look like snow melting.

There is a loud pop from the terrace below where two of the grown sons have disappeared. Their voices rise and fall in waves. The farmer trots off in their direction, his nose leading the rest of his body like a dog's. My father follows obediently.

After an interminable time, our father heaves himself onto our terrace. Even the flies have deserted us. He turns us back the direction we'd come from and begins trotting, expecting us to keep up, carrying his rifle by his side like a musician would carry his instrument, as though it was an extension of his body and he was unaware of its existence separate from himself.

The farmer and his sons are already at the tablecloth, which is still perfectly ironed. Bowls of steaming rice and sauces of stewed fruits and vegetables have been carefully arranged on the tablecloth. Their placement is very Arab—so artful it appears random.

Beside the tablecloth someone has arranged the bodies of twenty or thirty little black birds on brass hammered trays. It is hard to tell if their feathers have been plucked, they are so charred. Their little feet stick up in the air higher than their blue-black breasts, like Europeans lying on the beach by the sea in distinct rows trying to develop a tan when it is still too cold to go into the water. The charred corpses of the birds remind me of the American cartoons we sometimes see on Saturday mornings at the movie theatre near our house where the animal characters suffer gross insult and physical injury, then jump up as if they are just playing dead. Real birds don't jump up after being shot and charred; this I know. Still, I am nervous about eating them. I don't want them to come back to life in my stomach.

The birds have been roasted, my father says in English in a low voice, and are quite delicious. I don't know if we are supposed to eat their feet. Or their beaks. I watch the others out of the edge of my eyes. The farmer and his sons and my father are digging in with gusto.

"Eat!" says Dad. In our family, most of our conversations

are carried on in silence, beneath the words actually spoken. Under the command to eat is a subtext: Something about being guests and trying some of everything on the table. Something about eating enough to be polite, even if it makes you gag. Something about, don't shame me. Don't make me lose face. And even more importantly, don't shame them. Don't make our hosts lose face.

I look at the brass trays of birds, arranged like bodies in a morgue, waiting to be identified. The feet stick out. My brothers and I do as we are told, though I expect my younger brother to vomit any minute, his face is so green. I am full after crunching just two or three birds between my teeth, killing them for a second time. I feel like a traitor or an executioner, but I eat a few more to be polite.

The afternoon drags on like molasses but eventually we head down the mountain. Once we are in the city, we pass caravans of drab green trucks full of young men in drab green uniforms. Their heads have been shaved as though they had molested a woman. My brothers are in awe, falling over each other to impress our father about how much they know of military equipment and hierarchy.

I sit in the back seat and sulk. My father of the flat feet. My father of the Japanese ancestry who wasn't even allowed to walk the streets of his own country in freedom during World War II.

"Stupid," I say, more to myself than anyone else.

My older brother turns around from the place of honor in the front seat where he always sits when our mother isn't in the car. "You're just a girl," he says. "You don't understand anything."

"Shut up," I say.

"Protecting women and children is men's work," says my father, smiling at his firstborn son although we all know my older brother is not supposed to join the military. He is chosen, too special for mere fodder. But since I was born with a vagina and not a penis, killing and defending is something I am too unformed to understand. My lack of definition is between my legs. I have known this since I was an infant, somehow. I learned it from the way my father speaks to me.

It isn't a matter of age. I will never be old enough for my father to talk to me the way he talks to my older brother. I look out the window. This conversation in the car is a moral exercise, as far as I am concerned, to test my father's emotional honesty. He often fails. I always save his face by keeping my silence. I guess that makes me a liar, too.

That night after we go to bed we are woken by gunshot. My younger brother sits bolt upright in the top bunk. It has been his dearest wish to see a dead person since we came across an indefinable piece of meat in the trash can while walking down a long stone staircase on the outskirts of Dhure Schwire, the village where we usually spend our summers. The large, indefinable piece of meat had definitely looked like someone's buttocks. Someone who ate a fair amount of meat since it was fatty and flushed-looking. Blushing, my brother said at the time.

I lie in bed listening to the explosions in the street. My brother jumps down from the top bunk and starts pulling on his jeans, an article of clothing I am not allowed to wear. My mother sighs from the bedroom she shares with my father. She grunts softly as she sits up on the edge of her bed and fumbles with her toes for her slippers. Then the slap-slap-slap down the hall.

"Hush now," she says, leaning against the door jamb. She looks tired. She is still breastfeeding my sister. "Get back into bed, young man," she says. My little brother gives a big sigh and climbs back into his bunk with angry, jerking motions. "You never let me have any fun," he says, pulling the bedclothes over his head.

After she shuffles down the hall, we all lie on our backs in the dark listening to the gunshot, like a blind family enjoying fireworks until, one by one, we fall asleep.

The next morning my father hurries us into our sweaters and herds us into the lounge on the first floor of our apartment building. We are going some place special but he won't say where. My little sister is excited, expecting an Easter Egg hunt. She is so young and can remember so little.

My brothers and I whisper our suspicions to one another. It's a little like the authoritative arguments we have over the finer points of the American comic books, though none of us has ever been to America and between us we only have a handful of Superman adventures. Everyone in our family has a big mouth in private. My older brother finally says, "Dad is afraid you will open your loud mouth and ruin it," pointing to our younger brother. It is true. Our younger brother is the loudest, messiest, most argumentative, adventuresome and careless of our family. "Evacuation," says The Chosen One. It sounds like something the school nurse would say of a bowel movement.

My father stands us in a row by height a short distance from the window. My older brother, who is tallest, stands at one end of the row. The baby, who is a toddler, stands at the other. She is just learning to walk. "Don't move," says Dad, and goes to call a taxi.

He returns just as the barrel of a rifle edges its way over the window sill directly in front of us. We all freeze. It is as though we are arranged for a family photograph. We all know not to move, having posed for too many passport and visa photos to count. The photographer would be inconvenienced. We could be there all day. The rifle slowly enters the window closest to us. My little brother's eyes open wide. He stands uncharacteristically still.

"Get under the window, right now," hisses my father. We all crouch. I can hear the man with the gun on the other side of the window breathing slow, even breaths. He sounds frighteningly calm.

The rifle jabs my father in the chest. He ignores it, playing the urbane, congenial Arab host. For once I am glad my father speaks beautiful Arabic, spends his days in his study, and has learned the fine art of Middle Eastern etiquette. He is a true chameleon, blending in so completely with his surroundings that people somehow missed his Japanese features. Now he speaks reasonably, in a calm voice, to the young man with the gun, smiling politely and bending his head gently in a manner that indicates respect and accommodation, his hand on his heart to show he is sincere.

The young man slowly lowers his gun. "Get out," he says.

We are pushed into the taxi waiting outside, the pile of bags on the pavement dissolving like sugar. We hold our breaths while the driver rocks the car from one side of the narrow alleyways to the other in his round-about trip to the harbor. My father wants to avoid all major streets, though it takes longer. He is worried we might miss our boat. "Boat to where?" we ask, all talking at once. "You are going to Cyprus with your mother," he says, "and then to Switzerland."

"Aren't you coming with us?" I ask, feeling that familiar sinking feeling when the ground beneath me begins to move.

"Later," says Dad, "inshallah."

Inshallah, inshallah. Never yes, never no. Just inshallah. If God decides it's a good idea. The decision-making is out of my hands. Inshallah.

We stand with our mother dockside before embarkation and say goodbye to him. This is a bad idea, I'm thinking, feeling that old intuition that he's going to be killed this time. Maybe not last time, mashallah, thanks be to God, but this time for sure. This is risking fate one too many times.

I try to memorize this moment. But the only memory that remains is the image of his head swimming in darkness. I memorize those in the center of my field of vision to keep them alive in case they don't do such a good job themselves. We go up the gangway. It is exciting, romantic. Fleeing at night in the balmy Beirut breezes.

How I love Beirut, I think, my eyes suddenly tearing up. Am I crying because my father is staying behind and I will miss him? Or am I crying because I am suddenly intensely aware of my home, of how easily it can be taken away from me, of how little right I have to claim it as my own at all. This is the only home I know and now it is guns that are sending us away.

My father says it is because we are Americans but I look at him and however much of a chameleon he is, I always see him clearly: My one-of-a-kind Japanese-Canadian father. My brothers and sisters and I have never been to America. How can we be American when he is not? All the Americans we know are blond and blue-eyed and chew gum and drink Coke and wear sneakers. We are nothing like them, though secretly we would sometimes like to be. Another singular experience which I am sure will never be replicated. I sigh.

As the boat leaves harbor, we find a corner on deck and sit down on a blanket my mother has spread for us. "So this is what fleeing feels like," she says. "Christmas in May, like Mary and Joseph with the baby Jesus." She points to my little sister, fast asleep at the breast.

I wrinkle my nose. Whatever wanderers the rest of us are, she is an American and the Sixth Fleet, with the barrels of its weaponry pointed at Ras Beirut, is making sure she leaves the harbor in safety. Special, like the way my teachers treat "real" American kids at school. My father has told me a little about how the Japanese-Canadians and Japanese-Americans were put into concentration camps under armed escort during World War II. There is something equally nauseating about being sent away to Switzerland, but I can't name it. I don't have the words yet. I put it in the back of my mind, to chew on when I'm bored.

My mother, a Texan Anglo, seems oblivious to all this. I watch her scan the night sky for the north star, as she does every night. "For luck," she says. And then I think of my Japanese-Canadian father, staying behind in his adopted homeland. Our corner of the deck is cold and windy. The Sixth Fleet will not protect him.

I stay awake with Mama while the others sleep. We watch the lights of Beirut blinking on and off on its hillside as the boat plows through the harbor. I concentrate on the lights from our apartment building, where my father is sitting alone in his study, reading. No one stands on our veranda, signalling to us with a large mirror and flashlight, the way we always do when people we know are leaving. I wish someone would wave to us but there is no one in the dark. The sounds of the city, even the popgun noises, evaporate in the dark blue vapor over the green ish-black water. No one notices we have gone. We are not wanted.

So this is fleeing. I try to feel sad for my mother's sake or scared for my father's, but I can't feel anything. Fleeing is so familiar to me it is almost boring. I think about Switzerland, where we are heading, and the chocolate it is famous for. I think I will begin a collection of tin foil, collected from all those bars of creamy, delicious Swiss milk chocolate. I hope the Swiss do not think shooting birds is fun, or eating them whole on a platter.

I was born in Syria in 1954, raised in Lebanon and Iran, and immigrated to the U.S. in 1972. My father is Japanese-Canadian, my mother Euro-American. I am both sansei and an immigrant. I grew up under the Shah of Iran's reign of terror in which writers were disappeared, tortured and murdered. Because of their personal integrity and commitment to their beliefs, these writers are my role models.

I try to confront the serious issues facing us, and believe Asian American writers have an obligation to critically explore both anti-Asian steroetypes and our own internalized racism. Both are used to justify anti-Asian racism. It depresses me that Asian Americans lag behind other ethnic groups in understanding how cultural rape has crippled our identities as well as our willingness to fight back. A single mother by choice, I homeschool my son so that he will be an outspoken Asian American, able to think and stand up for himself like his mother, grandfather and great-grandfather before him.

Recently I have noticed an increase in racism towards mixed-heritage Asian Americans from both Anglos and, more disturbingly, monoracial Asian Americans. I believe the American preoccupation with "race" is pathological because in historical fact all "racial" groups are genetically and culturally related. My work focuses primarily on the politics of race and culture, cultural rape and displacement, and the Model Minority/Exotic Flesh Syndrome.

Recent work appears in "Premonitions", an anthology of new Asian American poetry (Kaya), and "Two Worlds Walking", an anthology of bicultural writers (New Rivers Press).